THE BIG HAPPY

THE BIG HAPPY

A Novel

Scott Mebus

miramax books

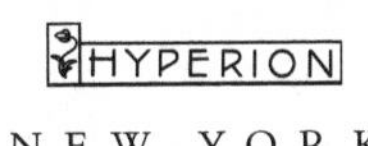

NEW YORK

Printed in the United States of America. For information address Hyperion, 77 West 66th Street, New York, NY 10023-6298

This book is a work of fiction. Names, characters, places and incidents are either the product of the author's imagination or are used fictitiously. Any resemblance to actual events or locales or persons, living or dead, is coincidental.

ISBN 1-4013-5256-1

First Edition
10 9 8 7 6 5 4 3 2 1

To Kristina, for showing me
how big a happy can be

Chapter One

Thirteen-Year-Olds Are the Devil

I have a long history of getting my ass kicked. It began sometime in the third grade, when I was forced to take penmanship classes to correct my illegible handwriting. As a guide for my chicken-scratch letters I had to sketch out these lines with a ruler, which, despite following the straight edge, I always managed to make look like the California coastline. I spent most of my time trying to make my guide lines come out right and never really got a chance to improve my actual handwriting, which still resembles Hebrew more than anything. Inevitably, Jimmy Esposito and Ken Hunt cornered me on the playground with rulers in hand, intent on forcing me to display my now legendary lack of line drawing skill.

It was a defining moment of my life. There I stood, faced with two bullies, one of which had the sad beginnings of an ill-formed mustache on his ten-year-old lip, and how I reacted would determine how I would be treated for the rest of my days at Manville Elementary, and perhaps my whole life. Would I lash out with a quick rabbit punch to the neck in defense of script-deficients everywhere, before booking it to the safety of the school halls? Or would I collapse into a ball like a hedgehog and hope the sight of my striped polo shirt shivering on the asphalt would disgust them enough to turn them away? Neither of those appealed. I'm more of a grand statement sort of guy. I knew that my muscles looked like individually wrapped snack cakes stuck on some sort of weedy vine. My punch would have felt like a kiss from Little Debbie. I also knew that I possessed far too much pride to stop, drop and cower. So I took hold of the one ability I knew would always come through for me. The only thing my father ever consistently told me I was good at. Saying the wrong thing at the wrong time.

"I could try to draw your mustache, Jimmy, but I don't know if even I could make a line that screwed up."

The beating I received that day would live on long after I left school. Principal McAndrews suspended Jimmy and Ken for a week, much to my satisfaction. She suspended me for a day as well, in a vain effort to teach me to control my mouth. But my mouth was never really the problem. It was just the loudest part of me.

For years my flapping mouth coupled with my Weeble-esque ability to wobble without falling down made me the favored destination spot for a whole host of fists. I had always been afflicted with verbal hemophilia, ever since I learned to put two words together in the least tactful arrangement possible, and I had no control over the bleeding. So from the official school bully, Frank Burns, to the dozens of unofficial pretenders to the throne, they all paid my stomach and arms and chest a visit. Never the face, for some reason. I think kids were afraid to hit the face. It was too real. The face was reserved for anger and truly violent grudge matches. Nobody was really angry with me. And God knows, I never sought out a fight. I just wouldn't shut up.

But then came that day when I was thirteen years old and the beatings ceased forever. Why they stopped is the most humiliating part of the whole story, actually, which is why I refuse to tell it. Annie played a big part in that. Annie, who was now finally coming home.

Thirteen, thirteen. To be thirteen. I wasn't thirteen years old anymore, thank God. I was almost thirty, and that next birthday scared the shit out of me. But on this particular Saturday I had thirteen-year-olds on the brain, maybe because of the fear in the pit of my stomach of what would soon be bursting through the fragile glass doors of the Pizza Hut. Or maybe because once this afternoon was over I'd finally be seeing Annie after her two years of exile in far-off Phoenix. Probably a bit of both. The problem was that the more I thought about thirteen-year-olds, the more I remembered what it meant to be one and it ain't a pretty picture. The boys are violent sex machines who are just as likely to hump your leg as shake your hand. The girls are social assassins whose forearms get huge from all the thrusting of knives into one another's backs. I know it's all the fault of those diabolical hormones rushing through their systems like food through a gremlin after midnight, but standing on the cusp of their attack, sympathy proved hard to hold on to.

So where was I, that a horde of newly pubescent berserkers was about to overrun me? Can't you guess? A bar mitzvah, of course. Okay, to be honest, it's a little bit worse than that. I am ashamed to say that I had been hired as the DJ. Yep, that's me. The lowest form of life, below even the thirteen-year-old kid. Let me paint the picture. The Pizza Hut stood empty and hushed, while a soft cloud of horrified anticipation drifted over the staff as they put the finishing touches on the decor. I set up in the corner, making sure to point my two puny colored lights in the general direction of the "man" of the moment's table. My suit smelled a bit like the inside of a jockstrap since this was my third event of the weekend and I hadn't had time for a dry clean, while my bright blue guitar tie broadcast the lameness of my profession. I rifled through my CDs, making sure all my bullets were in the chamber. I had the hip-hop, the punk, the pop, the R&B. Once those kids streamed through that door, we'd be in the gladiator arena and I had to be ready to do battle. The slightest misstep would result in failure and death and clumsy but surprisingly effective insults like "You're a douche," which shouldn't hurt a well-adjusted, mature guy like myself, but somehow . . . sniffle. A beaten cardboard box lay at my feet, filled with inflatable guitars, leis, tambourines, straw hats, sunglasses: If they were cheap and plastic, I stocked 'em. There would be a lot of scoffing and cool-ocity displayed when I handed them out and then a murderous battle over possession would leave some wounded and many pouting. Streamers hung from the Pizza Hut's ceiling, along with cardboard stars of David. A challah sat in the corner looking woefully out of place, as if to say, "What have the Jews come to? You cut me in reverence and then split a sausage and meatball? Disgrace!" The kids weren't there yet. I thanked Jesus aloud, and then felt guilty mentioning him.

The newly minted man's father, Mr. "Just Call Me Stu!" Mendlesohn, walked up.

"How's it going?"

I smiled a full 160-watt bulb of competence and excitement.

"Great, Stu! Where's the man of the hour?"

"They're coming in the other car. So, this is it, then?"

I had found in my year of working with the All-Stars DJ Company that people often become disappointed when confronted with our actual setup. I assume they were happy enough when they paid almost half of what most DJ companies charge, but then they got all droopy-eyed when they saw what their money bought them. The little table. The sad colored lights. Me. I felt bad for them and embarrassed for myself, but what could I do? I had to work with what I was given.

"Everything's ready. How do you want it to go?"

His eyebrows scrunched up in consternation.

"Um. Well. How are things usually done?"

I felt a nudge of mischief as it dawned on me that Mr. "Just Call Me Stu" was, in fact, a paper Jew. He had the birth certificate and that was about it. He was Hebrew enough to want to throw his son a party and try to milk his relatives for a few thousand (as well as take off every Jewish holiday to gamble in Atlantic City), but when it came to the actual specifics of the day, he was a babe lost in the woods of Judaism. The power I wielded at that moment was far greater than you can imagine. I could have created a whole new way to celebrate a bar mitzvah and he would have followed along blindly. The new tradition of screaming "Joanie loves Chachi!" and doing a Jell-O shot off Grandma's belly button could have begun right then. Unfortunately, I didn't want to anger the God I wasn't sure I believed in, so I kept it on the level.

"We can keep it simple. Just do a brief intro, cut the challah and play some games for the kids."

He smiled with relief.

"Great. We'll do a hora, though, right? Get my boy up in the air!"

Of course. What's a bar mitzvah without almost dropping the man of the hour and breaking his neck?

"Sure. There are chairs everywhere."

"Great. Just make sure they have a good time."

"You got it."

"Oops! Here they come!"

There's a part of me that doesn't want to believe that all thirteen-year-olds are bastards. That bright, shiny section of my soul really hoped that this young man was a pleasant, respectful, reverent fellow who just wants to dance and play an inflatable guitar. That was my dream. I looked toward the front of the restaurant with an expectant flutter of my heart. Maybe he'd be the one to prove me wrong.

"Hey, you dickhead, why don't you kiss my man's ass! That's right, this is now the butt of a man!"

Yet another dream crushed. The proud mother floated behind her scowling son, held aloft by every antidepressant ever made.

"Honey, this is a special day. Don't ruin it with that kind of language."

"Mom, I want my money! Pony up, be-yatch!"

"Please sit down."

The "man" ran past her and up to me.

"Hey, you got Eminem?"

I smiled benevolently, willing the irritation to stay inside.

"Yep."

"How about 50 Cent?"

"Yep."

"You'd better fucking play him, then. None of that pussy shit."

"Right. No pussy shit. Got it."

Another little preteen ran up. His tie was wrapped around his head like the saddest headband ever. He would probably meet his end in some dank frat house, when a keg stand goes horribly, horribly wrong.

"What about Good Charlotte? You got them?"

"Yep."

Yet another kid stepped up. He obviously sat on the bottom of the totem pole, as his nose had already been rubbed in what I hoped was dirt. He must be a momma's pity invite.

"What about Justin Timberlake?"

Oh, you dumb, dumb boy.

"What? What are you, a fag? Jesus Christ, you are such a faggot!"

As the chorus asserting this poor kid's homosexuality swelled, I felt some relief that apparently the J word was okay to use. Hey, it's good to know the rules. After a few vicious moments, the kids grew tired of mocking the alleged gay boy and ran off to sniff one another's butts. Maybe because I was feeling so nostalgic, I had the urge to comfort the poor kid struggling not to cry. Having been that alleged gay boy so many years ago, I knew that crying would only make things worse. So I spoke softly to him as I cued up my CD.

"What's your name, kid?"

The alleged gay boy looked up suspiciously.

"Why?"

"Just curious."

He swallowed his tears and answered.

"Fran."

Man, parents are cruel.

"Well, Fran, I can look into the future."

"You're a weirdo."

"No, it's true. You want to know your future?"

Fran thought for a second and then shrugged warily.

"Sure."

"Okay. I'm looking into the future. One day, you will enter a ShopRite to buy some bread. Behind the counter will be someone who seems vaguely familiar. After you've ordered, you'll study him and with a burst of recognition you'll realize that he is in fact Eddie Mendlesohn, your tormentor from years ago. He made your life a living hell, calling you a fag every five minutes your entire last year of middle school. You're still messed up about it, taking great pains to never coordinate your outfits just to head off any gossip. But now, he cuts your bread. And you'll smile to yourself, saying nothing to the guy, and walk out knowing that life is a little fairer than you thought. After a quick complaint to the manager about the way the guy behind the bakery counter was rubbing up against the dough inappropriately, that is."

Fran shot me a confused look.

"What the hell are you talking about?"

"Okay, in my case his name was Jimmy Esposito, but it'll still happen. I guarantee it."

Fran seemed unconvinced, looking me up and down as he took in the guitar tie and the beaten suit.

"So you were doing better than him?"

"Of course."

"Were you a DJ then, too?"

This kid seemed more like the thirteen-year-old version of me with every sentence.

"Hey! Being a DJ is a cool job. It's way better than some bread slicer."

"I guess. Do you DJ at a club or something?"

Damn kids and their constant questions!

"Well, no. I do weddings and proms and anniversaries. That kind of stuff."

"And bar mitzvahs."

I was feeling sorry for ever trying to cheer this ungrateful brat up. I set him straight.

"I'm not really a DJ. It's not my life's work, or anything. I'm a writer. I wrote a book."

He perked up a bit.

"Is it at Barnes and Noble?"

I sighed, wondering where they kept the vodka.

"Well, it will be. I'm looking for an agent right now. Anyway, I wasn't always a DJ. I used to be a television producer. I won Emmys and everything."

I don't think he believed me.

"Why'd you stop?"

Fran really loved the hard questions. He would probably grow up to be another Geraldo Rivera.

"You probably won't understand this at your age, but I quit because I wanted to be happy."

He processed this bold statement as the sounds of boys charley-horsing one another to death drifted over.

"So you're happy doing this?"

He sounded incredulous. I looked around at the kids across the room. Eddie had arranged a line of his best buddies and he was taking turns smacking each of them in the stomach for no good reason.

"I have a plan. Don't you worry about me. I'm five feet from the big happy, I can feel it."

Before Fran could answer, Just Call Me Stu stormed up.

"I'm not paying you to talk away. I'm paying you to keep my son occupied so he doesn't do anything too . . . rambunctious. Okay?"

"You bet, sir."

"Good."

He stepped away, waiting for me to get the party started right. I glanced back, but Fran had retreated to the corner, as far from his fellow classmates as he could get. I wished I could join him. Instead, I grabbed the mic and turned down the Black Eyed Peas.

"Can I have your attention please? Thanks! I'm David and I'm your DJ today. Let's give a hand to the man of the hour—Eddie Mendlesohn!"

Clapping and face punching all around.

"Before we serve the food, I need to see all the guys on the floor."

After a general brawl that resulted in four wedgies and an atomic melvin (it's as bad as it sounds), the floor was filled. Twenty kids staring at me, waiting to be entertained. Just Call Me Stu gave me an encouraging nod. I should have brought dancing girls.

"I've got some prizes here, so we're going to have a contest. It's a karaoke contest. . . ."

Just Call Me Stu winced. Miscalculation. I adjusted.

". . . But before that, we're going to do a little dance contest. . . ."

Mrs. Just Call Me Stu wore such a look of horror that I feared for all our lives.

". . . if there's time at the end of the day. Right now, we're going to play a little game called . . ."

I wracked my brain. What could we play? Just Call Me Stu lifted up his chair, begging for a hora. He really couldn't wait to break his kid's neck. But wait . . . of course.

". . . Musical Chairs! Yeah. Okay, guys, grab some chairs. Set them up in a row."

Mr. and Mrs. Just Call Me Stu took charge. Mrs. Just Call Me Stu actually cringed as she walked past her son. I wondered if she went shopping for dinner or if she just let her boy loose in the backyard till he loped back with a deer in his mouth.

"We need nineteen chairs."

A few of the smarter boys, realizing the painful implications of fewer chairs than guys, backed away, joining Fran in the corner. I did some quick math.

"Okay, ten chairs. Now stand around the chairs. Get ready to move, you know the drill. When the rap metal stops, your butt needs a seat. And please, no biting. We don't know who's had their shots."

The man of the moment sneered at me.

"What do we win, anyway? Not a stupid tambourine!"

Man, I hoped his relatives were cheap.

"No, you win a trophy."

This got a reaction. Trophies are big deals, no matter how cheap and small. The kids stood in a circle, expectant now, awaiting the start of the game.

"Ready, guys? All right. On your mark, get set . . . go!"

I started the music. The guys circled. The pushing had already begun. I almost didn't want to stop the music for fear of the consequences, but I had a duty. After thirty seconds or so, I pressed pause.

There have been a lot of seemingly innocent hand motions that have resulted in massive carnage. Caesar had only to point his thumb downward and the tigers were released. Al Capone drew his finger across his throat and an entire Italian restaurant went down. Truman just pressed one button. So did I. And in doing so, I unleashed the kind of slaughter not seen since biblical times.

"Boys, boys, not so rough!"

Mrs. Just Call Me Stu circled the teeming mass with her hands held up. She ducked just as the shoe of a misfortunate flew by. I can't be sure, but I think the foot was still in it. Mr. Just Call Me Stu wouldn't even approach the floor. He just called from the safety of the dessert table.

"Dammit, play fair, Eddie. Let go of his neck! That's an artery!"

A single chair remained upright, the lone survivor of this total societal breakdown. Some of the others were used as a blockade, with two boys joining forces and throwing plastic maracas like grenades from behind them. The air filled with straw from the hats some kids had stolen from me behind my back. I did nothing, just standing there paralyzed until I felt hot breath on my neck. I turned to find myself looking up Mr. Just Call Me Stu's nose. Considering he's four inches shorter than me, he must have been pretty pissed. I didn't think I could just call him Stu now.

"Yes, Mr. Mendlesohn?"

"Stop them."

"But they'll tear me apart like dogs on meat."

"Do it, or no tip."

Fuck. This was serious. I grabbed an inflatable guitar as protection and walked around the table. I could no longer tell which head belonged to which body. Then suddenly, from among the teeming masses, rose the familiar form of the man of the moment. He climbed over the struggling figures, kicking teeth and pulling hair as he went, until finally he sat atop the remaining upright chair, punching kids away as he lifted his fist into the air.

"Yeah! I won, you stupid dickheads! There can be only one! There can be only one!"

I felt privileged to be there at the exact moment a future psychopath realized that violence did in fact bring you valuable cash and prizes. I warily approached him.

"Hey, Eddie. Why don't you get your friends to calm down?"

He sneered at me.

"Where's my trophy!"

"I'll bring it over, just help me get your friends under control."

"Screw that! I am the king! I don't have to do shit! Where's my trophy!"

Before I could bargain any further, Mrs. Stu gingerly stepped up, holding one of my trophies in her hand.

"Here you go, honey. Now help the nice man."

The minute she handed it over she could tell it was a mistake, flinching as he snatched it from her. The Bastard of Honor stood up on the chair, brandishing the trophy like a Visigoth displaying the head of a rival war chief.

"Bow down, little bitches!"

His chair wobbled. Without thinking I reached out to steady him. A female voice rang out.

"Don't do it!"

Too late. Eddie reared back and swung his arm.

"No one touches the king! No one!"

The trophy whistled through the air and whacked me in the center of my forehead. The world imploded. I crumpled, marveling at how times had changed. They never used to hit you in the face when I was a kid.

As I lay on the floor, I pondered how I, who had won Emmys and directed hundred-thousand-dollar shoots during my television days, and had written one of the great novels (okay, novellas) of our time, had ended up surrounded by screaming teenage boys, half conscious, with the imprint of a man holding a torch thrust deep into my forehead. This is what happens when you try to be happy.

* * *

Everything seemed so cut and dried back in Mrs. Hickenbothem's first grade classroom. She handed out the Ditto sheets, passing them up and down the rows of children with her impossibly old fingers (she was twenty-five). I remember the sheets clearly, the blue-black ink smudged but still readable in my head. "What makes you happy?" they asked. You got to pick from a multitude of choices, such as swimming and construction and buying things on sale. After you checked the ones that applied, you turned to the second sheet, which matched your choices up to possible occupations. Mine matched up to being a writer. Well, that and homemaker, which I decided to keep to myself. So in my mind, what you did with your work life became intertwined with what made you happy. And in my case, that meant writing.

After all, my mom always lauded my compositions. She put them up on the fridge, which rivaled the Louvre for prestige. My dad told all his friends about my ambitions and they assured me of the respectability of the profession. My English teachers through the years encouraged me. Mr. Paulson from eighth grade told me I'd win a Pulitzer some day. That really got me excited, since I thought it was a type of machine gun. Everyone approved of my particular path to happy. They all believed in me. I believed in me.

But then college ended and I discovered that when I sat down to write, nothing happened. I'd sit and stare at the computer screen and gradually realize I was six months late on my rent. So I took a job as a production assistant on *The Puppeteers* (a cute little program about puppet pirates that sailed around telling children not to eat paste or laugh at German people), just to make money and do something interesting while I sorted it all out. I didn't dream of working my way up the children's television ladder or anything, I just wanted to do something different. Until my writing took off, I figured. Six years, a hundred episodes and three Emmys later, I was still there (to put the whole Emmy thing into perspective, bear in mind our main competition was an eighty-year-old man with a shoe fetish and a six-foot-tall naked orangutan in a top hat). Only now I ran the show. Was I happy? Not in the way those Dittos promised, no. They promised everything. My detour had become my life. It wasn't a bad life. But it wasn't the smudged-ink life I set out to lead all those years ago.

So at the height of it all, I made my grand gesture. I dropped out, leaving behind years of moving up and paying dues in order to follow that messy blue-black path. I knew what kind of happy I deserved. The big happy. The kind that comes with the fulfillment of potential and dreams, the kit and caboodle. Yes, I wanted both the kit and the caboodle. I was that greedy.

That was when I got lucky. I went through a messy breakup with the only woman I had ever loved, and during the ensuing emotional shit storm, out of self-defense really, I began to write. A few months later, I had finished my novel (okay, novella). Two hundred and twenty-five pages of David for all the world to see. It took more than twenty years, but I'd finally tapped into the potential first glimpsed in that elementary school classroom.

Next step? Send the sucker out! My words needed to be published, with a hefty advance included. So off I mailed my masterwork to every literary agent I could find in the helpful literary agent book my mom gave me for Christmas. My initiative taken, I had to sit back and wait. Only now, I discovered to my dismay that my savings had blown away like sagebrush in the desert, tumbling between two grudge-settling gunslingers before disappearing forever over the horizon. So I cast about for a job that wouldn't distract me from my goal while keeping me in the manner to which I'd grown accustomed (i.e., fed). One day I came across an ad in the paper looking for mobile DJs to work weddings, bar mitzvahs, anniversaries, birthdays and the like. Maybe it was the flexible hours, or the mental freedom, or the chance to wear a guitar tie, but I felt oddly drawn to the job. So even though everyone I knew was laughing at the thought of me in a secondhand tux trying to get this party started (quickly, of course), that's what I did.

As I began my (temporary!) sojourn into the world of the mobile DJ, I waited for responses to my novel(la). Gradually, they began to trickle in. Some people thanked me for submitting. Others just told me it wasn't going to happen. But they all ended the same. They all wished me success. This made me laugh every time. If they'd really wished me success, they'd have represented me. That'd be the quickest route to my success, I would think.

But I didn't get bitter. I had countless success stories to blunt my senses with. Tales of a writer receiving hundreds—no thousands—of rejection letters, and you know who that writer was? John Steinbeck! I love his work! He sold millions. Those agents must be kicking themselves! I surrounded myself with these thoughts, submerging my head in them. Reality would speak and I'd hear it like Charlie Brown heard his mom. Unintelligible and easy to ignore.

So I'm still waiting and working toward the big happy, plugging away as a DJ while waiting for the final letters to come in, including the one begging me to sign up for a one-way ticket to fame, fortune and lasting satisfaction. Anyway, I should probably get back to flailing blindly and struggling to regain consciousness now. . . .

* * *

"Hey, cowboy, you okay?"

I opened my eyes. Lip gloss. That was my first thought. This woman sure likes the lip gloss. Extremely, ridiculously long hair. Rapunzel-length hair that would get you up the side of a tower, no sweat. An unseasonable tan that spoke of many long hours spent in the oven. Long fake eyelashes. Nice, slightly mocking eyes. Hand outstretched toward me. I grabbed it and let her haul me upward.

"Thanks. Fuck!"

My head fucking hurt.

"There's a triumphant man dented into your head."

I felt the welt from my trophy encounter with my finger, cautiously.

"I wonder how far a dress shoe can go up a kid's ass."

"I tried to warn you. He's not good with the touching."

I blinked and took a wider view of my helper. She seemed pretty underneath the beauty aids. Her lips slipped sideways in a smirk.

"Shall I twirl?"

I coughed.

"Sorry."

"It's a free country. Take a good long look. Drink it in."

Embarrassed, I glanced around. The Bastard and his buddies had run off to eat some pizza. I took the opportunity to change the subject.

"Somebody should kick some sense into that shit-eater."

"I'd call him more of a shit-kicker, wouldn't you? I mean, you're the one who did the eating."

I didn't know what to say to that, so I staggered over to my table and threw on another CD. Just Call Me Stu stopped by apologetically, and I could tell my tip would increase according to the guilt. At least the pain was worth something. He quickly retreated and I turned to see that Lip Gloss had followed me. She leaned in to take a good look at my forehead.

"Damn, he got you good, didn't he? The little guy always did know how to take a man down. His cousin's missing a testicle because of him. No joke."

"He's quite a little Hitler, isn't he?"

"You better watch what you say, boy. Remember where you are."

Something about this girl was getting under my skin.

Maybe it was the total lack of tact. Or maybe it was the mascara. I couldn't tell. Something about her scent, maybe. She seemed in her early twenties and I could tell by her clothes . . . well, nothing. What the hell do I know about clothes? The only difference I can see between Prada and Old Navy is that Old Navy is obviously higher class because they can afford to parade around Morgan Fairchild. The only thing I could really tell about Lip Gloss was that her push-up bra was trying to make a full meal out of parsley.

She seemed to be waiting for something, but I was too dizzy to figure out what it was. Finally she gave up.

"Since your manners were obviously kept in your now-damaged frontal lobe, I'll help you out. My name is Janey. And no, I have no gun. Don't even ask me about a gun. And your name is David Holden. Don't get all excited, I can see it on the card."

"Nice to meet you."

"Nice to meet you, too."

I went back to my CD case. All I could think about was the smell of her, soft and sweet, making my nose twitch. A small burning sensation in my stomach tipped me to the fact that I felt a little nervous. A little on display. I focused on every motion I made as I flipped through my music, all too aware she stood next to me, watching. I didn't really know what to say. She broke the silence.

"I like the setup. Vintage. Especially the cheap lights and the faded company tablecloth. Very shabby chic."

"No need to mock my equipment. I may not be the highest-tech DJ in town, but that doesn't mean I . . . suck."

Ah, the great comeback. She smiled, her brilliant, recently whitened teeth reflecting the cheap lights onto my forehead, where I wouldn't be surprised to later discover a small tooth-shaped tan.

"Just because something's cheap doesn't mean it sucks. I still wear a ratty Minnie Mouse tee my dad bought me in Orlando when I was thirteen. It really pisses the prosecutor off when I show up at one of his trials wearing it."

I cued up a new CD, trying not to look at her, all the while constantly sneaking glances. She swayed on her feet, her eyes half closed. I realized she was drunk off her ass.

"So your dad's a lawyer, huh?"

She ignored my feeble attempt at conversation, distracted by the sound of the Bastard of Honor screaming for more pepperoni. She pointed her middle finger toward his table, shaking the digit vigorously.

"I hate that kid! Look at him! They give him fucking everything he wants! My uncle is such a pussy. I bet they give him a sponge bath every night before bed. Their house is like his personal dictatorship."

The vehemence in her voice struck me.

"He's a kid, what can you do?"

She leaned into me suddenly, breathing hot and strong in my ear.

"He's a bully. I hate bullies. I hated them when I was his age, little tyrants with the IQs of spitballs. And now I'm related to one. Fucking ironic, like rain on your wedding day. Or is that just a bummer? I can never remember which I'm supposed to smirk at and which I'm supposed to cry at."

Her breath seared my earlobe, clearing the area of any remnants of wax. Her tirade made me uncomfortable, so I retreated to my CD cases. She followed me, slipping around my table to stand at my side. I felt a jolt as her hand brushed carelessly against mine.

"I know I'm smashed, okay? You don't have to pretend or anything."

She swayed into me, rocking gently on her heels. I put out a hand to keep her upright.

"You're not that bad. You're just swaying a little bit. A lotta bit."

She flicked my ear, where the last remnants of my wacky, exploratory college years hung in a small loop of gold.

"Earrings are out, babe. You want me to take care of it?"

I leaped back, my hand shooting up to my lobe.

"No! Don't touch it! You'll pull off my ear!"

"I'm like a surgeon when I'm hammered. This is when I do all my eyebrow plucking. Come on, it's time to let go of your fake rebellion. No one bought it then, and they're not buying it now."

"Don't touch it."

She reached forward, clearly intent on ripping the thing out like an errant hair from its follicle, but thankfully a wave of dizziness overtook her, forcing her to use my table to steady herself.

"You know I'm gonna get it. Maybe not today, maybe not tomorrow, but soon."

"You keep your crazy hands off my jewelry."

Her eyes narrowed into sharp lines.

"You keep your opinions to yourself, all right?"

I could see the small shimmer of hurt I'd inflicted.

"Look, I'm sorry. I don't know you. I'm just doing my job."

Her eyes caught the sympathy in mine and she softened.

"Apology accepted."

We stood there, trapped, until my Sum 41 song ended. Our fragile connection shattered as I broke away, hurrying to throw on something equally pseudo-punk. I spoke as I searched, attempting to move past the moment.

"You said something about your dad being a lawyer?"

She coughed and looked away.

"Yep. He's good. I mean real good. I love to watch him work. I sit in the balcony and cheer him on during his cases. I even started the wave once. You'd be amazed what bored court spectators will do for a pretty girl."

"I bet you wrap them all around your pretty little finger."

"Oh, it is pretty. Gorgeous. Like the rest of me. Aren't I just fucking gorgeous?"

Her voice came out loud and dripping with disdain. A few of the parents leaned into one another, exchanging disapproving opinions under their breaths. Janey staggered back into the corner to get away from the whispers. She tripped and almost fell, prompting me to reach out and hold her. Her eyes flickered up to meet mine and I was surprised to see moisture.

"Are you okay?"

She blinked quickly, speaking in slurred, hurt tones.

"He said he was coming. That's the only reason I came all the way out to Long Island to see some kid I can't stand get handed an obscene wad of money for speaking in shockingly bad Hebrew. It was a family thing and he said he was coming. He promised. Look around, you see him? Anywhere?"

"I don't know what he looks like."

"I don't, either. He looks so tiny on the courtroom floor. He had a case, I bet. I should understand that. Right? Sure. I came out to Long Island! I mean, I'm in a Pizza Hut! Jesus! Isn't that love?"

She leaned in to me, holding on for dear life. I struggled to set her down easy.

"Sounds it to me."

She finally gave in, sliding onto the hard, fast-food-chain floor.

"He's probably teaching me a lesson. That's so like him. It's funny how you can't give up on them. Not really. No matter what they do, you can't give up. It sucks. I'm sorry. I think I mentioned I might be drunk."

"Don't worry about it."

She sat still for a moment, gazing at her feet. My contempt for a girl who'd get smashed at a bar mitzvah wavered, beaten back by her forlorn figure, so beautiful in its unhappiness. My stomach leaped again as I caught myself memorizing her, taking in the little details, like the freckles on her arm barely noticeable beneath her dark tan, her nose, slightly bumpy in the middle, the sound of her breathing as she sat lost in her sloshed mind. I didn't want to be looking so closely, but I did anyway.

She finally glanced up, catching my eye from behind the hair falling down over her face like a weeping willow.

"Can I have your card?"

I answered by instinct, unprepared for such a banal question.

"Sure, here. Got a party coming up?"

I turned back to my table, grabbing a card. After I handed it to her, I returned my attention to my equipment, checking my dials and faders minutely.

"No, I'm, in . . . in . . . in*volved* with a catering company and they're always looking for new DJs. To party hearty and all that. You know."

She stumbled over her pronunciation. I focused on my equipment.

"By all means, pass it along."

She stood up shakily as I spoke, her cheeks slightly red from embarrassment.

"Anyway, sorry about the concussion."

"Hey, it brought back memories of the whuppings of my youth."

"Nice to meet you, DJ boy."

"You, too."

She wandered off. I watched her go, telling myself I felt sorry for her. Telling myself I hoped she never called. Such an unhappy, angry woman. The last thing I needed on the search for happy was to be pulled off track by someone like that.

Chapter Two

Death by Apartment

I drove back to the city, passing through the scary underground of the midtown tunnel and popping up at Second Avenue. Whispers of lip gloss and soft perfume tried to take over my imagination, but I put those thoughts to rest. Once upon a time, I'd been in love with a girl I now affectionately call the Eater of Souls (at one point it wasn't so affectionate, but time is the great Ambesol to life's many canker sores). She became the impetus for my only real piece of writing to date, but her influence didn't end there. I'd tasted the forbidden fruit of actual romantic happiness, however short-lived and self-delusional it ended up being, and everything after that seemed somehow insubstantial. The only dating I'd done since was with a girl named Julie, the Relapse Girl. It lasted a year and never went anywhere. Two or three times a week we grabbed dinner and checked out a movie or a live band or something cultural, like a one-woman show about nipples or a one-legged breakdancer with gold teeth. Afterward, we'd have sex, usually in her apartment since she had good water pressure, and then we'd sleep. I'd be gone by breakfast and the cycle would begin anew. I'd probably still be locked into that *Groundhog Day* of banality if she hadn't gone back to her old boyfriend, Carl, who was forty-five years old with wrinkly balls. I mean, I never saw the balls, but I could just tell. Not that I'm bitter. She accused me of being fixated on something I'd once experienced with someone else, but I knew it wouldn't happen again. Love is never the same twice. Nothing will ever match that first rush. I probably wouldn't want it to. In fact, avoiding those big volatile relationships like I had with the Eater had become my mandate. Sing it with me, Mary J. Blige! No more drama.

I pulled up to my apartment building, parking in front of a hydrant, daring them to tow me. Considering how long the broken-down Chevy at the end of the street had been sitting on those four blocks, I liked my chances.

I've had to downgrade my apartment somewhat since I decided to be happy. My old place on the Upper East Side barely fit me and a TV. Now the TV and I share a bed. I live in a tiny, and by tiny I mean actually smaller than I am, studio on Avenue C. It costs two thirds of what I make to pay the rent, and on top of that I need to keep my car for the DJ business, so I am the dirtiest of dirt poor. My friends keep asking me why I don't move back home or out to Queens, where it's cheaper. They don't seem to understand. Manhattan says success, and I need to believe that. I may be king of the form rejection letter, but I can still see the top of the Empire State Building from my roof.

If my rent and room size issues weren't enough, ever since I'd moved into my new place, my apartment has been trying to kill me. My friends point to this as a sign that I should move, but I know it's just coincidence. Why should my apartment have anything against me? Who else would live in it? (Who am I kidding? There are thousands of idiots lining up to pay for the privilege of storing their clothes in the oven.)

It started with an allergic reaction to the carpet that left me unable to speak for a week. Ripping that sucker up helped me breathe easy until a bump the size of King Kong's ball popped up on my eyelid, forcing me to repaint the whole place (which took ten minutes) in order to kill any mold that may have been living in the walls. My eyelid went back to normal and I thought it was over.

But my apartment was set back, not defeated. Since subtlety had stopped working, it began to try more direct methods of homicide. I was awakened one morning by my heater spraying hot water all over my head. Thank God I sleep with my head under the covers (I miss the womb) or I would have been badly burned. Pictures fell off the walls, narrowly missing me. I stepped on a splinter from my wooden floor, driving it deep into my heel, causing me to limp for a month. So far I've escaped major injury, but the apartment has shown no sign of letting up. I wish it would either stop or kill me already.

I finished lugging my equipment up the stairs, shoving the second speaker under the cupboard before collapsing onto my bed. A pot fell off the top shelf, narrowly missing my head, but I was too tired to flinch. There I lay, lost in a cloud of lip gloss and perfume.

My cell phone rang, rousing me from my stupor to check the caller ID. I still lived in fear that the Eater of Souls would call me and I'd answer it unawares. But this was Annie.

"Hey babe! Could you pick up some wine on the way tonight?"

I wondered if she'd changed. I wondered if the desert really made you stronger. I wondered if she still had the fear. Annie had always been terrified of commitment. I mean *terrified* of it, the way most people are scared of spiders. She broke up with the best thing that had ever happened to her, Jacob, when he wanted too much, and fled to Phoenix to try to start again. That was a year ago. Then I get a call last week; she was coming home. She saw no reason to live alone in Phoenix when she could be with her friends back in New York. Solid thinking, I commended her. And I had missed her. All my friends seemed to be deserting me. Annie to Phoenix. My buddy Jim to his harem of goth women in Providence. I was starting to feel cut off here in my little murderous apartment. But now Annie was home. She'd sneaked into town a week earlier than she said she would and hadn't even called anyone until a few days ago. But we forgive.

"No prob. I can't wait to see you. I wish you had let me help you move back in."

"This is how I want to see everybody. A big party at my new place."

That stung a little. I was everybody.

"Who else is coming? Did you get ahold of everyone?"

"Most of them. Cameron and his new girlfriend are coming. Have you met her yet?"

"Not yet. I hear she's got big biceps, though."

"I think that's a safe bet."

Cameron only dates women who can beat him up. It's adorable.

"Dustin is coming with some girl named Carrie."

"The girl who laughs like a donkey being violated. Check."

"And of course, you. And a friend or two."

Annie sounded distant. Had we forgotten how to talk to each other? It's been known to happen. You lose that rhythm you'd always shared and you freak out, overcompensating by trying to force yourself back into familiarity, which never works. Nah, couldn't be. Some things last forever.

"Sounds great."

"See you in a few hours then?"

"You bet."

After she hung up, I glanced at the photos propped up against my television/nightstand. In between the shots of my parents and my brother rested an image of six happy kids mugging for the camera. I picked it up and stared at it closely, soothing my stomach with the sight of those smiling young faces. Most of them had turned fourteen by the time the picture was taken, all except me. The baby of the family. And like a baby, I'd centered myself in the photo, surrounded on all sides by my friends, protected and secure. A slight darkening around my eye was all that remained of a shiner I'd received a few weeks earlier (the last vestige of the humiliation that ended my ass kickings). But that didn't damper my stupid grin. Dustin leaned on my right shoulder, his tall lanky frame propped up against me with all the weight of a piece of Styrofoam as he smiled wryly. His large shock of untamed hair bulged out from his skull like he'd seen something particularly frightening just moments before, which coupled with his tall thin frame made him look like a recently lit sparkler. He wore his ever-present black coat that he strutted around in like a comic book antihero, cool and silent except for the well-timed quip. The chicks all thought he was dark and mysterious. Only we knew about the lightsaber in his locker.

Playfully driving his head into Dustin's arm, Cameron smiled widely with every tooth gleaming. The photo must have been taken after a football game (which we attended only for Cameron's sake), because he was fully decked out in his piper's kilt. He was not only Scottish, but also Jewish and Korean, which would often render the opposing team so confused they'd give up a touchdown in the first two minutes. He was a cool guy, but Dustin knew his fuse ran short and his mockery of Cameron's need to plot out his entire life through retirement on a huge spreadsheet could usually get the poor kid to blow.

On the other side, off on his own with a soft smile, stood Zach. He wasn't quite touching Hank, who was beside him, and therefore didn't seem quite so much a part of the group. I guess that was fitting, as Zach ran off soon after high school graduation to travel the world. He came back every once in a while, and I loved to see him when he did, but he never stayed long. Looking down at his clean, young face, I wondered where he was now. Probably sitting on some beach in South America with a bevy of young Brazilian women playing naked Twister for him while he perused his Sartre. More power to him.

Hank I hadn't seen since high school graduation. You can't hold on to them all. The last I heard he was married with two kids and living in Florida. He was the first defector, and I hoped to God he would be the last.

Finally, to my right, one arm draped around me and the other around long lost Hank, stood Annie, her mouth scrunched up in an impression of a fish drowning on dry land. She was the only girl in a group of boys, but that never bothered her or us. She'd lost her dad a year or so before, so maybe we were five fathers or five brothers or something. Or maybe not. Maybe she just had a boy's mind. After all, she could curse with the best of them, and she could out-sarcasm any of us at will. She could beat up Cameron in a fair fight, an occurrence I swear he would solicit (seeing his dating habits now, I think she kicked off a fetish). She was just a sharp, funny, cool chick. I'm sure it sounds like we all had mad crushes on her, but we never really thought of her that way. She was just Annie, the coolest girl ever created. When she took up with Jacob the punk rocker many years later, we all sighed in satisfaction at the cool nature of her selection. And when she screwed it up and fled to Phoenix a few years after that, well even that was pretty damn cool. Most people just let things fall away. They don't flee across the country like a cowboy running from his dark past. It takes a cool chick to manage that. God, I had missed her. But now she was back.

I gazed down at my frozen slice of childhood with no small measure of pride. They were still here, almost all of them, and waiting to drink wine with me tonight. I may have lost the esteem of my younger self, but my friends remained to encircle and protect me. Sure they'd mock me and push my buttons, but that's their job. Our entire friendship has always been based on jokes and button pushing. Nothing was more important than the joke. As long as it was funny, it was okay. As long as the circle remained, everything was okay.

Chapter Three

Invasion of the Rat Boy

I buzzed Annie's new apartment in Queens, embarrassingly cheap wine in hand. Her intercom was busted, so she had to buzz me in without speaking to me. Kind of defeated the purpose, but I wouldn't say anything. I walked up the four flights and stopped outside her door. I felt a little nervous. How much had she changed? Not too much. People don't change that much.

"What are you doing? Do you have gas or something?"

Annie's voice drifted through the door, making me smile.

"I'm just caught up in reflection."

"It's freaking me out."

"Then why don't you open the door?"

"That's not how's it's done. You have to knock."

"I don't want to knock. It's silly. You know I'm here."

"It's my party and I say you knock. Are we Communists? Here in America, we do things the right way."

"Fine. I'll knock."

"Thank you."

I knocked.

"Who is it?"

"Immigration. Now open the damn door."

The door swung open and I stepped back in shock.

"You're blond."

"You're observant. Your police sketches must be masterpieces."

She was blond! Even her eyebrows!

"I knew it was sunny in Phoenix, but this is amazing."

"I needed a change."

"Clearly."

"Well?"

She flipped her hair. She looked better than I'd ever seen her, sexy even. Like a real girl or something. I found myself admiring her, which is ridiculous since I've known her forever. That ship had sailed long ago. I covered my moment of insanity by whistling.

"Hot."

"Thank you. Come here."

She gave me a huge hug. Her hair smelled different. That brief second of awkward desire faded, replaced by the feeling that all was now right in the world again.

"Welcome home, Annie."

"It's good to be back. I missed you."

I felt my heart lighten even further as I realized I would no longer be the only single person in our little circle. After all, Annie has gone through literally hundreds of guys. And by literally, I mean figuratively. And every time she's rejoined me in the land of the happily unattached.

Annie stepped back out of the doorway.

"You should come in."

"Is anyone else here?"

"Everyone's here."

I walked in. Annie shut the door behind me and guided me down a long hallway toward the living room of her fairly sizable apartment. It seemed cheery and pleasant, with black-and-white landscapes and bright prints hanging on the walls, intermingled with framed photos of family and friends. Unlike most apartments owned by America's youth, this one felt like someone's actual home.

"Nice place. I know you're doing okay with money, but this place seems awfully big for one person."

She didn't respond. We made it to the living room. The fact that it took any time at all to get there should paint a picture of the un–New York nature of the apartment. These thoughts came and went as everyone I cared about still living in a five-mile radius looked up at me. Annie smiled.

"Hey guys! The party is now ready to begin."

Dustin sat in the corner with Donkey Girl, who brayed welcomingly. The sound seemed all the more shocking coming out of her petite, blond head. I'd spent only a little time with her, but already I could tell she fit right into Dustin's type, which could be summed up by "attractive" and "hopelessly optimistic." Dustin hated when women went around having expectations of him (he so rarely met them), but though they'd never admit it, they always did. His stick frame had filled out some, his crazy hair had been pruned down into closely cropped submission and his black coat had long since been retired by a particularly aggressive ex, but his laid-back and mysterious demeanor remained, along with its effect on the ladies. He seemed like the perfect blank canvas, and they took him on as a community service project, sure that that once they got their hands on him he'd transform into the perfect relationship citizen. And one by one they left him behind, scratching their heads at where they'd gone wrong. I'd noticed that lately these defections had begun to wear on Dustin, planting a seed of doubt into the mind of the man who refused to reflect.

Cameron lay on the loveseat, his head in the lap of a nice-looking, solidly built Catholic girl. I could tell she was Catholic by the beaten look in her eyes. We know our own. So Cameron was dating a Catholic. This boded well for his goal of having a child who actually imploded under the stress of his or her internal contradictions. Cameron looked exactly the same as he had in high school, down to the polo shirt and Dockers. He was in banking now, and he'd discovered that his bagpiping actually helped him get hired. Apparently people like a bit of color. Of course, they didn't realize exactly how much color they were hiring.

Behind the United Nations, sitting discretely in the corner, sat a young guy I didn't know. He had a bit of the rodent about him with his long nose and weasel teeth, and his facial hair hung weakly from his face like someone had sporadically attacked it with a Weedwacker. If you can't do the beard, don't, all right? Otherwise you look like a ten-year-old in a Halloween costume, chin covered in hair clippings and spirit glue. I nodded. He nodded back, his eyes strangely fearful. Before I could investigate further, Cameron waved from his prone position and pointed to his lady.

"David, this is Mary. Mary, this is the guy I was telling you about. The DJ."

"I'm a writer. Nice to meet you, Mary."

She tried to stand up, but Cameron's laziness lay in the way of etiquette. She settled for reaching over his head to shake my hand.

"I love that you do weddings. That is so romantic."

Oh Jesus. She sounded sincere.

"Yeah, well, I guess."

"How many brides have you slept with?"

I flashed Cameron a smile.

"We approve."

"I thought you might."

Annie walked over to the unknown rodent boy.

"David, this is Josh. He's a friend from Phoenix."

I leaned over and shook his hand.

"Hey, Josh. You here visiting?"

"No, I live here now."

"Great. Where?"

"Um, here, actually."

I gave Annie a quizzical look.

"So you guys are roommates?"

Annie moved behind him and put her hand on his shoulder. Uh oh.

"Actually, Josh and I are living together. This is our place."

I tried to process.

"So you're dating . . . him?"

Josh patted Annie's hand.

"More than dating. I moved here for her. I want her to be happy."

Annie smiled and kissed his forehead. My mind rebelled. This just couldn't be. Maybe he was a hypnotist or something. Or held her mother captive. I know! Alien mind control. Of course.

"How long did you date in Phoenix? You never mentioned him, Annie."

Annie threw her arms around his neck.

"It moved too quickly to tell you guys. Before I knew it, we were in love."

Cameron was sitting up now.

"How quickly? Six months?"

"Well . . ."

I knew where this was going.

"What are we talking here? A week? A week and a half?"

"Don't be so dramatic. It's been a month or so."

Dustin leaned in, worry marring his typically calm face.

"Or so?"

"Okay, a month."

Josh smiled, his feral incisors glinting in the light of the halogen lamp.

"It doesn't matter. When you know, you know."

I had to sit, almost breaking Cameron's ankle as I dropped heavily onto the couch.

"But moving in together, that's a big step. And no offense . . ."

Rat Boy! Rat Boy!

". . . Josh, but Annie hasn't been known for her quick decisions."

Annie shrugged.

"I just knew."

Dustin gave a shrug of his own.

"She just knew. End of story."

Donkey Girl let out another bray.

"This is so exciting. Another couple! I love it!"

Fantastic. And I was alone in the monkey cage, masturbating for the tourists. Rat Boy nudged Annie, who could already tell this wasn't going well.

"Oh, right. I have an even bigger announcement to make!"

I knew it!

"You're pregnant!"

Annie scowled.

"Don't make me banish you to the corner, David. I'm not pregnant."

Dustin yawned belligerently.

"Then what? What's behind curtain number three?"

Annie settled herself.

"We're getting married."

Silence. The kind of silence you could whittle wood with. Annie answered herself with an excited squeal.

"Ahhhh!"

Donkey Girl was the first to recover, joining Annie in a shout of joy that reminded me of a mule sex show you'd catch in Tijuana (or so I hear). Mary jumped in next, congratulating Annie with a big smile and a hug. Rat Boy looked around in complacent glee. But from her oldest, dearest friends: nothing. Dustin, Cameron and I remained motionless. Annie's face took on a look of desperation.

"Aren't you guys happy for me?"

As one, we turned on our fakest, "sure you look good in those stretch pants" smiles.

"Congrats!"

"About time!"

"Good luck, you two!"

The kind of performances that get replayed at Oscar time. But inside, I could hear our voices screaming in unison.

MISTAKE!

* * *

The squealing had died down and Annie moved into the kitchen to check on the chicken. After exchanging knowing looks with my two shocked buddies, I moseyed in after her. She took a small knife and cut a slice of chicken, checking the color.

"A little bit longer."

At least she understood patience when the threat of salmonella hung over her head. She flicked the point of the knife with her fingernail, refusing to meet my gaze.

"So what do you think?"

"I don't want to tell you."

"Why not?"

"You're holding a knife."

She put it down, thankfully.

"Now I'm not."

I considered my options. Nothing appealed. I chose to stall.

"Why didn't you tell me?"

She smiled wanly.

"I wanted to surprise you. Boo!"

"Yeah, you win."

"Are you happy for me?"

"Yeah, sure. I'm sorry, I'm still shocked."

"Hug?"

She opened her arms. I stepped in, giving her a noncommittal squeeze.

"Josh, huh?"

"Josh."

"What's his last name?"

"Mendlesohn."

Not another Mendlesohn. Is that the only Jewish name available?

"Annie Mendlesohn. Interesting."

"I may keep my name."

"Does he know you're Catholic?"

"His family isn't particularly observant, so he doesn't care."

"Does he know your aunts do?"

"He hasn't met my aunts. I need to make sure he's hooked securely before the trial by bitches."

Annie's aunts are evil. That's all I have to say about them. They'd get Mother Teresa to bitchslap them.

"Fair enough."

I fell silent, knocking my fingers against the fridge. I knew she was going to try again and I didn't want to hasten the moment. No way to dodge it, unfortunately.

"What do you think of him? Honestly."

Slicing right to the question I feared.

"Um. I don't know. I don't know him."

"First impression."

"You really want me to just judge off the cuff?"

"Not really, but I can take it. Smack me in the face with it."

"He . . . I don't want to say it."

"Say it. I want to know."

There's a commonsense approach that most people would take this opportunity to employ. I wouldn't recognize common sense if it flashed me. So I fell back on my one true talent.

"He kinda looks like a rat."

She stared at me. I felt the need to elaborate.

"Around the nose, you know? That's just my initial impression. Hey, I'm not saying anything about the beard, so don't give me that look."

Still nothing. I filled in the silence with more dirt for my grave.

"Maybe if he shaved the beard I'd see him differently. He might look older. I know most people look younger with a clean-shaven face, but something tells me he's the exception. Good, strong teeth, though. That's important. Nice, healthy . . . teeth. Interesting haircut. Obviously likes to try new things. Not afraid to fail. You have to like that in a spouse. Please put down the knife."

Some time during my grave digging she'd picked up the knife. I sent a quick mental thanks to my testicles to let them know I had appreciated working with them. Thankfully, she turned and cut a sizable chunk of chicken off one of the cutlets. She turned to me and threw it right in my face.

"Ahhh! That's hot! Jesus! Annie, don't kill me!"

What was it with the face today? She put down the knife.

"I think the chicken's cooked."

"Annie, I'm sorry. I'm sure he's very nice."

She called out into the other room.

"Dinner's ready, you guys."

"Do you need help?"

"This conversation is done, David. Go sit at the table and don't talk to me."

She turned her back to me and started transferring cutlets to a plate.

"Annie, I'm sorry."

She didn't reply. I sent her sorrowful vibes and exited into the dining room, tail between my legs. I made my way to the table to sit between Donkey Girl and Rat Boy: a newly minted Jackass.

Annie didn't talk to me all through dinner. Everyone else sensed the tension and tried to alleviate it through loud forced laughter. I didn't speak as I learned all sorts of things about Rat Boy. He was an Internet tech supervisor for a national bank, which was how he could move on a moment's notice. He collected Muppets memorabilia and knew every Monty Python sketch by heart. Okay, so maybe I do, too, but I don't go around *telling* people that. That's just asking people to take your lunch money. He belonged to Greenpeace, Amnesty International and PETA, making the trip out to the capital every year to protest the wholesale slaughter of chinchillas. He played guitar and thought Jeff Buckley was the messiah. Dustin pointed out that Buckley had drowned and if he had really risen from the dead, then he didn't tour to support it. Rat Boy didn't get the joke, which didn't bode well.

I just couldn't see it. I looked around at Annie's friends and we were all the same. Sarcastic, overly intellectual, competitive smart-asses. Those are her people! Rat Boy was so . . . nice. Sincere. Hopeful. Transparent. The entire novel was printed on the cover. Unless he was hiding a cock ring, I couldn't see the connection. Annie had obviously flipped over the idea of hitting thirty. Only a year away, it must be looming over her world like an eclipse, darkening her day. It just wasn't like her to rush into things like this. I couldn't understand it.

We moved back to the living room and I sneaked a look at Annie's face. She seemed nervous, laughing far too long at one of Cameron's Simpsons quotes. She needed us to like her new man, rat beard and all. A twinge of remorse popped up somewhere in the vicinity of my conscience. Maybe I was being unfair. I didn't really know this guy. So what if he had unrealistic hopes for a better world? So did I, right? I cared about stuff like the environment and the rights of chickpea farmers and baby ostriches. That didn't stop me from making fun of a bad weave. Maybe I just needed to delve a little deeper, for Annie.

Brimming with charity, I sat down next to (Rat Boy, Rat Boy!) Josh and smiled.

"So, how you doing? Okay?"

Rat Boy nodded gratefully.

"Yes. Thanks. I have to tell you, you're all nothing like I thought you'd be."

"What's she told you? All lies! Anyway, I never would have gone near that girl if I knew she was Amish."

Josh seemed confused at the joke.

"Annie never mentioned an Amish girl. Was she out on *rumspringa*? If so, I wouldn't worry. She was trying to taste secular life to decide whether to return to the faith. It's a common practice that I think is really important to why they've survived so long."

I didn't know which was worse, the fact that he completely missed my joke, or the fact that when I got home to my apartment I would end up Googling *rumspringa* and spending half the night reading up on it.

"So, what did Annie tell you about us?"

Josh tugged on his choppy chin.

"She told me how long you guys have been friends and that you're really supportive of her."

"So we're actually nothing like that, then?"

His face took on a frightened look.

"No! No, of course not. You're just a lot more, um, *opinionated* than I thought you'd be. After all, Annie's pretty easygoing."

What? The girl who isn't allowed near the floor at Knicks games anymore because she made Kurt Thomas cry is suddenly easygoing? Something smelled funny. Unfortunately, before I could delve deeper, Donkey Girl squealed.

"Oh my God! Are those pictures?!"

She had sniffed out a small book hidden behind piles of other books placed for the express purpose of hiding the pictures. Some women just have the knack. Annie smiled patiently.

"Yep. Don't make me look at myself, that's all I ask."

Rat Boy slipped away to stare over Donkey Girl's shoulders as she and Mary flipped through the old photos. Donkey Girl let out a loud honk.

"Jesus Christ! Look at your hair, baby!"

Dustin tried to hide, but he no longer had a black coat to disappear into. Instead he had to face the music.

"Yeah, that was my hair."

Mary smirked.

"You sure let that sucker grow free range, didn't you?"

Cameron laughed, prompting a dark look from Dustin.

"Laugh it up. The kilt's comin'."

Another honk.

"Is that a kilt? Cameron! I love your legs! They look just like mine."

Cameron made such a face that Mary rubbed his knee.

"I love your sexy hairless legs, honey."

Dustin smiled in satisfaction as another ship went down with him. Donkey Girl flipped the page.

"Annie! Look at you. You look so tough!"

Rat Boy glanced over at his fiancée in confusion.

"Why are you wearing combat boots?"

Annie looked like she'd just swallowed some uncooked chicken.

"It was just a phase."

Dustin leaned over to take a look at the photo.

"A phase? Eight years is a phase? Felt more like an epoch."

I looked over at Annie with a mischievous glint in my eye.

"What did you used to call them?"

Annie tried to look uncertain, but her eyes fried me like a turkey.

"I don't really remember."

Cameron didn't let that one pass.

"You wore them every day. How can anyone forget your famous Sack Smackers?"

Rat Boy didn't expect that one. He frowned.

"Sack Smackers?"

Annie shrugged, thinking fast.

"I played a lot of Hacky Sack."

There was a definite discrepancy between Rat Boy's Annie and our Annie and I wondered why that was. But before I could push any more buttons, Mary piped up.

"Why are you all waving chocolate at David? Is he allergic or something?"

Seeing the life preserver, Annie leaped to answer.

"David wasn't eating chocolate back then. He was on his chocolate strike."

Shit. Like waving meat at dogs, Annie had successfully captured Dustin and Cameron's attention. They both burst out laughing as Donkey Girl stared closer at the picture.

"Why weren't you eating chocolate? Was it like a protest?"

Dustin smirked at the idea.

"Yeah, he was the Biko of blackheads."

Cameron snorted.

"The Patrick Henry of pimples. Give me Clearasil or give me death!"

Annie walked over to take a look at the photo.

"It never even looked that bad. You are such an overreacter, David."

I didn't answer, hoping they'd all get bored and move on. But Mary was intrigued.

"What happened?"

Great. They loved this story. We'd be here all night. Annie brought the newbies up to speed.

"When David got his freshman pictures, he made the mistake of bringing them over to the alcove, where we all hung out."

I couldn't stay out of it. I had to make sure the right story got told.

"I wanted to see them! I didn't know she'd be walking by!"

Annie waved me off. After all, I was the one who lived it, what could I know?

"So there he was, poring over his new photos, when who walks by but Emily Watkins."

Cameron sighed at the sexy memory in his head.

"She was so hot."

Dustin chimed in, a melancholy look on his face.

"I ran into her a few years ago, actually. She's gotten ugly. Not fat or anything. Just ugly. It's like her deal with Satan expired and so her forehead went back to its intended size."

We sadly pondered the passing of a great hottie in silence. Annie respectfully waited a moment before continuing.

"So, hot-at-the-time Emily looks down and sees David's portrait photos laid out on the table. David is frozen by her, I mean he can't squeeze out a single word. He's just moving his mouth like a fish suffocating on the dock. So Emily leans over and takes a look at his photos and says, get this, 'Don't worry. They can airbrush those out if you ask.'"

I squirmed as everyone laughed.

"She was trying to be nice. She said I looked good. You're just remembering the bad parts."

Mary hit my shoulder, hard. Ouch. She was Cameron's type, all right.

"We've all been there, kiddo."

Annie held up her hands.

"Regardless of her intentions, she freaked you out. So you went off the deep end, as usual, and set out on your chocolate strike. Which for you was pretty impressive, because you were nutso for your cocoa."

I defended my rep with vigor.

"Look, my dad's obsessed with sugar and diabetic because of it. I was brought up to worship sweets as this forbidden fruit. My whole family was addicted. It's not my fault. It's environment and genetics ganging up on me. But I gave it up, didn't I? That was pretty impressive."

Cameron was still as unimpressed as he was back then.

"There are so many other ways to treat zits. Washing your face, say. Using some kind of medication, also effective. And anyway, I had just as many zits as you, and I didn't go nutso. It wasn't that bad."

"That wasn't the point! Emily saw them! Everyone must have seen them! I had to take a stand."

Cameron rubbed Mary's hand.

"I remember I made out all these graphs that proved that giving up chocolate did nothing to help you with your acne. I couldn't understand how you'd ignore simple science. I mean, the information was completely faked, but still, it's common sense!"

Annie smiled.

"Remember Zach? He's another friend of ours."

I laughed.

"Zach took the bus with me. He'd pull out all these exotic chocolates from all over the world and explain how I'd never know their joys. He wouldn't eat them. Instead, he'd tell me that he was holding them for me in trust for the day I realized that withholding pleasure was the most pointless endeavor anyone could ever undertake."

Annie walked over to flip the photo book to a picture of Zach.

"He never withheld pleasure from himself, that's for sure. Honey? What's wrong?"

We all looked up at Rat Boy, who had a look of disturbed disappointment on his face. Annie reached out and tentatively stroked his shoulder.

"Are you okay?"

"I'm fine."

"You sure?"

"It's just . . . David was trying something difficult, to try to make life better for himself. You're supposed to encourage him. It's hard to give something up that you feel a physical need for. I gave up pot after college, and without my friends' support, I never would have made it."

Dustin raised his eyebrows.

"Dude, it's chocolate."

Josh looked away, embarrassed.

"I'm sorry, I don't mean to lecture. I just can't believe you guys made fun of him."

Annie's face fell, devastated by her boyfriend's indictment. The room fell silent as we all searched for a response. I wanted to tell him that I never felt like my friends weren't supporting me. They made me laugh, which is all I really wanted. But I was already in Annie's doghouse and I didn't want to say anything that might make her angrier. Instead, Cameron jumped in.

"We supported him, dude. I mean, one time that dick Danny Esposito . . ."

Both Annie and I leaped to cut him off.

"Dude, it's not important . . ."

"Cameron, that's not the point."

Cameron stopped, surprised.

"I'm trying to explain to your guy that we were good friends to one another. We got one another's backs!"

Neither Annie nor myself wanted to revisit that incident (which was the one that ended my ass kickings at Manville High), so I talked him down.

"Of course we did. Look, Josh. They were great friends. We're telling these stories because they're funny. It's fun to shoot the shit about the old days, you know? But things always sound different than they were over fifteen years ago. You know?"

Rat Boy looked miserable that he ever said anything.

"I know. I'm sorry, I had no right."

Annie gave him a big hug.

"That's okay, honey. Really."

We echoed our agreements. But the night was obviously over.

* * *

We soon made our excuses and grabbed our coats. We were all disturbed and had to leave before we ran out of fake juice. I whispered to Annie as I walked past.

"I'm sorry about all of that. Are we cool?"

She didn't look at me as she answered.

"We'll talk tomorrow."

"Fine. But I really am sorry."

She closed the door behind us and we filed down the stairs in silence. We made sure to move out of earshot from her window before discussing.

"What the fuck was that?"

"I can't fucking believe it!"

"She's like a fucking Scientologist or something."

Donkey Girl looked puzzled.

"I don't understand. She seems happy."

Dustin scoffed.

"Happy? She's deranged. Marrying that guy would be insane."

Cameron took the route of logic.

"She's feeling the pinch of age and desperation. It'll end and she'll move on. She always does."

Mary hit him.

"Don't say things like that. Anyway, you don't even know him."

Donkey Girl nodded.

"I know. Who do you think you are, just dooming them to failure like that?"

Did she not witness what we just witnessed? I set her straight.

"I'm not saying he's a bad guy. But Rat Boy comes from a different planet than we do. We are Montagues and he's a Capulet. This can only end in ritual suicide."

Donkey Girl didn't like our completely justified pigeonholing.

"She looked happy. Isn't that what matters?"

Mary shook her head.

"It'll have to be a gradual thing with these boys. He'll have to grow on them, like fungus."

Dustin waved a finger.

"Never happen. Never ever ever. Not even if he knows kung fu."

I agreed.

"Look, I know it sounds like we're being unfair, but trust me, this is not Annie. You know what I think? I think she knows that she made a mistake with Jacob. She's desperate not to let this one slip away like the last one did. But I think we can all agree that sometimes they deserve to slip away. We need to make sure she sees what she's doing before she goes too far. That's my worry. She's stubborn. Too far is her favorite destination."

Dustin and Cameron agreed, promising to give the matter some serious thought. Which meant nothing. They'd go home with their ladies and have wild sex and forget all about it. I, on the other hand, would head homeward trying to decide which bothered me more: Rat Boy's total unsuitability or Annie's impending new life. I didn't want to be a third wheel forever. A third wheel is really one wheel, spinning alone.

Chapter Four

The Dance of the Cheap Old Man

My alarm went off for the fifth time. My hand shot out to disable it, but missed completely and slammed into the lamp. Pain shot up my arm and out my mouth.

"Motherwhore!"

I sat up, clutching my wounded paw to my chest. My alarm still rang incessantly, driving me insane. I walloped it into silence and glanced down at the time.

"Motherwhore in China!"

One shower of world-record brevity, two mismatched socks, a throat-slashing shave and a roll of my equipment down the stairs later, I hit the road, rocketing toward my gig, cursing up a storm, late as a motherwhore in China.

And what a gig it was. Quite possibly the worst gig you can get without having to do Salsa Night at the Bayside Retirement Home. (They go through at least ten seniors a month. Old people were not meant to partake of the steaming-hot Latin dance of love.) This was way worse than the most horrific bar mitzvah imaginable. That Sunday, I had drawn the short straw and been sentenced to work a Greek wedding.

I know what you're thinking. Oh my God, he is such a racist! Well, hear me out. It's not that I hate Greeks. I have nothing against them. I love the party itself. They dance right away without spending three hours sitting at their tables staring at you. But I, like every DJ around, am in it for the money. And there is a Greek custom that fucks with my money, and that is not cool.

Because I get my gigs through the All-Stars, I don't get a big cut of the actual price people pay for me. If I just lived off of what I'm paid by the company, I wouldn't be able to afford my bow tie. What saves me are the tips. The basic tip for a wedding is fifty bucks. If it's less than fifty bucks I could set the bride aflame on the way out and no judge in the land would convict me (unless the judge was really mean). A good night brings me eighty to a hundred. My fellow DJs and I still whisper about the time DJ Party-time got a two-hundred-dollar tip. We remember the date and celebrate it each year like Christmas. You don't go below fifty bucks. It's just not done.

The Greeks, however, have a cultural out. It's in the courts now, and we'll have to see if the American DJ Association will continue to recognize the exemption, but until that's settled I have to abide by it. Apparently, in Greece, it is customary for an older male relative of the bride to dance a special dance at the wedding. As he spins, people throw money at him, propelling him to spin faster and dance harder. Everyone surrounds him, clapping, spurring him on. Finally, he reaches a crescendo and finishes with a flourish to the cheering and frenzied applause of the guests. Then, custom dictates, he hands the money he collects over to the DJ and that is his tip. Beautiful custom, you might think. Adds color and spice to the proceedings. I would have agreed with you once. The first time I witnessed this spectacle, I watched entranced. When he handed me the money, I was touched. Finally, someone who appreciates the DJ. Then I counted it. Fucking bastard had handed me eight dollars and forty cents. When I complained to Jeremy, my boss, he laughed and welcomed me truly to the fraternity of DJs. A Greek wedding may be fun to work, but any DJ worth his wallet would avoid it like the clap.

Jeremy tricked me with this particular job. The last name of the bride was Anglicized. It wasn't until I spoke with her on the phone that I realized how far up shit creek I'd floated. She made sure I had the right music for the dance of the cheap old man. Of course I do, I replied. I'm an old hand at this. She sounded relieved. She should, she's at least fifty dollars richer than her other marrying friends. I can't think of a better argument for assimilation. I get paid more.

The All-Stars are an all-inclusive type company, so when the happy couple hired me, they also hired a photographer and a videographer. As I dragged my amp into the main room, I ran into Carlos, who was setting up his video camera in the corner.

"Hey, Carlos. How'd the ceremony go?"

"Okay, I guess. The bride's a little . . . well, you'll see."

"I don't want to see. I want to be warned."

He shrugged as he pulled open his tripod.

"I'm glad they didn't write their vows themselves, I'll say that much. And I swear she whispered 'like hell' right before her 'I do.'"

I looked toward the double doors nervously.

"Now I'm scared. I have to go meet Dr. Jekyll and Mrs. Bride."

"Just remember to bob and weave."

I walked back to my table. I hate working with unhappy couples. I come across them more often than I ever would have believed. Often, she is pregnant. I've done a few weddings with barely eighteen-year-old kids struggling to get out the "I do"s in their shaking voices. The world must look so small from up there. Sometimes the wedding is held in the basement of the community center, sometimes in the ballroom of the Plaza Hotel. But the look of desperation and longing for lost choices in the couples' eyes remains constant. Somehow I dodged the bullet. I just wish I had learned something I could pass on. But telling a kid to close his eyes and hope for the best like I did would probably be just as likely to land him in that used tux.

The nonpregnant unhappy brides are harder to figure out. Usually I assume that she's given up and married the rich man, or the nice man, or the man who asked. It's not happiness, exactly, but at least they don't get angry. Why was this woman so angry?

I couldn't put it off any longer. With a heavy heart, I grabbed my introductions list and headed off toward the bridal suite. As I stepped up to the door and knocked, I could honestly say I'd rather be anywhere else, even at a meat-packing plant, learning how hamburgers are made.

"Who is it!"

Oh shit. Not happy.

"It's David, the DJ. Congratulations!"

The door opened. A frightened bridesmaid stood there shivering. She wordlessly stood aside as I entered the room. To my surprise, there were no groomsmen inside. Usually the entire wedding party hangs out together. But here sat only the bride and her friends. No groomsmen. Hell, no groom. The bride glowered.

"What do you need me for?"

Abrupt with more than a splash of anger. Wonderful. I soldiered on.

"Actually I need both you and the groom. I'd like to go over a few things before I line you guys up."

"Go over them with me."

She was a machine gun pointed at my head. I just wanted to stay alive.

"All righty."

As I went over the particulars of the day, I sneaked some glances at the blushing bride. Her eyes were red as if she'd been crying but her mouth was small and hard. She nodded in all the right places, but I could tell she wasn't really there. Eventually, thankfully, I finished and she turned her back to me, the interview over.

I practically flew out of the room and headed back to the dining hall. Interesting. She was about thirty-five, which made the shotgun wedding idea fairly unlikely. Even if she was just giving in, that doesn't really explain the anger. Oh well, I wasn't going to worry about it. I had a job to do.

I stopped by the kitchen on the way back to my table. The reception was at a rented hall, which meant the catering was brought in from outside. I wondered who was doing it. A peek through the doors lifted my spirits immensely. Rialto! He was the best caterer I'd ever worked with. He always served us first, and well. His food was fantastic. And, most important, he hired really hot waitresses. I popped in to say hi.

Rialto stood behind some minions, ordering them around. If he weighed less than three hundred pounds, then I was the Albanian minster of defense. He looked up and saw me.

"David! Wonderful! Now I know the party will truly be rocking oh so hard!"

"I'm just excited about the food, Rialto."

"You should be. It is fantastic. Come here, taste this."

I walked over to the pans and snagged a small piece of chicken. The taste buckled my knees.

"Amazing."

"But I thought you like the filet mignon?"

"Can I have a little bit of both?"

"Sure. I have plenty. Will you play 'Copacabana' for me?"

Rialto was a huge Barry Manilow fan. I tried to be open-minded.

"I'll see if I can squeeze it in."

"That's all I can ask. If you'll excuse me, I have to go back to slave driving."

"Sure thing."

I turned and made my way back to the kitchen door. I stopped short when the door flew open to admit a waitress, her glossy lips twitching as she concentrated on not dropping her tray. I blinked in shock.

"Janey?"

She froze in her tracks. My heart jumped, which I attributed to my surprise at seeing her here. The surprise on her face trumped my own.

"DJ boy!"

She looked horrified as I took in her uniform.

"So, when you said you worked with caterers, you meant you worked *for* caterers."

She squirmed under my amused scrutiny. She was really bothered by her job. Amazing. She couldn't have been older than twenty-four. What's the big deal?

"I'm just helping out. It's my charity, really."

"Who cares? So you're a waitress. It's not like I'm running Microsoft."

"I have a trust fund, it just doesn't kick in until one of the parents croak. So I'm just . . . you know what? Screw you."

She grabbed a tray and stormed back into the main room. Maybe she was embarrassed by her drunken breakdown at the bar mitzvah. Ah well. I had a job to do and little time for distraction.

The intro went off without a hitch. There wasn't time for a hitch. I had them to the toast in less than five minutes. I took a good look at the groom, who seemed nice enough. A little uncomfortable, but nothing mean in his manner. She smoldered, though, and everyone could see it. As soon as the best man finished his halting, uncertain speech, the guests fled the drama, attacking the dance floor with determination. By the time the entrees glided out on high-stacked silver trays, I was exhausted. But not too tired to sneak a glance or two at Janey, bowed beneath the weight of a dozen cordon bleus. I wondered what had landed a girl like her in a waitressing gig. Maybe she was disowned or something. My mind raced through all the possibilities. Maybe she killed her maid for wearing her jewelry and now she was hiding from the police, but she couldn't disguise her true blue-blooded nature. Or maybe her dad was trying to teach her what it meant to be one of the common folk. It really could be anything. And I spent far too much time pondering the possibilities.

Before I knew it, the time for the cake cutting rolled

around. I walked over to wrangle up the bride and groom, but could find only the groom. He professed complete ignorance about his new wife's location, so I set off to find her myself. There were cakes to cut and schedules to keep. In the hallway, I ran into Janey heading toward the kitchen with a half-empty plate. She stopped short when she saw me.

"Okay, I'm a waitress. Go ahead. Laugh."

"Why would I laugh?"

"Everyone else laughs. So go ahead."

"I'm not laughing. I'm looking for the bride."

She grabbed her baggy dress shirt, flapping it in disgust.

"Look at this shirt! How can you not laugh at this shirt! Are there breasts in here? You wouldn't know it, would you? You need to be Dolly Parton to poke out of this shirt."

"I'm sure there are breasts in there."

She looked up at me sharply.

"What are you saying? You coming on to me?"

"No! No, I'm just trying to be . . . forget it. Look, have you seen the bride?"

"It's the shirt. That's why you're not coming on to me. This shapeless shirt! Or the pants. How high up can you put a belt, anyway? Am I an eighty-year-old man? You wouldn't even know I have an ass. I can't win, front or back."

I sighed, overwhelmed by the neurotic tidal wave.

"Look, I'm trying to find the bride. Can you help me?"

She stood there a moment, staring into my eyes before answering.

"She's back in the bridal suite. She's hiding, I think."

I had to look away.

"Thanks."

"You bet."

She strode away without looking back. This time, in a direct flouting of my previous decision, I watched her walk away, noticing that contrary to her belief, she did indeed have a butt (a nice one, at that). If only she didn't seem so out of her mind. I pushed the thought of that indignantly swaying posterior from my brain and focused on the job at hand.

I knocked on the door of the bridal suite. Greeted with silence, I slowly opened it, peeking in hesitantly. The bride sat in the middle of the floor, staring at her hands.

"Ellen? It's cake-cutting time. Are you ready?"

"Close the door."

Unsure what to do, I stepped inside and closed the door.

"Are you all right?"

She looked up at me. Her eyes could have been used as buckshot.

"You're a handsome-enough guy."

"Um. Thanks."

"I need you to do something for me. I'm not some distressed woman looking for comfort. I know what I'm getting into. There's just a debt that needs to be paid. I need you to help me pay it."

"I'm not really a killer, Ellen. I don't even step on plants."

"I don't need you to kill anybody. This morning, my wonderful new husband decided that he needed to unburden himself before entering into holy matrimony with me. He wanted to be clean, he said. Fucking selfish bastard."

I didn't like where this was going. Unlike before, when I assumed I was being asked to kill somebody.

"He sits me down and says to me 'Ellie.' Fucker calls me Ellie. Ruined a perfectly good nickname, selfish asshole. 'Ellie, I did something at my bachelor party I shouldn't have done. But it happened. And I'm sorry.' He's sorry. Fucker's sorry. Says it like I should give him a sympathy hand job for his hard life. Fucking sorry. I'm sorry I'm too afraid of jail to jam a bread knife up his ass."

I looked around to make sure she was weapon free. I saw a little drink umbrella on the side table and put it in my pocket, just in case.

"What did he do?"

"You fucking guys, always so curious. I didn't want to know! I never had to know! I would have been perfectly happy walking down that fucking aisle before the eyes of fucking God and said 'I fucking do!' without ever having to know his little secret. But he needed to be clean. I thought I could head off a little of the pain, you know. If I say it, then it won't hurt so much. So I say, 'You slept with the hooker.' And he said, all indignant like I'd just accused him of bestiality, 'No! Of course not. I'd never do that.' 'Then what?' I asked him. He looked down at his fucking shiny shoes, probably checking himself in the reflection, the vain prick. 'I slept with Robert.' Robert's the fucking best man, by the way. 'We were drunk and I don't know how it happened. It'll never happen again, I swear!' And then he starts crying like a little baby. Fucking Robert!"

Wow. I felt sorry for her, but I'd be lying if I said a small jolt of thrilled schadenfreude didn't dance up my spine. She continued.

"I'd never disappoint my family by not getting married. It's the right thing to do. But there is an imbalance. He's got one up on me. I can't live with that. I can live with his being boy crazy, but I can't have him be one up on me like that. I have no interest in women, so I don't see the point in punishing myself to get at him. You, on the other hand, are a nice-looking guy. You will be perfectly suitable to help me settle the score."

I guess I knew what she was getting at from the moment she started talking about hookers. The schadenfreude fled, run off by abject terror. I backed up to the door.

"I'm sorry. I wish I could help you, but . . . you know. The cake cutting should be happening any moment, so you should probably make your way to the dance floor. Would you like the old standard 'Going to the Chapel' or would you rather have everyone sing along to 'The Bride Cuts the Cake'?"

Not that putting a knife in her hand would be the best idea.

"Don't you dare walk out that door. You are going to help me settle this."

"I wish I could, but I haven't had a physical since college. I think I have scurvy."

"Just take off your damn pants."

"I really wish you the best of luck and happiness."

"If you walk out that door, no tip."

Normally, this would give me pause. I'd do a lot of things for a tip. But for once, circumstances worked in my favor. I thought about the small wad of dirty bills I'd be getting from the old man and decided that it would cost a lot more than eight dollars and forty cents to make me settle Ellen's score.

"Sorry, I'll just have to live without the super-size fries."

I shut the door and ran like hell.

I heard the door open behind me. As far as I knew, the bride was capable of anything. Maybe I'd just created a new score for her to settle. I was running, looking around wildly for a hidey hole, when I heard a voice.

"In here, stupid."

A door opened up and I slipped in. The door shut, encasing me in darkness. I heard the bride run by, her steps receding into silence. I took a few deep breaths as my eyes adjusted and turned to face my savior.

"Thanks."

Janey shrugged.

"I'm sorry. I should have warned you. But then I thought, that's what you get for making fun of my job."

"You knew!"

"Not really. I heard her tell the story to her stepmother. I didn't realize she'd try to take you down with her."

"How do you know what she tried to do?"

"I was listening at the door."

"Oh."

"I'm a great lover of melodrama."

"Well, thank you for saving my ass."

"You're welcome. She would have torn it apart like a party favor."

I took another good look at her. In the dim light, her features seemed strangely disquieting. Like she hailed from a different species. Not the kind of girl I find attractive, I told myself, conveniently ignoring my raging erection.

"What are you doing in here?"

"Grabbing a drink."

She pointed down at a small plastic cup in her hand.

"Not allowed to drink on the job, huh?"

She smiled and took a swig.

"And yet you can't get through this job without it. A cruel irony. Sip?"

After my last ten minutes, I needed one.

"Sure."

I took a sip. And coughed like a bitch.

"What is that?"

"Gin."

"Straight gin?"

"I'm in a hurry. I don't get a lot of breaks, so I have to make them count."

"Give me another sip."

As I drank, I noticed the sweet smell of her perfume surrounding me. We'd been stuck in the tiny room a few minutes and the closet smelled like her. This was a woman who left a mark. I found myself leaning in closer to take another sniff. I expected her to back away or crack a joke. Instead, she kissed me.

For a moment, I did nothing, frozen as her lips massaged mine. Then she moved into me and I was gone.

Like water bursting out of a newly cracked pipe, the desire I'd refused to acknowledge exploded out of me. We tore each other apart, mauling each other with frantic clutching fingers. She smeared her lip gloss all over me while I left red marks on her overly tanned neck. We didn't kiss, we *ate* each other, like crazed starving animals. Caution, responsibility, judgment, they lay strewn across the closet floor with our ravaged clothing. We made no sounds, no human sounds, and we showed no mercy. I banged her head against the low ceiling as I clawed at her. She ripped my earring out of my ear with her teeth (hey, she warned me). After an eternity (five minutes? ten?), spastically, emphatically, I pulled back, before I could do anything stupid like push into her. Quickly, I moved away as we fell back against the wall, trying desperately to regain my equilibrium. We sat there in the near dark, silent but for the labored sound of our breathing. After a moment, I brought my hand up to my ear. It stung. I pulled my finger back and stared at the blood. I half-expected her to lick it off. Instead, she stared at me, chest still rising and falling in big sweeping waves, her eyes uncertain. I stared back, terrified of what we'd done and almost done.

I broke first.

"I'm sorry. I don't know what just happened. I'm sorry. Are you okay? I'm sorry."

She shrugged, her nervous laughter tipping her hand.

"Typical wedding shit. Happens all the time."

"I didn't mean to . . . this wasn't what I thought was going to happen."

"Blame it on pheromones."

"I guess I'll have to. Can I have my earring back?"

She handed it over, a little ashamed.

"I told you I'd get it. Are you okay?"

"I'm fine."

I closed my shirt and pulled up my pants. I backed up against the other wall, holding my bow tie. I barely knew this girl. What was I thinking? I wasn't this kind of person. Reading my expression, she brushed her long hair back from her face.

"Shouldn't you get back to the party? Your song has to run out soon."

"Actually, I put in a special mix tape I use when I need some extra minutes."

"That's a good idea."

"Yeah, at one of my first weddings, I had a stomach virus, so I kept needing to take some 'me' time. By the end of the night, the groom came up and asked why I kept playing songs like "Bohemian Rhapsody," "Hotel California," and "Scenes from an Italian Restaurant." Apparently, "Paradise by the Dashboard Light" was the final straw. Especially since the groom's name was Diaz and they'd asked for merengue. It cost me a tip. I hate losing tips. So now I have a twenty-minute-long mix tape."

I was babbling. As long as my mouth was moving my mind wasn't screaming at me. She lifted an eyebrow.

"That's smart of you. You know it's been about twenty-five minutes since I passed you in the hall."

The blood rushing through my ears had buried all other sound, but now that she mentioned it, it did seem a bit quiet. I leaped to my feet.

"Shit! I gotta go. I'm sorry."

I burst out the door and ran away from her as fast as I could.

The room was silent when I entered. Everyone was staring at me. The bride waited in the middle of the floor, looking murderous, holding a big knife. I ran over to my table and grabbed the mic.

"Are you ready to cut the cake?"

Everyone clapped in relief. I emceed the cake cutting from across the room, well out of the way of the Bride of Death.

Thankfully, the groom dragged the Bride of Death into the limo before the end of the party, so I didn't have to deal with her again. The old man dance netted me a cool twelve dollars and eighty-two cents. I decided to celebrate by getting the hell out of there. Before I left, I sought out Janey, against my better judgment. She was clearing a table, not looking at me as I stepped up to her, not sure what I was doing.

"I'm heading out."

"Cool. Thanks for the perforation. It looks like my whole head's gonna rip off."

She pointed to the wealth of vivid hickeys I had bestowed upon her.

"Sorry about that."

"It's fine. It pays me back for the earring."

She stacked the plates, head still pointed down. I stood there awkwardly. I had no idea what to say.

"Look, I'm really sor—"

"You're sorry. I know. I'll live."

She reached into her pocket.

"Here's my number. Just in case you want to say you're sorry again. Now leave me alone, I've got shit to do."

She handed me a piece of paper without turning around. I opened my mouth to speak. Nothing came out. I closed it and turned, stuffing the paper in my pocket as I ran for the door. Once outside I hopped in the car, turned up the radio and sped off.

I could feel her number in my pocket, the scent of her clinging lightly to the paper. As my car carried me farther and farther from her, the memory of her smell faded, as did the feelings that inexplicably took over in that tiny closet. What had happened to me? I didn't understand it. It must have been some lingering aftershock from my last breakup with Relapse Girl. A rebound thing, like people have been rebounding since the dawn of time when Thundar the Hunter first got dumped by Kruki his Neanderthal girlfriend and accidentally found himself in the storage cave getting it on with her sister Gruki. Man, Kruki was so pissed when she found out, she beat her big-browed sis senseless with a mammoth bone. It was not pretty. The experience scarred Gruki so badly she couldn't touch a leg of mammoth again, from that moment on becoming mankind's first vegetarian. The moral? Thundar is off limits, because that Kruki is one crazy bitch.

The image of Janey shifted in my mind, her glossy lips and too-deep tan overtaking her bright eyes and sweet breath in my ear. She just wasn't my type, I knew that. Closet indiscretions notwithstanding, I knew she'd only be trouble, or at best, more work than I needed to be putting into a girl right now. I'd leave this whole experience behind me, receding rapidly in my wake as I sped onward. Mistakes happen. The point is to learn from them and never make them again. While I was sublimating, I pushed the whole wedding out of my mind. I didn't need to dwell on the unhappiness in that bridal suite. That wasn't why I became a DJ. The whole point was to buoy my spirits, not sink them. Just turn the radio up and think about my book. Concentrate on the goal, and happiness is bound to follow.

Chapter Five

The Portrait

I was halfway back to Manhattan before I remembered that I'd promised to stop by my parents' place to move some wood. My dad loves his fireplace and he loves his fires, so when he discovered that one of his trees was diseased, he became quite excited. He hired some locals to fell the tree, but for some reason decided that he'd haul it around back himself. Which meant I'd haul it around back myself. Don't ask me why he'd pay for one and not the other. He's a little funny when it comes to saving money. He saves money the way white people dance: It's something he'd like to do but he has no natural aptitude for it, so he ends up making silly choices. He'll blow hundreds of dollars on a ceramic duck, then refuse to pay for shipping. He'll stay in a five-star hotel in Monte Carlo, but he'll fly over on ValuJet. He'll pay for hundred-dollar seats on Broadway, but he'll smuggle in a Diet Pepsi under his jacket, because drink prices are *outrageous*. I have no problem with frugality. I have no problem with largess. Just pick one horse and ride it, that's all I'm saying.

Because of this natural defect of my father's, I drove deep into Westchester to tote some wood to the backyard in the dark. It always feels comforting to head back to my old haunts. My jarring day faded as I passed by the familiar streets and houses. When you live in a big city by yourself, it's good to know that out beyond the ring of skyscrapers something is constant. You don't need your tiny apartment to be the perfect home, because somewhere up the Saw Mill River Parkway the room where you grew up fingerpainting on the walls and the streets where you and Craig Dumont raced bikes and the driveway where you built snow forts that collapsed within minutes waited for you always, forever untouched. That world doesn't change. It may feel smaller and unfamiliar faces may walk their dogs past your front door, but it's always there for you to hide in. A womb where everything is the same as it ever was.

I pulled into the driveway just after eight. The house was ablaze with light. My mom takes the "Look, we're having a party!" approach to home security. In order to balance out the Con Ed bill, my dad, in his typical fashion, had left the outside light turned off. I stumbled up the walkway and pushed through the front door.

"Hello? Where are you guys?"

"We're right here. You don't have to scream your head off."

My parents sat in the living room, across from each other. They never sit together unless they're out to dinner with Dad's work friends. Then my mom holds on for dear life.

"Hey, guys."

"Hey, David."

"Hello, honey."

Mom seemed expectant. Almost excited. Dad sported an evil twinkle in his eye. What was going on?

"How was your wedding, honey? Nice?"

"Yeah. It was okay, I guess."

The parents didn't need to hear about the attempted rape of my innocence by an insane bride. Not for free. What the hell was Mom smiling about? Dad shook his head.

"Did you eat?"

"Yeah, I had filet mignon. What is wrong with you, Mom?"

She pouted.

"Don't you notice anything about the living room?"

"Not really. It's the living room. It doesn't have a wheel of torture or . . . oh."

I sputtered out as I caught sight of what made my mom look so pleased with herself.

"Oh man. What is that? Oh, Mom. Please. Tell me that's not me."

Dad smiled.

"It sure is, sonny boy. It sure is."

Right behind my mother, dominating the wall, floated a huge portrait of yours truly. Huge. Like I was an old English king or something. Though "king" wasn't the royal designation my pose immediately brought to mind.

Mom almost burst with excitement.

"What do you think? Does it look like you, do you think?"

"Um . . . yeah. It really does."

My mom is an excellent portrait artist. She'd done a painting of my uncle Jeter that captured him perfectly. He's sitting on a motorcycle, hair streaming, motoring down the open road like a latter-day wild child. It looked just like him.

This looked just like me. Unfortunately, I wasn't on a motorcycle.

"Mom, why am I wearing a see-through shirt?"

Yep, you heard me. My hair stood up in a jaunty pompadour. My shirt gaped open at the top, not that it mattered, as you could see my chest hair through the translucent material. My stomach was in full view, with a treasure trail of hair leading down into my tight leather pants. That was all bad enough. But the pose. What was she thinking when she decided to put me in that pose? That awful, terrible, horrific pose.

"I was trying to capture your essence."

My hand was flung back as if I were Siegfreid riding one of his white tigers like a rodeo bull. And my large happy "Oh!" expression seemed simply delighted with the experience. I was Ricky Martin crossed with Rip Taylor. I was just so . . . absurd. I looked like a foppish disco jester. This was my essence?

Mom looked crestfallen.

"You don't like it?"

I had no idea how to respond.

"Um. It looks just like me."

Dad nodded.

"That's true. I guess we should give up on the grandkids."

Mom snapped Dad's way.

"Shut up, Ed."

"Mom, why did you paint me like that?"

Her voice hovered on the cusp of breaking.

"I wanted to capture you the way you look when you dance. I know you love dancing. So this is supposed to be you dancing."

Dad wasn't helping contain the damage.

"What kind of club is he dancing in?"

"Shut up, Ed!"

The edges of her eyes began to tear up. Dad sighed in exasperation as I sat down next to her and put my arm around her shoulders tenderly.

"I love it, Mom. I do. It's really good. It's just . . . why am I wearing the see-through shirt? Even the big 'Olé!' I'm doing would be fine without the shirt."

"It was for my art class. The assignment was see-through material. So I did a shirt."

She quivered. I felt like the lowest form of offspring.

"It looks great. I wouldn't be thrown if you hadn't done such a perfect likeness of me."

"And the shirt . . . ?"

"It works great. You can see right through it. Right to my hairy . . . chest."

"So you like it?"

Dad leaned forward with interest. I avoided his eyes.

"You bet."

Mom hugged me.

"That's great! You know how I did it? See, I painted part of it from this picture I took of you dancing at cousin Amy's wedding. I think of you DJ-ing all those parties and heading out onto the floor to lead everyone in a conga line, and this is what I see."

So this was her portrait of David the DJ presiding over all those weddings and anniversaries and bar mitzvahs. And I was a joke. I could see the thirteen-year-old version of myself looking up at this caricature and despising him. Was this what I gave up everything to become? Was this how everyone saw me? A big joke?

No. Stop it! I got a grip on myself before I began flagellating. My mom did this for a class. She copied it from some picture where I probably was making a stupid face and posing like an idiot. Calm down, you crazy asshole. It's just a portrait. It was nice of my mom to take all that time to try to capture me like this. So what if I'm not . . . thrilled with the outcome. I'm a writer trying to make some money. I like doing parties. I'm not a joke. Not yet.

We sat still for a moment, peering up at my mother's masterpiece. I broke the silence.

"So, how long do you think you'll keep it up, do you think? A day or so? Not more than a week, right?"

She stood up quickly and pulled away.

"I need to check on my tea."

"Mom . . ."

"I'll be back in a sec, I promise."

She retreated, leaving me feeling awful. Dad watched her go, the impish glimmer in his eye replaced by concern.

"Nice going, David."

I sat back down, the biggest asshole in the world.

"I didn't mean to hurt her feelings. I just hope she won't keep it up forever."

"No, I think she wants to give it to you. After she shows it in the gallery."

My stomach rolled.

"Gallery?"

"Everyone was very impressed with it at art class. It'll be showing at a gallery in the city in a few weeks."

"Please no."

"Oh yes. And then you'd better have it hanging up in your place when we visit, otherwise we'll go through all of this again."

"Yay me."

"Count your blessings. She wants to do me next. Who knows what she'll make me wear? It'll probably be ass-less chaps week at that art class of hers. I can't wait."

* * *

After I'd lugged all the wood back to the pile in the backyard, I made my way inside to grab a drink before I hit the road. I had apologized again to my mother and now she was sleeping. I sat down at the kitchen table and grabbed a bag of Goldfish. I heard a creak as my dad walked in behind me.

"Thanks, David. I couldn't have gotten all that wood back there by myself."

I refrained from any pointed remarks.

"My pleasure."

He sat down and grabbed a handful of Goldfish out of my bag. I gave him a look and moved the bag away from his prying fingers.

"Don't eat my snacks. You have your own snacks."

We were taught to know what was ours in my house.

"Fine."

He pulled out a bag of jelly beans. I gave him a look. He tossed a few in his mouth and waved me off.

"Don't worry, they're sugar-free."

"They'd better be. I'd hate to have Mom tear them out of your fingers with a crowbar."

As I mentioned earlier, my Dad's diabetic. We all have to be on the alert because he's a junkie for sweets. It wouldn't surprise me to hear he bought them in dime bags down in Washington Square Park. It's a problem. If for no other reason than his addiction makes him eat sugar-free candy, which gives him the farts. I just can't win.

"We're thinking of selling the house."

This knocked me right off my tracks. Where did this come from?

"What do you mean? This is our house!"

"It's too big. I'm retiring soon. Our savings aren't what they should be."

I refrained from commenting on my dad's spendthrift ways. My appendix was going to burst under all this internal pressure.

"But we've always had this house."

"Things change. We had a different house when you were born. This wasn't always your mother's and my house. The new place will just be another stop down the road."

"Are you staying in town at least?"

Please leave me something.

"We can't afford it. We're looking at the Danbury area or something else in Connecticut. The taxes here are too much because of its proximity to the city."

"But this is home."

He popped a jelly bean in his mouth.

"The only thing that's certain in life is your family. We'll still be a train ride away. We'll still be around. It's not the end of the world. It's just a change."

"Are you guys okay with it?"

"Your mom's not doing too great. That's probably the real reason she broke down tonight. She doesn't do change very well. But I won't miss the taxes, I'll tell you that."

"Yeah, I guess."

We lapsed into silence. My home was going away? My shelter? Where would I sleep in this new place? The couch? The cellar, next to the rusty old manual lawnmower? Would they even have a lawn? I was already changing. I didn't need any more change. And what did he mean by not as much savings?

"Are you guys going to be okay for money?"

"We'll do okay. I can't buy so many ceramic ducks, but that's probably a good thing. Don't you worry about it, we'll be fine."

But if they don't have money and I don't have money, who has the money? Suddenly I found myself halfway across a tightrope when, looking down, I noticed that the net has been stashed away and nothing stood between me and the cold hard ground but a thin piece of wire and my balance. I have no balance. The stakes were so much higher now. I was in the real world, where there are no safety nets. I'd better be the best fucking writer in the world, because it's easy to want to be happy when you always have the guest room to crash in. I fought down the panic. There's a bright side. There had to be.

"Do you think Mom would include my portrait with the house? It'd be a nice gift with purchase."

"I wouldn't ask her that if I were you."

I upended the bag of Goldfish into my hand.

"Dad?"

"Yep."

"If you're going to sell the house, and summer's almost here, then why did you have me cart all that wood back behind the house?"

He shrugged.

"It was good wood. You don't waste good wood."

I couldn't argue with that.

Chapter Six

The Writer at Work

I woke up at one thirty Monday afternoon to a face full of books toppled off my bookshelf. I sleepily shook my fist at the wall.

"You won't beat me! You fucking . . . apartment!"

What do you want, Oscar Wilde? I had just woken up.

Life is bizarre when you don't have a day job during the week. Time loses its meaning. You fall out of sync with everyone else. I often found myself calling friends at two in the morning just to chat and not understanding why the mumbling malcontent on the other line was threatening to Taser me sterile. When I stepped out to grab some lunch at four in the afternoon, the restaurant was usually almost empty. I felt like I was walking in one direction and everyone else passed me by, heading downstream. It sounds like it would be an easy life. Maybe to some it would be. But my rhythms were off. It was such a struggle to keep the hours from slipping through my fingers that I often went days without leaving my place. My gigs were all on the weekends. Why go outside, otherwise? It was such a struggle to swim upstream. Tiring. I might as well stay home and write.

Ah, writing. It occupied my every thought. When I woke up in the morning (early afternoon), I thought about writing. Then I went out for food or ordered in. As I ate, I thought about writing. Then I watched some afternoon cartoons. While I watched *The Powerpuff Girls,* I thought about how I could write for that show. Inspired, I would turn on my computer. Waiting for it to start up, my initiative would dissipate, so I would lie on my bed and read a book, since reading is like stretching for writing, as I frequently told myself. After which I'd order food, to refuel for my long day of composition. As I ate, I didn't think about writing, not wanting to overtax my already weary mind. I usually daydreamed about whether anyone would ever buy my book. Maybe I'd make so much money, I'd never have to work again. I'd be like one of those geniuses who writes only one novel before disappearing into the annals of legend. After my musings, I'd force myself into my chair and stare at the computer for thirty-five minutes. Finally, I'd open up the file containing my book and pick a chapter to reread. I wouldn't revise it. I'd just read it. This would satisfy my creative impulses and I would fall asleep in my chair, ending yet another day of hard work.

Still slow from waking up, I brushed my teeth and stepped back into the bedroom. I was hungry, seriously considering stepping out for something quick from the deli downstairs. But today, I would break the chain! I returned to my computer, sitting alertly in my small swivel desk chair designed for maximum comfort and back support for those long hours of writing I couldn't quite bring myself to endure. I brought up Word. I was thirsty. A black cherry soda would hit the spot. But first, genius! I placed my fingers on the keypad. Time to be happy.

I sat there for five minutes, still and silent.

I began to lightly tap my fingers on the keys, not hard enough to register. They made a light percussive sound. I began to tap faster, seeing how hard and fast I could make my fingers go without shooting out a letter onto the screen. Soon, I could hear a horse in full gallop, steaming over the cobblestone streets of some nineteenth-century city, lost in the fog. Full throttle I raced through the gray toward the freedom of the countryside when suddenly out of nowhere I tripped and crashed. The letter "h" had appeared on the screen, pushed out of the clapping symphony. The key was jammed. Ah well, it was too good to last. Jesus, I was a scaredy cat. After all, I'd given up everything to do this. Sure, that's a lot of pressure to put on some plastic keys. So much uncertainty. But I'm no DJ joke.

I pried up the key and tapped delete to dispose of the errant letters on my screen. Nothing happened. Fuck. The computer had crashed during my finger frenzy. The weight dropping off my shoulders, I turned off the power and headed out to get a sandwich.

* * *

I sat staring at Janey's number as I scarfed down my turkey club, when my cell rang. I glanced down, making sure it wasn't the Eater of Souls. Thankfully, the LED read "Cameron."

"Hey David. What are you up to?"

I picked some turkey out of my teeth.

"Just working on the writing. You know."

"Cool. What are you doing Wednesday night?"

"I'm not working. I've got some writing to do, but I can always rearrange my schedule. Why?"

"Mary is moving out of her apartment and she wants to have an empty apartment party."

"And what is that exactly?"

"She thought she'd invite everyone up for one big blowout now that she doesn't care what the neighbors think."

"Who else is coming?"

"All of us. Her friends. Rat Boy, too."

Rat Boy. Just the thought of him showing up at my friends' gatherings made my teeth clench.

"I've got to talk to Annie about that guy before it goes too far."

"I'm with you on that one. Oh, do you have Rollerblades?"

"Um, no. Why?"

"Some of Mary's friends are going to be skating. They thought it'd be kinda cool."

"What do you think?"

"That I like to get laid on a regular basis."

"How big is her apartment?"

"One bedroom."

"This will end badly."

"You can always hide out in the kitchen."

We hung up. I stared at the number some more. I could smell her skin again, wafting up from the paper. Maybe it was pheromones. But I was stronger than nature. She answered on the second ring.

"Hello?"

"Um. Hi. This is David Holden. The DJ? From the closet?"

"Ah yes, the apologetic lothario. What's going on?"

"Just calling. To see how you are."

"Well, I'm a-okay."

"Has your head fallen off yet?"

"What?"

"From the perforation."

"Oh. No. It wobbles a bit in the shower, but I have high water pressure, so that happens all the time."

"I'm glad to hear it."

I had no idea what I was doing. I had no idea why I was calling. Her voice leaped out at me like the flick of a blade at a fencing match.

"So did the bleeding stop?"

"What?"

"On your ear. Is it all right? I did feel bad about ripping your earring out like that. It got caught on my incisor. I meant to snatch it off when you weren't looking, not pull a Mike Tyson."

"It's fine. You didn't tear anything."

"So you got to bite me up and I didn't leave any marks on you? That's hardly fair."

"Life sucks, sometimes."

"And sometimes it blows. The trick is to predict which is about to happen."

What were we talking about? She was actually kind of funny. In a depraved sort of way.

"Well, I'm sorry about your neck. I hope I didn't get you into too much trouble."

"Where did you go to school?"

This came from nowhere. I adjusted to the change in direction.

"Um. Tufts."

"Hah! I went to Brown!"

Wonderful. She went to the school that rejected me. The one I had always wanted to go to. Great.

"Bully for you."

"So I'm smarter than you, huh? All right."

"I could have gone to Brown if I wanted to."

"You went to Tufts. That means you got rejected from Brown."

"Not necessarily."

"Am I wrong?"

"That's not the point. What if my dad had gone to Tufts?"

"Am I wrong?"

"Maybe I like their modern dance program."

"Am I wrong?"

"It was a bad year for English majors."

"Hah! I knew it. Don't feel bad. I'm sure Tuft's DJ program is top notch."

"Well, Brown is famous for its waitresses."

That struck a nerve.

"Yeah, well. Look, I'm not really a waitress."

"I'm sorry, would you rather be called an eating assistant?"

"I'm interning at a television production company right now. I'm just waitressing for a little extra cash."

Hello hello? She wants to be in television? And look at me, the Emmy-winning producer.

"Television. Nice work if you can get it."

"Oh, I'm gonna get it. Maybe, if you're lucky, I'll let you DJ our Christmas party."

"Here's hoping. What company?"

"Jamestown Productions. They do that reality dating show on F/X, *Why Buy the Cow?*"

I knew it well. Jamestown had offered me a job producing another one of their reality shows. Something about people's pets living in a house and getting voted off. Staggeringly stupid. But it paid well. I was on a mission for happiness, however, so I turned it down.

"Who's your boss? Tony Demillio? Or Audra?"

Silence. Her voice came out smaller.

"Kim Taylor, actually. Tony and Audra are the executive producers. How do you know them?"

"They wanted me to produce one of their things. But I turned it down. Not for me, you know."

"You're a producer?"

She sounded off balance. Finally.

"Was. I quit."

"To be a DJ? Are you on smack?"

"To write, actually. Someday I'll tell you all about it."

"Okay."

I felt exultant. Like I'd scored a knockdown in a heavyweight bout. Which is why I ignored my better judgment.

"What are you doing Wednesday night?"

"Why?"

"I'm going to a roller-skating party at a friend's apartment. Want to come with?"

"Um. Sure, why not. I haven't fallen on my ass in almost a week. It'll be refreshing."

Now why did I do that? Heady with victory, I guess. I got caught up in the witty banter and forgot myself. Too late now. Can't uninvite someone. I'll just have to live with it.

* * *

I rushed up to the outdoor café a few days later already apologizing. I'd finally coaxed Annie out to meet me, and here I was twenty minutes late. Being Annie, she let me know it.

"What was it this time? I really would like to know what pressing plans held you up."

I sat down and picked up a menu. I'd been running late and, in my haste, had a little zipper incident. It took me a few minutes just to free myself and another five minutes or so to test the equipment to make sure nothing was broken. But I didn't feel like mentioning my penile humiliation.

"I was writing. Sorry."

"I was writing" is my all-purpose excuse. I could be late, I could forget birthdays, I could accidentally set fire to Cameron's kilt (long story) and this excuse covered for me. Creativity relieved me of the need to be civilized. My next experiment involves not wearing pants at the Museum of Natural History. I'm sure the *New York Post* will let you know how that turns out. Thankfully, Annie accepted my explanation without a fight.

"I've already ordered."

"Is that the waitress? Miss?"

The waitress walked over nonchalantly. She wanted to be an actress. You could tell by her total lack of personality.

"Yep?"

"I'll have the breadsticks."

"The breadsticks are complimentary."

"Then we're all good here."

She scowled and stomped away. Broadway, probably. She had that certain lack of anything resembling grace that is so in vogue nowadays. Annie sighed.

"Why did you invite me to lunch if you can't afford it?"

"I can afford it. Especially since these fantastic breadsticks practically fell from the sky like manna from heaven."

"I'm paying for myself."

"No way. Let me. This is the first time I've been able to sit down and talk with you in months. It's only fitting that I pay for the privilege."

"Fine. Whatever you say. Thank you."

She leaned back and looked around. We were sitting right by the street, so people strolling by could see what disgusting eaters we were. There's nothing like catching a hot woman looking your way while she's out for a stroll. Especially while you're eating ribs with a bib.

"I'm a little hurt, Annie."

She scoffed.

"You're hurt. How are you hurt?"

"Why didn't you tell me about . . . Josh? You could have called or something."

She softened.

"I'm sorry. I don't know why, really. It was quick, that's true. But also, he was such a change from you guys. When I'm with him I don't want to spoil it with the outside world."

Because maybe we'd point out what a huge fucking horse's ass you were marrying.

"Why would we spoil it?"

"He's not like the other people in my life. Most of all, he's nothing like you. I knew he wasn't your type of guy. I wanted you to like him, but I had to be realistic. So I can't say I was surprised with your whole 'rat' thing. Not that it didn't hurt to hear you say it."

This wasn't supposed to happen this way. Annie was finally back and I was making her cry. Was I really that mean? I needed to see all sides.

"How did you guys meet? How did all this happen?"

The crappy actress showed up with Annie's lunch. Annie picked up a fork and waved it as she spoke.

"It was pretty funny, actually. I was working with this one kid, Morgan, pro bono because of his dad's income level. I had to see him at the local elementary school because that's the only place I could get a free room."

Annie works with children with autism. It's a rewarding job filled with flying fists, frequent biting, and unexpected urination. But she loves the job and she loves her kids. The world is slightly closer to being civilized because of her, while I, on the other hand, am usually setting it back. She took a bite and continued.

"Morgan was being very difficult. I'm usually pretty good with the violent ones, but this little bugger was some kind of evil mayhem machine. He threw toys at me. He tossed Doritos at me. He bit my arm so hard I had to pop his jaw to get him to let go."

She showed me the mark. It looked vicious.

"How long ago was this?"

"A month or so."

"Wow. That's quite a set of teeth."

"Finally, I was trying to get him to ask for his Tonka truck when he launched himself across the table and grabbed it. I'm a trained professional, so I did what any highly educated expert would do."

"You fought a little kid for a Tonka truck."

"He had a grip like a little lobster. He kept screaming and

digging his nails into my fingers. I stood up and up he came with me. I swear, the kid just dangled from the toy truck in my hand. I couldn't help myself. I tried to shake him off. I wasn't angry, I just couldn't believe the will of this kid. I swung him to the right and to the left. The child was welded to me. I skipped around the room, hoping he'd give, but he hung on like Will Smith dangling from a helicopter. Finally, I ended up in the hallway, defeated, staring down at this little face just hanging there. I guess I made some noise, because Josh came out of another room to see what was going on. He had agreed to help set up the school's Internet for free, to help out. He didn't even know anyone going there. He just wanted to help."

I hated him more.

"What a guy."

"So he walked up holding a small piece of cookie and told Morgan to let go if he wanted it. Morgan drops right away and grabs the cookie. That was my next move, by the way, but of course I didn't tell Josh that. We got to talking and it turns out that his cousin has autism. He asked me out and I said yes. He's such a decent, nice, good guy. I didn't have to try with him. I could just relax. He felt so . . . comfortable. He doesn't tell a thousand jokes or ask me a million questions about my political stance on whatever useless crap some idiot with a megaphone is spouting that week. I can just chill out with him."

"So he doesn't challenge you, that's what you're saying."

"You challenge me. Cameron and Dustin challenge me. Jacob used to challenge me all the time. I don't need that from Josh."

"What about ten years down the road? Won't you be bored to death?"

Annie sat back, sighing.

"Look, I've changed, David. Or at least, I'm trying to change. I don't want to be the person I used to be, sarcastic and mean, commenting on the world as it passed me by like some asshole judgmental spectator."

"You're not an asshole. I love the way you are."

"I love how I feel around Josh. I love the person he makes me want to be. I feel good about myself."

"Annie, you work with kids with autism, for Christ's sake. You're a saint."

"That has nothing to do with who I am, that's just what I do. After I fled to Phoenix, I thought I'd find some kind of balance, something to put me back on the right track. But I could do all the yoga in the desert I wanted and nothing changed. I was no different inside. But once I met Josh, I got a glimpse of what I could be. For the last month I've been like a different person with him. An open, aware, nonjudgmental, loving person. And it feels better. So now I'm trying to follow that feeling. I don't want to be so coarse and rude and biting and snarky. I want to grow up."

No! That was the Annie I loved! You can't lose the snark! We love the snark! The Annie I loved was special and original. This new Annie sounded boring as hell. And, more important, she didn't sound like Annie. It seemed more likely to me that Annie had hit the crisis point and now she's overreacting, big time.

"Annie, that's great, really. But you can't change completely. Some part of you is always going to be snarky. You can keep fighting it, by all means, but it will never go away completely."

"That's not true. It does go away when I'm with Josh. I'll

still be me, I promise. I just want to be the woman Josh sees, the woman he loves. I like that woman and I want to be her."

"What about Josh? While you're changing who you are, what does he do for you? That doesn't sound fair."

Annie brushed back her blond hair, the foreign color framing her face.

"He's changed for me, too."

"Really? How?"

"Well, for one thing, and don't tell any of the guys this, please, his parents are nudists. For real! I haven't seen them nude or anything, thank God, but every time I had dinner with them I could picture it, believe me. Josh grew up with that and he used to go with them and be . . . you know . . . nude. I think he enjoys it, to be honest. I told him I wasn't comfortable with that and he promised to change for me."

Come on. Seriously. This guy had to go.

"So you change your personality and he puts on a pair of pants? How is that equal?"

She put her head in her hands, frustrated.

"I love him, David. It's real. I'm going to marry him. Please be happy for me?"

She wouldn't listen to reason. How could she not be bored to tears already? I was losing Annie to middle-class, middle-age mediocrity. This was unacceptable. Annie had always been different. Smarter, funnier. Hell, she wasn't one of my best friends for nothing. But this life she was describing . . . this wasn't her. I couldn't have a conversation with her without having to fight off some barb or another. To give that up would be to give up a piece of her soul. This happiness she felt couldn't be real, not if it meant she had to subsume who she was. She wouldn't be able to keep it up forever. At some point, it's going to burst out. And Rat Boy won't know what hit him. Everything about this was wrong.

A thought popped into my head.

"Josh is the Bride of Death!"

Thunder crossed Annie's face.

"He's a nudist, not a cross-dresser, David. Jesus, I'm sorry I told you."

"No, I did a wedding this weekend where the groom had a secret . . ."

I recounted the story to Annie, expecting her to see the correlation. Instead she gave me a wary look.

"What does that have to do with me?"

"A whole side of her husband was kept hidden from her. And you see how she reacted!"

"Like a lunatic. You slept with her, didn't you?"

"God no. But imagine Josh discovered that you could be sarcastic and sharp and all those things you say you'll never be again. How will he feel knowing you've kept that from him? That there's a whole side of you he can't ever understand? Who knows how he'll react?"

Finally she looked alarmed.

"But he won't find out! The problem in that story is that the groom told her what he did. And you slept with the bride!"

"I did not. You know that wasn't the problem, Annie. The problem was that he couldn't help doing it."

"You know what the problem is? You just don't know Josh. You'd feel better about this if you got to know him. You'd like him. Okay, well you'd at least tolerate him if you knew him better. Go out for a drink. Talk. For me. I think we can all be good friends, I really do."

I pictured Annie, me and Rat Boy skipping through the grass holding hands. Cameron and Dustin popped up from the brush holding sniper rifles. Bang. Then it was just the four of us, skipping along, making fun of Rat Boy's shoes, the way it should be.

"You can't just ignore this, Annie."

"I'm in love, David. Please, for me?"

She wouldn't listen to reason. What could I do? The only thing anyone can do when unable to convince a friend of her folly: lie and try to do what's best for her behind her back.

"I'll try to get know him. For you."

"Thanks."

People walked by, intent on their destinations and the fine day. For a moment, Annie and I joined them, lost in our separate thoughts. I decided to change the subject.

"A girl is stopping by at Mary's party tonight."

"A potential ex?"

"Nah. Just some girl. She's a little crazy. She bit my earring off."

"That doesn't sound too smart of you, David."

"Since when am I a smart man?"

"You're not exactly picking out the best long-term investments for yourself. You seem to keep making these same mistakes. You don't ever learn, do you?"

"I learn all the time. Just like I learned calculus. I crammed for the exam, got an A, and forgot it all the next day."

"Sad."

"Don't blame me. Blame the American educational system."

She shook her head and finished her sandwich while I

discreetly rummaged through my pockets trying to figure out how the hell I was going to pay for lunch. I had to come up with some way to keep Annie from going through with this. I didn't want her to change. Especially since the person she didn't want to be anymore bore a striking resemblance to me.

Chapter Seven

Fun with Roller Skates

Cameron's ladyfriend lived on a pleasant little side street not far from my place. I pressed the buzzer next to the number written on the little sheet of paper on my hand. I hoped her apartment wasn't too much better than mine. I didn't need that right now.

"Hello?"

"Hey Cameron, it's David."

"You're early. Come on up."

Mary's apartment waited way up on the seventh floor in an elevator-free building. By the time I made it to her door, I couldn't feel my legs. Cameron stood in the doorway.

"You look awful."

"I'm going to pass out. You need Gatorade stations along the way. I'm completely dehydrated."

"Come on in and have a beer."

"Yeah, that'll solve my water deficiency."

Mary's apartment was completely barren. No chairs, no tables, nothing. Just wooden floors and an air conditioner. I followed Cameron into the little kitchenette and grabbed a glass of water. The countertop was completely covered with alcoholic beverages just waiting to be vomited up.

"This seems like a questionable decision. There will be people on roller skates, right?"

"Don't worry. It's perfectly safe."

"What about that huge open window over there?"

I pointed to the huge open window.

"Look, this is Mary's idea. I'm just along for the ride."

I looked around.

"Where's the lovely hostess?"

"She ran out to grab some last minute items."

"I thought you said nine o'clock? Isn't it nine?"

"Who shows up on time? Certainly not you."

He had me there. I must be slipping. I usually wouldn't be there till after one, when all the people I didn't care for had either passed out or gotten each other pregnant.

"So are you roller skating?"

He grabbed a beer and led me back in to the main room.

"No way."

"What do you think of Mary's skating?"

"If that's her thing, then let her do it. As long as I get laid at the end of the night, I'm happy."

"You must really like her."

Cameron took a swig, emptying the bottle. I noticed a hint of desperation in his eyes. He grabbed another beer.

"This is headed to failure, I can feel it."

"Stop it, dude. You always do this to yourself."

"I'm destined to die alone."

"You won't be alone. We'd all pool our money and get you a dominatrix to send you out happy. Anyway, things look good from where I'm standing, so what's the freak-out for?"

"She's moving back home for a month till she finds another place."

"Why is that a problem?"

"Her mom. She's Irish and she hates slanty eyes."

"That's not nice."

"She's not too happy that Mary's dating a Korean, no matter how Caucasian I sound on the phone. And now I have to see this woman when I pick Mary up."

"Just honk."

"This is doomed to failure. I don't know why I start these things."

"You're bumming me out, dude. At least you're getting sweet, tasty— Hey! Look who's here!"

Mary pushed her way through the door carrying eight bags. We stared at her. She stared back, swaying under the weight of her burden.

"Cameron."

"Sorry!"

He rushed over and grabbed some bags. I took a few myself. They were heavy.

"Hey, Mary. I guess I'm the first one here, huh?"

"Where are your roller skates?"

"No, I don't do stuff like that. Too many lives at stake. Mostly my own."

"Well, Cameron and I will be having a great time and you'll just have to watch."

"But Cameron isn't . . ."

Cameron gestured wildly from behind Mary, cutting me off with his fevered throat slashing.

"Isn't what?"

"Scared, so why should I be? I'll tell you. Because I'm a big pussy."

Over the next hour, a bunch of people trickled in, mostly Mary's friends. They all brought roller skates or Rollerblades. As they tried their best to re-create the heady disco days of the Roxie, I reflected on how group participation can make anything seem okay. Put any of those sad skaters in with normal people, and they'd be as embarrassed as I was for them. But stick them in a group of like-minded, delusional fanatics, and they dance around like the coolest kats on earth. Cameron stood to the side, holding himself up while grasping the last tatters of his dignity to him like a shredded robe, muttering under his breath as skaters passed him by. He threw me a pleading look. What can I do? I shrugged back to him silently. He was the idiot wearing the shoes with wheels. My shoes had no wheels. Hence, I wasn't falling down. It's simple science.

Around ten thirty, Annie finally showed, Rat Boy in tow. It did not surprise me at all to hear him squeal with joy, throw on an ancient pair of skates and join in on the tiny circles. Annie walked over to me and sat down. She pointed at my shoes.

"Party pooper."

"Right back at ya. Though Josh looks happy."

"He was excited about the skating. He's an avid roller-skating fan."

"I can see that."

Josh did a split. Okay, not bad. Annie clapped while speaking to me out of the side of her mouth.

"Where's your woman?"

"She'll be here."

The door opened and Dustin entered with Donkey Girl. They both looked flushed as they came over. If Dustin had smiled any wider, the top of his head would have slid right off.

"Sorry we're late. We stopped to do it in the cab."

Donkey Girl honked in embarrassment. Dustin spotted Cameron.

"Oh God. He's joined the cult."

Annie shushed him.

"Be good. They're innocents. Let them have their fun."

We fell into silence as we watched the mini skating party unfold. Someone was going out that window, and I wanted to see it when it happened.

Two hours later there was no Janey. Cameron had retreated to the kitchen, ostensibly to make drinks, but really so he could hold on to something steady. Mary twirled on, oblivious. Dustin and Donkey Girl had disappeared somewhere, and unless Mary kept a kangaroo in her closet I could guess where. Annie and I sat with our backs against the walls. Annie laughed as Rat Boy moonwalked.

"He's got some moves, doesn't he?"

I watched him do the wave.

"They are certainly moves, all right. Why aren't you out there? Wouldn't that be something the new Annie would do?"

She flicked my leg.

"Don't give me crap. It isn't my thing. He knows that. We're cool."

And she did seem cool. Wonderful. Rat Boy tried to do the robot and almost killed a short medical student. Whatever the reason, he was a menace. Annie touched my knee and gasped in surprise.

"Is that Zach?"

I looked toward the door. Holy Shit.

"Did you know he was back in town?"

"No. Hey, Zach!"

Annie waved. Zach walked over, smiling.

"Hello! How are you!"

Slightly shorter than me, with closely cropped hair and expensive clothes, Zach looked the picture of *Great Gatsby*–esque American aristocracy. His dad had died of prostate cancer when we were all juniors in high school, and since Annie's father had passed away a few years before, she tried to help him by bringing him to her grief counseling group. This kind move backfired, as Zach went on to piss off the counselors by showing no signs of grief whatsoever. He explained to us that it all came down to a man's job. His dad had been a great doctor and when a man chooses medicine as a profession, he must decide who will get his compassion and soothing sympathy: son or patients? It had to be one or the other. According to Zach, you can't be a great doctor and a great parent at the same time. The two are mutually exclusive. Dr. Holzman chose a wing at the hospital named after him in memorial and a son who couldn't stay in one country longer than an hour and a half. Too bad he couldn't live to see the fruits of his labor. Zach's mom leaped back into the single scene as soon as the caterer packed up the cold cuts and I haven't seen her since. Zach was on his own.

I sometimes thought about what strange countries his trust fund led him to. He'd come home for a week and we'd see him a few times. He'd wow us with his adventures and then disappear again. Just like he would disappear again in a week, or the next or the next. As inevitable as the sun setting.

We both got up. Annie tried to hug him, but he flinched. Hugging Zach was a gradual experience. He had to see it coming and prepare. Upon the second try, Annie succeeded in getting her arms around him. Zach patted her back awkwardly.

"You look fantastic, Annie. The blond hair makes you look like a movie star. Hey, David. How's the author?"

I shook his hand. He looked tan and fit. I tried to imagine where he'd last been. Somewhere near the sea, I guessed, with white sands and perfect blue water.

"I'm just waiting to hear back from some agents."

"I'm sure it'll be sold in an instant. I can't wait to peruse it."

It was as if the voice of a sixty-year-old Harvard English professor lived in the body of a club kid. I brushed past his inquiries into my work.

"When did you get back in town? How long are you here?"

Annie piped in.

"Tell us everything. How many baron's daughters did you impregnate?"

Zach waved his hand.

"Please. I had a wonderful time in this little village in Spain, right on the Mediterranean. I lived with a contessa in her villa for a time. The sight of the gulls skimming inches above the water could melt your heart. It was heaven."

I laughed.

"A contessa? How old was she, forty?"

"She was twenty-five. We'd walk along the beach drinking Ribera del Duero and talking about art and music. She was beautiful. We'd wake up and have breakfast, lunch and dinner in bed. The air in Spain, you have no idea."

Annie smirked.

"It sounds like you spent more time between the sheets than you did on the sand."

Zach shrugged unapologetically.

"I've come to a great realization. All the best moments of my life have unfolded in my bed and all the things that annoy me tend to happen away from it. So in order to minimize my discomfort in life I'm trying to minimize my time away from my boudoir. I plan on being out just long enough to lure a lovely lady back to my bed and then we'll spend hours enjoying ourselves in it. I think that's the recipe for a fulfilling life, don't you?"

Annie scoffed.

"I take it you've never seen a bedsore."

"Don't sink my battleship, Annie. Leave me my aspirations to perfection. Who are these people, David?"

A hippie on wheels shot by with arms flailing. He ran into the wall and slid down it slowly. It was very satisfying.

"Ask Cameron. His girlfriend has made some strange personal choices in the past."

Annie interjected.

"How long are you here for?"

"I'm not sure. I can't decide if I want to jet up to Montreal, dye my hair red and go clubbing in my new silver lamé outfit or go on a bicycle tour that retraces the steps of the pilgrims across northern Spain. At the finish, you actually receive an indulgence from the Church that wipes your sins clean. On second thought, maybe I should go to Montreal and then the pilgrimage. That would give me incentive for a spiritual scrubbing."

Annie broke in again.

"Zach, you have to stay for a little bit. I'm getting married!"

"What! That's fantastic! Best wishes!"

Another timid hug.

"Who's the lucky guy?"

Annie pointed at Rat Boy, who chose that moment to do a pirouette. Zach carefully maintained a blank expression.

"Wonderful. I'm sure you'll be very happy."

"Thank you."

Zach ran his hand through his hair as if to rub away the memory of what he'd just seen.

"I'm going to say hi to Cameron and procure a beverage. I'll be back."

He walked off. I couldn't tell if Annie had noticed the reason for Zach's hasty retreat. She stood watching her man boogie down for a while. Something that had been nagging at me popped to the surface.

"Have you noticed that since your boy's taken to the floor, your comments have gotten a lot more biting?"

Annie gave me a look.

"Leave it alone, David."

"It's not a bad thing. They were funny."

"It's because I was so unprepared to see Zach. Can you believe that story about the contessa? The two of them in bed all day? Does he do anything useful? Sometimes I wonder if he even thinks like a normal person."

"Now you're being judgmental."

"Look, I love Zach, you know that, but I'll put nothing past him. He's like a child that way. Part of me doesn't know if I want Josh to meet him. It's hard enough with you guys intimidating him. Zach will eat him alive."

I cocked my head like a dog spying food on the counter. That was an interesting thought.

"I'm gonna grab another drink. I'll be right back."

Leaving Annie to mull over her indiscretions, I walked

into the kitchen, where Zach and Cameron were talking. I butted in.

"Zach, you have to help us with the Rat Boy situation."

Zach took a sip of his Shiraz. That's funny, I didn't see any wine when I was helping set up.

"That is an unfortunate man in there. Though I don't know what I can do about it."

Cameron interjected excitedly.

"Take him to one of your freaky sex parties and he'll disappear forever into the New York underworld."

"I don't do those parties anymore. I'm more into the hula-hooping thing right now."

This derailed both of us. I had to ask.

"Hula hooping?"

"It's the big thing in Europe. You should try it, it's great cardio."

"Hula hooping?"

Cameron couldn't even speak. But Zach's next sentence put the world aright.

"It's done in the nude, of course. Naked hula hooping is fantastic. You'll have to try it. There's a club here in Manhattan. They'd love to have an up-and-coming writer and a high-powered investment banker join them for an evening."

It always amazed me how Zach could make anyone feel like the most successful guy around. He just had this way of assuming that since he was upper crust, all his friends must be upper crust as well. It was impossible to be a true failure as long as you had Zach around to put his spin on it. In his eyes, I will always be William Faulkner, because how could I not be? He made it difficult to keep things in perspective.

"You should take Rat Boy. He's all about the nude thing. Annie would flip."

I meant it as a joke, but Zach gave me a hard look.

"What? You're actually going to get involved? Why? I don't see how this is your problem."

Cameron pointed at the roller-skating beau.

"Look at him. She's making a mistake."

I concurred.

"Exactly. We need to get her to see what a mistake this is."

Zach finished his glass.

"I don't know if I agree. But I'll help you out if I can. I've got an indulgence on the way, so I can be as much of a bastard as I feel the energy for. Though I don't want to stay out too late, that's all I ask. I'm trying to get to bed at a reasonable hour now. To minimize my annoyances."

I patted him on the back. He winced but bore it. Old friends have privileges.

"I'll think of something suitably evil and centered around early evening."

Zach looked past me into the main room, his eyes narrowing into the thin slits of a hungry predator.

"Who is that lush woman?"

Janey had come at last. She looked fantastic in the dimly lit living room. The difference in level of hotness between her and the silly girls spinning out of control on their mobile footwear staggered me. I hadn't seen her dressed to kill, and the sight left me breathless. She still hadn't seen me, so I watched her unnoticed, suddenly hesitant to approach her. Zach didn't have that problem. He was by her side before I could warn him off.

"Hello, my name is Zach. You are the most beautiful woman in the room, do you know that? Simply stunning. May I get you a drink?"

She smiled at him and patted his cheek.

"Wow. Did you read that in a fortune cookie? Are you going to tell me my lucky numbers next?"

Zach's smile didn't even flicker.

"I am completely sincere. You are a beautiful woman and I would love nothing more than to pour you a glass of wine."

"How about a seven and seven? Wine's a little pretentious after ten thirty, don't you think?"

This time Zach's smile did fade a little. I finally regained my legs, striding over.

"Glad you could make it, Janey."

"David!"

She kissed my cheek. I tried not to breathe too deeply. Her scent owned me and I needed my wits.

"I see you've met my friend Zach."

"He was about to make me a drink. Could you?"

Zach looked off balance.

"I'll see what I can do."

He turned and walked in the opposite direction from the kitchen. I looked at my watch. It was eleven thirty.

"A little late, aren't you?"

She smiled sloppily.

"I had to hit a few other intimate gatherings before this one. One must be fashionably late at all costs. Your friend is a little funky. I think he wanted to bone me."

She swayed, eyes focusing and defocusing on my face. I reached out to steady her.

"Man, you came prepared for a party, didn't you?"

"You never know what kind of shitty booze these dinky apartment parties are going to serve. I always come pre-moistened."

She leaned against the wall, pretty far gone. I felt a surge of irritation. It was one thing to have a drink or two before going out. It was a completely different thing to show up to meet a guy so completely blasted you could barely stand. This just wasn't cool.

"I'm gonna grab you a cab, okay?"

"No! I just got here."

"I'll walk down with you. We'll get some air."

"Okay. Air is all right. I love the air. The air's my bitch."

I opened the apartment door and led her down the first set of stairs. She stopped me on the landing and leaned up against the railing.

"Just let me stand here a minute."

I watched her. She didn't hold up as well under the hard glare of the hall lights, but she remained invitingly seductive. She wiped her mouth with the back of her hand and reached for the railing. She lost her balance, overcompensated and fell into me, knocking the two of us to the floor.

"Sorry. Sorry about that. Do you like my shoes? Prada!"

I looked at her shoes, which were hanging precariously on her feet over the first step of the next set of stairs. They had a bow on them. I guessed that was style.

"They look nice."

"They're the best shoes in the world. I lust after my Prada shoes. They're my only obsession."

Something told me that wasn't entirely true. She let her head go, releasing it onto my shoulder. Her scent shot past my defenses up into my nostrils before I could limit my exposure. Her breast brushed up against my elbow. Her other hand found its way magically to my crotch, inciting more magic to occur. She turned her face up toward mine and I had no control. I dived into her glistening lips without thought or restraint.

Eventually, I felt a tap on my head. I looked up from my face-sucking to see Zach standing over me.

"I'm heading home. Give me a call, my cell's back on. You know the number. We'll talk about the sting operation. She's beautiful, well done."

He stepped over our tangled limbs and disappeared down the stairs. Closing the top of my shirt, I shook my head to clear it and sat up.

"Janey? Hey Janey, I think you should get home."

"Could you hurry up? I ordered a seven and seven twenty minutes ago! Did you get lost? Did the bimbo at the end of the bar with the fake tits trap you with her gravitational pull? Just get me my damn drink."

At first I thought she was talking to me, but then I realized she couldn't possibly be. She was actually facing the railing. How she mistook a railing for an inattentive bartender I had no idea. I hoisted her to her feet as she rattled on.

"I want my seven and seven! Damn it, if I were pregnant I'd get what I wanted! Pregnant women get whatever they want! That's because it's a *craving*! How do you know I'm not pregnant! Maybe I am! I *crave* a seven and seven! Don't make me break my water all over your ass!"

I half carried her down the stairs, with her fighting the whole way, unwilling to leave without her beverage.

"It's not like I even want it anymore. It's the principle of the thing. I won't let you get away with ignoring my drink order. It's just not right! I'm an American! I demand drinks with umbrellas in them!"

She was still protesting indignantly as I stuffed her in a cab. Thank God she had a phone bill in her purse or I wouldn't have known where to tell the cab driver to take her. I slipped him a twenty and sent her on her way.

No more, I told myself. I'd had enough of drunken party girls, no matter how her smell tried to invade me and replace the clear-thinking David I knew myself to be with a sex-crazed fiend lacking restraint and common sense. Still, long after I'd had the opportunity to breathe in dozens of new scents, hers remained, stubborn, unwilling to let go. She was caught up in the back of my throat like a small hair I couldn't dislodge no matter how I coughed. She just wouldn't budge.

Chapter Eight

The War Against Pheromones

On my way to a fiftieth anniversary gig on Long Island that Saturday night, I reflected on the nature of pheromones. What are they exactly? What do they want from me? I know they don't give two shits whether I'm happy or not. They're nature's way of getting somebody pregnant, plain and simple. People keep saying that nature knows best, but making the decision to create a new human being doesn't seem like the kind of life-defining choice one should make based on whether the girl smells nice. Who's in control here, anyway? My mind or my nostrils? I'm a civilized human being, for Christ's sake, not some aroma-enslaved monkey. If we all went around being with whomever our noses told us to, who knows who we'd end up with. Probably the kind of woman who'd devour your head after you mated. The Eater of Skulls.

Out of curiosity, I'd looked up pheromones on the Web. One article informed me that I'm attracted to the smell of the woman whose immune system most differs from my own. So it's all based on what makes you sick. You're supposed to spend the rest of your life with the one person you won't share a cold with. If you can't share misery, what can you share? It seems like a dumb way to fall in love. It's not even about love. It's about some kid you're supposed to create. I'll like the smell of the woman I'd make the strongest baby with. We'll get married and pop this healthy child out into the world and proceed to fuck his mind up with our fighting and alternating sicknesses until it doesn't matter how robust his body is, his brain will shrivel up from all the neuroses we saddle him with. We'll go to a marriage counselor, and she'll tell us to suck it up, take a strong whiff, and get back to the baby-making. 'Cause that's all those pheromones want. More babies. They don't care about favorite TV shows and religious backgrounds. Fuck sly senses of humor and the discussion of a good book over breakfast. It's not about musical tastes and sports obsessions. Food cravings and political leanings. Views on the number of drinks per evening and the number of pills per morning. It's about getting those fucking babies baked up and ready to go. What happens to them out of the oven, and what happens to the poor bastards who kneaded the dough, is not a concern. That's nature's way, and it sucks. So fuck pheromones. I've overthought every choice having to do with women that I've ever had to make, and I'm not changing now.

I pulled up to the venue and double-parked outside. They'd decided to throw their party in some kind of community building, a short ugly cement structure devoid of anything resembling charm, which almost made it charming. It was better than that barn I'd had to work in last fall. I was crammed in the corner, flicking spiders off of my head all evening. The floor was so old and rickety, the vibrations from the conga line kept skipping my CD, prompting Buster

Poindexter to feel "Hot hot hot hot hot hot hot hot hot!" I kept waiting for someone to jump too hard on a floorboard, causing the other end to shoot up like a seesaw, sending me flying through the roof. Thank God they didn't hire River-dancers.

I walked in to scout out the joint and stopped up short. Rialto stood in the corner supervising the buffet. Shit. This was a Rialto gig! I looked around, trying to spot Janey before she could spot me. At first glance, I didn't see her. Maybe she wouldn't notice me behind the DJ table. Then I spotted the DJ table, high up on the stage behind the anniversary couple. I didn't stand a chance. I stood in the doorway furtively trying to spy her until someone stepped up behind me.

"Excuse me, may I pass?"

It was the kind of voice that you prayed slipped out of a beautiful woman. Because if it didn't, then you had to come to terms with the very real possibility that all that phone sex you've been having really is with a two-hundred-pound housewife. And the accent! She had an accent! Oh please, don't be two hundred pounds. I looked around. Blond hair, full lips, soft smile, hazel eyes. Thank God.

"Sorry about that."

She had on a white shirt and black skirt, the Rialto uniform. That fat bastard sure knew how to hire. She smiled, holding the tray of hors d'oeuvres up to me.

"Spring roll?"

That accent! The only way she could be sexier now was if she decided to boycott underwear. Taking a spring roll, I leaned in confidentially.

"Who else is working today?"

"Just me and Alice."

She pointed to a pleasant-looking girl across the room. I let a grateful sigh escape. She seemed confused.

"You are relieved?"

I brushed by her question, determined to take advantage of my good fortune.

"I love your accent. Where are you from?"

"Argentina."

"Where?"

"Argentina."

"Please say it one more time."

"Argentina."

"You could just say that word over and over and I'd be happy. We wouldn't need to have a real conversation at all."

"That would make life very easy for me."

"You speak wonderful English."

"Thank you. I have been practicing all of my life."

"Well, I've been practicing my curveball all my life and I still throw like a girl, so don't sell yourself short."

"All right."

There was a lull for a moment. I took in her perfectly shaped face and open, glowing smile. I gave the air a cautious sniff. Nothing. She looked worried.

"Do you smell something?"

"No, it's just allergies."

"Okay."

Pheromones had nothing to do with this one. This was all me. Conveniently forgetting that I had just been hiding from the last woman I flirted with, I smiled winningly.

"So have you been catering long?"

She made a horrified face.

"Oh no. I began very soon ago. I am not a waitress! I mean, not professional, like you are a DJ. I am a student."

Ouch. She must have seen the change in my face, because she quickly followed with more painful truths.

"I am not speaking bad of DJs, or waitresses. They are noble professions, being in charge of people's parties. Rialto thinks you are very good, he said so when he saw you walk in. You are lucky to be good at what you do. Please do not take offense."

Trying to regain my footing, I answered her with more force than I intended.

"Well, I'm a writer, actually. I write. Books. That's what I do. All of this . . . it's just cash, you know? 'Cause I write. As a writer."

I had to stop myself from repeating it again. I just had to hope she picked up on my point. She glanced over at Rialto, who was waving a meaty hand in her direction in the international signal for "Spring rolls won't give out themselves."

"I should get back to my working."

She turned to go, but I stopped her. This was all fate, I could tell, and I was determined to get as far away from Janey's scent as possible.

"I know this is strange and I don't know you or anything. But do you think you'd want to grab a drink some time?"

She hesitated, then smiled.

"Do you have a pen?"

I ran back to my table and grabbed a pen and a card. I ran back. The whole trip took three point two seconds. She scribbled it down for me. I took the card back with a smile.

"Great. So I'll call you."

"Don't you wish to know my name?"

Whoops. I'd promised myself never to make that mistake again.

"Of course."

"Malena."

"That's beautiful."

"Gracias."

"De nada."

She got excited.

"Habla Español?"

"No. Just *de nada* and *que pasa* and *puta.* The usual."

"We will have to teach you some new words."

"Sounds good."

She walked away. I went back to my table feeling pretty damn pleased with myself. This was more like it. I was in control now. I was not my nostrils' bitch, damn it.

* * *

While thinking up the specifics of my Annie's marriage aversion campaign, I found my friendship with her getting in the way of my coming up with a suitable plan to destroy her relationship. I needed to put myself into the mind-set of someone without regret, without moral fiber, without empathy. Someone who once broke up with a girl because she bowed out of Sunday brunch to go to church, unable to comprehend why she chose God over eggs Benedict and a mimosa. Someone who wouldn't even date a woman unless she passed his gymnastics test, including the vault. Someone who actually prefered premature ejaculation because it gave him more time to sleep. I needed Zach.

As Zach stepped into my apartment, a look passed over his face that I was becoming increasingly familiar with. My parents, my friends, even my landlord struggled to keep it off their faces and failed. Pity. They felt pity for me when they saw where I lived. There are entire families living in closets in Tanzania, but they feel pity for me. So what if the only place Zach could sit was on top of the TV? So what if he could use the toilet without actually getting up? Who cares, it's just an apartment. It's not me. It's romantic, actually. I'm a struggling artist. Sixteen-year-old girls would be very impressed. Zach smiled with vigor.

"Nice place. Bohemian. You must get a lot of young ladies up here."

"Sure. I am a chick magnet."

"Of course you are. You're a writer. All writers attract women. That's just what they do."

"Of course."

He looked around, squirming a bit while trying to get comfortable on the cable box.

"This reminds me of my college days. Living the good life up in Boston, drinking wine late into the evening with some pretty young heiress from Wellesley, then back to my tiny apartment, lady in tow, ready to consummate the flirtation."

"You had half a floor. Hell, one room had a grand piano you couldn't even play."

"Always have a piano, in case the lady plays."

"I'll keep that in mind."

"I'm not saying it's exactly the same. It just takes me back. I don't miss the stress, though."

Stress? He majored in modern dance.

"It must have been tough."

Zach turned around to look out my window. A whirling

sound started up as my VCR began taping whatever channel Zach's ass had flipped the TV to.

"Not a bad view. I looked down on the street in those days, as well. Three stories down. A friend from university and I would watch the people walk by during exams. God, I hated exams. I'd get so stressed out about my interpretations. I could never get my trees right. They always came across more as cactuses."

"Disaster."

"Laugh all you want, but I needed that degree. I earned that degree. I knew nothing about dance before I started majoring in it and I graduated summa cum laude. So somewhere along the line there was some major stress."

That was true. Zach did tend to throw himself into whatever inane obsession he'd gotten caught up with. Summa cum laude is nothing to sneer at. I looked over at my blank computer screen, which seemed to sneer at me.

"I know all about stress."

"You should do what we did. I have a theory. Stress can neither be created nor destroyed. It can only be transferred."

"Okay."

"So if you're stressed out, you need to transfer that stress."

"Start writing or something?"

"Perhaps. Though that sounds fairly complicated. I'm a simple man. My friend and I would pop our heads out the window and look for happy people. When we saw one walk by, we'd throw an egg at them. Then he or she'd be standing there, dripping, screaming and cursing. You should have seen these poor people looking around, all pissed and just generally stressed out. We, on the other hand, would be laughing and carefree, stress vanished. It's a great system, you should try it."

"That's horrible. You threw eggs at helpless people. What did they do to you?"

"That's the point! They did nothing to me! If they did something to me, then they'd know who I was, or at least suspect me. How could I be stress-free while worrying about that angry devil getting back at me? No, strangers are the only way to go. Do you have any eggs?"

"No! I can't believe you. What if someone threw an egg at you when you were walking by?"

"That's different. That would be awful. God, I hope that never happens. I'd be horrified."

"You're a bad person."

"No I'm not. I'm just stress-free."

"I'm going to change the subject before I throw you out the window at a passing stranger."

He shrugged, unconcerned.

"Okay. So what are you thinking about Annie and her rodent friend?"

I laid out the situation, stressing how Annie would be subsuming herself unhealthily in this relationship.

"So we need to get her to see how wrong all of this is."

"What can we do about it, really? It is her life after all. Anyway, breaking people up is very difficult. Nobody listens to their friends' advice until it's too late."

"We've got to take it beyond just giving our opinion. We need to take action. That's why I need you. I need the mind that comes up with that whole egg thing. I need that kind of almost childlike uncaring attitude toward the concerns of others."

"Well, the first thing, off the top of my head, would be to show her how she can't change, and in fact isn't changing at all no matter how hard she's attempting to."

"Okay, that sounds good."

"Or maybe we can show her how her rodent friend isn't in fact changing for her the way she assumes he is. Perhaps she's overestimating his role in their meeting in the middle. Maybe she doesn't realize the middle is in fact so far over on his side of the line."

"How do we do that?"

"I'll have to think about it. I'll need a little time."

"Okay. Just don't take too long. They'll be married before we know it if we don't do anything."

"So you say."

We sat in silence for a moment. I got up to grab a drink of water when the CD case next to my bed fell over right where I'd been sitting. Zach jumped a mile, coming down hard on a VHS tape of the world cheerleading championship.

"How the hell did that happen?"

I shrugged and poured us both some water.

"It's just my apartment. Don't worry, I'm smarter than it is, so I'll be fine."

"If you say so."

I swept the CDs to the side and sat back down, handing Zach his glass.

"So how long are you here for, anyway?"

"I don't know. I'm thinking of going back to Spain in a few weeks. It all depends."

"On what?"

"On whether this guy I'm seeing will come with me. I hope so. But it's too soon to ask, you know."

Hold on. Hold up. Apply brakes. What the hell? Calm down. Don't spook him. Time to be delicate.

"You're doing a dude?"

"Oh, that's right. I'm not telling you guys about it. I forgot. Well, I don't mind your knowing. Yes, I'm giving homosexuality a test run. Just to see if it suits me."

"To see if it suits you? Like a nice sweater?"

"Most people I meet think I'm gay anyway. I thought I'd see if there was something I was missing."

Zach does have an effeminate manner about him, which some would call aristocratic and others would call . . . curious. I'm more in the aristocratic camp, myself. It's not like he bursts into a room screaming "Hello!" and rears back like, well, like my infamous portrait. But there is an androgynous quality to him that gives his sexuality an air of mystery to those who don't know him (and to those who do, apparently).

"So now you're gay."

"I didn't say that. I'm giving it a try."

"Just a try?"

"Something like that."

"Why didn't you want to tell us?"

"I didn't know how comfortable you'd be. Well, I'm not so worried about you. You talk a big game, but you never seem to judge me. I don't know if the others will be so understanding. Please wait until I'm comfortable, all right?"

I couldn't see the issue. Annie wouldn't care, Cameron is open-minded and Dustin already assumes it. But it's his life. It just pissed me off that I couldn't go telling everyone I knew. It was a waste of damn good gossip, if you ask me.

* * *

An entire day of computer-screen staring passed by me painlessly. Exhausted, I lay in bed, casting a suspicious eye on the lighting fixture above me (I could have sworn it twitched), thinking about Annie's new life and Zach's new life and Cameron's new life. All this change made me nauseous. I started to welcome the thought of the light crushing me. Instead of loosening the bolts, I picked up the phone.

"Hola?"

"Hi, Malena?"

"Yes."

God, her accent was so fucking hot. She could recite a recipe for banana bread and it would be banned throughout the Bible Belt. I had to stop myself from asking her what she was wearing.

"Um. *Hola,* I guess. This is David. The DJ?"

"Oh, yes. Hello. I am so happy to hear from you."

She sounded excited. Doing good, David, real good. Skipping down the path to happiness like Dorothy and the Scarecrow. Just have to keep my eye out for any flying monkeys. I really need to stop watching TBS after midnight. The commercials make it impossible to make the Dark Side of the Moon thing work anyway, so I should just give up.

"*Sí.* Um, good. *Que pasa*?"

"I am doing fine, thank you."

"Good. Me, too."

"Good."

We fell silent. I rallied.

"So what are you doing right now?"

"I am studying the draping."

"What's draping?"

"It is when you put cloth on a dummy to make a dress."

"Why are you draping?"

"It is for my class."

Oh shit. She's still in school. She has classes. She takes tests. She eats in a cafeteria. She can still remember where she went to her prom. She's so young! Which meant she didn't know any better. My panic attack subsided.

"Where do you go?"

"Fashion Institute. I am studying design."

"So now you're draping?"

"Yes, I am draping. I hate it. I feel like the mannequin is mocking me."

"They've been known to do that."

"I have been here for hours. I just cannot get it right."

"Well then, I won't keep you. I was wondering if you'd like to grab a drink sometime?"

"Okay. That would be nice."

"Cool."

"Can I bring a friend?"

A friend, eh? Pictures of the Argentinean and, I don't know, the Croatian, flanking me like an international booty sandwich flashed through my head. I forced myself back to the task at hand.

"Sure. Bring whomever you want."

"Thank you. Do you think you could bring someone for her? A guy friend?"

A guy friend? Fuck. Fuck fuck fuck! I hate double dates. I hate them worse than rice pudding and movies that follow dogma. They always end up with no one getting any. The guys spend half the time undercutting each other in a backward attempt to look good in front of their dates and the girls spend the rest of the time in the bathroom doing reconstructive surgery or whatever the hell they do in there. Talking shit about me, most likely. Women in groups are evil. And a double date is the worst manifestation of that evil.

"Sure. It sounds great."

"Great."

"Cool."

More silence. This was like pulling teeth.

"So how about tomorrow night?"

"I will check with my friend and give you a call back."

"Sounds good."

I gave her my number and we hung up. So she's not a phone person. That's great! I spend too much time on the phone. I need real human interaction. And did I mention the accent? I felt good about this one, I really did. I was taking charge. Things were only going to get better. As long as I could get through the horrific double date.

Who wouldn't sabotage me? Time to call in the troops. First stop, Cameron.

"No way. Mary would kick the shit out of me."

Fair enough. Second stop, Dustin.

"That's the last thing I need, dude. Another fucking woman."

Apparently, Dustin was in a tizzle. Which sounded just like Dustin not in a tizzle, only with more "dudes."

"What's wrong with the woman you have now?" I asked.

"Judy wants to have a talk."

"Okay."

"Talks aren't cool."

"What does she want to talk about? Haute couture?"

"I don't know. Shit. Everything has to have its own talk. Did you like that movie? Why? Did it remind you of something from your childhood? Come on, you can tell me. You hate milk? Why? Were you not breastfed? Come on, you can tell me. You like kung fu movies? Why? Do you like the thought of lashing out at an uncaring society and taking back your pride? Jesus. I like watching people with bad haircuts kick each other. It's not complicated."

"I know that and you know that. But she just wants to get to know you, dude. Sneak inside the Dustin stronghold and take some pictures."

"There's nothing to see. She keeps pushing me to tell her shit that isn't true. I'm just a guy with a normal job and a normal life. What the hell do these women want from me?"

Dustin never could see himself from the outside. The odd thing is, he's such a great guy. Funny and smart and interesting. He's just not particularly complicated. If he likes something, he says that he likes it. If he doesn't, he doesn't. In many ways, he's what women should want: the strong silent type with a sharp mind who never demands too much. But women tend to gravitate toward masochism. How else do you explain Billy Bob Thornton getting married five times? A gender capable of looking after its best interests would never let that happen.

"I don't know what women want, Dustin. Hidden depths, I guess."

"Hidden fucking depths? What the hell are those? Serial killers have hidden depths. Sociopaths and pedophiles and foot fetishists have hidden depths. Why can't I just be a good guy?"

"Fucked if I know, dude."

"And now we have to have a talk. Dude, this sucks ass."

Poor guy. A victim of his own lack of issues. We hung up, leaving me with my last resort.

"Zach! Wanna go out with some pretty women with me tomorrow night?"

"I thought I told you I was trying to be gay."

"Come on. You still like women, don't you? Just because you're gay doesn't mean you need to stop having sex with women, does it?"

"You make a good point. Is the woman cultured?"

"Extremely. Every other word out of her mouth is Voltaire."

"What about her politics?"

"Strictly nonpartisan."

"Is she used to comfort?"

"She'd expect a park bench to recline."

"Sounds promising. But wait, I can tell by your solicitous manner that this is a favor for you, isn't it? I'm running interference, aren't I?"

"Of course not. Not really. Yes."

"What are her physical defects? Hairlip? Mustache? Peg leg?"

"She's hot, really."

He sighed.

"All right. I will take one for the team. But if she has uncontrollable flatulence or something of that nature, I am out the door."

Man, I hoped this chick wasn't a dog. Though knowing

Zach, he'd be more likely to walk out if she used the wrong fork with her salad. For this mystery woman's sake, I hoped there weren't any good-looking men there to nudge him back to the other side of the plate. There's nothing more embarrassing than when the guy you're on a date with hits on the waiter. That's gotta sting.

Chapter Nine

Cockroaches and Kisses

I waved at Zach as he entered the Hungarian restaurant. He waved back hesitantly, looking around apprehensively as he made his way over to me and sat down.

"Why did you pick this place? Are you really doing that bad financially?"

"What do you mean? What's wrong with it?"

I acted offended because I knew the minute I walked in that I had made a horrible mistake. The wallpaper was peeling and the waitstaff looked like they belonged in a George Romero movie. The guy who sat me actually wiped off the menus before he gave them to me. Classy.

Zach was obviously thinking of a different word.

"It has . . . character."

"Dustin recommended it. He said he took Donkey Girl here on their first date and she loved it."

"That is insane. This place is ridiculous. I don't even see a salad fork."

"A lot of places don't have salad forks. TGI Friday's doesn't have salad forks."

"And that restaurant is right at the top of *Zagat*."

"A lot of these small restaurants don't look so hot, but the food is great. Isn't that all that matters?"

"No! You've invited women here! Don't you know anything about women? They'll barely eat anyway. Ambiance will be all they get. And you give them something out of an *Indiana Jones* movie."

I looked around furtively.

"Keep it down. We don't want to piss off the waiters. If they get angry at us, they could serve us anything and we'd never know. Do you know the difference between normal Hungarian food and pee-soaked Hungarian food? Because I don't!"

He brought it down to a whisper, leaning in to complain conspiratorially.

"I don't think either of us is getting coitus tonight, David. Not with these place settings."

"Look, let's just make the best of it. There she is."

I waved at the Argentinean who was walking in the door. She waved back. Zach nudged me.

"What about the consolation prize? Oh, there she is. Not bad at all. A little too much lip gloss maybe. Actually, she looks a little familiar. Do I know her, David? David, are you all right?"

I couldn't talk. It just wasn't fair. The Argentinean walked up, followed closely by a smirking Janey.

"Hello David. And you must be Zach. This is my friend Janey. I think you've met."

"Hello, David. So nice to see you again."

Janey smiled sardonically. I tried to breathe through my mouth to keep her out of my olfactory glands. Zach stood up and shook Janey's hand.

"Hello, Janey. I don't know if you remember me, but . . ."

"Of course. The fortune-cookie guy with all the great original sayings. Do you have one for me today?"

"Not one you won't tear apart like a ravenous wolf. But give me time."

They all sat down. I still hadn't spoken. Janey wouldn't stop grinning at me, her smile sharp enough to slice my balls off. The Argentinean turned to me.

"Are you all right, David?"

This cracked my wall.

"Yeah. Of course. You just look so beautiful tonight."

She smiled. Janey lifted an eyebrow.

"So you've changed roles. Tonight, you're the fortune cookie."

The Argentinean looked slightly annoyed.

"I think it is sweet. Thank you. You look nice, too."

Zach, thankfully, guided us past the awkward moment.

"So have either of you had Hungarian before?"

Janey picked up a menu.

"Not at such a fancy place."

I looked at her sharply, but she kept her eyes on the specials. I picked up my menu.

"Let's figure out what we want."

For the next hour, I could get no read on the Argentinean. I mean, we tried to talk, but between Janey and Zach, a reticent woman like her had no chance. And Janey was in fine form. She mocked the food selection. She mocked the wallpaper. She mocked me, especially. I could tell she was getting on the Argentinean's nerves. Finally, after a comment comparing my build to the goulash soup, the Argentinean snapped.

"Janey, I need to go to the bathroom."

And she grabbed Janey's shoulder and practically tossed her into the restroom. I leaned back and rested my head on the frayed wallpaper behind me.

"Dude, that girl is nuts."

Zach was still looking after the two ladies. He spoke without turning.

"She's fascinating. She's so angry."

"What do you mean? She's not angry. She's mean."

This time Zach did look at me.

"She's furious at you. You really got to her."

"You can't get to someone like her. She's too snide."

"Can you imagine her in black latex with a whip? She would be so sexy. God. I can just see her grinding her heel into my face."

This was disturbing. I didn't want to see this side of Zach.

"Let's not talk about this anymore."

"I'm going to think about it, though."

"You do that."

The girls appeared in the restroom doorway, Janey looking slightly abashed. Zach gave me a leering smile, prompting me to kick him under the table. He didn't even have the decency to look embarrassed.

The next hour went by much more smoothly. I don't know what the Argentinean said to Janey in the bathroom, but it must have been harsh. Janey stopped mocking almost completely. Zach was disappointed, I could tell. We were able to concentrate more on our food, which, while not completely poisonous, didn't rise to the level demanded by the shabby decor. My plate's off-white color seemed somewhat suspicious to me, as well. I resisted the urge to pick at it with my fingernail. I probably didn't want to know what color it used to be.

Without Janey to distract us, the Argentinean and I were able to concentrate more on talking to each other. After about fifteen minutes, I realized we had a problem. We just couldn't get into a rhythm. We'd start down a conversational avenue, but the stoplights of stepping on each other's words and waiting too long for the other to fill a silence would keep us from getting too far. She wasn't a dumb girl. We had a very nice forced conversation about the role of government in the arts during which she constructed plenty of well thought out sentences for me to cut off. We just couldn't figure out how to talk together as a team. We were tennis players swinging our rackets at the same time regardless of where the ball was. I attributed it to the language barrier. We just needed a little practice. I didn't pay attention to what Janey and Zach were talking about. It was enough that they weren't talking to me.

We finished our meal and Zach suggested we get dessert. The Argentinean looked apprehensive and Janey made a face.

"You guys are lucky I ate the main course. I don't think I have the character to lie about enjoying my dessert."

Zach clearly wanted to keep talking to Janey.

"Come now. It can't be that bad. It's dessert. No one can screw up dessert."

"Okay, fine, whatever."

So we ordered dessert. Janey's looked particularly nasty, being some kind of black pudding with hair.

"This looks like insect poop."

Zach smiled.

"That's an ethnic delicacy. And no, the Hungarians do not consider insect feces to be a culinary favorite. In fact . . ."

Zach stopped speaking. He stared at the wall behind me.

"Don't move, David."

Janey froze with her fork in the air while the Argentinean blanched and quietly spit her food onto her plate. Janey leaned in slightly, her eyes fascinated.

"Look at the size of that thing."

I didn't know what to do. What the hell were they looking at?

"Is it a spider? Why can't I move? Where the fuck is it?"

Zach stayed calm.

"Just don't move."

"I want to move! Why can't I move?"

"It's very close to you. I don't want you to move into it."

"So do something. Jesus. I'd like to be able to move again, someday, somehow."

The Argentinean didn't move either. Janey slowly put down her fork.

"That looks remarkably like my dessert. I think I'm going to be sick."

"Why won't any of you do anything? I want to be able to move! Is it on me? What the fuck is going on?!?"

Thump!

I felt something slam into the wall next to my ear. I jumped ten feet into the air and almost peed my pants. I heard something heavy hitting the floor. A low chuckle drifted over from my left, where an elderly man sat at the table next to us, calmly putting his shoe back on.

"Pussies."

Shaking his head, he returned to his meal. I looked down at a dead cockroach the size of a Shetland pony lying belly up on the floor. The rest of my table stared at me, rigid with shock.

Finally, I tentatively lifted my hand into the air and made the weakest signature gesture in the history of snooty bill requests.

"Check?"

Janey took Zach's plate and placed it over her nasty pudding.

"All right, boys. You owe us a beer."

* * *

We stepped up to the unmarked door, Zach leading the way with a confident smile. A lone black man who would tower over Andre the Giant sat out front, separating the weak from the strong. Zach turned back to us, his open face beaming.

"I adore this place. You'll love it. Hi, Maurice!"

Maurice's face remained impassive.

"IDs."

"But of course. Anything for you, Maurice."

Maurice refused even to look up. Zach simply waited for his ID to be handed back to him and bounced forward, a jubilant puppy whose spirit remains eternally unsinkable. We followed through the door and into androgyny.

I guess I shouldn't have been surprised. After all, Zach had warned me about his new direction in life. But I couldn't help but feel out of step with my old friend's new persona. Janey leaned into the Argentinean and me to whisper.

"Are we the only ones in here with genitalia?"

I shrugged, because I didn't know the answer and I wasn't about to check. The club spilled over with rail-thin, bald-headed, almost completely hairless (except for the perfectly tweezed eyebrows) men-women hybrids in shimmering silver and black clothing that hung like dresses on hangers. The music thumped along in that nonthreatening club style with frequent drum-free breaks filled with meaningless synth space chords, each one an open invitation for the shiny-domed aliens to wave their arms above their heads like tripping air-traffic controllers trying to land a plane. Zach pointed toward the floating green and yellow neon bar manned by the ship's physician from *Star Trek*.

"Who wants a beer?"

Incredulity leaked out from Janey's face.

"They have beer here?"

"Sure!"

"What kind? Space beer? Moby beer?"

"Ask and find out."

We stepped up to the bar and Janey attempted to order her beer. To our considerable surprise, the only beer they served proved to be Guinness on tap. A strange bedfellow to all the Zimas and Smirnoff Ices. After we grabbed our drinks, Zach led us to a small table off in the corner where we set up shop, staring out at the sea of undulating ambiguity. The Argentinean didn't say a word, sitting by my side in obvious discomfort. I leaned into Janey, who'd been chatting up Zach.

"Is Malena all right?"

Barely turning around, Janey spoke out of the side of her mouth.

"She's kinda conservative. She's spent the last twenty years working up to oral sex, so you can imagine all this would be quite a shock. Anyway, I'm not talking to you."

She pointedly turned back to Zach and continued her conversation. I tried a few more conversational start-ups with the Argentinean, but between the loud music and the louder statement of sexual experimentation surrounding us, she'd been barraged into silence. I asked her to dance, but she refused that as well, content to sip her beer and disapprove. I quickly became bored and wedged my way into the conversation next to me, which had just reached the point where Zach's vow of sexual discretion got broken by a Jack and Coke.

"I just like gay men, I think."

Janey pointed to me, giving me a moment's heart attack before I registered her comment.

"Not straight men? What's wrong with them?"

"They're too . . . messy. Untidy and sloppy and . . . uptight. I need a man who's slight and in good shape, with nice clothes and an open, well-traveled mind."

"So why do you hang out with him?"

Janey pointed to me again, sending my head jolting back as I flinched. I resolved to send her my chiropractor bill. Zach raised his vaguely phosphorescent drink to his lips, taking a moment to tilt it my direction.

"He's an old friend. And he doesn't judge me."

Her eyes flashed, a pinhole of pain nestled in the center of mocking brown.

"I wonder how that feels."

Zach smiled, oblivious.

"I wish my other old friends accommodated my wanderings as easily as he does."

Janey still stared at me, arresting me with the hint of weakness in her face. She grabbed my hand.

"I wanna dance."

"But the music sucks."

"I wanna dance to sucky music. Humor me, I'm the only one in here with hair."

She pulled me onto the floor. The last thing I saw was Zach sliding over to talk to my practically catatonic date before pale thin bodies cut off the light. I spun to face my tormentor, who'd begun moving her hips to the cheezy electropop. She grabbed my hand and pulled me close. I breathed through my mouth, trying to keep those pesky pheromones out of my system. Her naked expression prompted me to yell into her ear any small talk I could rustle up.

"So . . . I noticed you didn't get a seven and seven."

She leaned into my cheek, her warm, slightly moist breath slipping into my ear, carrying a voice so soft I shouldn't have been able to make out the words.

"I decided to stick to beer around you."

"Why?"

"I don't always act the way I want to, or talk the way I want to. Especially after the week I've had."

"What do you mean?"

"Have you ever gone through a particularly bad patch, where everything seems to be going to shit? You ever wonder what would happen if someone met you for the first time during that bad patch? They'd think you're insane, right? Well, that's been my week. I don't think I gave you a real picture of me. Of course, I don't think you're looking too hard to find it, either."

What was she talking about? I already knew who she was. Pheromones and lip gloss, Rapunzel hair and staggering steps, mocking smiles and biting barbs. What else did I need to see?

"I'm sorry. I don't understand."

She pulled back from my ear to stare me in the face. I had never seen this expression before. I had never seen this Janey before. So uncertain and needing, like a hungry child. She leaned in slowly, laying her hands lightly on each of my cheeks, fingers gliding up my skin, leaving tiny goosebumps in their wake. I watched, immobile, as her eyes drifted shut and her lips moved unerringly to cover mine. This was no dark-closet, hands-clutching-at-each-other-wildly kiss. This soft, light, warm kiss meant things. What, I didn't know. But I couldn't be kissed like that and not be affected. I found my lips moving under hers, matching her slow circles pressing into me. After a lost, unforgettable moment, she slipped her head to the side and slid her chin into the hollow of my neck, kissing the base of my shoulder lightly as she wrapped her arms around me. I heard her voice drift up to my ear.

"It killed me when I saw you there at that table and I don't know why. I don't even really know why I keep thinking about you. It must be some lingering guilt over that ridiculous earring. I don't understand it. But there it is. I know things got fucked up, on both sides. But can we give it one more try, for real this time, and I'll try and you'll try and who knows? You don't have to say anything. Just squeeze once for yes."

We'd slowed down as the music sped on by us, the gyrating space creatures leaving us in their wake. I didn't want to do this. She'd be trouble, I could feel it. We didn't even move well together. Our hips swayed to two different metronomes, knocking our bones together jarringly. It just wasn't right. I breathed into her long full hair, and squeezed, once.

She smelled so good, after all.

Chapter Ten

The Healing Properties of YMCA

"I don't understand the problem, David. It sounds to me like you're making it more difficult than it has to be."

Annie would think that. Ever since she'd dropped the Rat Boy bomb on us, she'd been optimistic about everything. She'd been pointing out particularly pleasant flowers and smiling at playing children for weeks now. Had she been replaced in some evil *Stepford Wives* scheme? Or have the pharmaceutical companies finally figured out how to manufacture a pill that eliminates sarcasm? Wasn't Viagra bad enough? I hate Viagra. We finally get to the point in our lives when we can get some relief from the relentless demands of our penises and medical science goes and fucks it up for us! I'd been looking forward to the restful impotence of my sixties, when I could finally stop talking like an idiot to women because they happen to have breasts. But now I will never find peace.

I'd just finished telling her all about my Janey problem, revisiting the night in question with great attention to detail. The kissing didn't last too long, as we both knew we weren't being exactly fair to our respective dates. But after we left the dance floor, we discovered both Zach and the Argentinean missing. A quick check of my cell phone later revealed the painful truth. As has happened every single time in the history of illicit lip locking, the Argentinean had spotted the two of us making out on the dance floor, and she fled with Zach in tow. In his message, Zach assured me he would take care of her. Ashamed of ourselves, Janey and I separated, each heading home alone to our cold beds. Janey didn't even make me promise to call. But I had squeezed. That meant more than any tossed off assurances.

The next morning, I tried calling the Argentinean to apologize and explain, but no one would pick up. I considered phoning Janey to make sure her roommate got in, but before I could make the call, my cell jangled with Janey's name on the screen.

"David! Have you heard from Malena?"

Crap. This better not be a *Days of our Lives* moment, where the Argentinean, despondent and alone, throws herself to her death from atop the Statue of Liberty. They never tell you how she pulled herself up there. It's not like you can just hop on a ladder and climb up to the head. She just appears there in a jump cut, hanging on to Lady Liberty's crown before hopping out into space. Soaps can really screw with your paranoia, giving you new, completely unrealistic fears to worry about. By the way, I know that stuff about the Statue of Liberty only because my mom tells me the plotlines every once in a while. I personally don't watch soaps. I swear. Stop snickering.

"She's not home?"

"This is all my fault! There I am with my lips all over

you, not even thinking about her feelings! I'm going to hell! I hope she didn't throw herself off the Statue of Liberty or something!"

See what I mean? *Days of Our Lives* is the devil.

"I'm sure she didn't . . . hold on, my phone is beeping."

I clicked the call waiting. A despondent voice leaped out at me.

"My sheets are ruined."

"Zach?"

"Six-hundred-thread-count Egyptian cotton! Those sheets were more expensive than my bed!"

"Zach, Malena's missing!"

"What? She just left here ten minutes ago. That's hardly enough time to go missing. Don't you have to wait twenty-four hours or something?"

Thank God.

"Hold on."

I clicked.

"She's on her way home."

Janey's sigh of relief lasted five minutes at least.

"Thank you, Jesus! Where was she?"

"She spent the night with Zach."

Her sigh morphed into a horrified cough.

"What! She's a good girl!"

"I don't doubt it."

"Did they do anything . . . bad?"

"I don't know."

"Well, find out! I'm going to kill Zach if he took advantage of that poor sweet girl!"

"All right. Finding out. Hold on."

I clicked.

"Zach!"

"This won't come out in the wash! Ruined!"

"Focus, Zach, and tell me what happened!"

"What do you know about sheets, David? You buy your linen off the guy selling used batteries on the street corner. You can't understand my pain."

"Just talk to me, okay?"

"Fine. You acted like an asshole."

"I know. I'm sorry."

"Tell her, not me. Anyway, she dragged me to another bar, where she proceeded to drink every brand of vodka they stocked, including Skyy, which I warned her was overpriced and vastly overrated. You need to meet a certain standard, I feel, and just because Heather Graham is clutching a martini on the billboard doesn't make it quality. She wouldn't listen, of course, and the next thing I knew we'd landed in a cab headed toward my apartment. She wouldn't keep her hands off me! And the things she said! She is far more fluent in English than I ever would have guessed. I didn't even recognize some of the terms she suggested we put into action, and I've been to Thailand. We get back to my room and she attacks me, ripping one of the buttons of my Paul Smith shirt, which I still haven't found. She throws me on my bed, tears off her top, screams something in Spanish that they never taught me in Barcelona, and proceeds to vomit all over me. Thank God I'd slipped out of both my injured shirt and my DKNY slacks, or the carnage would have been far greater. But my sheets! Ruined!"

"What about you? Are you okay?"

"I come clean in the wash. Egyptian cotton isn't so lucky. It's the story of all romantic entanglements, isn't it? You break her heart and my sheets pay the price."

"Is she okay?"

"She passed out soon after. She left this morning without saying much to me. She should be home soon, I'd think."

"I didn't mean it. It just happened. You know I didn't mean for this to happen!"

"Tell it to the six hundred threads."

I clicked back over to Janey, who remained waiting anxiously on the other line. I explained the situation, leaving out the strange obsession with bedding.

"I'm gonna call later and apologize. Tell her that, okay?"

"Trust me, kiddo. Your apologies are nothing compared to the groveling I'm about to sink to."

She hung up before I could reply. A few hours later I called the Argentinean, apologizing from the word "go." She didn't have too much to say, not surprisingly, and we didn't talk long. Janey never called me back and I didn't call her. I wasn't sure what I wanted to do. Which is what prompted Annie to tell me how easy my decisions really were, despite all evidence to the contrary.

"What's so easy about it? Look what we did to the Argentinean."

Annie smirked as she leaned over a wedding bouquet display case.

"It was one date. And you hooked up with the girl you'd hooked up with before. She'll get over it. Anyway, if anyone is in the doghouse it's her roommate. She's the one who put her lips on her girlfriend's guy. That's pretty, don't you think?"

Annie pointed to a small flower arrangement in the corner. I nodded absently.

"It's still embarrassing."

"Fine. But that's not why you're not calling her. Let's look at thank-you cards."

She led me down the aisle to the next booth, pushing past a few groups of intent women on her way to the thank-you card table. She had on a low-cut pair of jeans that almost dipped too low, which I pointedly didn't notice. I grabbed a thank-you card and didn't look at it.

"Of course it is."

I knew it wasn't. I just hated how easily everyone else saw through me. Annie thumbed through a display book of cards while an attentive salesman stood by, ready to step in.

"You're not calling her because you're afraid you like her."

Now this wasn't what I'd been thinking. Annie, once again, has let her engagement blind her to reality.

"I'm not calling her because she's crazy. One kiss doesn't change that."

Annie closed the book and moved on, leaving the salesman behind to look longingly after his lost sale. She wove through the gaggles of prospective brides and their support staffs with practiced ease.

"I don't know why you keep calling her crazy. I didn't get a chance to meet her at that party, or anything, so maybe I'm missing something. But she sounds less crazy and more . . . feisty."

I struggled to keep up, lacking her innate shopping skills.

"You are missing something. Every time I talk to her it's a . . . a struggle. I have to be on my toes. It's tiring. And she looks so strange, with that tan and those shiny lips."

"Makeup comes off. Skin lightens when left unburned. Is it a struggle to keep a conversation going?"

She stopped again, so abruptly I had to dig in my heels to keep from impregnating her purse. She picked up some framed portraits of happy wedding couples, all of whom seemed perfectly matched down to their eye color.

"Not a struggle to keep it going. More like a struggle to . . . well . . ."

"To keep up?"

"I can keep up. It just takes a little work."

"That doesn't sound quite so bad. These are a little generic, don't you think?"

The photographer standing to the side blanched. Annie moved on, oblivious. I trailed after her, trying to make her see.

"It's just always work with her. It shouldn't be so much work. It's like my grandma used to tell my dad that it was just as easy to fall in love with a rich woman as a poor woman. Sure, my mom's dowry consisted of two mixing bowls and a broken carburetor, but doesn't the principle still make sense? My uncle married a rich woman and so did his sons."

Annie gave me a look of profound scorn.

"So she's not rich enough for you?"

"No, that's not it. I don't need a rich woman. But isn't it just as easy to fall in love with a stable, centered, level-headed woman as an off-kilter, unpredictable one? Why can't I fall in love with the girl who doesn't come with so much baggage? Why can't I control that much?"

"That's a load of shit. That woman doesn't exist. Look at the guys being dragged around this place. Ask them if a relationship is all sex and strawberries."

You're probably wondering where this little talk was

taking place. Across the country, from the smallest burb to the largest metropolis, brides-to-be need to be sold on the most expensive weddings known to the human race. In order to achieve this, wedding expos have sprung up from coast to coast, from church meetinghouses to Sheraton ballrooms to the huge glass Jacob Javits Center on Thirty-fourth Street by the Hudson River, where Annie was currently dragging me around. Every type of wedding accoutrement, from invites to mammoth circus-size tents, could be found at one of the hundreds of tables lining the walls. A huge stage dominated the center of the main room, across which trotted wedding band after wedding band, with the odd DJ company sprinkled in, each promising that only they could make your special day perfect. The musicians cranking out well-worn versions of "Respect" and "The Way You Look Tonight" looked so dead-eyed I felt sorry for their souls. By day they played in Broadway pits or recorded with the brightest stars in music, but to pay the bills they all ended up here, jamming to "We Are Family" while a cheeseball in a glittering tux strutted around surrounded by underdressed dancing girls. Nothing pays as well as a wedding gig.

I'd promised Annie I'd help her with some of the wedding plans since her mom couldn't get away from work in California. I'd actually sneaked her into this particular wedding expo, though on one condition.

"By the way, David, where's your booth?"

I scowled. Yes, the All-Stars DJ Company maintained a booth. And this month I had to be one of the resident DJs. I'd taken an hour break to help Annie, but then back to the grind I had to go.

"You're not allowed to know where my booth is."

"I'm gonna come across it, you know that. This place is big, but it's not that big."

"Then you'll just keep walking."

"But I want to see the show!"

"You know our deal!"

Since we catered to a slightly less affluent market, the organizers wouldn't let us onto the main stage with the big-time DJ companies. Therefore, the All-Stars DJ Company decided to stage its own little shows on its own little stage. Meaning, at four o'clock, yours truly would be up there with three other DJs, trying to get a pretend party started. And Annie was forbidden to watch.

"Fine. Wuss. Look, free samples!"

She ran ahead to a catering table, eyes lit up like a child's. I followed at first, but what awaited me at the catering table froze me in my tracks. Janey stared back at me, holding the plate of hors d'oeuvres that Annie was busy emptying. Rialto had a booth. I should have known. I'd been decisively spotted, so no sneaking away under the tables. Steeling myself, I walked up.

"Hey Janey."

"David."

Annie looked up, quiche pastry flaking down her chin. She hurriedly swallowed, wincing as a large, unchewed piece refused to go down quietly, then forced words out of her mouth as soon as her esophagus freed up.

"You're Janey?"

Janey's face shone especially sun-kissed (a big wet kiss) today. She barely looked at Annie.

"That's me."

"I'm Annie. I'm engaged."

She held up her ring. I could tell by her wild eyes that she hadn't planned on mentioning this, but panic got the better of her. Janey gazed down impassively.

"It's gorgeous."

"Thanks!"

Annie looked back and forth from stone face to stone face for a moment before coming to her senses.

"I'm headed down toward the place settings. Meet me there, David, okay?"

"See you there."

She scurried away like a rat from a sinking ship. Janey raised her eyebrows.

"Quiche?"

"No thanks."

"What about some rugalach? It's fantastic."

"That's okay."

"You've got to have something. After all, it's free."

"I'm sorry I haven't called."

"That's fine. I'm sure you're still pissed about your friend's sheets."

Her face hadn't changed, still as hard as the brick it resembled.

"No. I just . . . I don't know what to do. It's a screwed-up situation."

"Malena and I are fine now, if you're wondering."

Great. My last excuse fluttered away.

"Wonderful."

"So . . . if you don't want any quiche, you should probably get moving. There's a lot to see."

"I'm working the expo. I'm helping Annie on my break."

"How chivalrous of you. Well, I guess I won't keep you."

She still stood there, staring. I found myself locked onto those lips, remembering them on my neck. I found myself recalling the feel of that quick squeeze, overcome by her scent and her hands on my back. I found myself opening my mouth to speak.

"Do you want to go out sometime?"

She snorted, finally looking away.

"I don't want your pity invite, just because you ran into me and you're embarrassed."

"No. I really want you to go out with me."

"Just go back to your friend."

She wasn't looking at me now. I gave it one last go.

"I'm working down in the Lower Pavilion. If you want, you can stop by. Before four. Or I'll call you. Anyway, I'll talk to you soon."

She didn't look at me. Eventually, I just walked away.

Annie waited for me around the corner, practically pouncing on me as I walked up.

"So? That's the girl, huh? She seems cute. Did you patch it up?"

I shook my head, my stomach tightening like I'd just eaten lamb vindaloo.

"She's pissed. Extremely pissed. I think this one is fucked up for good."

Annie put her hand on my shoulder, casually flicking my ear with her fingers.

"It's your own damn fault, idiot. Try her again in a day or so. Why don't you like her again?"

"I don't want to talk about it."

"Fine. Look at these place settings!"

I followed her around like a moping puppy for the next

forty minutes. She never seemed to buy anything, though she picked up enough business cards to build a paper replica of Versailles. Thankfully, the subject of Janey was dropped, and I learned even more about how perfect and wonderful was the Rat Boy. It was a struggle to keep my tongue in my head, but somehow I managed. No one rewards you for the stupid things you don't say. There should be Oscars for that feat as well. I'd be a multiple winner by the end of your average hour.

My time up, I took my leave of Annie by the ugliest wedding gowns ever devised. I even saw one with a bare midriff. Not a two piece per se, just a long gown with a bare midriff. Fashion designers need to be federally legislated. I gave Annie a quick hug.

"Good luck. Remember, don't come downstairs!"

She laughed.

"I promised, didn't I? Listen, thanks again David. This meant a lot. This hasn't been easy for me, especially since my family either can't or won't do a damn thing. So it means a lot that you're here to help. Even though you think my fiancé is a tool."

"I never said that."

"You've been saying it without saying it for the past hour."

Academy Award revoked, I guess.

"I don't really know him."

"But you're going to, remember? Please, for me, try to make him feel at home. My biggest fear is that he'll see my real life and run screaming."

To my shock, her eyes teared up. I leaped in to dam the flow.

"Annie, you're fantastic. You know that. Guys fall all over themselves for you. Literally. Insurance companies charge extra premiums because of it."

"He doesn't know how I can be. My family's a mess. His family is perfect, you know. Two loving parents and four eternally sunny older sisters, all of whom still go camping together every summer. I wish I had that. I wish I was that."

I couldn't understand her. Annie was the perfect one, the one too good for that shiny happy wacko. Why did she think she could ever be wanting?

"Annie, you have friends who love you. You can't choose your family, but you can choose your buddies, and we'd do anything for you. I'm looking at floral arrangements for Christ's sake. That is unconditional, if ever I heard it. You're too good for him, if anything."

Her head shot up, eyes burning.

"Stop that. You promised to be nice."

"I am being nice. Sorry. I'm just trying to make you see how great you are."

My resolve deepened. I had to save her from a lifetime of feeling like this. Her eyes softened, the fire dying down.

"I know you are. I appreciate it. But can you do something for me? Can you give him a real chance? For me? I want you guys to get along. I don't want to lose you just because you don't mesh with him."

"You're not going to lose me."

Of course, that assertion's truth rested on my firm belief Annie would never actually go through with this. Because she was right. If Annie actually married Rat Boy, we'd never see her again. It wouldn't be her fault. We just wouldn't mix. The Rat Boys of the world with their earnest folk music and simplistic senses of humor have nothing to say to the Davids of the world. We're too sharp. Too caustic. Too real. He'd keep her from ever seeing us. She'd be trapped in that house in suburbia eating macrobiotic muffins and wondering why the hell her car runs on electricity, lost as to why the new, nicer version of her didn't make her happy the way she thought it would. How long before she reverts, little pieces of her real self slipping out from behind the plastic? And by then she'd be all alone, an island of sarcasm surrounded by a sea of sincerity, cut off from the ironic mainland. She sighed.

"Okay. Go do your job. I'll be up here, I promise. No peeking."

I hugged her again, giving her a probing look.

"You okay?"

She forced a smile, flipping her hair back.

"But of course. I'm amazing, after all."

* * *

Jeremy, my boss, fumed as I walked up to the booth fifteen minutes late.

"Kid, where have you been! Bill needs to pee!"

Bill, our newest rookie, stood in the corner, legs wrapped around each other like the contortionist at the fair.

"Why didn't you just let him go while you minded the store?"

Jeremy snorted.

"I need to be free to schmooze. I don't have time for brochure duty."

He waved at Bill, who shot off like the Road Runner. I took his place by the brochures, making sure everyone got one as they passed by.

"Where are Jean and Father Kim?"

"They'll be here by four for the demonstration, don't worry."

Our demonstrations always followed the same hellish pattern. Jeremy would introduce us and go over how we work a party. Then, one by one, we'd each demonstrate a dance, leading the crowd in our "specialty." Jean, our only female DJ, always took on "Hands Up," made famous at Club Meds, on cruise ships and wherever single women drink too many brightly colored coconut beverages and suddenly feel the need to raise their hands in the air at regular intervals for no apparent reason. Father Kim, an actual Catholic priest who DJ-ed in his spare time to make extra money, was a whiz with the "Electric Slide." He's been known to preside over a wedding and then immediately hop behind the turntables to rock the party late into the night. The sight of his white collar sliding across the floor to the faux island beat never fails to get even the most hardened, party-hating soul up onto the floor. DJ Party-time usually took care of the Dollar Dance, a particularly pointless piece of choreographed mob mentality. But DJ Party-time couldn't make it this time, as he wouldn't miss his grandson's graduation for the world. Since DJ Party-time had a tendency recently to trip over his cane and curse loudly in Yiddish, this wasn't such a blow. Being the new guy, I'd been relegated to the lowest line dance of all: the "YMCA." Even as I began to get a reputation as one of the more popular DJs, Jeremy made me stick with it for the demonstrations. It's my own fault, really. I couldn't help it if I really sold the moves on the crowd. But this time, I was looking forward to moving up to the Dollar Dance and leaving "YMCA" to the newbie.

"So is Bill ready for 'YMCA'?"

"He's doing the Dollar Dance. You're still on 'YMCA.'"

"What? But he's the new guy!"

"And he can't seem to figure the thing out. The Dollar Dance doesn't require so much hand-eye coordination."

"'YMCA' isn't that hard. It's all spelling!"

"Well, you're the writer, so of course you'd think it's easy. You're sticking with it."

I simmered, handing out brochures with a scowl. Bill came back from the bathroom to take his place next to me.

"I'm real sorry, David. I don't mean to screw things up. I just don't have the hips."

"It's okay, Bill. It's not your fault."

How hard is it to make a "Y" in the air? Honestly.

Three thirty rolled around, bringing with it both Jean and Father Kim. Jean always wore the same thing, a jeans and white shirt combo straight out of Tennessee, down to the string tie. Her hair wouldn't move if you fired a scud at it. Father Kim also had a uniform, kind of a shiny tuxedo with a sparkly priest's collar. Even though I had long since left the Church, there still remained a tiny Catholic inside me who screamed in righteous horror every time I saw his get-up.

"Hey, guys. Looking good."

They smiled back at me. Jeremy ran up.

"It's time to start. Get ready while I draw a crowd."

My watch said twenty of four.

"Isn't it a little early?"

Jeremy waved me off.

"I don't want to be stuck here all day. Bill, how're those guitars coming?"

Bill popped up from behind the table, a half-inflated plastic saxophone hanging limp from his lips.

"I'm gonna pass out."

Jeremy frowned in annoyance.

"Go help him, David. We don't have time for medical attention."

Five minutes of furious blowing later and we stood off to the side, staring at the small crowd milling around in front of the small black curtain with the All-Stars banner square in the center. Couples, parents of couples, small kids of couples (hey, it's the new millennium) stood shoulder to shoulder, restlessly awaiting our little performance. The interesting thing about the next fifteen minutes wouldn't be the abject humiliation we'd be subjected to as we pranced around pretending to be working a party. Rather, the strange thing would be how much I enjoyed it. I mocked the demonstration mercilessly both to my friends and my fellow DJs; I complained about it to Jeremy every chance I got. But once I stepped out in front of those people, I had a damn good time. So I'm a masochist. Go figure.

A drum beat and light guitar riff announced both the start of "Celebration" by Kool and the Gang and the start of our show. Jeremy leaped out from behind the curtain like a Vegas magician and ran around waving, inciting the crowd to some bewildered, polite clapping.

"Are you ready to party!"

The small crowd nodded.

"I said, are you ready to party!"

The crowd murmured, that yes, they were ready to party.

"That's not good enough! Are you ready to party or not!"

Finally, everyone shouted, "Yes!" Mostly to shut him up.

"Then let me introduce you to my crew! The DJs that form the backbone of the party animal that is the All-Stars DJ Company! Put your hands together for Jean Meadows!"

Jean ran on to mild applause.

"The holy MC, Father Kim!"

Father Kim ran on to louder applause and surprised muttering.

"The dancing DJ, Davey H.!"

I never expected it, but every time my name got called, I felt a leap in my stomach. All my derision and mockery fell away and I found myself trotting in with a huge smile, waving at the crowd, fully in the moment. What can I say, it was kind of a rush. The crowd clapped a little louder, getting into it as we got into it.

"And the king of swing, the man with the plan, the silky-voiced devil. Ladies, get ready to catch your breath! Here's DJ Bill!"

Bill ran on, full speed, like he needed to win the sprint. Unfortunately, Bill didn't have a whole lot of experience with any kind of running, which, coupled with his lack of anything resembling coordination, did not bode well for a smooth jog. Sure enough, his ankle caught on the edge of the curtain pole and he tripped, right toward me. Without thinking, I reached out and grabbed him just as he fell forward, catching his leg as he fell toward the ground. Working on instinct, Bill threw out his hands as I pulled his feet up and past me, his shoes passing under my nose. Somehow, he managed to bring his feet back down to the ground and Jean reached out to grab his arm and steady him on the way up. Thus, from the audience, Bill seemed to execute a perfect cartwheel. I saw the tape later and it was a pretty piece of acrobatics, except for the terrified look on Bill's face. The crowd went wild, applauding and cheering. Bill looked bewildered for a moment before breaking out into a grin. Jeremy's voice shot out from behind us.

"See what I mean! The man stops at nothing to make sure you have a good time!"

They were putty in our hands.

One by one, we took them through the dances, moving through the crowd to hand out tambourines and inflatable instruments. Even Bill's Dollar Dance didn't go off too badly, with only three chairs and a maraca as casualties. Finally, the show came down to me.

"Are you people ready to really get down?"

The yes from the audience was loud and enthusiastic by this point. I grabbed the mic and leaped out in front. The horn riff blared out behind me as the disco beat took over my hips. I began to bob in place as I pointed toward the crowd.

"This is one of the greatest party songs of all time and I need you all to move with me. The dance is easy. It's just letters, four of 'em. You can all spell, can't you? All right then. Get ready to go back to school!"

Yes, I said things like that. What can I say, I was in the moment.

I stepped back and forth, clapping as the verse played behind me. All the couples and parents and kids clapped with me, smiling widely, as into the show as I was. After a moment I kicked it up a notch, pointing a circle from one end of the crowd to the other. They followed me, matching my booty shake for shake. The music crescendoed, and, lost in the moment, I punched the air with the horn hits, feeling no small satisfaction as the crowd, to a man, threw their fists in the air. We moved together, made one by the magic of the Village People. Finally, we reached the apex, the top of the mountain, the reason for it all.

"It's fun to stay at the Y-M-C-A!"

Lifting my arms into the air, I led them through the chorus, forming the letters with my outstretched limbs, my death grip on my masculinity finally loosened under the warm adoration of the dancing crowd. Nothing could touch me while I led and they followed. Until I cast my gaze to the corner, drunk on the power of line dancing, and it came to rest on the smirking face of an extremely amused Janey.

I tore my eyes away instantly, terrified. Why did I invite her down here? What was I thinking! Why did we have to start so early? Why did I have to look so damn stupid! I stumbled a bit, losing my place in the song. I glanced to my left, where Bill stood clapping to his own little beat that bore little resemblance to any rhythm we could hear. Somehow, the sight of him calmed me. If he could trip over himself and come out a rock star, I could get through this dance in one piece.

Determined to do it right, I became even wilder, with twice as much energy. I raced through the crowd, dancing with old ladies and getting little kids to shake their tambourines. I leaped atop the table for the second chorus and, peering down the row of booths, I could see all the photographers and flower arrangers and thank-you-card purveyors throw their hands in the air, tossing aside their jaded ways for a brief moment of "YMCA" euphoria. Down the aisles in every direction, as far as I could see, people were dancing. Looking down, I spotted Janey, her smirk widened into a full smile. We hit the last line and suddenly she threw her arms in the air with me, forming the letters with abandon. I smiled at her, lost in the silliest song in the musical canon. And at that moment, somehow, everything seemed simple. I wanted to kiss her again. It was that simple. I just had to throw everything else away, my pride, my decorum, that mocking voice inside me that never seemed to sleep. We formed the last "A" and the crowd swelled into applause. Janey joined them, her arms still raised above her head. So simple. And it took the Village People to show me the way.

* * *

The crowd bled away after the show, most even forgetting to grab a card. (Bill's comatose form lying behind the table, drained from all the excitement, probably had something to do with that.) I walked up to Janey, who stood with raised eyebrows by the brochure table, reading about my services. She put up a hand as I started to speak.

"Look, idiocy like that dance does grant you some dispensation. I don't know why, it must be some cosmic rule I've been unaware of until today, but I'm willing to give you a chance. But I put myself out there, way out there, and you didn't treat me very nice."

"I'm sorry."

"You're sorry, I know. Let's make it simple. Do you want to go out, really go out? If you don't really want to go out with me, I'll be fine, trust me. To speak in your language, I will survive."

Still high on my seventies-classic-induced realization, I didn't feel a single doubt. This Janey? The one with the calm demeanor but slightly trembling hands? The one not showing up hours late drunk off her ass just to be hip? The real Janey (I hope)? I wanted to kiss her. That's all I needed to know. So I did just that, leaning in and placing my lips on hers gently before pulling away.

"I honestly want to go out with you."

Janey smiled, her eyes crinkling at the corners.

"All right then."

Chapter Eleven

The Perils of Arm Cream

The small Italian bistro on Prince Street, so small it didn't even have a name, just the word "PASTA" above the door in block letters, stood empty except for the four of us. A perfect place for plotting the downfall of one scraggly bearded imposter. Cameron and Dustin fought over the last piece of calamari as I hogged the breadbasket with no remorse. All of us listened intently to Zach, the adventurer from outside the city gates.

"Morocco is such a decadent country. Simply fabulous place, truly. I meant to stay a week and remained for four months. I rented a small set of rooms and simply lolled about drinking wine and absinthe and eating grapes off the lips of whatever beautiful thing would come up for a chat. We'd sit on my veranda overlooking the Mediterranean, underneath the African night sky, and listen to the soft plucking of some stringed instrument drifting up from the opium den across the street. I remember once I invited over two lovely ladies, whose names I never quite caught, and we laughed and drank and talked about art late into the night. The country is awash in Byzantine architecture, simply beautiful. Truly a perfect evening."

Dustin sat entranced, the last piece of calamari half hanging out of his mouth.

"Did you do both of them?"

Zach shook his head.

"Threesomes are a bore. They never work properly. I refuse to do them anymore."

He couldn't have shocked us more if he'd pulled off his face to reveal the alien from *V.* I choked on my bread as Cameron leaned forward in agitation.

"Are you insane? Sex with one woman is amazing! A threesome would be twice as amazing! I mean, you can't argue with the numbers!"

Zach shook his head at our simple ways.

"It's far too much work. Someone is always neglected, usually me. There are just too many parts to keep track of, too many things to massage and slap and pinch. It's exhausting. I don't have the attention span. I have a hard enough time satisfying one vagina. Two is just far too much pressure."

Cameron couldn't believe what he was hearing.

"Do you know how long I've tried to make a threesome happen? Do you know the effort, the planning, the 'accidental' meetings I had to arrange? And it never worked. You bastard! How dare you rip apart my dream!"

I patted his shoulder, trying to calm him.

"Zach, how many threesomes have you had, anyway? One? That hardly counts, right?"

Zach looked down at his hand, ticking off his fingers.

"Four. I think. Okay, four and a half. Trust me, they're

never worth it. Sex requires concentration and attention to detail and, above all, a connection, even if the connection is fleeting. A threesome does not lend itself to the fulfillment of these requirements. Someone is always getting less attention, someone always ends up sitting back and watching, someone is always left out of the connection. And in my experience, a threesome happens because two women are curious to sleep with each other and need a man to mediate. The guy is an icebreaker, nothing more. And once the conversation gets going, he is relegated to the role of bystander. And let's say that doesn't happen, let's say he is involved, he is one of the active participants, then one of the women is left on the sidelines, idly running her fingers along someone's skin or holding someone's limb out of the way, but not really part of it. What's the point of that? It's the ultimate in gluttony. Two people, diving into each other, inciting each other, ripping each other apart and then mending the tears with kisses, that is sex. Anything more is a carnival sideshow act."

Cameron sputtered helplessly while Dustin threw up his hands in disgust.

"It's like what they say about money being wasted on the rich. Sex is wasted on you, Zach."

"I stick by my opinion."

I couldn't bear to hear anymore about Zach's dismissal of all that men held dear, so I changed the subject.

"Zach, you said you'd thought of something we can do about the Rat Boy situation."

"Yes, I think so. It's simple, but it might be effective."

The waiter appeared with our food, laying the plates down in front of us. Cameron checked over his chicken marsala to make sure they left off the mushrooms like he'd asked. The waiter rolled his eyes as he walked away, a gesture Cameron caught out of the corner of his eye.

"Italians are so snooty about food. It has to be their way or no way at all. You'd think I'd asked for something insane."

Dustin speared a piece of penne.

"Cameron, the main ingredient of chicken marsala, besides the chicken, is the mushrooms. It's like ordering nachos with no tortillas. He's right to think you're an idiot."

"I'm not an idiot. I like the mushroom sauce, I just don't like mushrooms. They're too . . . spongy. It's freaky."

I steered us back to the topic at hand.

"Zach?"

"Well, I was thinking about how she's had difficulty reconciling her two worlds. What if we bring out how different they really are? And how less attractive his world seems now that she's back home?"

Cameron slammed his hand down on the table.

"We can go to Hogs and Heifers! I love that place. She'll get drunk and dance on the bar! He'll run screaming like a pussy and she'll see how useless he really is!"

I pictured the place in my head. Fear was not the first emotion that came to mind.

"Cameron, why would he be put off by his fiancée dancing on a bar?"

"It's a biker place!"

Zach looked over sharply.

"Do they have fights?"

"Sometimes."

Zach furrowed his brow with worry.

"I don't know if I like the sound of that."

I smirked at the thought of the "bikers" at Hogs and Heifers.

"Cameron, most of the people at Hogs and Heifers are frat boys and tourists. You can find the same crowd at Webster Hall."

"He doesn't know that. He'll see the bikes and stuff and watch Annie dance around and get freaked out. I'll bring my bike to add to the worry."

"Come on. You have a Vespa. Kate Moss drives one of those."

"I have a helmet, don't I?"

Dustin laughed into his bowl of pasta.

"I love you in that helmet."

"Shut up! It's badass!"

Zach inserted himself back into the conversation calmly.

"We need to step back here, friends. You're all thinking too big, too over the top. That's not how you break up a relationship. It's the small things, the annoying things, the nagging things that end up tearing it apart. We don't want to do anything drastic. We want to plant seeds. After all, a relationship is two people on a seesaw, constantly adjusting their balance, trying not to hit the ground. We need to disrupt their rhythm, make it hard for them to shift to keep up."

This sounded awfully wise for a man who thinks a three-day weekend is a long-term relationship.

"How did you learn so much about relationships? During your failed threesomes?"

"No, David. I read. I watch. I just can't do. And those who can't do, teach. Right?"

We all saw the wisdom in that one. Zach continued.

"So we need to plant some doubts that they can proceed to take home and quarrel over. They'll do most of the work, not us."

I pointed out the problems.

"Annie is on the lookout for stuff like that. She's watching everything she says."

"I anticipated that problem. I feel that getting her in an altered state of mind is essential to our ends. That's why I picked this up."

He fished around in his bag while we waited uncomfortably. Dustin furrowed his brow.

"You didn't get crack, did you?"

"This is more effective than crack, my friend. Far more effective. Here we go."

Zach pulled out a small colorful jar and placed it in the middle of the table. We leaned in to take a closer look, treating the strange object like a meteorite recently fallen from the heavens. I poked at it, rotating it to read the label.

"Slim Limb?"

Cameron frowned suspiciously.

"What the hell is Slim Limb?"

Zach smiled in self-satisfaction.

"It's a cream that tightens the skin and reduces the flab on places like your upper arms. It's a miracle product."

Cameron snorted in disbelief.

"Arm cream. Instead of crack, you bring arm cream?"

"Yes."

Dustin leaned back, distancing himself from the insanity.

"Because when she takes a good look at her taut upper arms she'll suddenly realize she's wasting her life?"

"No, of course not. Look closer. Read the label."

I picked up the jar and spun it around to read the bright pink lettering.

"A circulation stimulating cream with caffeine encapsulated in Jujomes. What the hell are Jujomes?"

Zach shrugged.

"Beats me. Better not use it without permission though. It's trademarked."

"I see that. What is this supposed to mean?"

"It's like a nicotine patch for fat. It uses large doses of caffeine sent directly into the bloodstream to somehow tighten your arms. I don't know why it works, but believe me, it does."

Dustin couldn't let that one go by.

"So you've used it? For your flabby arms?"

Zach lifted his arms into the air, staring at his forearms woefully.

"They just seem to be going with age. Though they look nice now, right? I'd been using the cream for two days before I stopped."

I had to admit, his upper arms did looked tight and shapely. Cameron took the jar from me.

"Then why did you stop?"

Zach lowered his arms.

"The caffeine drove me crazy. It's like drinking ten cups of coffee or guzzling Red Bull after Red Bull without end. It drives you up the wall. I would sit in my bedroom vibrating. I was a mess. Jumpy, irritable, punchy even. Trust me. If we put this cream on Annie's arms, she'll be unable to keep her inner smart-ass down. This is PMS times fifty. Smell it."

Cameron tentatively lifted the lid. We all recoiled in unison. Cameron blinked his tearing eyes as he moved to replace the top and contain the olfactory damage.

"That is nasty! How are you going to get her to put it on? She doesn't have flabby arms and the stuff stinks. Why would she ever use it?"

Zach leaned back in his chair, shaking his head fondly.

"Ah, Cameron. You truly don't understand women, do you? She'll try it. She may not admit it, but if we mention it and then leave it in the bathroom, she'll try it."

I took the jar from Cameron and handed it back to Zach, eager to have him put away the dangerous contaminant.

"Okay, so she lathers up in crazy cream. Then what?"

He stashed the jar away, thankfully, and then leaned in to lay out his plan. It was simplistic, which most great plans tend to be, and I wasn't sure it would work. Still, what else did we have? If we didn't move soon, we'd be down a friend. And that just wasn't acceptable to any of us.

After deciding to spring the trap at a little gathering in Cameron's apartment the next Sunday, we split up. On the way out, I sidled up to Dustin to see how his little "talk" with Donkey Girl went. His face told me the entire story.

"It didn't go over well, dude. She's convinced now that I'm hiding something. She thinks I'm being secretive on purpose because there's some big bombshell in my past I'm afraid to tell her about. It's all fucked up. I just can't win."

Maybe I should lend Donkey Girl the arm cream to use on her guy. When she saw that the hyped-up, uncontrollable Dustin was pretty much the same as the everyday, normal Dustin, maybe then she'd understand. Or maybe she'd be convinced he was a CIA operative who'd undergone extensive Slim Limb training and could now withstand up to three coats of the poison. It's amazing what a convoluted mess people will make of a perfectly straightforward situation. I'm sure there's an ironic message there, but I let it pass me by.

* * *

Zach decided to walk with me to my apartment, taking in the sweet early-summer air. We strolled up to Houston Street and headed along the busy thoroughfare, past the shops and restaurants still bustling in the early evening. Zach walked along easily, his arms swinging gracefully at his side. I matched him in stride, if not in ease.

"So, how are the sheets?"

He shot me a dark look.

"Ruined. I bought new ones the other day. Who knew such a tiny thing could emit such copious amounts of Hungarian food?"

"Sorry again about that."

"How is your friend Janey?"

"We're going out this weekend."

"That's good to hear. She's an interesting girl. The kind of deep family trauma that keeps things interesting for years to come."

"What did she tell you? "

"More than she meant to, I think. We know our own. I have daddy issues and so does she. Don't worry. That doesn't really mean anything. I turned out all right, after all."

That didn't comfort me as much as he thought it should have. We passed by a park, the kids still shooting hoops in the fading light.

"I'll have to ask her about it."

"Don't do that. Oh no. She'll bring it up."

"Okay."

We walked on in silence for a moment, coming up on the Sunshine Cinema, which had replaced the Angelika as my independent movie mecca. A small line blocked the sidewalk, forcing us to wade through the intelligentsia on their way to seeing the next big subtitled Belgian cartoon. Zach brushed off his shoulders once we pulled free.

"I hate crowds. So much dirt passed from one body to the next."

"It is a nightmare."

"Apropos of nothing, how is the writing going? Heard back from anyone yet?"

"Just mounds of rejection letters. Still waiting for the big break."

"What about the next project? Enjoying the creative process? I've always admired you for that. Being able to lose yourself in the writing like you do. I wish I could sink into something like that."

I hadn't actually written anything for months, but he didn't need to know that.

"It's going okay."

"What's it about?"

"I'd rather not talk about it while I'm still in the middle, you know?"

"I understand. Can I ask you a question, though?"

"What?"

"What's it like to have a passion like that? I mean you dropped everything to follow it. It must consume you. What does it feel like? I have nothing like that need for one thing.

Nothing big like that at all, really. But you, you have that big overwhelming purpose to your life. What does that feel like?"

I opened my mouth to answer, before I realized that I had no answer. What did it feel like? I know I had a passion. You don't drop your well-paying job to be a wedding DJ for anything less. How could I describe it? The days of sitting in front of the computer, not typing, not wanting to type. Just rereading what I've already written. I love to read something I've written, but I hate to write it. So I have to force myself to put something down. I have to force myself to feed my passion. That's part of the reason I quit my job. I procrastinated writing so much that I couldn't get it done if I had anything else to distract me. My DJ job didn't require as much of my mental energy, giving me more headspace to focus on making myself write. How could I explain that? It didn't resemble what he expected. How could I explain that the day to day wasn't all that special? That the whole point of what I was doing, the whole payoff, came at the end, when the book shot out into the world to be read. That was my passion. To be read. And one day, I'll get a letter from an agent that tells me my passion is about to be fulfilled. And all of this blank day after day would be worth it. Everything would be worthwhile, then. All the emotional valleys and long, lonely days would be left in my wake like ballast tossed off a ship that could no longer be held back. Everything would be burned away in the blinding light of the big happy.

"It feels good. I feel good."

Zach accepted this without question.

"It sounds good. I can't hope to reach what you reach."

"Your life seems pretty full."

"I just want to experience things. Sunsets over the Seine, a glass of wine in Mexico City, a brief romantic encounter on the beaches of San Tropez. Nothing oversized. No one will remember me when I'm gone. Just nice stories to tell you guys when I roll into town."

"That doesn't sound too bad."

"It's not. I'm pretty happy."

"Me, too."

We walked on, each thinking about our different paths to happy. We quietly passed the people of New York, out on the sidewalks, headed toward a good time wherever they could find one. It seems so cut and dried when they set out, but inevitably they end up bouncing from place to place, trying to find the right spot to spend the evening. It was never as easy at it looked.

* * *

A letter awaited me when I reached my apartment. From the return address on the envelope I realized it came from one of the two agents still left on my hope sheet. Tearing it open, I quickly scanned the brief paragraph. By the end, I could sing along. We wish you success. La la la. I bet you do. I tossed the letter onto the counter, falling back onto my bed. The ceiling above me seemed to rush toward me, boxing me in. I cast my eyes helplessly about my home, my sanctuary, my enemy, the rough sounds of the street below my window shrinking me until I could feel myself disappearing. The blank computer screen offered no relief. The poisonous air and the menacing walls that pop out nails and drop bookshelves mockingly surrounded me, shrinking me faster, forcing me into a tiny ball of nothing. Soon the apartment would give up on the warnings and simply drop the ceiling on my head, smashing the cockroach with one swift blow. And then I'd be gone like I never was. That was the purpose of rooms like these, wasn't it? To make you disappear. To bury you alive. It took all my strength to keep the place at bay. But I was weakening.

Chapter Twelve

The Mystery of the Fizzing Cup

My first date with Janey. We'd mauled each other in a closet, kissed furtively on a stairwell landing, she'd even ripped my earring out of my head, but we'd never actually had coffee. Why did this feel like such a bigger step? I thought about planning some elaborate first date, involving a five-star restaurant and the Cirque du Soleil, but somehow I didn't think watching French clowns cry on the inside would be the best way to figure each other out. We knew too much about each other for the elaborate first date. When you've already drooled on each other, you've moved beyond the big production. What is a crazy, overplanned first date anyway but smoke and mirrors? You're trying to convince some girl who doesn't know you from Fabio that you actually eat at these places and attend these cultural events. You love the symphony and can't wait to catch the next Cuban film about Che Guevara in kindergarten, highlighting how eating paste set him on the path to political revolution. Later, weeks later, you'll finally feel comfortable enough to drop the bomb that you TiVo *Fear Factor* and it depresses you when the girl at the Chinese takeout place doesn't recognize you by the way you say "Hi" on the phone.

But with Janey, it all seemed unnecessary. I didn't want to wow her. I wanted something much simpler. So coffee seemed like a good idea. Of course, I don't drink coffee, but that shouldn't get in the way of a great cultural preordained meeting place. I'd have a Snapple or something. Of course, I don't drink Snapple. Black cherry soda? I could do that. Sure, that would make me the biggest dork on the island, but I have to answer to my taste buds. I decided to pour it in a coffee cup, just to stave off the comments.

I sat at a small table in Sunburst, a small coffee shop a few blocks from my apartment. My covered cherry soda–filled coffee cup sat in front of me as I awaited Janey's arrival. I hate waiting for dates. I always feel like everyone else is staring at me, pitying my obvious loneliness. I make a point to check my watch frequently, sighing hugely at my ridiculously late companion, but not fatalistically, so as to avoid communicating any fear my companion might not show. It's all very complicated, very *Alias*. Suffice it to say, everyone around cannot fail but come to the conclusion that I'm making up a friend in order to not appear pathetic. Works every time.

I was in the process of staring at my watch for the fourth time, mid-sigh, when she appeared in the doorway. I sat up quickly, swallowing my breath, far too quickly, it turned out, putting me in the awkward position of suddenly needing to belch. I forced the burp down as I stood, wincing as the air bubble put a kink in my chest. Janey noticed me and quickly walked up.

"Hey. What's wrong with you? You look like you need to let one go."

I forced a laugh, barely keeping my air bubble inside.

"I'm fine. How are you? You look great."

She smiled with restraint, trying not to appear too pleased. I didn't lie. In her jeans and form-fitting T-shirt (which instructed me that love is like gravity, everybody falls), her hair long and full down her back and around her face, she did look extremely attractive. Her face held less of the makeup overload, and nothing could mar her pleasant smile and bright eyes. It struck me that this was one of the few smiles she'd shown me that didn't hold a hint of mockery within, aimed at either me or herself or both.

"Thanks, kiddo. I'll just grab a coffee. Be right back."

She sauntered up to the counter behind me, ordering with practiced ease. I took a sip of my clandestine cherry soda. It tasted all the better for being my secret. After a few moments, I could feel her approach, picking up her scent way before I could hear her footsteps. She eased around me and into the seat across from me.

"I need this, let me tell you. I'm dying."

She took a sip, eyes rolling in caffeine-induced ecstasy. I took a swallow of my faux coffee, squeezing my face into a similar orgasmic expression.

"I hear you. It hits the spot."

Eyes narrowing, she leaned over, bringing her ear up to my covered coffee cup.

"Why is your coffee fizzing?"

"Um. It's a new brew. The beans are still settling."

"Why did you invite me to a coffee shop if you don't drink coffee? And hide it from me, no less."

The short-lived open smile curled into a hint of the dreaded mockery. I shrugged, embarrassed.

"I like coffee shops."

"That's cool. So drink the soda from the can. There's nothing to be ashamed of."

"Okay."

I pulled the black cherry bottle out from under my chair. She snorted.

"Okay, never mind. There is something to be ashamed of."

"Fine. I'm putting it away."

"Sorry. I'm sure it's very sweet, like liquid candy."

"It is."

I sipped my soda sullenly. She dropped her smile completely.

"Really, I'm sorry. I don't want to make fun of you. Much. I bet it is tasty."

"You want to try some?"

"No thanks. I already had some sasparilla back at the General Store. But Mama says I can have some ginger beer with supper if I do all my chores."

"Don't make me hit you with the bottle."

The smile had reappeared in all its original glory.

"Yes sir. This is a nice place."

"I like it."

"Do you write here often, like on a laptop or something?"

She must have seen the shadow pass over my face, because she suddenly looked uncertain, wondering if she had said something wrong. I pushed the cloud away.

"Not really. I need my routine."

"Okay."

Sensing my unwillingness to continue on that topic, Janey

looked down at her coffee and we sipped in silence. Some of her lip gloss was transferred to the coffee cup, leaving her mouth dull and human-colored. I welcomed the change. She looked around again.

"So, where are we going next?"

Next? We had to go somewhere next? But this is a coffee shop! We talk here! We get to know each other better! I wasn't supposed to impress her! Fuck!

"Um. Well, actually . . ."

"Is this one of those drink dates, where you grab a drink together so you don't get trapped by a meal? Because I can talk a lot, so I could just as easily trap you here as at a nice restaurant."

"No, I just wanted to find a nice place to talk. Keep it simple, you know?"

"You're not being cheap, are you?"

"No. Of course not. I just thought this would be nice. Just us, talking."

She smiled again. Every time she did, her face grew warmer. The bubble in my chest remained, though I began to wonder if the air hadn't seeped out a while ago.

"It is nice. Maybe we can grab some food or something, graduate to actual sustenance."

I felt chastised, even though her tone stayed light.

"Sure. Why not."

We lapsed into silence again. Why was I suddenly so nervous? Somehow the stakes had risen behind my back. Some time between the cola joke and the restaurant plea she'd gained importance. I suddenly wished I had tickets to Cirque du Soleil. I felt the need to apologize.

"I should have planned this better, Janey. I'm sorry. I just didn't want to go overboard and book an evening of Broadway shows and everything. I want to get to know you."

She took a long sip of coffee, staring at me over the lip of the cup, the steam hiding her expression in a cloud of fog.

"Then I'm glad we're not stuck in the second mezzanine watching *The Lion King*."

"Good. Because that show makes me cry, and I'm not ready for you to see that side of me."

She laughed again. Why wasn't she my type? Because she looked a little strange and kept me on my toes? Because she seemed a little on edge all the time?

"Why are you staring at me? Are you thinking about how much you could get if you sold my hair?"

"No. Just thinking about the next thing I want to say."

"Thinking about it, huh? It better be good then."

"Oh, it is good."

"The kind of insight that changes the way a gal looks at the world. That's what I'm expecting, you know."

"I won't disappoint. This kind of wisdom and incisive out of the box thinking has a tendency to blow the unprepared mind. So be warned."

Her eyes danced.

"I'm warned. Take me higher."

"Okay. Here goes."

And just then, to my eternal chagrin and unending mortification, the air in my chest raced up and flew out of my mouth in the world's tiniest, highest pitched burp. Janey froze, eyes wide with shock. My hand shot up to cover my mouth, my face the color of my cherry soda.

"That's not what I meant to say!"

Laughter burst out of her mouth, hard and real. She clutched her stomach as she bent over double.

"Oh my God, that was fucking amazing! Priceless! Yes, I'll marry you!"

I started to laugh as the tension and expectations drifted way. After all, once you've burped around a girl, you've pretty much lost your grip on the mystery. After our laughter died down, we started in on real conversation, the awkwardness dissipated with my tainted air. I finally began to get to know the woman I kept hooking up with.

She was funny, she was smart, she was self-deprecating. She tossed off pointed barbs, true, but she could take a joke, too. We definitely made each other laugh. She grew up in Manhattan, going to private schools and learning to fight for survival among the Paris Hiltons of the world. Including the actual Paris Hilton, incidentally. I had to laugh.

"Any underground tapes of you floating around?"

"Not that I know of, though God knows I've seen my share of crazy shit. I'm good at hiding from the camera, though."

"So you're still daddy's little girl, huh?"

She forced a laugh, though I could tell I'd hit something I shouldn't have. I moved quick to apologize.

"Look, I don't mean to get into stuff I shouldn't . . ."

She put on the mocking smile again.

"We're getting to know each other, right? I'm not ashamed. My parents split when I was, like, thirteen I think. God, I hated my mother for it. I just couldn't forgive her. I don't think we spoke for a year, except to ask for the salt. My dad moved across the street on West End Avenue, so I spent most of my time over there. He's an interesting guy, my dad. Lawyer, real good at his job. I used to love seeing him work, watching him from the balcony. He'd always smile at me from the floor when I caught his eye. He told me he liked me there because I distracted the opposition with my pretty face. And he liked to take me to his client meetings, showing me off I guess. He always told me how pretty I was. Every day, you look so pretty! When I graduated from Brown, he came up to me, gave me a hug and whispered how pretty I looked in my cap and gown. Maybe he thought I was playing dress-up. That's what he made me feel like. I always felt like a pretty, empty doll around him. Though, the last time I saw him, he didn't say I looked pretty, so maybe he's changed his mind."

She swished the remains of her coffee idly. I wondered if her dad had anything to do with the deep tan and the lip gloss.

"When did you last see him?"

"That night I met up with you at that strange roller-skating thing your friend had going. He'd just found out that I'd started working for Rialto rather than let him support me while I do my internship. He didn't really understand why I was doing what I was doing. Neither did Mom, but she never tried to talk me out of it. She's embarrassed by me, they both are, but she just stays out of the way. I think she kind of understands what I'm doing. On some level, anyway."

"What are you doing?"

"I'm doing my thing. Why are you DJ-ing?"

"It's my day job while I write. I'm trying to be happy."

She smirked, the mockery in her smile directed inward.

"Me too. I graduated with an economics degree, all ready to hop into law school. I interned at Dad's firm, learning all about the trade. I wanted to be on that courtroom floor, holding everyone's attention, making brilliant points, winning the case. It was all I wanted."

"What changed your mind?"

"I sucked at it. No, really, I did. I got into NYU, took the first semester and practically failed every class. It bored me to tears. I couldn't wrap my mind around any of it. I just couldn't think that way. So cold, you know? I wanted to, but I couldn't. I realized by Christmas what a horrible lawyer I would be."

"I doubt you'd be that bad."

"I wouldn't be great. And why do it if you can't be great at it? My dad's great. I don't want to be a half-assed version of him. So I dropped out. And everybody freaked and blah blah blah. All those old standbys got tossed around . . . I'll disown you! You're throwing your life away! No daughter of mine would ever do this! It sounds extreme, but that's my family. I discovered that my mom still told her friends I was in law school and doing great. I embarrassed her. My dad couldn't understand it. He told me that with my looks, I'd dazzle any jury. I was crazy to walk away from that."

"Wow. He sounds like a real self-confidence builder."

"Yeah, well, there isn't anything I can accomplish that he can't belittle by sticking a bow in my hair. I had to get away from that, but I didn't have any idea what I wanted to do. A friend of mine introduced me to Malena and I ended up moving in with her. She hooked me up with the waitressing job. It's no big deal, I'll do this while I figure stuff out, if I really want to work in TV or do something else entirely. My parents were so ashamed when I told them. They spent the whole meal blaming each other. It was kind of fun to watch, actually."

"It's just a short-term gig. It's not the end of the world."

"It's funny, I didn't really feel ashamed of it until I met you at that bar mitzvah. Somehow, I felt the need to impress you. I regressed ten years, riding my daddy's coattails. I knocked my head against the wall for five whole minutes after that conversation, believe me."

"Why? I was just some DJ."

"I don't know why. I just . . . did."

We stared at each other a moment, hands frozen around our cups. We might have stayed like that for hours if someone hadn't dripped burning hot coffee in her lap, squealing in pain. We both looked away, startled, shifting nervously. I shrugged in her general direction.

"It was probably the trophy guy emblazoned in my forehead. Chicks really dig that."

She chuckled softly.

"It probably was. What about you? Parents still together?"

"Yep. Thirty-four years, I think."

"Do they live around here?"

"They're moving actually. Selling the family home. I'm heading out to Westchester tomorrow to pack up my stuff, which will be sad."

"Sounds it."

"I just hope they don't have sex while I'm there. They're always having sex. It's not right. There comes an age when you really should hang up the old whip and handcuffs, that's what I say. But they won't listen."

"Yeah, it sounds awful."

She looked down at her hands awkwardly. I nodded.

"Yeah."

"How are they with your DJ job?"

"Well, I have the writer thing going for me, so that makes it okay."

"Oh."

Obviously time to get off parents. She wasn't even looking at me anymore.

"Hungry?"

* * *

Dinner went great. We talked, we laughed, we mocked, we ate, we mocked some more, and we eavesdropped on other conversations. One couple by the wall really brought the drama out on the town with them. The guy was married and the woman was his mistress. She used the word "love" at least eighty times. He used the words "keep it down" just as often. We gave it two more years at least. Another couple didn't say a thing. We kept an ear out for any conversation at all, but they ate in simple silence, comfortable and secure. They didn't even seem all that old, but maybe a comfortable silence can strike at any age. Unless you're me. I haven't let a comfortable silence occur since my days in the womb. And even then I used to whistle. Janey and I agreed that we could never live like that. We'd have to grab our partner by the lapels and scream at them to say something! Anything! For the love of God, speak! But in a loving way, of course.

After dessert, I hit the curb and tried to flag a cab for Janey. She stepped up beside me, staring up at me standing there with an outstretched arm.

"Thanks for dinner. Eventually."

"You're very welcome. Now."

She looked up the street into the traffic, trying to spy a cab. When she turned back toward me, my lips were there, pressing into hers. We kissed, one long, lovely kiss, my arm still waving in the air like a spastic kid in class begging to be called on. Eventually, we pulled apart. We didn't say a word, unconsciously emulating the silent couple we so vehemently denied ever becoming, lost in each other until a loud blaring horn shook us back to life. Looking around in confusion, we spied a cab idling, waiting right beside us. Calming my nerves, I leaned in for one more kiss.

"Bye."

She opened the door, stealing a peck from my lips, quick and sure.

"Bye."

She dropped down into the cab and it sped off. I watched her go, full of mixed feelings. How would this new development affect the search for happy? It could be hard to tell the distractions from the clues. I turned around to stroll home, wishing I could strain out the uneasiness and just revel in the joy. I guessed for now I'd have to learn to live with both.

Chapter Thirteen

A Jarring Discovery

David's got a girlfriend! David's got a girlfriend!"

My brother Alex's singsongy words would have really stung if he had managed a date in the last four years. Instead, the sight of my football player–sized brother dancing around like Baryshnikov and singing in falsetto only served to make me chuckle. Until my dad walked in the living room.

"Who has a girlfriend?"

"David! A new flame!"

My mom hurried in from down the hall where she'd been packing up knickknacks.

"A girlfriend! How serious is it? Do you love her?"

I tried to kick Alex, but he swung his arm around and lifted me easily above his head.

"Sure he loves her! And baby makes three!"

Dad coughed heavily.

"The girl's pregnant! Sweet Jesus, David!"

My voice vibrated from the force of Alex's bench press of my body into the air.

"She's not pregnant. It's nothing. We just started. Put me down, dork!"

Alex dropped me easily to the floor, laying me on the varnished wood with a soft twist of the wrist. He may be five years younger than me, but between his large frame and huge, ill-advised muttonchops, people often thought he was older. Not that anyone ever guesses we're related. People assume he's holding me for ransom and I'm too scared to ask for help.

Mom rushed up to me.

"What's her name? Where's she from? What does she do? Are her parents still together? Does she like seafood? How old is she? Does she like to sing? Does she live in the city? How many boyfriends did she have before you? Has she been tested?"

My dad added his own inane questions.

"What does her dad do? Does she have sisters for Alex? Is she foreign? Was she ever an acrobat? Does she have money? How about a kid? Two kids? Is she older than you? Not over ten years, right? Does she like kids?"

And almost in unison.

"When do we get to meet her?"

I grabbed Alex's ear.

"This was for your ears only. Now the crazy people have the bit in their mouths."

Alex shrugged, pulling his head away from my tightening fingers.

"I need to get them off my back. They keep asking me about when I'm getting married and having grandkids."

Dad smacked his back.

"Of course. You're the dependable one. David here is the

flake. But now . . . maybe we'll finally get some little babies around here!"

Alex smiled with satisfaction. Mom gave him a big hug.

"Don't you worry, dear. I'm sure someday you'll meet someone great. There's no rush."

I stared at her incredulously.

"What do you mean, no rush? I'm not married with kids, you know!"

Dad punched me in the shoulder lightly.

"Not yet."

Alex sighed happily.

"This is what it must feel like to be you. Worry-free."

My parents never put much faith in my ability to settle down, a conclusion I nurtured diligently since the day I went out on my first date. Alex, on the other hand, made the mistake of proving to be dependable and steady, always ready to fix things and take out the garbage. The end result being whenever the two of us come home, he always has a million jobs waiting while I'm barely trusted to wash off the lettuce. The perfect setup, if ever I saw one. It's not his fault, he just caught on too late. So he's always been expected to deliver the grandkids, while I've always labored under lower expectations, like not choking to death on my own vomit. But now Alex was having his revenge. He wasn't done.

"Hey David, did you see the new portrait Mom just finished?"

Mom lit up, pulling me into the dining room and pointing to the wall. My spirits sank into my shoes.

"I put it side by side with yours, my two boys together!"

Fantastic. I didn't think my immortalization could get any worse, but I was wrong. My portrait hung from the wall, resplendent in its cheesy, *Dance Fever* absurdity, even more horrifying than I remembered it. But to make things infinitely worse, she'd hung a new portrait beside it. Slightly bigger than mine, it showcased a smiling Alex astride a zooming Jet Ski, almost bursting out of the frame as spray surrounded his wide, bare shoulders. He sported a devil-may-care smile, his curly hair rakishly askew, shining under the barrage of water kicked up from his manly motorcycle of the sea. Everything about this portrait screamed manly heart-throb. Alex beamed.

"It looks great, Mom."

I smiled weakly.

"It does. It looks just like him."

She smiled, putting an arm around each of her boys.

"This way I can enjoy my two sons every day. Until I have to send your portrait to the gallery, that is. I'm sorry, Alex. David's is the only one they have room for this time and it is the one they've seen."

"That's fine, Mom. I can't wait to see it up for everyone to enjoy."

Out of the corner of my eye I caught sight of my dad, his face red from keeping in the laughter. I scowled at him, and he had to leave the room. Alex patted my shoulder, pleased with himself. Ah well. I'm the one with the girlfriend, so who gets the last laugh, really?

* * *

Hours later, I sat on the floor of my old room, staring at the bottom of my closet. My mom's voice drifted in from down the hall.

"Don't forget to box everything, David. You know how your father is. If you don't box it, he'll donate it."

Ain't that the truth. I remember once back when I was a kid I really wanted to read *The Princess Bride* one more time, so I scanned my shelves for my copy. I couldn't find it, much to my chagrin, so I decided to head down to the library to take it out. I grabbed it off the shelf of the young adult section and flipped through it to make sure all the pages remained. And there I found my name, on the first page, eked out in my horrific handwriting. My dad had donated my favorite book without telling me. Suddenly suspicious, I began to leaf through the other books around me. Sure enough, first page after first page carried my moniker in scraggly ink. My childhood tomes made up more than half the library's young adult collection. They should name the entire section after me. After all, I built it. When I confronted my dad about it, he just shrugged and told me to stop leaving my books on my floor. As if I had any books left. If I'd fallen asleep on the floor I probably would have woken up in a thrift shop downtown, a price tag for four dollars tied around my neck.

Thankfully, much of my childhood stuff remained, hidden in the back of my closet. It's always strange to go through your old things. Your triumphs never seem as bombastic when you revisit them fifteen years later. I dredged up a script for a play I'd been in when I was ten, an experience I recalled as being nothing less than Shakespearean. I started to read. Two pages in, after the twentieth bad pun, I tossed it aside. Complete crap, of course. But it felt so important at the time.

I scrounged through old pictures, baseball cards of all the least important players from the eighties, some comic books, a leaf project my mom did for me in seventh grade. Got an A, too. All my report cards. My hands closed around a black-and-white notebook. There it was. My first composition book. The one that, along with my first-grade ditto, really put me on the road to writing. I still remembered my eighth-grade English teacher, Mr. Paulson, telling me how special I was. How I was going to be a great writer some day. I cracked the book, ready to be dazzled.

Ten minutes and eight compositions later, my stomach started to hurt. This kid was crap! Awful! The worst writer I'd ever read! A poem about chickens? An essay on how *Star Wars* rocks? A short story directly ripped off from *The Goonies*? What the hell was going on? How could my teacher have ever thought I would amount to anything after reading this? But there lay his comments in red ink at the end of each atrocity, telling me how wonderful it was and how I did it again. Almost made him throw up in his mouth again, probably. Was this a sick joke he liked to play on his students? Tell them they're good at something they suck at and then wait for the reunion to come around so he can see if they fell for it? Hah! You became a writer! My God, I was only kidding! You wouldn't have known a metaphor if it crawled up your ass and died! And even that metaphor is better than anything you'd come up with! You made my day, sucker!

I threw the notebook on the ground. It meant nothing. I've learned so much since then. Of course I'm better now. I was twelve years old. Who writes well at twelve? Besides Doogie Howser, I mean? But I couldn't deny it shook me. This was the basis of my confidence. Mr. Paulson telling me I could be something special propelled me like nothing else could. If he was wrong . . . but he wasn't. And who cares, anyway? He was just some stupid teacher from a long time ago. How important could his opinion really be? Not important at all! So why did I want to vomit?

Mr. Paulson wasn't why I became a writer. Neither was Mrs. Hickenbothem. Right? I became a writer because I had to. It's my passion. Right? It's been my passion for as long as I can remember. Right? I thought of that last agent's letter, floating out in the federal post office system. This would be my last chance. If the agent wanted me, then I had made the right choice. If not . . . If not, what?

Alex knocked on the door, disturbing my unsettling chain of thought.

"Hey, David. How's it looking?"

I climbed up onto my bed, as far from that notebook as I could get.

"Good. Just skipping down memory lane."

"Yeah, me too."

He sat down on the floor, closing the door. He looked worried.

"What's up, dude? Something wrong?"

"It's Dad."

I sat up, all other thoughts banished.

"Is he okay? Is he sick?"

"Nothing like that. I overheard them talking. Dad's being forced to retire. That's why they have to sell this house."

A shock ran through me. I'd never expected this.

"What? But he's only fifty-seven. He's worked there for what? His whole life?"

"I know. From what I could hear, they don't want to tell us yet. They're waiting until after the move. What are we going to do?"

"What do you mean?"

"They're going to be living on a pension."

"Okay."

"Where's the money going to come from?"

"The pension."

"You know what I mean."

A year ago, I would have laughed this off. Alex worked for next to nothing in a computer software start-up, trying to help get a new business off the ground, so he never had any money. He'd borrowed a bunch of money from our parents in order to survive. I, on the other hand, always did fine. Even now, I didn't touch a dime, mostly out of pride. But the safety net was always there. A pension . . . that would barely support the two of them. So the safety net disappeared. They would insist on helping if they knew we needed it, of course, but we'd never let them know.

"Man. This is not good."

"I know. I don't think Mom's doing so great with it, either."

"Well, we can't do anything until they tell us. At least he gets a pension. I think he has some stocks. He'll be okay."

"Dad loves to work. He gets to travel all over the world. What's he gonna do now?"

My dad's life is traveling. There's nothing he loves more than discovering new countries and revisiting favorite cities around the globe. Working for an international firm sent him everywhere he wanted plus some. What would he do now? No wonder he was so keen on grandkids.

"I don't know."

"Maybe we should tell them we know."

"No, we can't do that. It's up to them to tell us."

"Everything is changing. We're going to have nothing left to stand on."

It sure felt like it. When you can be forced out of your job at fifty-seven, years before you're ready, what can you rely on? His job always made him so happy. What now? Alex and I sat staring out into space, wondering what in life could be counted on. Nothing remained constant, nothing at all.

Chapter Fourteen

Killing Grandma

Maybe I could have given the Monroe wedding out by the lake a little more attention. Sure, it was the first job I worked with Rialto since my Janey date, which meant Janey herself flitted from table to table, taking dinner orders while smiling at me. And sure, the Argentinean was also present, avoiding my gaze as she stayed as far away from the DJ table as humanly possible. But that was no excuse. The fact was, by the end of the evening I had almost killed the bride's grandmother, and that is just a major party foul no matter how you look at it.

Rialto really outdid himself this time with the reception. They hired him to do the full-on job, including the tent beside the beautiful lake and the wedding arch down by the water. A small tent between the two held a piano raised five feet off the ground, the ivories nicely tickled by some fifteen-year-old kid in an ill-fitting white tux. The bride and groom themselves were adorable. Late twenties, blond hair and blue eyes, the two of them did the Aryan Nations proud that day. But even their perfection and unfeigned joy didn't put them in line for a hit on Grandma. Others were to blame for that.

As I popped in an old standard for the middle-aged and above, a sultry voice whispered in my ear.

"Tell me a secret."

I turned to look into Janey's big brown eyes.

"I can't find my Sinatra CD. I'm gonna play the Rod Stewart CD instead and see if anyone notices."

"Come on. Just one secret."

"Here? Is this really the place?"

"I'll tell you one."

"Tell me first."

She glanced out at the crowd quickly before leaning into my ear.

"Okay. I once threw up while giving a blow job."

I recoiled. I thought these would be silly secrets.

"My God! Why did you tell me that! That's disgusting!"

Her head shook as she held in the laughter.

"It's a secret, isn't it?"

"And it should remain a secret! Jesus!"

"You should see your face."

"Is this your idea of a sick joke?"

"Well, it happened. I was so embarrassed."

"That's not something you tell a guy you just started going out with."

"I wasn't going to, but it just flew out. Sorry. Pretend I never said it."

"Were you sick at least?"

"The idiot insisted I do the deed while in the cabin of a boat, even though I told him I'd get seasick."

"When was this, last week?"

She hit my shoulder.

"No. Years ago. Now tell me a secret."

"I don't want to. I'm frightened."

"Come on, quick, before Rod finishes up."

I pondered. It was kind of early to be telling secrets. I was still getting to know the girl. I'd have to play it smart.

"I'm gonna give you a level-one secret."

She pulled back, her face scrunching up in confusion.

"What the hell is that? Who says that?"

"It's too soon for a level-two secret or above. You start at level one."

"Is that the way you think? Is every stage of the relationship mapped out by level?"

Of course.

"No. Do you want my level-one secret or not?"

"What could it be? You're white?"

"If you don't want it . . ."

"Fine. Tell me your amazing level-one secret."

"I'm partially color-blind."

"You can't see colors?"

"No, I can see most colors. Just certain shades of purple look like red to me."

"So that's it? You have trouble seeing purple?"

"Yep."

"Does anyone else know this about you?"

I hedged.

"Um. Well, my closest friends. My family . . . you know . . ."

She turned and called out to Rialto.

"Do you know David is partially color-blind?"

Rialto waved merrily.

"No purple, right?"

She turned back to me, disgusted.

"Your level-one secrets suck."

She walked off, dismissing me with a wave of her hand. I was a little irritated by her disdain. Did she expect me to just reveal my whole self in one go? At a wedding in a tent? I had to do the slow reveal. The last time I fell in love, I moved way too quickly. When we broke up, I realized that I never really knew her at all. So this time, I was determined to take my time. I would be king of the slow reveal. It was the only way not to make the same mistake twice.

Janey ignored me for the next two hours. Apparently, she meant it when she gave me her secrets ultimatum. I found myself unsettled by this, losing track of my music and mispronouncing the couple's name, which was Bart. (Trust me, I found a way.) I even led the conga line around the table she was clearing up four times before the guy behind me got pissed off and broke off to lead his people back toward the floor. But she didn't break.

They cut the cake, doing the same thing all couples do, pretending to smear the cake all over each other, but in the end not even leaving a dab of icing on the lips. I guess the rented tux and lavish wedding gown were far too expensive for such dangerous games. I took a moment to approach the Argentinean, determined to clear the air between us at least.

"Hey, Malena."

"Hello, son of a bitch."

I could feel the air clearing already.

"I'm really sorry."

"I can tell that by the way you laugh and smile with Janey. The sorry is all over your face."

"Look, we're going to run into each other since I'm dating your roommate, and I never meant to hurt you, I swear. Can't we put it behind us?"

The Argentinean cocked her head in thought, trying to decide whether to put it to rest or rip my eyeballs out with her long fake fingernails. Eventually, she nodded.

"All right. We will put the water under the bridge. But if you are an asshole with her as well, I will destroy you and everything you love. I will dance on your genitals like it is carnival. *Comprende*?"

Horribly frightened by this pretty young girl's promise of total destruction, I quickly nodded. She smiled, returning to the nice, quiet girl I kinda knew.

"Good. Then we are friends again."

"Good. I'm glad. Really. Can I ask you a question?"

"Okay."

"Why is Janey acting weird? She won't even walk toward me."

She shook her head sadly.

"You men and your skidding of the feet. What is this level-one secret? That is shit. Where is the passion in that? The romance?"

"But it's too soon for a level-two secret. We need to do the slow reveal!"

"Take too long and you will be revealing yourself to the door she shuts in your face."

She walked away, already done with me. I scanned the tent for Janey, but she seemed to have disappeared. My song was almost over, so I ran back to the DJ table. The older folks seemed ready to dance again, so I threw on Al Green's "Let's Stay Together." A great tune to dance to, one of my all-time favorites. Unfortunately, the only version I owned lay deep inside the *Pulp Fiction* soundtrack, which has the irritating habit of alternating songs with swear-laden quotes from the film. I made sure to program the CD player to stop after the song played, just to keep things PG. The sultry, sexy strains of an R&B classic poured out onto the floor and the dancing began anew. I ran out of the tent to try to find Janey.

After a few moments, I spied her over by the generator, the long extension cord leading me to her from where I'd plugged in my equipment. She gave me a haughty look as I approached.

"I hope you've got something good."

"Look, I'm sorry about the level-one secret thing, but I don't understand why it's a big deal. We'll probably be on level ten by next Wednesday."

Suddenly uncertain, she twirled a piece of grass in her hand, pulling at the end.

"That's not the point."

"Then what is the point?"

"It's like you put these boundaries on us before we even have a chance. Can't we just let things happen? No levels or stuff like that."

"I just think it's a little early for deep, dark secrets, that's all."

"Maybe it is, but you don't have to lay it out there like that. You're making me feel like if I wanted to tell you something, a real secret, you'd stick your fingers in your ears and whistle."

I reached out and put a hand on her arm.

"I didn't mean that. Look, no more levels. I'll just play it by ear."

As much as I could. I still believed wholeheartedly in the slow reveal. I could tell, however, she wouldn't understand the concept. She looked up at me with those brown doe's eyes, wanting to be reassured. I wanted to reassure. So I leaned in and kissed her.

She kissed back, hard, grabbing my head and pulling it toward her. We fell backward under the force, tripping over something on our way down to the grass. Noticing a shift in the air, I raised my head. Janey peered up at me, grass hanging in her hair.

"What is it?"

"Does something sound different to you?"

"I don't hear anything."

"Neither do I. Fuck!"

I bolted upright. The music had stopped. I could see everyone on the dance floor inside the tent milling around, staring up at the empty DJ booth in confusion. What happened? A sneaking suspicion occurred to me as I picked myself off the ground, helping Janey to her feet in the process. I looked down at the grass at my feet. Sure enough, we'd kicked the extension cord out of the generator when we fell.

"Fuck! This is just perfect."

"Well, plug it in."

"I am."

I leaned over and stuck the cord back into the generator socket. Immediately the small colored lights on my table came to life and the CD player began to spin again. I breathed a sigh of relief. Janey's brow furrowed.

"Where's the music? It just sounds like shouting or something."

"What? I don't hear . . ."

My face dropped as I picked up the words drifting over from the tent. My worst fears come to life. Somehow, when I plugged my equipment back in, the CD had restarted from the beginning. And what begins the *Pulp Fiction* soundtrack, you might ask? Well listen close, and you can hear it.

"Any of you fucking pricks move and I'll execute every motherfucking last one of you!"

Honey Bunny's speech from the movie, leading off the CD with a bang. For a moment I couldn't move, but with the next profanity-laden burst, I sprang into action. I took maybe two steps on my way across twenty feet of grass, tearing through the side of the tent and leaping atop my platform, finger outstretched like Superman in a dusty tux. I hit stop right as the guitar strains of the first song began, practically driving my hand through the machine. Looking up, I came face to face with a dance floor full of people staring at me in disbelief. And in the center stood Grandma, eyes wide, apparently certain that Honey Bunny was about to shoot every last motherfucking one of them. I could hear her mutter.

"We didn't invite a Honey Bunny. I know we didn't!"

Her daughter came onto the floor and led her away. I found out later that she recovered completely, though she still thinks the groom's family invited killers, just as she'd warned they would. I smiled weakly into the mic.

"Sorry about that folks. Small technical difficulty. Let's get back to the smooth R&B, shall we?"

I pressed track nine and Al Green reappeared to make everything all right. I sat back heavily, horrified. Gradually, the people on the floor turned to each other and began to dance again, though the sense of shock never did dissipate completely. I knew my tip had left with Grandma. I felt a tap on my shoulder.

"Nice going, kiddo."

I turned to retort, but her kiss cut me off before I could form the words. My heart still hadn't returned to its normal rhythm, not since the words "level-one secret" popped out of my mouth. Out of the corner of my eye, I could see the Aryan twins dancing in the corner. Mixed signals. I only seemed to get mixed signals. Ah well. I should make like the Argentinean suggested and just let it happen. I can do that. Of course I can. Can't I?

Chapter Fifteen

The Dirty Telephone Game

Cameron lived way out in Bronxville, which meant a train ride far into suburbia for our little Sunday get-together. I met up with Zach to ride in, as we were the only two without dates. I didn't feel ready to bring Janey fully into the fold yet, not until things were a little less . . . nefarious. We didn't speak much as we rocketed along through the slightly upstate New York countryside. Zach's bag lay at his feet, its deadly passenger waiting to be unleashed onto its unsuspecting victim. I pushed the guilt down. No time for sentiment. This was a rescue mission. Apologies come after everyone's safe.

We walked over to the apartment complex from the train station, two assassins in the night. Cameron opened the door to his place, looking irritated.

"Hey guys."

I gave him a quick hug (in a manly way, of course, beating the shit out of his back with my hand), concerned.

"What's up? You don't look happy."

Cameron led us into the living room. As his apartment

lay out in the countryside, what he lost in location he more than made up for in space. Living room, dining room, kitchen, bedroom, office, the place had it all. I could get lost for days in the myriad of rooms. Walking through them sent me back in time to my younger days. His walls were covered in bagpipe paraphernalia mixed in with a few old swords and pictures of all of us in high school. His diploma hung proudly above his university graduation photo. His high school varsity letter in fencing sat next to his prom photo. The man was proud of his schooling, ain't nothin' wrong with that. We sat down on the couch as Cameron dropped heavily into his overstuffed easy chair.

"It's nothing. We had a nice quiet dinner with Mary's she-devil of a mother."

He looked like he wanted to snap that she-devil's head right off. Cameron's temper always fascinated me. He seems so laid-back and go-with-the-flow until something pisses him off, and then he totally loses it, going ballistic on everyone from the driver in front of him to his boss to the airport security guy (never a smart move—he couldn't sit down for a week). I've seen him actually get out of his car and run at the vehicle keeping him from forward motion, ready to tear apart the Volvo in righteous anger. I can only guess at what the driver must have been thinking, watching this preppy Korean guy striding toward him with fury in his face. He put down the cell phone and drove through the green light, that's for sure. I treated him with care.

"What happened? Did you hurt anyone?"

"No. No, I controlled myself. She had some . . . pointed remarks."

Zach leaned in, interested.

"What did she say to you?"

Before he could answer, Mary walked into the room.

"You talking about my mother?"

Cameron smiled wanly, trying to calm himself down.

"Nope. I'm fine. Are you fine?"

"Of course. I was born fine."

She appeared under control, though I thought I detected some tension. It seemed like Mary was willing to dance on by it, however, so we moved right along without comment. A loud knocking signaled the arrival of Dustin, who walked in sans Donkey Girl. Cameron peered behind him.

"Where's the lady?"

"She had something. She sends her regrets."

He threw himself onto the floor and refused to elaborate. His voice drifted up.

"You got any beer?"

Mary set off to grab the poor kid a beer as Zach reached into his bag to bring out the jar and place it on the table. The doorbell rang again, which could only mean Annie and Rat Boy. Climbing to his feet, Cameron gave the jar a conflicted look before running to let them in. I busied myself with rearranging the chip bowls as Annie and Rat Boy stepped into the room. Rat Boy had decided to don some sort of T-shirt detailed in a haphazard aborigine pattern, which made him look like he'd been stepped on by a giant wearing Pumas. Annie moved by us to go say hi to Mary in the kitchen. Rat Boy lowered himself onto a hassock and we all sat there a moment, staring at one another in silence. Finally, Rat Boy pointed to the jar on the table.

"What's that?"

Zach tapped the lid.

"Slim Limb."

Unnerved, Rat Boy nodded as if that made sense. Cameron ran into the kitchen and returned with Annie and Mary in tow, drinks in hand. As they handed them out, Annie's eyes lit upon the jar sitting innocuously in the center of the table.

"What is that?"

Zach shrugged.

"That's just Slim Limb. I bought it as a laugh. I thought you guys would get a kick out of it."

"What is it?"

"Arm cream. To tighten up the flab, you know. You certainly don't need it."

Annie gave her arms a look and moved them slightly. I thought they looked quite shapely, actually. Annie always did have nice upper arms. I looked away, a little embarrassed at checking out my friend's arms, as Mary made a face.

"Come on, Annie. You don't need it. I'm the one who needs it."

Annie rolled her eyes.

"You don't need any cream, Mary."

I broke in.

"Neither of you need it. Man."

Zach tapped the lid.

"It's funny though."

I nodded.

"Really funny. I almost tried some myself."

Annie shrugged.

"Do you think it works?"

Zach lifted his arm.

"You know, I think it might. I'm looking pretty good. But

it's just a joke, really. I'm giving it to Cameron to cheer him up. He can stick it in the bathroom or something to give his guests a chuckle."

Cameron stared at him a second before I flicked his arm. He jumped in.

"My mom'll get a kick out of that when she visits."

He grabbed the jar and disappeared inside the bathroom, reappearing after a moment.

"Right on top of the toilet. Kind of like a joke book, in cream form."

He sat down and we moved on. For half an hour we talked like the old friends most of us were. I brought up some old high school antics that had us all reminiscing. This seemed to make Rat Boy a bit uncomfortable, probably because it reminded him of how he didn't belong. Mary spent most of her time in the kitchen trying to make some cinnamon bread happen, which helped add to the Rat Boy–as–outsider effect. Everything was going according to plan. After a bit, Annie stood up, stretching her legs.

"I'll be right back. Anyone need anything while I'm up?"

We assured her we were fine and she wandered off toward the bathroom. We continued talking, shooting knowing glances at one another while discussing arcane pop culture references until Rat Boy didn't know what to think. He didn't really say much, except to comment on how we seemed to know a lot about eighties music and the actors from *The A-Team*. Annie stepped back in, looking slightly sheepish. As she passed by, a strange scent wafted up to my nose.

Busted! Zach sure knew the ladies. I had to keep myself from chuckling at her predictability as she sat down next to Rat Boy, who wrinkled his nose like his namesake.

"Are you all right, honey?"

"I'm fine. Why?"

"Nothing. Just checking in on my angel."

I stifled a laugh. The guy thought his fiancée had let one go. I had to give it to him, he was polite about it. But polite was about to be burned away like so much cellulite.

A few minutes later, Mary joined us, setting down some sliced cinnamon bread in the center of the table before heading off to wash her hands. A minute or so later she returned, sliding into Cameron's chair. Zach gave her a look of alarm. He tried to catch my attention, thumbing his nose like a cokehead and rubbing his arms furiously. Though Mary became concerned and moved to the other side of Cameron's chair, away from him, Zach's message came through to me loud and clear. *Mary was on the stuff, too.*

Nothing we could do about it now. We just had to hope she didn't get as excitable as Annie, or the whole night could turn into a WWE pay-per-view event. We pushed onward with the plan, heading into phase two.

It began with Zach suggesting a game.

"It's been sweeping Europe, so I thought I'd bring it over here. It's hilarious. They call it the dirty telephone game."

Cameron read from the script.

"What's the dirty telephone game?"

Zach was only too happy to elaborate.

"You know when you're trying to make yourself understood over the phone, you spell it out? Like when you say 'The name is Zach. 'Z' as in 'zebra,' 'A' as in 'alabaster,' 'C' as in 'Chianti,' 'H' as in 'hotelier.'"

Annie gave him a strange look.

"Those are the words you choose? Chianti? You too good for 'cat'?"

So the cream was starting to work already. Excellent.

Zach did not deign to answer her, continuing on with the explanation.

"Well, this is just like that. Only the point is to be as dirty as you can. It's great fun."

Annie's eyes narrowed.

"Dirty? Like curse words?"

Zach stared back at her innocently.

"If you aren't particularly imaginative, maybe."

I jumped in.

"It sounds fun. You don't have to curse if you don't want to. It's probably funnier if you don't, right?"

Zach nodded.

"Exactly. For instance, you could give me the word 'apple.' And I'd say something like, um, 'A' as in 'aureola,' 'P' as in 'prick,' 'P' as in 'poopshoot,' 'L' as in 'labia' and 'E' as in 'erectile dysfunction.'"

Mary leaned forward.

"Come on. Those aren't even that bad. Give me one."

This was going to be easier than we thought.

"All right. 'Tiger.'"

"Okay. Tiger. 'T' as in 'tea-bagging,' 'I' as in 'in the face,' 'G' as in 'gag reflex,' 'E' as in 'enter the exit hole' and 'R' as in 'rumpspunker!'"

We could only gape in amazement. I nodded approvingly to Cameron.

"You got yourself a winner there."

He smiled halfheartedly. Zach pointed to Cameron.

"Now Mary, you give Cameron a word."

Mary's eyes glinted as she bounced on the chair arm.

"Stubborn."

She immediately looked regretful at what she said.

Cameron wasn't too happy with this assignment, grunting in displeasure.

"All right, honey. Stubborn. 'S' as in 'sucky sucky,' 'T' as in 'tasty titties,' 'U' as in 'Um, tasty titties,' 'B' as in 'big tasty titties,' 'B' as in 'big-ass tasty titties,' 'O' as in 'Oh my God, big-ass tasty titties!,' 'R' as in 'Really, look at those big-ass tasty titties' and 'N' as in, uh . . ."

Mary jumped in.

"'No more big-ass tasty titties.' Please!"

We all laughed. Cameron turned to Dustin.

"Hey Dustin. Here's an easy one. Felon."

Dustin lifted his head from the floor.

"'F' as in 'first-date fisting,' 'E' as in 'extreme booty bangin',' 'L' as in 'liquid magic,' 'O' as in 'Ouch, oh!, Ouch ouch, oh!' And 'N' as in 'nut butter nougat.'"

We all applauded at this fine show of verbal agility. I sneaked a glance Rat Boy's way and liked what I was seeing. You'd have thought by his face that we were eating a baby. His skin had paled under the onslaught of crassness, and he actually flinched when Dustin mentioned Liquid Magic. Hell, I don't even know what that is. Annie, on the other hand, alternated between casting worried glances at her man and getting drawn in to our world of aural depravity. She'd always loved cursing, since we were kids. Not your average, everyday cursing, mind you. She loved elaborate, long-winded, satisfying curses. Phrases like "teutonic twat" and "cock-nibbling cornhumpers." That's how Zach knew this game would intrigue her. But so far, she'd kept herself in check, forcing herself to be aloof from the depravity while furiously stroking Rat Boy's biceps until his arm hairs began to smoke. Turning lazily, Dustin shot me a word.

"Turkey."

I sat up straight and cracked my knuckles.

"Okay. Turkey. 'T' as in 'toothbrushes don't go there,' 'U' as in 'Underage is a state of mind,' 'R' as in 'Rinse that off if you're gonna eat with it, trust me,' 'K' as in 'Keep the gerbil calm until I remember where I put the Cheddar,' 'E' as in 'Enough with the Brillo pad you're gonna give me a rash,' and 'Y' as in 'Yo' Mama!' "

Annie couldn't help herself. She scoffed loudly.

"Were those long enough? Jesus. You're such an amateur."

Her caffeine-inspired outburst drew a disapproving glance from her man, who obviously felt that the best way to deal with this storm was to sit quietly and ride it out. Annie caught the look and a flash of irritation shot across her face. It wasn't there long, but I caught it. Finally, a kink in the armor. I dug my fingernail in while the hole was exposed.

"Annie, you want to try?"

She shook her head.

"Not tonight."

Pause.

"Okay. Fine. A short one."

I needled further.

"Short? You afraid you can't come up with enough examples? I guess I used all the good ones."

Her hackles raised, she snorted.

"Please, David. I don't know what the hell you're talking about. I fell asleep halfway through your little *War and Peace* recitation."

"Sorry my imagination intimidates you."

Her eyes burned with the unholy light of Jujomes.

"Give me a good one."

Rat Boy shrank back under the force of her glare. He was about to be introduced to a side of Annie he'd never heard before. It wasn't the major piece of her, just a simple facet of her personality that didn't come up too often, but it definitely wasn't a side he'd ever pictured existing in this laid-back, loving teacher of children with autism.

I threw it down.

"Cornucopia."

The room grew hushed at the word. Cameron and Dustin exchanged frightened glances, like bartenders stuck in a saloon shootout. Annie didn't miss a beat.

"All right. Give me a second."

She sat there, staring at me belligerently while she went over the word. I'd really grabbed her attention now. There would be no pulling of punches. Rat Boy stared in sick fascination, waiting breathlessly with the rest of us. Finally, Annie nodded.

"Okay. Here we go. Cornucopia. 'C' as in 'cockgobbling cumdumpster,' 'O' as in 'Open Jizsamy,' 'R' as in rod-reaming rimjobbers, 'N' as in 'nutnuzzling,' 'U' as in 'Unsheath your meat missile,' 'C' as in 'Camel felching for fun and profit,' 'O' as in 'odiferous buttfuckery,' 'P' as in 'Pop the prim punnany,' 'I' as in 'itchy tit monkey,' and 'A' as in 'Anal Anthropologists attack with ass-polishing analingus.' Cornucopia."

She sat back, exhausted.

The entire room fell silent, staring at her in mute astonishment. She had risen to the occasion and far, far above. Slowly, and then with gathering speed, we began to laugh. I nodded, giving her a small golf clap.

"That's what I'm talking about."

She smiled widely, drinking in the accolades. And then she

turned to her man, triumphant. The look on his face drained the victory out of hers. He blinked, slowly.

"Wow. Um. Well. Wow."

The room quieted as Rat Boy's horror became apparent. Annie glanced down at her shaking hand, instantly regretful.

"Maybe we should go."

Zach wouldn't hear of it.

"Come on. Please. I'm sorry my game caused trouble. We can stop."

Cameron, still stung by the "stubborn" comment, chimed in.

"No, let's do another one. How about 'Yellow'?"

Mary erupted, spurned on by the venom rushing through her.

"Will you let it go! She's a bitter, bigoted old woman, but she's still my mother. You need to respect that!"

Cameron needed no cream to leap into this fray.

"She disrespected me all night long. Hell, you called her a bitch on the ride home."

"I'm allowed. She's my mom! But you can't. You have no right!"

While we'd been busy stoking the flames of Annie's and Rat Boy's differences, we'd been ignoring the fight brewing in the corner. But the cream recognized no intentions, it worked its evil magic evenhandedly. By this time, Mary was shaking with fury, but Cameron had reached his own little Krakatoa point and pushed on, heedless.

"The things your mother said to me tonight were unforgivable!"

"She's set in her ways."

"Set in her ways? First she hates the Chinese. And I'm

Korean, for fuck's sake. Okay, so that's bad enough. Then I mention that I'm Scottish."

"Why did you say that?"

"I thought it would help! How could I know she thinks all the Scottish are British turncoats?"

"She's Irish!"

"Your mother has special prejudice powers."

"Then why did you have to throw that last grenade? I swear I saw you cock your arm right before you tossed it out there."

"She pissed me off."

"So *kapow!* You had to tell her you're a Jew. The only thing she hates worse than the Scottish and Asians. I asked you not to do that."

"I wanted to make her flinch. She's a horrible woman. What was the first thing she said after she stopped sputtering? 'So that's what this is all about. You're a whore for his Jew money.'"

"I told her you didn't have any money."

"Yeah, thanks for that. It was nice to hear her say, 'Then why are you with him?'"

"I know she's terrible. I've lived with it for my entire life! But she's still my mother! And I don't want you saying those things about her! Even if they're true!"

"That doesn't make sense! She's a bitch and I'm not afraid to say it. A bitch!"

"I can't look at you!"

With that, Mary ran out of the living room and into the bedroom, slamming the door. Cameron immediately looked ashamed. We sat there for a moment, stunned, until Dustin pushed himself to his feet.

"I guess this party's cooked."

And so we dispersed, blown apart by our own irresponsible dabbling in devil cream. But our initial plan had taken root. Rat Boy and Annie were barely speaking as they filed out. They might make up on the way home, but the seeds had been planted. We'd leave them to water them on their own for a while. Cameron had calmed down by the time we left, assuring us that he was just about to go in and make nice. As we slipped out, he leaned in to let me in on a little secret.

"I think I'm going to marry her."

"What about her mother?"

"Can you think of any better revenge than giving that hateful woman Korean Scottish Jewish grandchildren?"

One man's roadblock is another man's reason to live. It's amazing how people work things out in their heads.

* * *

For the next week, I stayed out of the situation. Annie called once or twice and hinted at some small problems, but since she knew my stance on the Rat Boy situation, she never gave me much info. But I could tell Zach's instinct had been correct. Small nudges, tiny reveals, and let the poor kids do the work themselves. After all, they weren't right for each other anyhow, so let them realize it on their own. With nudging.

Chapter Sixteen

The Naked City

The following weekend found me up on 116th Street, in a small courtyard in the middle of Columbia University's Teacher's College. Summer semester had recently begun and already the professors needed to let off some steam. Thus was I hired, brought in to give four hours of background music while old men in tweed jackets mumbled to one another over the decline of Western civilization. Or so I figured. You can imagine my shock when, a half hour in, a fairly young guy in jeans and a T-shirt that read ATARI approached me as I ran through my Motown set.

"Sorry to bug you. Do you have any OutKast?"

Who'd a thunk it? They were a hip-hop crowd. Even the old ones in tweed jackets. Pot must really be making a comeback—or had it ever really left? After switching it over to some old school De La Soul and Rob Base, I had the whole picnic jumpin'. A couple of middle-aged professors of the feminine persuasion hijacked me and made me shake my groove thang to some Run-D.M.C. After a while, we ended up by the snack table chatting as I ran back and forth to and from my table to keep the beat thumpin'. I liked these teachers of teachers. They were some of the finest minds teaching other fine minds how to teach young minds. Georgia, a forty-ish short and frumpy prof with way too much of a jones for the brownies, let me in on her frustrations.

"Kids are getting dumber, I swear."

Kerry, in her mid-thirties and already mostly gray, reproved her mildly.

"Come on, that's not true. They're just harder to motivate."

"Because they're dumber! They don't read. They don't think. They certainly don't write. Do you hear the rhymes in hip-hop nowadays? Thank God for Kanye West, otherwise I'd have to write off the whole bunch as a group of lazy meter junkies. None of them could hold a candle to even a Young M.C., let alone someone like Posdnuos."

Atari shirt guy, whose name was Lydon, nodded.

"She's right, there. Nelly wouldn't know imagery if it was rubbing its naked boobies in his face."

Georgia put up one sadly agreeing finger.

"Exactly. And the kids are the poorer for it."

Kerry let the point go.

"You still have to motivate them. That's what we have to stress to the new teachers. How do you motivate them?"

Georgia shook her head at the lost glory of it all.

"You tell the ones with no talent they're destined for greatness. Sad."

Wait a minute. Did that mean what I think it meant? I cut in.

"You lie to the kids?"

Kerry nodded.

"Sure. We tell all our students to learn to lie to the kids.

It's a great motivator. I mean, we don't lie all the time. And *lie* is such a strong word."

Lydon clarified.

"We tell them to overstate talents, you know, to give the kids a reason to try. To tell the kids that they could be rocket scientists someday when in fact they'll probably end up in middle management or driving a snowplow. It's a tragedy, but it's policy."

Georgia looked disgusted.

"And then you get Lil' Jon and you're surprised?"

I focused on her.

"So you don't tell your students to do that, right?"

Georgia didn't even look embarrassed.

"Of course I do. It's a vicious cycle. Somebody's got to encourage the children, and it sure ain't comin' from the home."

"What about writing?"

Georgia laughed.

"Oh, that's the mother lode of ass kissing. Everyone's a genius, right guys?"

Lydon and even Kerry joined her in rueful chuckling. Kerry shrugged.

"It's the easiest to overstate. What makes a good writer after all? And if you get them interested in writing, suddenly they're reading more and thinking more. You get real results."

I thought back to the days of Mrs. Hickenbothem and Mr. Paulson. Sure enough, I did read more and pondered more. Hell, I haven't stopped pondering. But that was so long ago. And I doubt that either of those teachers ever went to a school like this for their degree. Maybe they lie now, but there was no reason to lie back then. Hip-hop was damn good in those days, after all. I opened my mouth to ask them how long the web of deception had been in place, but I couldn't form the words. I didn't want to know. And by then, the three of them had wandered off behind the side building to eat more brownies. I pushed those disquieting thoughts out of my mind, but I couldn't help but picture my composition book filled with those glowing red lines of praise, so untrustworthy. I didn't know what to believe anymore.

* * *

On the way home that afternoon I was blessedly distracted by a phone call from Annie.

"David, what do you know about hula hooping?"

Hmm. Unexpected.

"Not much, really. Why?"

"Apparently Josh ran into Zach down in the Village and they got to talking and discovered they have a mutual love of hula hooping. How the hell that happened, I have no clue. But Zach invited Josh to go hula hooping with him one night at some movement salon or something. Do you know anything about this?"

Hearing her mention hula hooping did tickle my memory, but I couldn't come up with the thought. So instead, I pleaded ignorance.

"Nope. Sounds like Zach, though."

"But now Josh wants me to go with him! And I have to go. After all, I feel bad about all the arguing we've been doing this week. But I don't want it to be just the three of us. Please, you've got to come."

A small warning bell went off in my head.

"I don't think I can."

"Why not? You're afraid of a hoop of plastic? Come on,

you promised to spend a little time with Josh. Can you give me one good reason why you can't come?"

I couldn't come up with one. Which pretty much roped me into going hula hooping the following week. As soon as I got off the phone with her, it rang again. I answered it to Zach's voice.

"Annie's probably gonna call you. You should come up with a good reason not to go hula hooping."

"Shit! She just called and I had no such reason."

Zach's voice took on a slight edge of mild panic.

"Say you said you couldn't go, David."

"What the hell is going on?"

"I had a day free this week, so I decided to case out Annie's apartment. It was quite exciting. I felt like a dapper young spy. I followed Joshua into the city and contrived to run into him downtown. I figured I could feel him out in order to fashion the next phase of the plan. But instead, the next phase dropped out of the sky and into my lap. He's a hula hoop enthusiast! Just like me! And remembering your comment about his prior love of nudity, I realized that this was the perfect opportunity."

"Opportunity for what?"

"To invite him to my nude hula-hooping party. Isn't it brilliant?"

That was what that tickle in my brain meant. Oh shit, which also meant . . .

"I can't go to that. What were you thinking!"

"With a little light digging I found that our young friend is quite resentful of having to give up his nude pastime. He's done it only in the spirit of compromise. But as they've been arguing, I was able to convince him to spring it on Annie as his little line in the sand. After all, if she can be herself, he should be allowed to be himself. So Annie will be walking into a nude trap. I am amazed by my own ingenuity."

"Shit, what am I going to do? I've already promised to go!"

"I don't know, David. But you better figure something out if you don't want to see us both naked."

I knew I had to back out somehow, especially because the idea itself was nothing short of brilliant and I didn't want to screw it up, but I couldn't figure out a way. Annie wouldn't do it without my moral support. When I explained it a few days later to Cameron and Dustin over sandwiches, Dustin shuddered theatrically.

"Man, I don't want to think about that little man naked! Disgusting!"

I popped a potato chip in my mouth.

"I find the idea of a whole room of naked people hula hooping disgusting."

Cameron leaned forward.

"Yeah, about that. Where the hell does Zach meet these people? It's a little . . . strange."

I shot him a look of derision.

"Hey, you don't have to go, so don't tell me what's strange."

Dustin reached out across the table to retrieve his chips.

"Wait! Silver lining! Won't there be naked chicks there, too? That's pretty sweet."

I shook my head at his naïveté.

"Hot women never show up at nude gatherings. Nude beaches, clothing-optional day in college, strip poker games, go to any of these events and you will definitely see a decided lack of sweet sweetness. Male genitalia, now that you will find everywhere, hanging off the poor assholes just like you who thought for sure that Giselle Bündchen came to these parties every Tuesday like clockwork. Maybe a fifty-year-old woman or two, if you're extremely lucky. Besides that, it's a barren fucking wasteland. And Wednesday night will be no different. I will be seeing a lot of penis, boys. And I may never recover."

* * *

"Can I come? I love penises!"

Janey laid her head on my shoulder, her hand comfortably inside the back pocket of my jeans. We strolled haphazardly along the brick path that follows the East River, the soft light spreading out from the hanging lamps above us mixing with the fading twilight to create a strange glow that surrounded the benches and trees while obscuring the city behind us. The air seemed warmer, more seductive, almost unreal, like we had somehow made a wrong turn and ended up in a strange fairytale Manhattan where the light had weight that covered us like a down comforter. Nothing around us seemed real, even the people we passed, the lovers wrapped up in each other on the hard wooden benches, the lone fishermen casting lines out into the dark water, the joggers who began as a hard clap against the brick before sliding out of the haze, huffing, brief humans in spandex shorts, lost inside the world of the headphones hanging from their ears, here and gone in a flurry of footfalls; they all wavered around us, fading into our shadow. Evenings like these seem outside of time, outside of our lives, a brief sojourn into a New York set aside for lovely moments destined to become perfect memories. And I always feel that I squander them, never having the kinds of moments worth becoming those remembrances. Even now, with my arm wrapped around a great girl I think I might really like, my head flies away, spending time with other things that don't have anything to do with lamplight or softly lapping water. I feel her hair brush up against my face and I want to be there, completely, drinking in every second, storing them inside an inner cubbyhole for when I truly need a perfect moment to keep me going. Instead, I'm with my novel, and with Annie and Rat Boy, and with my parents. I'm with everyone but the one I'm with.

"No you can't come. Rat Boy's got a reputation now. What if you see his lovely penis and run away with him! He has that effect on people."

She squeezed her hand in my back pocket, tickling me through the denim.

"I'm sure it's small, with very little character."

We reached the end of the walkway, the small marina empty before us, its ships gone on their evening cruises around the island.

"I did a wedding on one of those boats."

"Which boats?"

"One of the boats not here now. Big boat. Sorta blue, I think."

"You paint like van Gogh with your words."

"It was a gay wedding, actually. Not official, of course, in a legal sense. In every other sense."

"Did they have a good time?"

"The funny thing is, I don't think so. They gave me all this music to play, which none of their guests wanted to hear.

They had all these planned events, none of which worked out. Dance contests, stuff like that. Maybe they were nervous. But their parents seemed fine with the wedding, smiling and drinking and requesting Bobby Darin tunes. Those two guys were a mess, though. Some guests were late, so the boat had to wait for them, which cut into how long they could be out on the river. Nothing seemed to go the way they wanted it. They bickered, they spent ten minutes not talking to each other. Then they made up, dancing to their song, until the CD started skipping. Not my fault! They provided it for me, after all. Of course, when we docked, one of them carried the other one off the boat in his arms, which was nice. They kissed on the dock before hopping into a limo while everyone cheered. So it ended well. But all in all, not the perfect wedding, gay or otherwise."

Janey kissed my cheek.

"I think that's beautiful."

"Why?"

"I think a marriage should probably start with bumps. Like testing a car, except you're the crash test dummies. It may hurt more that way, but I'd rather sprain an ankle than break my neck. I mean, my parents had ten years of problem-free marriage. The first bump in the road broke them."

"What was the bump?"

Janey stared out at the empty docks.

"Me."

"Oh."

"Dad was never good at the day to day. He's more of a long range, big picture guy. That didn't sit well with Mom."

"I see."

We listened to the cars on the FDR shoot by above our heads, my arm sheltering her from the breeze off the water.

"I'm seeing him Friday. Nice little family dinner."

"I thought you weren't talking."

"I called. Why not? Can't be angry forever."

"I'm impressed."

"We'll see."

We turned and headed back down the river the way we came. On impulse, I turned my face toward hers and kissed her, much deeper than I meant to. The kiss raged out of my control, forcing us to a halt as we wrapped our arms around each other. Eventually, we pulled apart, her half-lidded eyes peering up at me in surprise.

"Where did that come from?"

I was so shocked at myself I answered honestly, squandering the chance to gain brownie points.

"I don't know."

"Trace it. I want more like it."

We kissed again, my fingers gliding through her hair. I lay my forehead on hers, noses almost touching. She smiled.

"Yum."

Slipping her hand back into my pocket, she slid around to my side, grinning like a kid into my shoulder. We resumed walking, lost inside the lamplight. Where had that kiss come from? It sprang out of something within, something I'd been ignoring. Like my head had been deciding one thing while the rest of my body took a vote behind its back. Her call to her father did impress me. That was a hard thing to do. And she's not afraid of bumps, which is good to hear. How about me, though? My brain flew past that thought without stopping. She felt so good, nestled in my arm. I felt calm and present. I no longer flew with my job and my parents and my life. I stayed there by the river, next to a woman I liked more with every word that she tossed me, confidently sticking the moment into that inner cubbyhole for a rainy day. A small moment, true, but perfect.

Chapter Seventeen

Rising to the Occasion

To my relief, Zach and I worked out a game plan that would keep my exposure to nudity to a minimum. After all, it wouldn't do for Annie to walk in with Rat Boy. She had to catch him sans trousers, swinging in the breeze. So my job entailed meeting up with Annie and heading over to the nudity fest together so she and I could walk in on the sausage swing together. We'd tried to come up with some vast, intricate plan involving wrong times and missed taxis and a drug deal gone bad in an effort to delay Annie so that Rat Boy was naked and gyrating when she arrived, but thankfully Annie solved our problem for us by needing to work late, promising to meet us there. At least, I was thankful until she made her request.

"Could you be there when Zach and Josh meet up? I'm not sure if I want Zach to spend too much time with him alone, you know?"

I tried to keep the panic out of my voice.

"But, I thought we'd go together . . ."

"That's stupid. I don't want you waiting around for me

while I finish up with my kid. Go on ahead. I won't be more than a half hour late, I promise."

I hung up, worried. So much could go wrong. I had to keep my pants on.

I met up with Zach outside his building. He waved, keeping a slight distance between us as I grabbed his hand hello. I cut right to the chase.

"I'm scared. I don't want to see him naked."

"Who?"

I whispered, in case the man in question stepped up behind me.

"Rat Boy."

"I'm sure he's well proportioned."

"I don't care! Hell, I don't want to see you naked."

Zach shook his head, bemused at my vehemence.

"It's no big deal. It's a lot of fun! It's only my hula-hoop team and a few friends."

Hold on a second.

"Hula-hoop team? You didn't mention this was a hula-hoop team."

"Yes. We all belong to the movement salon where I do my Pilates. We're quite good."

"How can you have a team? How do you compete?"

"It's fairly competitive, actually. Like cheerleading with hoops. Though we're in exhibition season now."

"Hula-hooping exhibition?"

"Hey, it's broadened my horizons. I mean, I've been on Spanish television and I have my hula-hoop team to thank for it. Though I wouldn't mention that tonight. Things didn't go quite as planned that night and the memory still stings quite a bit down at the salon. Here he is!"

Rat Boy walked up, smiling, his incisors glinting under the streetlamps. He'd dressed up, wearing a button-down shirt and long shorts with sandals. Not that it mattered what he was wearing where we were going. His intermittent beard remained as scraggly as ever. He stuck out his hand to me.

"Hi, David. It's great to see you again!"

"Good to see you . . . whoa! How are ya!"

My exclamation came as he pulled me into a hug I did not want or need. He pulled back and grabbed Zach's hand. I could see the terror in Zach's eyes as he realized that he might be hugged as well. His other hand had already shot up in front of him to prevent body contact. Rat Boy had been well briefed, however, and he kept it to a handshake.

"Zach! Hello! Thank you so much for this, it's really nice of you."

Zach pulled his hand away as politely as he could.

"My pleasure, Joshua."

Rat Boy stood back and put his hands on his hips, Superman style. We stood there, stuck in the pause, uncertain what to do or say. Finally Zach stepped out and flagged down a cab.

"Let's get this started."

* * *

Rat Boy sat between us on the bitch seat of the cab, his legs scrunched up uncomfortably. For a while we rode in silence, none of us sure of what to say. I was apprehensive about the nudity to come, Rat Boy seemed pensive trapped between two guys he barely knew, and Zach was probably walking along the beaches of San Tropez. I finally broke the silence.

"Say, Zach. I want to take Janey to a nice restaurant, someplace special."

Zach nodded sagely.

"Aureole. Has to be."

"Is it that good?"

"I've enjoyed three of my top twenty meals there. It's extremely good. Breathtakingly excellent."

Rat Boy shifted uncomfortably, trying to work the seatbelt buckle out of his ass.

"You remember your top twenty meals?"

"I can do you one better. I recall my top one hundred meals, in order."

Wow. That's some obsession at work.

"By number?"

"Of course, by number."

Rat Boy thought this over.

"Can you remember them at will?"

"Try me."

"Forty-seven."

"Steak tartare at Bordeaux, this tiny bistro in Monte Carlo. They had these lovely murals of Greek gods violating mortals on the wall. I felt quite at home."

I jumped in.

"Twenty-two."

"I remember that one well. Risotto at Il Mulino. The waiter's cuff links were dirty, but I said nothing."

Rat Boy seemed fascinated. Hell, I was fascinated. Rat Boy kept the game going.

"Fifteen."

"Three stalks of asparagus at Aquavit."

Now, I know bullshit when I hear it.

"Come on. How can three spears of asparagus be a meal?"

Zach leaned back, his eyes misting over.

"When I sat down to eat, I thought as you do, David. Twenty-five dollars for three lonely stalks? I wasn't going to order them, but then I realized that I had no choice. How could I not taste such outrageously priced vegetables? The chutzpah hooked me. I had to know. When they were placed before me I poked at them, hesitant, not certain what I had gotten myself into. They certainly looked tender, three slender shafts simmering in butter on an otherwise empty plate. I cut off a tip, brought it up to my mouth, and . . . fireworks! My taste buds sprang up and applauded. This was what asparagus aspired to be. This twenty-five-dollar vegetable trio was the ideal of all asparagus, everywhere. Just perfect. It knocked sushi at NoBu down to sixteen with barely a protest."

Rat Boy didn't know what to say.

"Wow. You really like to eat."

"I believe the culinary arts stand as high as painting or music in our cultural hierarchy. Each meal is a small moment of pure happiness, if treated correctly, and this moment can be planned and repeated as long as you have the time and to a lesser extent the money to seek it out. I have never known a moment of passion that could equal any one of my top ten meals."

I sighed.

"Do you know what the sad thing is? Somewhere in my top twenty there's a Wendy's."

"Don't be ashamed of it! There's a McDonald's value meal in my top fifty."

Rat Boy's macrobiotic heart skipped a beat.

"That stuff is horrible for you!"

"So much is, these days. But that meal at the McDonald's in the Gare du Nord in Paris will always linger with me."

I interjected.

"Wait a sec. That's a location meal. That's great because it's not just a Big Mac, it's a Big Mac in Paris. My Wendy's came from downtown White Plains."

Zach leaned back against his door.

"You're probably right. We are nothing alike. You may be a writer, a lover of art and literature, a world traveler, but at heart, you're an old man who eats nothing but toast."

* * *

The movement salon sat on the second floor of an old white building, which was covered with carvings and sconces like tattoos on the chest of a biker. Annie called to say she'd meet us in the studio in a half hour or so, which should give us plenty of time to get Rat Boy naked. We made our way upstairs, the sounds of early-nineties dance music filtering down to our ears. I cocked my head.

"Is that Deee-Lite?"

Zach shrugged. Popular music not by Britney Spears never seemed to stick with him. As we climbed upward, Rat Boy whispered to me.

"I hope Annie understands. She's never been too comfortable with this side of me. The nude side, I mean."

"She should see how important it is to you. It's your passion!"

He had to nod.

"Yeah, it is kind of a hobby."

"And a man has a right to his hobbies! She needs to understand that. Even if it doesn't work for her, she has to understand that it's important to you."

"You're right. She should understand that it's part of my heritage."

Heritage? Did his forefathers fight the Civil War with balls bouncing in the breeze?

"It sure is. Just because it may not be for her, that doesn't mean she should keep you from doing what you love. You deserve to be naked! I mean take this hula-hoop troupe. You heard about the Spanish television thing, right?"

We reached the landing and stepped through the door. Rat Boy turned to me in the doorway and replied loudly.

"What Spanish television thing?"

The room hushed. Remember, comedy is all about the timing. Apprehensive, Rat Boy slowly turned to look inside the room he'd just entered. The studio took up the entire floor, with hardwood floors and a long mirror along one side, like any dance studio across the country, only larger. Filling the room were around twenty-five people between the ages of twenty and sixty, stretching and getting limber. They were, to a person, buck naked. A large man in his fifties with an immaculately trimmed gray beard strode toward us, his face, hell, his whole body, red. I tried desperately not to look, but my head was attached to an anchor that dragged my line of sight down . . . Damn! Definitely not Jewish! He began to yell as soon as he reached us.

"You do not mention those Latin bastards here, is that clear! We may be fooled once, but we will not be fooled again! Am I right, people?"

Everyone behind him gave a halfhearted cheer. Rat Boy stammered under the assault.

"I'm sorry. I didn't know . . ."

"I find that hard to believe! The entire Spanish-speaking population of America seems to know! The Edgar Kraus Hula-

Hoop Expression Troupe is no one's sap! We are no one's play toy! We are serious, here! Deadly serious!"

The entire time he yelled, his little snake in a turtleneck swung to and fro, emphasizing each point like a flaccid little index finger. Zach put up his hands.

"We're sorry, Edgar. It won't happen again. He didn't know."

"Those Spanish bastards! We'll get them, you'll see! We are no one's laughingstock!"

"You're right, Edgar."

"Who are your friends?"

Zach pointed to the two of us, who by now were cowering in the corner.

"This is David and this is Joshua."

"All right, get ready. We're starting in a few minutes."

He strode away, buns shaking with righteous anger. The show over, conversation resumed. I took a good look at all the naked people, trying not to stare. Just as I thought: guys and middle-aged women. Zach nudged me.

"Don't stare. Come on."

He led us into the corner, where he started to disrobe. Rat Boy looked around, undoing his belt buckle with nary a second thought.

"But what are we going to do, actually?"

This was something I'd wondered myself. What did one do at naked hula-hooping Friday? Just stand around, idly spinning the hoop atop your bare ass, trying not to get it caught on your member? Zach pulled off his pants as he explained.

"Well, some exercises to limber up, some jumping jacks

and the like. Then we work on our speed and endurance for a bit. After that we concentrate on the routine. At the end, Edgar and some of the other experts pull off some crazy stunts. Very much like a gymnastics team."

"But bare-assed naked."

"Yes, David. That's what makes it so beautiful. Are you taking off your shirt or not?"

Zach reached down and pulled off his boxer briefs, exposing himself to his oldest friend. I tried not to look, I swear I did, but I'm only human. The strange thing was, once everything was exposed, it was just a penis. I've seen porn. I know what a penis looks like. Though in porn they're much larger, so more than anything the sight of Zach's normal-sized rooster filled me with a small measure of relief. It wasn't bigger than mine.

Rat Boy grabbed his shirt and pulled it off. His underdeveloped chest stuck out, begging to be played like a xylophone. He grabbed his pants and struggled with the button. A naked Zach nudged me.

"You're staring, David."

Elbowing him back, I turned away, right into Edgar's face.

"Are you getting naked or are you leaving! It's your choice!"

But I had no choice. Where the hell was Annie? Fuckbeans.

"I'm getting naked."

"Then nude up, mister!"

Sighing, I grabbed my shirt and pulled it over my head. Disrobing as quickly as I could, I came down to my boxer shorts, which, because of a massive brain fart while dressing, were covered in tiny Charlie Browns. Everyone else was naked. Zach, Rat Boy . . . Rat Boy! I stepped back in shock.

Rat Boy's penis was . . . well, it was porn-size! A little of the mystery of the Annie attraction had been solved. He had the chest of a starving child and the unit of Milton Berle. It's amazing how life balances out. Suddenly I didn't want to take off my boxers. But I had no choice. With a soft sigh, I yanked them down. Edgar called over.

"Are you done with the strip show? Good! Let's go, people!"

Everyone lined up, five deep, each with a brightly colored hula hoop at their feet. Edgar faced us, his silver-spangled hoop in his hand.

"Normally we'd be doing some light speed and technique work, but in light of the Spanish incident, we will be working hard on our choreography! We will not be fooled again, and that means being prepared at all times! Keith, come up here!"

A well-built young guy with an easy smile and, of course, no pants, walked up to the front, smiling at Zach as he passed him. Zach smiled back. I looked closer. Was that . . . could it be? Yes. Zach was blushing. It's harder to hide when your entire body changes color. Yet another mystery solved. This must be the boy. Keith reached the front of the room and faced us. There was entirely too much penis in this place.

"Yes, Edgar."

"Show them how it's done. Look closely, people!"

And Keith began to spin. I won't describe the hula-hooping extravaganza put on by Zach's crush, because I don't think I know how. That hoop spun and swooped and did all kinds of crazy things, around all kinds of crazy limbs. Even his willy, which should have looked ridiculous shaking around like a flag in a hurricane, instead seemed almost aerodynamic in its movement. Zach's eyes shone as he watched, entranced. Finally Edgar stopped him.

"That's good. Did you guys see that? That's how it's supposed to be. Now the worst thing about the Spanish incident, okay, the second worst thing, was how sloppy we were. If we're going to be exploited, we better at least look professional! So let's work on it!"

We split up. I kept an eye on the door, ready to hide in the corner when Annie showed. Zach stepped over.

"I'm sorry guys. I thought it would be looser today."

Rat Boy waved him off.

"That's okay. Really."

I had to ask.

"What happened with Spanish television?"

Zach grimaced and leaned in to whisper.

"Let's just say they didn't play the music at normal speed. Our second best hooper still can't walk. He's over in the corner there with the ice pack."

He pointed to a short guy sitting by the window, injured but still naked, determined to be there for his team. I shuddered, reflexively shifting my hips around as my groin tried to hide from all the pain in the world.

"Ouch. Sorry, man."

"Stretching. It will save you every time, even when your hoop is spinning so fast your chest hair alights. Thank God I wax. Not everyone was so lucky, let me tell you. Anyway, have fun!"

And then he bailed on us, running over to join Keith's practice group.

"That little bastard. He ditched us!"

A strange voice cut in.

"You guys need help?"

What the hell! Long legs, bright eyes, round buttocks, pert . . . a girl! A cute naked girl! But that wasn't how it worked! Everybody knows that only guys and ugly old women do these nude things. Not hot chicks! I could hear Dustin in my head, leering, telling me how lucky I was that I got to see this girl naked. And she did look very nice. But that was not a good thing. Men and ugly women served a very important purpose. They made sure I never got too . . . excited. Because I was naked. And there were no secrets here.

Rat Boy gave me a concerned look.

"David, are you all right?"

She put a hand on my shoulder, concerned. Warning! Danger!

"Are you okay?"

I had to answer, even though all my mental energy was focused on picturing the moon landing and my father eating ribs.

"Sure. Just a cramp."

"Do you need a quick massage?"

"No!"

She pulled back at my yelp. I apologized.

"Sorry. Spasm. I'll be fine."

"Okay. I'm Eve."

Of course you are. If you're a naked girl, chances are your name is Eve.

"I'm David. This is Josh."

Rat Boy reached out genially, pumping her hand with nary a lecherous glint.

"Nice to meet you, Eve."

Did he have no testosterone in his body? How could he

be so nonchalant? I was dying over here. Rat Boy had moved on to asking Eve a question.

"I really like the choreography, but I'm not sure how the second part goes. Is it like this?"

He picked up his hula hoop and began to twirl. My God. The astonishments never cease. He was fantastic. The hoop spun around him like he'd been doing it all his life. He did a quick turn (causing me to leap back in case his oversized johnson swept my leg like in *The Karate Kid*) and finished. Edgar stepped up, clapping.

"Very nice. Very nice. See that people! That's natural talent! You didn't get the moves right, but you've seen it only once, right? Who'd expect you to? But the raw talent! Where did that come from? Don't tell me this is the first time you've picked up a hoop!"

Rat Boy kicked his foot into the ground, embarrassed.

"I used to hula hoop in camp. I guess I still have it."

"I guess you do. You have to be one of our regulars."

"I'll think about it."

Edgar slapped him on the back.

"You do that! Back to practice, people! Show's over!"

Eve clapped her hands.

"That was great, Josh! Don't you think so, David?"

I could barely answer, as the sight of her bouncing up and down in place had sent my mind scurrying for images of my grandfather putting on suntan lotion.

"Yep."

Josh lowered his head, pleased.

"Thanks. Though I want to get the choreography down."

Eve picked up her hoop.

"Watch me do it."

She put the hoop around her waist and gave it a quick spin. From that moment on, I was a goner.

What could I do? No amount of baseball players or lists of venereal diseases could hold back this assault. They all fell beneath the juggernaut of her naked breasts and her naked hips and her naked ass and her naked everything moving in circles, jiggling, all of it in constant motion. I could hold back no longer.

"David. You okay?"

Rat Boy stared at me, horrified. Eve turned to see what was the matter and she stopped, shocked. Edgar strode up.

"What's wrong with . . . oh, my dear lord! What do you think you're doing!"

Even Zach glanced up from his conversation with his crush, peering over to see what was the matter. He took one look and dropped his head in shame.

I guess there is a certain karmic justice to it all. On the night that I planned to shock and embarrass Annie into dumping her nude-loving fiancé, I was the one standing there, beet red, mortified beyond belief, as the entire Edgar Kraus Hula-Hoop Expression Troupe stared in sick fascination at my huge, obvious, unyielding erection.

Edgar turned me toward the mirror, for some reason deciding that the reflection of my huge, obvious, unyielding erection was better than the sight of the real thing. His haughty expression said it all.

"David! That's not the way we do things here!"

I could see people nodding in the mirror.

"I'm sorry."

"That's my daughter you're pointing at."

Oh great. Even better.

"I really am sorry."

"I think you should leave."

I turned and walked toward my clothes, my tail not yet between my legs, but nonetheless a beaten man. Edgar continued.

"Zach, I think you and your friend better leave as well. And don't bother to come back."

"That's not fair, Edgar. It's completely natural. You're just trying to get rid of me."

I turned back to see Zach, livid, up in Edgar's face. Edgar stammered.

"That's preposterous."

"Come on, be honest."

Edgar burst.

"You're a distraction! He's our best spinner. We need him. And we don't need you!"

"You can't just kick us out!"

"I'm in charge."

"Then I challenge you!"

A gasp went up. I guess you didn't just challenge Edgar. Edgar smirked.

"You must be joking."

"An endurance test."

"Well, since you're challenging my ruling to eject you and your friends, it'll have to be all three of you in the challenge."

Zach gave us a pleading look. I nodded.

"Of course."

Rat Boy didn't hesitate.

"I'll do my best. I don't want you kicked out."

Zach looked more pleased with Rat Boy's assistance than my own. We lined up in the middle of the room, our hula hoops at the ready. I glanced down, relieved. At least my erection had fled under the pressure. I would lose with dignity. Edgar stood to face us, flanked by an older guy with an extremely hairy ass and, directly across me from, Eve. My penis stirred, already comfortable with the pressure and ready to take another good look at the hottie across the way. I tried to focus on the hairy ass, which kept me in check. Edgar lifted his hoop.

"The last person left twirling wins for his team. Very simple. No tricks. Just plain old hula-hooping like our ancestors did. Tex here has been doing this since nineteen sixty-two, so don't think that he's the weak link. The weak links are all on your chain."

Zach sneered.

"We'll see about that, Edgar."

Keith took up position between us, a white handkerchief hanging from his fingers. He lifted it high into the air.

"Ready! Set!"

He shot a quick air smooch of good luck over to Zach before waving the handkerchief wildly.

"Go!"

And he dropped it, leaping back out of the way. With a furious twist, we spun the hoops around and were off.

First, let me say that I have never tried to hula hoop in my entire life, except for one instance in tenth grade, when I lost a bet and had to wear a wig while spinning the hoop around my hips and whistling the theme to *Eight Is Enough*. So my only association with the hula hoop did not engender me to success. But for my friend, I desperately tried to make a good showing of myself. For a while the hoop did stay up on my hips, amazingly enough. But my concentration began to slip soon after. Why, you might ask? Let's just say that Edgar placed his daughter across from me for a reason. Yes, despite all the pressure, the sight of her various body parts moving and shaking, twisting and gyrating, lifted my shame up again for all to see. The boner had returned, and there was nothing I could do about it.

Eve glanced down with distaste, quickly looking up and away. I tried staring at Tex's hairy ass, but my eyes would not be controlled. Eve's undulating bosom pulled me back like Michael Corleone into a life of crime. To make matters worse, I could feel my hoop slipping, heading south toward the ground. I would be the first casualty. I couldn't control the rapidly falling hoop, sending a swift mental apology to Zach for failing him. The hoop slipped off my hips and I waited to hear the clatter of plastic hitting the floor.

It never came.

Confused, I took a look down to see what had happened. To my amazement, the hoop still twirled right below my hips, unable to fall past my big ol' erection. It held it up like a pointy roadblock, a stiff barrier between the hoop and the ground. Immediately, I focused my attention back on Eve's bouncing body. I knew a good cheat when I found one. And this might just win the day.

When he saw me still in the game, Edgar began to show small signs of worry. He glanced down, blanching when he caught sight of my helping hand, but there was nothing he could do. His body shook, slabs of fat rising and falling like the ocean during a storm, as he struggled to keep his hoop aloft. Feeling a small softening at the sight, I quickly turned my attention back to the sexy girl in front of me. I knew my method and I would stick to it.

To my surprise, Zach was actually the first one to fall. I heard the clatter and risked a look, watching him pick up his fallen hula hoop with his face full of embarrassment and worry. He shouted encouragement.

"You're doing great, guys. Don't worry!"

But I could tell he was worried. I focused on one of Eve's breasts, which seemed to be hypnotizing me. I didn't want to let him down.

Tex fell next, to my relief. The thought of his hairy ass had loomed as a real obstacle for my chubby. Now it was just the four of us. Edgar was sweating, his big meaty hips rotating like a pig on a spit. Rat Boy didn't seem to be slowing down. He just kept moving, his hips gyrating at a steady pace. But I couldn't rely on him. I was the one with the magical erection. I had to stay strong for all of us.

Edgar's face took on a calculating look. He whispered softly to his daughter, too soft for me to hear. But I knew something was up when Eve suddenly missed a beat, her hoop clattering to the floor.

"Oh shit. I guess I'm out. It's up to you, Dad."

And she picked up her hoop (which was nice, don't get me wrong) and walked out of my line of sight. Not sure what to do, I glanced over at Edgar. His huge man tits spun in a grotesque imitation of his daughter's beautiful motions. His pudgy arms, held out like he wanted to hug me, vibrated, displaying an urgent need for arm cream. And worst of all, his small, hooded man serpent flung back and forth like a burrito caught in the jaws of a ravenous dog. I couldn't help it. All the odds were stacked against me. I felt everything fall down.

Clatter.

Defeated, I bent over to pick up my fallen hoop. Edgar's face was awash in triumph, and he shook his fist in the air. Unfortunately, this threw off his rhythm, and as if in slow motion, his face turned from elation to horror. His hoop began to spin wildly out of control, a wheel off its axle, and before he could do a thing about it, the circle of bright plastic sank down below his hips and to the floor. Rat Boy calmly completed three more revolutions before stopping his hoop with his hand.

We'd won. And it had been Rat Boy who saved the day.

During the ensuing celebration (no one was particularly fond of Edgar and most of the troupe relished his defeat), Zach sidled up next to me and whispered in my ear.

"I can't help you anymore with this. It was a satisfying diversion for a time, but now I owe him. You understand, right?"

I nodded helplessly as he danced off to cover Rat Boy in thank-yous. As I watched him fawn over the lucky bastard—it had to be luck; the guy has the hips of a ten-year-old; it could only be luck—I felt cold jealousy gnaw at my belly. First he steals Annie, now he digs in with the one friend I could say was mostly mine. Would it never stop?

"Josh?"

The victory celebration clanged to a halt as Rat Boy turned to see Annie standing in the doorway, her horrified face taking in all the sweaty nudity. I quickly ran for the corner before she could see me, too. She stepped up to Rat Boy, trying not to look at all the bared skin surrounding them.

"Josh, you promised."

Rat Boy couldn't say a word. He looked over at Zach, trapped. Zach gave him a look of profound pity. He opened his mouth, probably to spill the beans and ruin our whole plan as some sort of restitution, but he never got a chance. Annie spun in place and ran out. Mission accomplished. As Rat Boy struggled to put his clothes on to run after her, I tried to feel triumph. But nothing came.

Chapter Eighteen

The Princess and the Serf

I trudged home, haunted by the look on Annie's face. I did that. I put that look on her face. Why? Why did I need to go to such an extreme? Didn't she deserve to be happy? I shook my shoulders, trying to dislodge those self-defeating thoughts. What was the big deal, anyway? It wasn't like I tried to set Rat Boy up with a woman or anything. It was just a little harmless nudity. Just a symptom of a bigger problem.

Why is it so wrong to want people to go on being the people I knew them to be? Everything wobbled out of control around me. My computer screen intimidated me, my mailbox mocked me with rejection after rejection, my entire plan for happiness hinged on some unknown person out in the ether approving of me. I had no control. I just wanted a little control. Some things in life should happen the way they're scripted. Otherwise we'd go crazy waiting on unfulfilled expectations. I had a right to my expectations. Without them I'm stuck in Space Mountain, rocketing around on a roller coaster in the dark, never knowing when the next violent turn will strike. I needed to see where I was going.

My cell rang, as I knew it would.

"Annie. Are you okay?"

"I told him! I specifically told him! I don't ask him for anything! I just didn't like the idea of my fiancé parading around naked! That's all! Why is that so much? I'm uncomfortable with it and I told him. Why am I even bothering with this if he won't listen to me?"

Her thought process followed my trail of bread crumbs to perfection.

"Where are you?"

"I'm on a train heading up to Cameron's. I need to get out of the city tonight. I'll deal with Josh tomorrow, when I can think about it rationally. I knew I shouldn't trust Zach! But how could he know? Fuck! Did you know, David?"

Did I think I could get off scot-free? She'd figure it out at some point. I couldn't hide my involvement forever. But what should I say? I had no idea. Thankfully, my call waiting beeped, informing me that Janey waited on the other line.

"Could you hold on a sec, Annie? Sorry, it's Janey."

She indicated her impatient approval and I clicked over.

"Janey?"

"Can you come over?"

I could hear hysteria lingering on the outskirts of her voice.

"Are you all right?"

"Can you?"

"Of course. I'll be there as soon as I can. Are you okay?"

"Just come over, please."

She hung up. I clicked back over, stunned.

"Annie, I've got to go. There's something wrong with Janey. I'll give you a call later, I promise."

"Is she all right?"

"I don't know."

"Then go. We'll talk later."

She hung up, leaving me to hail a cab frantically, almost getting run down by a delivery van as I shot out into the street with my arm raised. Fifteen minutes later, the taxi dropped me off in Williamsburg, Brooklyn. I'd never actually visited Janey in her apartment, though I'd walked her to the door. I got the feeling she felt more embarrassed about her place than I did about mine, if that was possible. I rushed up to her buzzer and pushed, holding it down until the front door clicked and I could get in.

She waited for me at her open apartment door, her face streaked with tears. I gathered her in immediately, brushing my lips against her hair.

"Hey, it's okay. What's wrong?"

She didn't answer, clutching at me. I moved the two of us inside, closing the door behind us. Looking around, I took in her embarrassing apartment. A one bedroom. Motherfucker. Her embarrassing apartment was bigger than mine. Tastefully decorated with nice prints on the walls and sparse but well-arranged furniture in the living room, the entire place made my studio look like a shithole. I had no time for jealousy, however, as I held her close.

"Hey. Hey, come on Janey. Tell me what's wrong."

She finally answered me, swallowing her emotion.

"I'm sorry to sound like such a crazy person on the phone. I'm just trying not to handle this the way I usually handle it, so I'm kinda fragile."

"It's okay."

"I'm not some emotionally bent loser who needs to be

constantly reassured or anything. I just needed to hug a sane person. Someone who isn't related to me in any way, shape or form."

She was rambling, obviously off-kilter. I delved.

"What happened? Is it your dad?"

She took a deep breath and looked up at me. Her voice came out calm but her eyes refused to back it up.

"My mom. She's crazy."

That seemed to be a theme lately. Thank God for my sane, perfect, saintly mother.

"What did she do?"

"It's so stupid. I don't even know why I'm getting so bent out of shape."

"Let's sit."

So we sat. And gradually it came out.

"She called to talk about my father. Ever since the divorce, which has been a while, she's had this need to make me choose sides. It's ridiculous. She always has to be the good guy and he always has to be the bad guy. It never stops. And then, for some reason, she calls me up and starts in on how crazy he's gotten about my refusing his money. How guilty it makes him. So according to her, he's plotting to get me to move back home and go back to law school. She doesn't know how yet, but she knows it's underhanded. Where she's getting this, I have no idea. Sure, he's not exactly happy with me, but come on. This is conspiracy stuff. He's not like that. Hell, we're having dinner next week. Finally things are getting better and she can sense it, so here she is trying to fuck it all up with her crazy delusions. The whole thing is like something from *Melrose Place.* Everyone's trying to destroy each other. So I yelled and she yelled and we called each other horrible names until we hung up on each other and then I called you. My safety rope to normal."

Her eyes teared up and she pulled my arms around her, tight. She needed me so much, it frightened me. There was nothing I could say. All I could do was wrap my arms around her and not let go. I felt lost, out of my depth, completely unprepared to handle the woman clutching me. Her pain ran deep, much deeper than I could ever reach. I was useless to her. A bad ex-boyfriend I could replace, but her family? That would never get better, not without a lot of work. What was I signing on for here?

Eventually she regained control of herself. She buried her head in my shoulder.

"You know something funny?"

"What?"

"A month ago I would have been lying on that floor, dead drunk, beating my fists into the wood until my downstairs neighbor started pounding through the floor. But tonight, I didn't. I wanted to, but I didn't. I needed you to be with me tonight."

"I didn't do anything."

She leaned up and kissed me, the salt tangy on her lips. I leaned in as she buried her face in mine. Her kiss seemed to breathe me in, to pull at me, needing me. After a long moment, she fell back, wiping her eyes with the back of her hand. I felt like a small piece of me went with her, slipping down her throat as she swallowed. She noticed something in my face.

"Are you okay?"

"Of course. I'm fine."

"You sure I didn't freak you out?"

She looked up at me so vulnerable, I had to lie.

"Of course not."

She was so beautiful and sad and defiant and needing that I had no idea what to feel. Part of me fell in love and another part ran screaming. I felt trapped between the two desires. Something would have to give. I pushed that thought from my brain, kissing her forehead repeatedly until she smiled and made me stop.

"Will you stay with me? Just, you know, sleeping. I don't want to be alone."

I stayed, lying awake next to her the entire night, encompassing her as she slept on her side, clutching my hand like a teddy bear. I tried to sleep, but my head kept falling forward into her long waves of hair, which filled my nostrils and left me gasping for air. So instead I stood watch, unable to sleep for fear of choking, listening to her breathe and wishing for morning.

* * *

I must have fallen asleep at some point, because I woke up to the sound of a woman frantically tearing apart her closets. Janey moved around her bedroom like the Tasmanian Devil, leaving T-shirts and jeans in her wake. I must have sat up in confusion rather noisily, as she looked over her shoulder at me.

"I knew it. I can't find it anywhere."

"Find what?"

"I thought the last time we had a blowout I picked it up, but I must have brought it back when we made up over Easter. Damn it, I'm not leaving it at her place another day."

"What are you talking about?"

"My BE COOL tee."

She tossed that off like it was the most normal thing in the world, like everyone including Tara Reid had one.

"What is a BE COOL tee?"

"My second favorite sleep T-shirt. I need to get it back today."

"From where?"

"My mom's place. When I first moved out, I left it in my old room to make my mom happy. It made her feel like I would be coming home, or something. But I won't be sleeping over anymore, so I'm not leaving it there. You want to come with me?"

Which is how I ended up getting out of a cab with Janey on the corner of Seventy-second and West End, staring up at one of the nicest luxury apartment buildings I'd ever seen. She had to tug at my hand to get me to move.

"Don't worry, she's not home; she's got club meetings all day. We won't be long."

She dragged me past the doorman, who welcomed her back, and to the gold-plated elevator. We reached the fifth floor and stepped out into a small alcove. The space looked exactly like someone's front stoop, including some flowers in the corner and an exact replica of a normal everyday front door with knocker and doorbell. Janey noticed my look and shrugged.

"My mom always missed the country. So she had it done up."

She fumbled in her purse for her keys as I looked around at the walls.

"Where are the other doors for this floor?"

"There aren't any. This elevator goes to my mom's door and the other elevator goes to Mr. and Mrs. Goetenburger's door. Here they are."

She pulled out her keys and unlocked the door.

"Welcome to home not so sweet home."

My soul suffered a small seizure as I entered Janey's childhood apartment. Everything New York in me screamed in protest at the sheer size of it. After all, it took up half the floor, the *floor,* of the building, with windows facing out in three directions. A balcony, small greenhouse, fireplace, digital cable: The place screamed opulence. I felt like I should genuflect before crossing the threshold, but Janey kicked me when I hit the floor.

"Don't be a smartass."

I guess she just didn't understand the racial peasant impulses that still lingered in my DNA. The only contact her ancestors had with my ancestors was when my ancestors would petition hers for fairer distribution of the sod. Invariably, justice would be done and my ancestors would proudly till their land with only slight nostalgia for their testicles. As Michael Moore will tell you, nobody likes a reformer.

Mom loved the Far East and she had most of it on the walls. Prints, wooden fans, ancient instruments and entire panda bears with bemused expressions covered the walls like 3-D wallpaper. Strange weapons familiar to kung fu movie enthusiasts stuck out from every corner, waiting to impale the poor bastards with inner-ear infections. The rugs were woven out of strange, exotic materials unknown to the common American floor owner, like straw and human skin. Everything about the place beat me down into my proper social place. Janey moved through this intimidating world in her Pogues T-shirt and ratty Converse sneakers five years past tattered.

"You want something to drink?"

"Water strained through the eyelashes of a young slave boy?"

"Gatorade?"

"Sounds good."

I sipped my bright red drink while Janey searched her bedroom for her wayward shirt. Her room seemed cozier, but still opulent. She had a huge four-poster bed and a large wooden armoire. Don't ask me how I knew it was an armoire, it just leaped into my head (it's amazing the weird shit that pops up in your brain for no good reason, and yet I keep forgetting my phone number). Black-and-white prints adorned the walls, sparse against the white paint. I leaned in to check out one, a close-up of a gnarled old man who looked like he'd been brushing his teeth with a vacuum cleaner.

"Who's this? Your dad?"

She glanced up from the armoire.

"No, that's an Avedon print. It's a limited edition. I'd steal it if it weren't worth more than the furniture."

A Richard Avedon portrait in the bedroom. All right. My dad had an animation cel of Pepé le Pew set against a cartoon Paris framed in my old bedroom. When you pressed a button, Pepé would bounce around and try to kiss the cat while music from the old cartoons leaked out of a speaker on the side. So I could relate.

"Here it is!"

She pulled out a faded old T-shirt; it looked older than she was.

"Wow, you hold on to stuff."

"Isn't it cute?"

She spread it out so I could see the design. Sure enough, it read BE COOL, except instead of the word "Be" it said "Bee" while a large smiling bee buzzed above wearing sunglasses and sipping a margarita. I could see why she had left it here. It really went with the Avedon.

On the way out, she stopped to stick my glass in the dishwasher while I dawdled by the mantel of a huge fireplace. An array of photos were spread out across the shelf, all of them of Janey: young Janey, smiling Janey, too cool to care teen Janey, Janey on horseback, Janey next to a smiling older woman with the same long hair who could only be her mom. Janey stepped up next to me to look over my shoulder.

"Ready to go?"

"She's got a lot of pictures of you."

"I know. See this one, with the two of us wearing the hula skirts? She cut out my dad. He used to be right here, where the frame is now. But now he's gone."

"But you're still here. You're everywhere."

"Can we get out of here? I don't want to be here anymore. Let's go to your apartment."

"After this place? Jesus, do you want to make me cry?"

"Come on, we'll get a little takeout, we'll watch some movies. It'll be fun."

There was no way I could say no to that, even if it did make my teeth hurt to think about my tiny room coming on the heels of her childhood mansion. Maybe I'd build a mantel over the radiator. It kept threatening to catch fire, so it could look pretty authentic.

* * *

We sat on my bed, eating dumplings with forks, while *When Harry Met Sally* played on the television. I knew most of the lines by heart, which began to annoy my poor ladyfriend.

"Will you shut the hell up and let the movie play? Man, it's like when people sing to the radio in the car and won't let you listen to the song."

"I sing to the radio."

"Well, no singing to the television. Hand me the soy sauce."

We kept sneaking glances at each other, as our knees tapped together lightly. We were feeling each other out. It's amazing how you can date someone for weeks, months even, and still know very little about what makes her tick. Janey must have been skipping down similar paths, because she poked my elbow with her fork.

"You know, I'd like to read your book."

The dumpling I'd been swallowing suddenly staged a sit-in halfway down my esophagus and refused to budge. I coughed, working to crush the agitator before I choked to death, and finally broke its resistance and sent it down to be dissolved and digested. Janey patted my back worriedly, as people often do in these situations for no apparent reason whatsoever. I smiled weakly.

"Sorry. Wrong pipe."

The worry faded, replaced by a wry smile as she detected my bullshit.

"Wrong sentence, more like. Why don't you want me to read your book?"

"You will read it. I'm just waiting to hear back from the last agent first."

"What does that have to do with anything? Does he have the only copy or something?"

"No. No, of course not. I just . . . I don't want people reading it if it sucks."

"I'm sure it doesn't suck."

"How can you be sure? People always say that, as if by looking at me they can tell if I can form a snappy sentence or not. Because I'm a nice guy I must be a good writer? Some of the worst people in the world were great writers. Alexandre Dumas? Awful person. Kicked puppies. Well-documented fact. And even that isn't a good indicator. Some of the worst people in the world were shitty writers, too. Hitler was a terrible writer. Sappy as all hell. The point? You can't tell."

"Wow. So when are you gonna give me a copy?"

"I don't feel comfortable enough."

"Oh, I'm sorry. Is your book a level-five secret?"

She will never let that go.

"Someday, I swear."

"Even if I hate it, I won't care. It has nothing to do with you as a person. Though I won't hate it."

"It has everything to do with me as a person. How can you be with someone you don't respect?"

"This is stupid. If you believe in your book enough to quit your job and send it to all those agents, then you should believe in it enough to let me take a peek. Come on."

"One day, I will. Really. Just not now."

I wasn't hiding anything from her. I really didn't want her to judge my book. And there was no way to win. If she says she doesn't like it, I'm devastated. If she says she does like it, I don't believe her, sure that she's just being a good girlfriend. Either way I'm a mess. She sighed with frustration.

"You're going to have to open up, just a little, you know that, right? Maybe after I've taken a bullet for you or something. I'll be bleeding to death on the ground and you'll lean over and whisper that your mother never really hugged you as a child. And as my sight dims to black the last words I'll ever hear is how you're finally ready to tell people we're dating."

"I'll make sure to read you a chapter of my masterpiece before you pass on."

"You're a prince."

"I tell people we're dating."

"I'm flattered beyond words."

We watched Billy Crystal tell Meg Ryan that she was the dog in this scenario. After a moment, Janey brushed her lips against my arm.

"I'm sorry. It's just that I've been open with you, letting you see stuff most people don't see. It's made me a little vulnerable. And I've barely even met your friends."

"Look, why don't you come to my mom's gallery opening next Friday? You can meet my parents. So, no pressure."

She gravely accepted my peace offering.

"I would love to come. I have my dinner with my father that night, but I'll swing by afterward."

I thought about the painting on display and added a caveat.

"No mocking the portrait. That's my condition."

Her eyes fluttered innocently.

"Why would I do that? From what you've told me, it looks just like you."

"It's a little . . . less than manly. Just be nice."

"Of course. Anyway, you have nothing to worry about. You are very manly."

I shook my head.

"Yeah, right."

"I don't understand why you're so worried about being manly. It's such a silly thing to obsess over."

"I don't obsess."

"Yes you do. Come on, there must be a reason. What is it?"

How could I explain the fear of failure, the testicle-chopping terror of being rendered an impotent loser? I guess I could go back to the source. After all, I owed her something.

"All right. I'm going to tell you a story that only my closest friends know. It's horribly embarrassing, which is why I never tell it. But I'll tell you. If you promise to keep it to yourself."

Her eyes shone.

"Of course."

So I proceeded to recount the tale I never wanted to tell anyone, that both Annie and I have struggled to bury. Of how my adolescent ass kickings ended for good, and how true and clueless a friend Annie could be.

The Story of the End of My Adolescent Ass Kickings

The story of how my beatings finally came to an end starts with the chocolate strike. Everyone knew about it, my big stand against the crime that was teenage acne, and kids would often stop me to comment on how the fight was going. I basked in the attention, even as I squirmed under the "I don't see any difference" comments that inevitably followed. And trust me, it wasn't easy not to give in and cheat. I loved chocolate. I will go so far as to say I needed it, chemically, like a crackhead needs his stash or Oprah needs self-help books. So how did I manage? Well, grand gestures always prompted me to rise to the occasion. Because zits and the idea of zits made me desperately unhappy and I wanted to be happy, I quit cold turkey. I simply put down the M&Ms and never looked back.

I really should have expected what happened. After all, there's nothing people hate more than someone putting a positive spin on an affliction they should be humiliated over. Especially when you're as obnoxious as I could be. So I should have seen it coming. But I didn't. And I paid for it.

The day my beatings came to an end, I was walking behind the school on the small path that led down to the performing arts center. Play auditions loomed in a few days and I wanted to try out my monologue on the actual stage. The Manville Performing Arts Center was designed by our only famous alum, architect Kenneth Parks, and thus the acoustics were absolutely perfect. If I spoke loud enough, I'd hear myself coming back at divine levels of amplification. It made me feel like God, or a wrestling announcer. Unfortunately, in front of me stood a small hiccup in my plans in the persons of Jimmy Esposito's older brother Danny and his lumbering friend Big Ted. Neither of them was too bright, which actually worked against me. My mouth got me into much more trouble when the objects of my smart-ass-itude didn't understand what the hell I was talking about. Danny was waving a large brownie in front of him.

"Davey! I was just looking for you, you know?"

"Hey guys."

I looked around warily, trying to figure out some sort of plan. Big Ted had fists the size of my skull and as everybody knew, Danny fought dirty. I could try to run, and had just resolved to do so when a shadow fell upon my back.

"Hey, Davey."

Little Jimmy Esposito, all growed up from the third grader who introduced me to ass whuppin's and yet still the same height, stepped up behind me. There went the escape route.

"Hey Jimmy. Wow, the gang's all here. You guys trying out for the play, too?"

Danny smiled and shook his head.

"Nah, we're not pussies. Not like you."

Jimmy bumped into me, hard.

"Yeah, fucking pussy."

I don't know if you've picked up how deficient my sense of self-preservation was, but my next move should bring you up to speed.

"Wow, Jimmy. You think *I'm* a pussy? The girls must love your grasp of anatomy."

"Shut up, asshole."

"Am I pussy, am I an asshole? You're fine either way, right? I'm all your dreams, rolled up in one."

Jimmy kicked my knee, sending me to the ground. Danny stepped up, holding out his brownie while Big Ted looked over his shoulder, grinning like a crazy person.

"I heard about your little bet or whatever. No chocolate, ever. What a stupid bet."

Big Ted snorted.

"Yeah."

I kept up my bravado.

"It's not a bet, it's a lifestyle choice."

Jimmy grabbed the back of my neck as Danny leaned in.

"It's fucking stupid. And you're about to lose your stupid bet. Open his mouth."

Jimmy pulled open my jaw. I tried to fight, but Big Ted reached down and grabbed my shoulders, holding me firmly in place. I was helpless. Danny held out the brownie, waving it in front of my face.

"I'm gonna finally shut you up."

He started to shove the brownie into my open mouth. Reflexively, I tried to chew, but Jimmy's grip on my jaw kept me from biting down. Suddenly, I realized that if I couldn't chew, I would choke. And who knew if they'd let go. It was all probably a big joke to them, up until I lay purple on the ground. We were all kids, after all. Kids are invincible. Except we aren't. And it would take my death to prove it to Danny and Jimmy and ol' Big Ted.

"Stop that, you assholes!"

Abruptly the hand on my jaw disappeared and I fell to the ground, spitting out chocolate and taking big gulps of air. Turning over, I saw Annie staring down my three tormenters, one of her little followers standing meekly behind her. Annie attracted a specific sort of girl to her. They're all damaged in some way, either physically or mentally or emotionally. At any one time she'd have up to four or five followers trailing after her. They never hung with us. When she'd show up at our corner of the hall, they'd melt back into the crowd. We never made fun of her for attracting these girls to her. Probably because in the backs of our minds, we wondered what that said about us.

Annie's eyes burned into the bigger boys.

"You assholes were choking him."

Jimmy sneered.

"We were just giving him a little chocolate."

Annie's jaw hardened.

"You think this is funny, numbnuts? You think you're badass? You wouldn't have been laughing so hard when the police were questioning why you choked a kid to death with a brownie."

Big Ted shrugged sheepishly.

"He's okay. It's just a joke."

"We'll see how funny it is."

Danny's eyes glittered dangerously.

"You're not gonna say nothing, right? I'd hate to have to feed you, too."

He stepped forward. Annie's follower shrank back, but Annie never budged.

"You threatening me?"

"I don't threat, I promise."

I really think Danny was about to take her down. Sure, she was a girl, but those things didn't really matter to Danny. But then Annie opened her mouth and unleashed the fury.

"You have the balls to threaten me, fuckface? You have the stones to lean into me? You have no balls, ass-tickler. None! They're withered little boy sacks, half sucked up into your little girl pelvis. You are all such cock-gobbling goat fuckers. Threatening a fucking girl! You twat monkeys don't have the sacks so just turn around and walk away."

On and on it went. None of us had ever heard such profanity. And it flowed out of her mouth like she'd written it down the night before. Like it was the monologue she'd memorized for her audition. I'd never heard her curse before, and the sheer volume and creativity of the swears surprised even me. By all rights, Danny should have just pushed her or smacked her or something. But he couldn't believe it. None of them could. They were in the presence of a profane master and they could only bow their heads to the symphony. Before Annie could finish, they'd already turned tail and run.

There was nothing more embarrassing than being reamed out by a girl who knew more dirty words than you did. They never bothered me again. I think I reminded them of their humiliation, and they had no wish to revisit the memory. In fact, somehow word must have spread, because no one ever bothered me again. They all must have feared Annie's mouth just around the corner, waiting to tear them a new one. By the time Annie sputtered to a halt, the long era of my ass kickings had drawn to a close.

And how did I feel? Proud, happy, grateful? Of course not. Annie had just used my weapon against my tormentors far more effectively than I ever could. Humiliated, castrated, belittled; those were the emotions rushing through me as I lay on the ground, brown chocolate smudged over my mouth and cheeks like so much shit. So as she reached out and asked me if I was okay, I pushed away her hand, without noticing its tremble.

"I had them, you know."

Annie's eyebrow rose.

"Did you."

"We were just fooling around. I was fine. You didn't have to come barging in."

I dragged myself to my feet and wiped the last remnants of brownie from my lips sullenly while trying not to cry like the weakling she'd transformed me into. I glanced over at Annie just in time to see the fist rocket toward my eye.

Smack!

I staggered back. Annie waved the hand that had just slammed into my eyesocket like she'd broken a knuckle, wincing in pain. I whimpered.

"What the hell was that for?"

"What do you think?"

Rubbing my stinging eye, I stared back resentfully. That's when I noticed that she was shaking visibly, her cheeks red. She'd been terrified the whole time. I felt even smaller than before. I guess the Hollywood version of this would have had me rushing over and giving her a huge hug in gratitude and understanding of what she did for me. But Hollywood doesn't remember thirteen all that well. The best I could manage was a sheepish look at my shoes.

"I'll get your back next time."

She nodded.

"I know you will."

Her follower stepped up meekly and handed Annie her dropped textbooks and we headed on through our day. No one bothered me again. My freshman yearbook picture sports a pretty shiner, much more noticeable than any zit, which I could never look at without mixed emotions. I'll be forever grateful to Annie for what she did, but it had to remain a secret because it hurt so damn much. Some things are too hard to face up to. But I'd learned a valuable lesson. Sometimes you need to be saved from yourself.

* * *

I finished my story and refused to meet Janey's eye. I felt wet nuzzling on my neck.

"It takes a man to admit he needs saving."

And she pushed me down, knocking the dumplings to the floor as she kissed me hard and hungry. The television sputtered on as Billy Crystal kissed Meg Ryan on New Year's Eve, but I didn't pay any attention to those last well-remembered lines. I was busy, after all.

* * *

There comes a point when you're making love that you realize something more is going on. I wish I could chalk it up to chemistry or pheromones or something just as scientific, because then I could dismiss it. I wouldn't be beholden to it. But when your heart starts to pound and your shoulders shake and you want to clutch her so tightly there's a real danger of popping her head from her shoulders, then you have to admit that you're not simply horny. You're not so excited to be inside a vagina that the very thought of it makes your eyes roll back in your head. I'm almost thirty years old. I've been inside a few vaginas before, not as many as I tell my friends, but enough to know what it should feel like. It feels nice, I won't lie, and the more expertly she moves her hips and flips her hair and grabs my neck, the nicer I feel. But this other feeling, this overwhelming urge to hold her so tight she sinks into me, this need to laugh as we move, to smile as we kiss, to whisper forbidden words in her ear (not nasty, inciting words, but gushing, declaring words), this feeling is so much more dangerous than the need to push in and out until it's over. That need dissolves like sugar in rain after the final thrust, disappearing until the next storm. And after it's gone, you feel a little uncomfortable, a little hollow, because once the need seeps away, you're just left with mild embarrassment as you wonder what came over you. The memory of the desire fades and you can no longer recall why you needed so much. Why you acted the way you did and said the things you said. Once the need seeps away, you're left with less than nothing, like a balloon stretched out until it's full of air, then let loose to release the oxygen within, leaving it emptier than before. And for a moment, you don't know why you would ever do this to yourself. Why fill yourself up if you're only going to be emptier at the finish? But you get up and you leave and hours or days pass and that memory fades as well, until the desire takes over, overruling common sense, needing to move in and out again, needing the storm. You can write yourself a note, or tattoo it on your chest like the guy in *Memento,* but it won't mean a thing. Not unless you're very strong, or very wise, or your testicles get caught in your zipper, taking the entire argument out of your hands. I've told myself to ignore my desire, to remember the empty balloon, but too often I sucker punch myself into silence. Only one thing has ever saved me. I was riding in a cab with this girl I'd just met, heading toward emptiness, when she grabbed my hand and held it. The feeling of holding someone's hand doesn't communicate with my desire. It is wired directly into my happiness, my feeling of well-being. Holding someone's hand is not sex, it's comfort. Holding this strange woman's hand made me feel emptier than a thousand meaningless stormy nights. I never made it to her apartment. So ever since, I grab the girl's hand, just to see. If I think of it. If I want to think of it.

As I've mentioned, I've been in love once in my life. It ended badly (sparking an entire book on my part, so it could have been worse, I guess), but while it lasted, it meant everything. So I could recognize certain warning signs. They weren't exactly the same, much to my relief. The last thing I would ever want would be to feel the same thing twice. But I could pick out certain symptoms. So when Janey began to kiss me, as I pulled her onto the bed, and we began to shed clothing as easy as we'd blow dust off a mantel, I did receive a jolt of recognition. Very slight, just enough to give me pause for a brief moment before the wave of more familiar desire overtook me. Then, when I entered her, so agonizingly slow, I felt it again, something familiar and yet so new it scared me. As we picked up speed, wrapping around each other until our skin grew moist with the heat, I marveled at how good it felt, this first time, even though we fumbled a bit and took a while to agree on a rhythm. The gaps in our technique were filled by something else. But the real kicker came after that last moment, that big finale, when the final firework winked out. I collapsed onto her as she held me close, and I didn't want to leave. I wanted to stay above her, stay inside her, to stay. Somehow the balloon never opened and the air never came hissing out. The need never faded. A part of me wanted the need to fade away. It can hurt to need so much, all the time. It can hurt to stay full. It scared me, because once you feel like this, you can never completely let it all go, not even if everything goes horribly wrong and you never see her again. Something will always stay caught inside you. Love may not always last, but it is permanent all the same, like the long-healed wound that still twinges when rain approaches. You may look the same as when you were new, but you are altered forever. She smiled as we kissed. I liked how her smooth teeth felt on my lips. She opened her mouth as I retreated from the kiss.

"Hi."

I kissed her forehead in reply. She giggled.

"Low."

I kissed her chin.

"Middle."

I kissed her mouth. Her eyes opened wide as I pulled back,

her lips sliding apart to uncover two teeth biting into her skin. She looked up at me like a delicate, helpless child.

"You take direction well."

I laughed at the compliment.

"It's a gift. You're sexy."

"You're sexy."

"You're shiny, too."

"And slippery. I'm a lot of things right now."

"Like what?"

She turned over in bed, stretching luxuriously as she answered me.

"Oh, lots of things. Sleepy, happy."

"You're happy?"

She suddenly looked scared at my question, like she'd leaned out too far without holding on to the railing.

"Aren't you happy?"

"I'm very happy."

She relaxed as I leaned down to kiss her. I was happy. Comfortably happy. I still didn't want to pull away so I kissed her mouth, slipping my tongue inside, feeling a stir of excitement when her tongue answered mine. She giggled as I licked her lips, then fell silent for a moment, her smile fading slightly.

"You're not sorry, about any of this?"

"Not even a little."

"You're not scared?"

"Maybe a little."

"Me too. I like you a lot."

"I like you, too. You're sexy."

Her eyes closed slightly at my light tone.

"Is that all?"

"You're funny and smart, too. Didn't I mention that?"

"You better."

"I should probably pull out."

"You probably should."

But I didn't. I lay down on her slick, perfect breasts and closed my eyes. This felt far too good. I could remember how badly it turned out last time. It could be worse, this time. I wanted a happy that didn't turn sour. But how could I tell? Only with time. I had to be smart, keeping my eyes out for warning signs before I sank too deep into this. I'd been buried before. I would be sure to take my time, not just fall in love, but rather manage more of a controlled descent. But for now, I'd rest here, within her. I'd have to pull out some time, I knew. Just not right then. Right then, I'd enjoy what I had while it lasted.

* * *

A bee danced up to my face, darting around me as I tried to avoid the stinger. But I moved through rich, thick syrup, unable to dodge the assailant, and the sting blossomed right on my ass as the bee whispered in my ear.

"Your door is buzzing."

I blinked, coming out of my dream fuzzy and unprepared to react. The room had lightened, the morning peeking in through the blinds. Janey lay next to me, her pillow firmly over her head, trying to block out the incessant buzzing that rang throughout the apartment while pinching my ass with irritated fingers. I heard a muffled banging on my wall from my next-door neighbor. Stands to reason, if I can hear him watching porn, he can hear my door buzzer. I stumbled out of bed, landing on the floor.

"It won't stop. David, make it go away!"

"I'm trying."

I crawled across my floor, eyes still three-quarters shut, trying to find my way from memory. I slid over some crumbled plaster, the remnants of another failed murder attempt during the night. Feeling around blindly for the intercom, I turned on the faucet.

"David! Could you get me some water, while you're up?"

"Sure."

I used the fridge handle to pull myself upright, opening it once I made it safely to my feet.

"Brita okay by you?"

"Sounds wonderful. You should get the door though."

Other neighbors had joined in on the banging, making a sound not unlike elephants in a conga line. I opened my eyes wide enough to locate the button, pushing down to unlock the downstairs door. The buzzing stopped, prompting mock applause to ring throughout the building. I lay my head on the door, listening to the footsteps make their way up the stairs. Finally, a knock sounded on the other side of the wood. Without checking, too tired to look through the tiny hole, I opened the door to admit an Annie far more crazed than any amount of arm cream could account for.

"If you want me to say you were right, you will be waiting a long time."

I yawned.

"You came out here to tell me that?"

She was a mess, her eyes alight with some ferocious inner fire. She pulled up when she caught sight of Janey.

"Um. Hello."

Janey sat up, holding the covers to her chest.

"Hi."

Thrown for a moment, Annie turned, recovering nicely.

"Okay, there have been setbacks. He's still got a jones for nudity. Okay. And maybe I'm not little miss homemaker yet, either."

"What do you mean, yet? You never will be."

She cut me off.

"That's not the point. The point is I love him. Not why I love him or how I love him. Just that I love him. I'm happier with him than without him. You think I can't change, I can tell. All of you do."

I tried to head her off before she got too far.

"Of course you *can* change. But that doesn't mean you should."

"It's not about what I should do or what I want. It's about what I need. And I need him."

Great. So she still hasn't seen the light. Well, maybe the doubts need more time to blossom. After all, we have a little time. I sat down calmly.

"So you came over to tell me that?"

She sighed.

"No. I was up the other night, all night, worrying about losing him. And then Josh came out to see me at Cameron's yesterday and it felt so good to make up. It felt so right. So I've decided I need to push up the wedding."

My calm blew apart.

"What? Are you insane! You've been dating a few months!"

"I want to be his wife. I don't want to lose him because of stupid self-serving shit. So the quicker it's official, the sooner I can settle down and be happy."

I sprang to my feet, gesturing wildly as I sputtered.

"He won't make you happy!"

"You know that, huh? You're a wizard who can peer into my brain? Get off your high horse! You don't know what will make me happy!"

"Yes I do! You need sarcasm and wit and interesting conversation. You need so much more than he can ever give you!"

Now she was the one to speak calmly.

"Come on, be real. This has nothing to do with him. This is about you, David. You're afraid I'm changing into someone you don't know. You're afraid I'll be happiest with you out of my life. I mean, it makes sense, right? If I'm trying to leave all that negative behavior behind, and that's the behavior you value, then aren't I really rejecting you? Isn't that what this is all about?"

I sat down heavily under her words. I had nowhere else to go. Janey sat silent up against the wall, trying to make herself invisible. So what? So maybe I wanted to place the people in my life back into the slots where they made me happiest. They'd always been happy there, too. Why was I such a bad person for wanting people to stay where I knew we all fit together so well? We'd tested the arrangement for fifteen years, we knew what worked. I answered her quietly, tired of shouting.

"But aren't you? Aren't you rejecting me when you reject everything that held us together for so long?"

She shook her head at my wounded tone.

"If that's what you think held us together, you don't have any right to tell me about happiness. You don't know the first thing about it."

Her self-righteous assumptions burned me. She didn't know anything about what I'd been going through the last year. She didn't know anything. I pushed my anger aside as I tried to get through to her.

"Look, Annie, you may not want to admit it, but I know you. Not many people know you better than I do. And okay, I don't know who you are when you're around Josh, and why you feel the need to be this new woman. But I know who you've been. And the woman I knew would never be satisfied with this relationship. Maybe I'm wrong, I'll admit it. But you're not even stopping to think about it. You're not even considering the possibility."

She leaned back against my door, her face suddenly sad.

"I hope someday you find something you want to be worthy of. Something you're willing to change for. There's nothing for me to consider. I almost pushed Josh away over something so stupid I can't even bear to think about it. When he came up to Cameron's last night, I didn't even want to see him. But he talked to me and explained how hard it is to compromise sometimes and I understood that. I live that. It seems the longer I'm back here in my old life the harder our relationship gets, and it's because I feel this pull back into my old ways. I need help fighting it. I need everyone to realize that this is not going away. That's why I'm pushing up the wedding. There are too many distractions, with you and my crazy family and everything, and I need to get back to the purity I felt in Phoenix. So it's gonna be this month. I don't need it to be huge, I just need it to be. I can get the basement of the church in Hartsdale, I know I can. That's been my church since I was four. All the people who can't rearrange their schedules don't deserve to come. So I came here to ask for your help. Can you get me a DJ?"

"Of course not! This is crazy!"

"Please, David. It's going to happen. I need your help."

I didn't answer right away, staring at her sullenly. What could I do? I could scream and cajole and try to point out every mistake, but I couldn't turn my back on her. My words came out flat.

"I'll give Jeremy a call at work. I'll see if someone's available. Which day should I tell him?"

"I'm not sure yet."

Janey shifted, inserting herself into the conversation.

"Do you have a caterer?"

Annie turned, startled, to answer her.

"We can do potluck."

Janey smiled.

"Rialto had a cancellation for two weeks from Friday. I'll bet I can get him for you."

I gave her an incredulous look. Why was she getting involved? Annie's eyes welled up.

"Would you do that?"

"Sure."

Annie gave her a big hug, startling the hell out of her.

"Thank you! You have to come!"

Janey glanced at me.

"I'd love to."

Annie dried her eyes with her hands. I sat defeated, apart from both of them.

"Please don't ignore what I'm saying. Don't turn yourself into someone you're not just because you're afraid."

She gave me a look of pity that twisted my soul.

"I'm not afraid, David. I've found what makes me happy. If I don't change for that, I'd deserve feeling lost like I did in Phoenix. Who would want that?"

But what if she can't change? She never seemed to face that fact. All the wishing in the world doesn't always make it so. But I said nothing. I had no ground to stand on.

After she left, Janey and I sat in silence for a bit. Eventually I spoke.

"There has to be something I can do."

Janey sighed.

"David . . ."

"Something. Maybe . . . maybe I should call Jacob. He's in that punk band now, the Fuck Annies. Maybe I can take Rat Boy to see their show, show him the kind of guy Annie usually dates. He's got, like, eighteen piercings. That should intimidate him. I just have to make sure they don't actually talk. If he ever finds out Jacob once wrote Annie a poem about bluebirds, all the tattoos in the world wouldn't cover it up. But from long distance it should send a message, right?"

"David, come on . . ."

I steamrolled over her.

"Maybe I can introduce him to Annie's aunts! They'd eat him alive, like a human sausage and pepper hero. There's got to be some way—"

"David!"

Janey grabbed my arm and I sputtered out.

"What?"

She gave me a serious, searching look.

"Do you have a thing for Annie?"

I was thrown. What? A thing for Annie? Was she nuts? I was too shocked to actually answer, so she continued on.

"I can't figure it out, otherwise. Why are you going to such lengths to break them up? It's over the top."

I regained my voice.

"It's not just me. Cameron and Dustin are doing it, too."

"And yet they never seem to be leading the charge. You're always the one pushing and pushing. I keep telling myself it's because you're such good friends, but you're not stopping. So the only answer I can come up with is that you have a thing for her."

That was crazy. I'd known Annie for fifteen years. We grew up together. Can't a guy have a platonic friend? Is this Victorian England?

"Janey, come on. That's ridiculous."

She didn't look mollified. If anything, her eyes seemed even more uncertain.

"Never? Not in all the years you guys hung out? She's not ugly, you know."

"I know. It's just . . . some things aren't meant to be, you know?"

She sat back against the wall, looking at me, not saying a word. I took her hand.

"Here's the deal. She asked me out when we first met, but it didn't work. We never clicked that way."

"Then why are you going crazy? She's happy, she's finally got her life together, you should be happy for her. Instead you're running around like a Bond villain. Why would you go to all this trouble if you didn't have some sort of feelings there?"

I thought of Annie in her doorway, her new blond hair

falling into her face. She'd looked brand-new, like someone I hadn't met before. Did I feel something?

"I don't have feelings for her like that. I promise. We're just good friends."

Janey didn't look convinced.

"Okay."

Why did everything have to be romantic? Why couldn't I just be afraid of losing a friend? Isn't that catastrophic enough? Lifelong friends are rare, and I refused to let go without a fight. I refused to be left behind. How could I explain that to her if all she understood was a guy hung up on a girl? How could I get her to see that it was change that was the enemy, change being forced upon me against my will. As I got older my life picked up speed like a river nearing the waterfall and as I drifted down it I could feel myself losing control over what I could hold on to. If I waited too long I'd be stuck with whatever my failing hands could curl around. That was so much more frightening than losing out on a crush. That was worth a little crazy behavior.

She didn't believe me, I could tell. She'd pulled her hand away and sat staring at me from the corner, like she had no idea who I was. I didn't want our weekend to end this way. So I reached down under my bed and pulled out a large sheaf of papers. Wordlessly I handed it over to Janey. She peered at the first page.

"This is your book. I thought you weren't going to give it to me."

"Well, here it is. Try not to mock it too much."

Her face lit up. She kissed my cheek happily and scanned the first chapter. And all I could think about was Annie's face, blond and tan, peering out at me from her doorway and smiling.

* * *

Soon Janey left for her place, my novel stashed inside her big purse. I felt no small dread at her reaction to my book. What if she hated it? I guess I'd find out. That night I dreamed of Annie, though by morning I'd forgotten everything but the sensation of fear in the pit of my stomach.

Brushing these feelings aside, I called Jeremy to see if anyone would be able to work Annie's emergency reception.

"Besides you, I have only one guy free."

"Don't say it."

"Just Bill. Sorry, man."

"What about Father Kim?"

"Doing a bar mitzvah out in Newark. Jean's doing an anniversary in Katonah. And Paulie G is working the annual crab festival in Riverhead. Even DJ Party-time has a preschool dance."

"What about you?"

"Sorry, guy. It's Bill or nobody."

I didn't know which would be worse. But I'd promised.

"Okay, Bill it is. But tell him to listen to me, all right? I don't want any mistakes! This is important!"

"You got it."

It may seem strange that I was so vehement about the quality of the DJ for a party I didn't want to happen. But though I knew it was a bad idea, I wanted her to experience the momentary happiness of a nice wedding. I've seen enough weddings to realize how important a good DJ, and tasty food, are. Though the couple rarely gets to enjoy them. They're too busy thanking everyone for showing up. There's something wrong with a custom that has you thanking people five minutes into the reception. At least let the poor bastards have some salad.

Chapter Nineteen

A New Wrinkle

Union Square bustled in the early summer sunshine as I sat at the table outside the Coffee Shop, waiting for Zach to show for lunch. Small white tents filled the open area in front of the park, making up the farmers' market that set up shop every other day. You could fill all your organic needs, down to bison meat, at the market if you so wished. All natural, the signs proclaimed. All the more reason for me to avoid it. I don't trust natural; I have a sneaking suspicion they don't wash it. I always enjoy grabbing a meal at the Coffee Shop, with its bevy of models for waitresses. I don't know where they come from, but somehow every person working at this pretentious establishment looks perfect. Even the guys look flawless. Of course, no one has ever screwed up my order more frequently than the lovely staff here at the Coffee Shop. And that's the main reason I love it so. Nothing makes me happier than pretty people fucking up. It's tonic for the soul.

"Sorry I'm late. I got caught up in Pilates class."

Zach slipped into the seat across from me, his sunglasses glinting expensively. I waved his apologies off.

"Don't worry. Pilates class wouldn't be a euphemism, would it?"

This sad excuse for innuendo confused him.

"A euphemism for what? I worked on my core muscles for an hour."

"You say that and you don't see where I'm going?"

Comprehension dawned.

"Oh. I see. You want to know if I've been fucking. Oh, well yes, but that was before Pilates class. That's not what caused my tardiness. Keith taught an especially long workout, because he saw his ass in the mirror this morning and freaked out. For a man who exercises as much as he does, he has no reason to be insecure about his form. You saw him. He looks magnificent."

"He is a good-looking man."

"His muscle tone is impeccable. I'm the one trying arm cream. But no matter how many times I tell him, he won't believe me."

He smiled slightly to himself, lost in his morning. I smiled with him.

"Wow. You really like him."

This brought him back. I could see him shiver as a small jolt of alarm shot up his spine.

"He's a great person. I'm not saying I'm in love. I enjoy his company."

"You've been here for almost two months now. I haven't seen you this much since senior year."

Zach took a sip of water, grinning as he set it back down.

"You know, he said the most wonderful thing to me this morning. We had been discussing this book he'd read, something he'd been begging me to peruse for some reason. By some person named Brown. Appalling book about Da Vinci. Total waste of wood pulp. The man has the writing skill of a West Virginia hillbilly. So I am telling him all the reasons I hated the book, and he simply lies there, smiling, watching me talk. Then he told me, in this wondering voice, how surprised he was that I read it. He never thought I'd actually listen to him and read it. I told him that he said I should read it, so I read it. Why wouldn't I? He talked about it enough. He patted my cheek and told me that for all that I'm an egotistical, narcissistic, shallow, thoughtless, vain, elitist layabout, deep down I have a really good heart. I almost cried. Isn't that a beautiful thing to say?"

"Um. Yeah. Real nice."

I didn't know what to think. You really have to be starved for compliments to let that one touch you. But Zach removed his sunglasses to wipe his eyes just thinking about it. He laughed at his own reaction.

"Sorry about the . . . well, you know."

"It's fine."

"He's such a wonderful person."

"Are you going to ask him to travel with you?"

Zach picked up the menu, flipping through it idly.

"I don't know. I've never been in this situation before. I don't know what to do. If I hadn't met him, I'd be long gone. The city is so boring in the summer. But he's here . . . I don't know. I'm not bored, I'll tell you that much."

"It doesn't look it."

"Though I'm getting fat from all the dinners we share."

His form-fitting shirt said otherwise.

"Zach, you've been doing his Pilates class every day. You could open a bottle of Coke with your ass."

He lifted his arms, giving them a wiggle.

"Look at these things. I stay off the cream for a week or so and they're already back to flab. Those products are heartbreakers. They're worse than E, I tell you. You come down hard."

"Can I ask you something?"

Zach stopped jiggling his arm fat.

"Certainly."

I took a deep breath. Zach was the only one I could talk to about this, since he had the distance I needed.

"I've been having weird dreams. All week I've been having them. Every morning I wake up feeling strange."

"Okay. So what are the dreams about?"

"Annie."

Zach grabbed his lettuce wrap.

"Not surprising, considering the events of the past month."

"No. It's a little more than that. They've been . . . strange."

"In what way? You haven't been ravishing her or anything, right?"

He laughed and took a bite. After a few chews, he noticed I wasn't laughing, that in fact I was red and miserable. He swallowed quickly.

"These have been . . . sex dreams?"

I nodded unhappily.

"I don't know what's going on. Janey accused me of having a thing for her, which is just not true. But ever since,

I've been dreaming about her and we've been . . . doing stuff. It's freaky."

Zach took another fascinated bite, thinking this over as he ate.

"Describe the dreams, every detail."

"Well, last night we were dancing together and then I kissed her and then we . . . well, you get the picture."

"No, I don't. I need every detail described. What happened next? Was there rubbing?"

"I'm not going to recount my pornographic dream to you, Zach. You'll just have to imagine. Actually, on second thought, don't imagine. Keep your thoughts chaste, Zach."

Zach smiled in a way I didn't like. I flicked his elbow.

"You're imagining it! I can tell."

"Yes, I am. And it's fantastic."

I gave up and moved on to the point.

"I don't know what to do. I've never had a thing for her in the past. But now . . . what do you think?"

"Hmm. Well. You have been going overboard in these breakup machinations of yours. I have wondered about your fervor privately. And Annie does look better now than she ever has. The blond hair suits her and she is in wonderful shape. Plus, the glow of love gives her that extra something. And after all, you two have so much in common. You laugh at the same things, hate the same things, find the same things ridiculous. There's always something to be said for being able to relate to your partner like that. So, who knows? Maybe it's true. Stranger things have happened."

This was not what I wanted to hear.

"But I've known her fifteen years! We've had plenty of

chances! It never even crossed my mind until Janey stuck it in there."

Zach shrugged.

"Life is timing, David. And we have no control over that whatsoever."

"What should I do?"

"The way I see it, you have two choices. One, ignore it, push it out of your mind. Not only is she one of your best friends, but she's about to get married. And you're dating a fantastic girl yourself. There's no need to complicate matters. Or, if you really are mentally unbalanced you can go for option two."

"Which is?"

"Confront Annie and see if this is in fact true. See her face to face and put it to rest on way or the other. Kiss her, or look deeply into her eyes, or do whatever people do in those situations. This is what I like to call the idiot option."

"Why?"

"Because no good can come of it. The timing is all wrong, even if it's true."

"Then I guess I'll go with option one."

He raised his glass in salute.

"Wise choice. A hundred dollars says you'll end up following option two."

"Well, then I definitely won't do it. I don't have a hundred dollars."

"Saved by poverty."

We both took large sips of wine, and I tried to ignore the itch in the back of my head that always seems to show up when I am about to do something colossally stupid.

* * *

After lunch, I parted ways with Zach and headed home for some quick relaxation before my afternoon of getting nothing done. Janey and Annie did laps in my brain until the sounds of tinny salsa ringing out from my pocket brought me back to reality. I didn't recognize the number, but I felt reckless and answered anyway.

"Is this David?"

"Yep?"

"This is Craig Schuman, from the Julian Becker Agency."

I stopped short, midstep. I knew that name by heart. I'd pinned my future on that name. The Julian Becker Agency, literary agents extraordinaire. I tried to keep my cool.

"Hello! Hi! How are you doing? Great to hear from you! What's shaking?"

I resolved to tone it down a bit. He didn't seem to notice.

"I read your book."

"That's great! Really, really great. Did it suck?"

"On the contrary, I'd love for you to come in and let me talk to you about it. I think you really have something here."

I almost fell down the stairs.

"Sure. Sounds great. Peachy, even. Really peachy. Peach-tastic!"

"Cool. How is Friday?"

"Friday is perfect."

And we set it up. For me to talk to an agent about my book. My novel. My slice of literary heaven. I danced into my apartment, too excited to sit down. I wanted to throw on a chipper song and boogie around the room, though I knew I'd probably end up falling through the floor and onto the ninety-year-old Lithuanian woman in 3D. Who to call first? My parents? My friends? Life was finally back on track! The way I'd planned it! I needed to celebrate! Janey answered on the third ring.

"Are you in the mood for some fine dining?"

"Okay. When?"

"Tonight!"

"What's the occasion?"

"I am bona fide, baby. I am bona fide."

Chapter Twenty

Eating Above My Station

I refused to tell Janey where we were headed, figuring that this would be the perfect opportunity to take her to the land of so many of Zach's top twenty meals. Amazingly enough, I managed to score a reservation. Zach gave me permission to drop his name, which actually did some good. He's famous there, apparently. Maybe because of all the yum yum noises he makes during his meal. He's the next best thing to an Herbal Essence commercial.

I dressed up a bit, wearing dark shoes instead of Converses and tucking in my shirt. Janey, on the other hand, dressed up a lot. She slipped into the sexiest dress I'd seen in a long time actually worn by someone not plastered on the back of a bus, this black number with the kind of cleavage dip normally reserved for Jennifer Lopez or Trey Parker. I don't know if it was her intention (knowing women, I'd say probably), but all thoughts of Annie fled at the sight. I kept tickling her knee in the cab because I had to be touching her. She flicked my probing finger away.

"Tell me where we're going! I'm dying."

"It's a surprise."

"Why is there a surprise for me when it's your celebration? That makes no sense."

"It's a celebration for both of us."

My hand magically reappeared on her knee. She half-heartedly scowled at me. She seemed distracted.

"Are you okay?"

She put on a strained smile and nodded.

"Of course."

"Um. Okay. Good."

Before I could delve deeper we pulled up in front of our destination. I slipped out of the cab excitedly, holding the door for Janey as she followed. She looked up at the restaurant, nodding slightly.

"Oh. Aureole. This place is nice."

She talked about it the way I mentioned Bennigans.

"You've been here?"

"Sure. My parents love this place. My mom still takes me here for lunch sometimes. It's nice, really."

Great. The top-rated restaurant in *Zagat* is nice. I tucked in my shirt, for Christ sake. This is the big time! She stepped up to the front entrance, waiting for me to open it for her, then stepped through nonchalantly, like it was an Applebee's. I followed her into the land of above my station.

People who try to tell you there is no class system in America are usually either politicians or idiots or both. A very real class structure was put into place by the founding fathers, who wanted to substitute the "pursuit of property" for the "pursuit of happiness" in the Declaration of Independence, and didn't trust the Irish further than they could get them to chase a whiskey. Abraham Lincoln was born in a log cabin, and they didn't let him hang out in the White House too long, now did they. Everybody is somebody's bitch, that is the true American way. And deep within our genes, regardless of how high we've risen in life, something remembers where we belong. They may not turn us away at the door, they may not say a word, but our genes get the message. My grandfather owned a butcher shop in Yonkers. My other grandfather still sits in his log cabin that he built with his own two hands up in the mountains of Virginia, holding on to his shotgun, just waiting for the Jews to try something. From no angle did my blood appear blue, despite all my parents' accomplishments and my own. So stepping into the top-rated restaurant in the entire city, it shouldn't have surprised me that I became overcome by the urge to head around to the servants' entrance and grab a tray.

People, white—and carelessly, expensively dressed—sat throughout the beautiful dining room, talking easily about whatever people in Versace underwear talk about: how to make paper airplanes out of hundred-dollar bills, probably. As we stepped up to the maître d', I could feel them all looking at me, in my scuffed black shoes and Macy's button-down. Staring at my lower-class eyeballs, willing them to look down like they're supposed to. I knew they could see me for what I was, a peasant in a Halloween costume, holding out money like Julia Roberts trying to buy a dress on Rodeo Drive in that prostitute movie, without realizing that money means nothing if you don't have the breeding to spend it. The maître d', no doubt wondering how long it would take for a security guard to Taser me into submission and toss me on the street, looked up as we approached.

"Hello. Name please?"

I froze. I opened my mouth, but nothing came out. I was too busy resisting the urge to order a Whopper and fries. Catching my expression, Janey smoothly stepped in.

"Hello, Jean. It should be under David Holden. For two."

The maître d' lit up.

"Ms. Finegold! Nice to see you again. Of course, here it is. Right this way."

As we followed him through the maze of tables, I tried to walk tall, smiling and nodding at all the people not looking at me. If I could just make it to my table, everything would be fine. We reached a small table in the corner, probably by the kitchen, and I rushed to pull out the chair for Janey. Not going to be caught out on that one. After she sat down, I moved to my side, almost pulling the tablecloth off with my shaking hand as I quickly took my seat. Smiling politely, the maître d' handed us our menus and wished us a wonderful meal, probably cursing inside that I slipped in on the coattails of a slumming blue blood. I nodded to a passing Mexican busboy like we were homies. He gave me an odd look and hurried off. Great. Now I had to check my food for strange condiments.

"Are you all right, David? I like this place, really."

"Of course, I'm fine. I didn't realize you came here so much. I thought it would be special."

"It is special. A meal at Aureole is always special."

Special like a birthday party at Arby's, you mean. An errant thought popped into my head (*Annie would be impressed*), but I shushed it up before it could gain volume. We looked down at the menus. I didn't recognize half of the foods listed. What the hell was Florida grouper? Or baked ruget? Rubbed duck? What the hell did you rub the duck with? Did you rub it before or after you killed it? Who the hell massages a duck? I guess loose, relaxed duck tastes better than uptight, stressed-out duck.

"What are you having, David?"

I looked down the list of uncharted culinary territory.

"I don't know where to begin."

"Well, the halibut is very good. So is the goat cheese Napoleon."

"Ah."

I don't do goat cheese. Cheese comes from cows. Nothing should come from goats, except other goats. I also don't do strange fish with the word "but" in it. The waiter came over.

"Would you like something to drink?"

Janey glanced at me quickly.

"Just a Perrier."

I nodded.

"Me too."

He walked away. I gave Janey a look but didn't say a thing. No wine. A little unnerved by the complete lack of alcohol, I went back to my menu of Sophie's choices. Janey didn't talk. Looking up, I noticed her menu closed in front of her.

"You okay?"

She answered my question with a question.

"What about you? You don't seem as happy as you were on the phone."

"I'm just settling into the happiness. That's all."

Why did I pick this place? It took all the fun out of being a soon-to-be-successful author. I'd have to come back after I became famous, to bask in the glow of recognition. Because authors are instantly recognized wherever they go. Aren't they? Everyone knows what James Patterson looks like. I mean come on. Michael Chabon can't get a cup of coffee without having to sign some woman's breasts. It's the cross all authors bear. So I'd have to come back and regain my sense of self worth, which I left crumpled at the foot of the maître d' table. Janey nodded, unconvinced.

"If you say so."

"You don't look so thrilled either."

"It's nothing."

"No it isn't. Just tell me."

She took a breath, forcing herself to face me.

"I finished your book."

She hated it! My God, she hated it! And now she hated me! She was going to dump me, only now I've taken her to a nice restaurant so she can't do it. That's why she looks so down! She'd been all ready to leave me at the curb like yesterday's trash, when I got a stay of execution, courtesy of Aureole and the Julian Becker Agency. Janey caught my expression.

"You're already freaking out, calm down."

I forced myself to be calm, probably rupturing an internal organ in the process.

"What did you think?"

Janey took a deep breath.

"I feel weird."

Weird? What did that mean?

"How so?"

She searched for the words, as I writhed in agony, waiting.

"It's hard to explain. You wrote all about this girl you really cared about. You loved this girl. And I'm reading about how you felt about her, how much you loved her, and how hard it was to get over her, this girl you broke up with."

"It just didn't work out. It's one of those things."

"I know. I understand that. It's only . . . Look, I shouldn't be saying these things. We haven't been going out very long. I know it's not how you should do things. But I . . . I really like you. And reading about this woman and how you felt about her, it was awful. Especially after that talk we had about Annie. I know there's nothing between you two. But that put together with this . . . I know you've had girlfriends and experienced love before. Of course you have. I have, too. But to be confronted with the blow by blow . . . it made me feel small. How could I ever live up to all of that or make you forget it? How could you ever feel like that again? How could anybody? I don't want to be the only one feeling like this. You know, this is stupid. Why am I telling you this? It's too soon. You're probably about to run out the door or something. Look at you."

Okay, I'll admit this threw me. This was pretty much the opposite of a slow reveal. I mean, I liked her. A lot. But this . . . this was more than that. Janey looked away, down at her closed menu.

"I'm sorry. You're freaked. I shouldn't have said anything."

"No. No, of course not."

"Let's just forget about it."

"No. Look, you have nothing to be worried about. We're doing great. I'm just more about the slow reveal, you know?"

"The slow reveal. Right."

"I like you a lot. Okay?"

She looked back up at me with those big, open eyes. "Okay."

But inside, was I okay? She practically said she loved me. I could hear the words lurking in the background, whispering. I was not ready for that. Then I'd have to make a decision about what I'd say. I'd been in love only once before and it felt nothing like this. That was obsession, mostly self-created. This was . . . different. Maybe better? Hopefully better. But I couldn't tell, not yet. Janey's face broke my heart.

"Are you sure you're okay, David?"

"I'm fine. Really."

"Look, if you think we're moving too fast, I don't have to come to your mom's gallery opening."

"No! No, please come. I really am all right."

I leaned over to kiss her. Even though our lips met, I could feel a barrier between us. But what could I do? Should I lie and tell her I loved her just to knock it down? I wanted to be sure. And I didn't want to lie. There was so much I didn't know. What about her friends? How did she act around her mother? How often did her father reduce her to tears and could she really resist the angry drunken rampages that followed? I needed this stuff. I needed to fight this rushing water, keep my place for just a little while longer before I got swept away. I needed to know we'd be as comfortable as I was with . . . my other friends. I sat back down and returned to my menu. I had no idea what to order. And on top of everything else, now I'd never know what she really thought of my book.

* * *

Janey stayed over and we had sex, though I felt far more removed than I had that first, perfect time, and I had the sneaking suspicion she did, too. Afterward, we just clung to each other, willing the dinner not to have happened. By morning, we'd forced ourselves into some semblance of normalcy. It almost felt natural. Almost.

Chapter Twenty-one

The Little Agent Who Could

I pushed my uncertain feelings about Janey and Annie and everything between far from my mind, focusing instead on my big meeting with Craig Schuman. This would be it, I knew it. The beginning of the happy stage of my life, the last stage. I woke up the morning of our meeting at eight AM, even though my appointment wasn't until three. I couldn't do anything all day except surf the Internet and shake uncontrollably. I tried to write, thinking that I'd better get back into the swing of things, but I couldn't sit still. Finally, after hours of watching the seconds march by on my computer's clock, 2:30 rolled in. Time to go! I had to get all the way across town, of course, but I'd never been on time to a damn thing my entire life, and I wasn't about to start now.

I stepped out of the cab at 3:15, right on schedule. The Julian Becker Agency waited for me on the eighth floor of a normal, generic apartment building on the Upper West Side. I probably should have checked in with the doorman, but I hate the hassle, and anyway I've found that as long as you look like you know where you're going, they don't ask questions. I made it through my first job without doing any actual labor by following that maxim. I'd walk briskly through the ShopRite supermarket, always deadly intent on where I was headed, and no one ever stopped me. I could go through an entire seven-and-a-half-hour shift just walking in circles, eyes focused, never slowing down, and, more important, never actually doing a damn thing. I was known throughout management as a relentless workaholic. You should try it. It's good for the calves.

I stepped out onto the eighth floor into a long, dim hallway lined with featureless doors. I walked down to the end of the hall, right up to the number written on the back of my hand for safety's sake. No sign or other feature differentiated this door from any other door on the hall. Unsure, I pushed the buzzer. The door opened to reveal a munchkin.

"David! You made it! I'm Craig. Come on in!"

Okay, he wasn't really a munchkin. He probably topped five foot two, barely. He could go on most of the rides at Six Flags Great Adventure. But when your heart is fluttering as you contemplate stepping into the heady world of literature, you expect a tall, perfect-featured, Hollywood-type agent. Not Gimli, son of Gloin. I reached down to shake his hand.

"Hey! Nice to meet you!"

"Come on in. Everybody else is out to lunch, so it's just the two of us. Come on into my office and we'll chat."

I followed him through the offices of the Julian Becker Agency, which proved to be a converted two bedroom apartment with the bedrooms and the dining room turned into private offices. The kitchenette remained unchanged, however. It's disconcerting to be in the waiting room of an agency and from your vantage point on the couch be able to see the Hungry-Man dinner heating up in the microwave. Craig pointed to a tiny desk sandwiched between a copier and a fax machine.

"Our secretary, Robin, sits there, but she's out sick today. Julian's office is over there. Karen, another of our top agents, sits back there, behind the StairMaster. And I'm in here. Come on in."

Right on his heels, I stepped into the world's smallest office. It had a window, and thank God for that, because otherwise I would have suffered a claustrophobic fit on the spot. A tiny couch sat pushed up against the window, with about four inches of room between it and Craig's desk. Craig plopped himself behind the desk with a sigh, a tiny head floating above the massive city of papers and manuscripts like the baby's face in the sun on the Teletubbies.

"Have a seat."

"Okay."

I wedged myself onto the couch, my legs jamming into Craig's desk, immobilizing me. I'd need some serious lube just to shift in my seat. Craig sat back, almost fading from sight completely. His voice came from somewhere behind a stack of manila folders.

"I am so excited you're here. I just love your book."

I beamed. I don't care how bizarre the situation, praise always sounds sweet.

"Thanks."

"I'm expecting big things. Big things!"

"Really?"

"You bet."

"So it's that good?"

Craig blinked.

"It's different, David. Very different. And the timing couldn't have been more perfect. Have you heard of dump lit?"

"Um. No."

"It's the newest genre to hit the fiction world. Simply huge!"

"Wow. Best sellers, huh?"

Craig kept his smile.

"Well, none of the books have actually hit shelves yet. But once they do, it will take right off! I'm talking bigger than lesbian true crime!"

"Wow. That's . . . pretty big."

"You bet."

"What is dump lit exactly?"

Craig leaned forward, his small face lighting up.

"It's so ingenious. There is a huge hunger for fiction dealing with men dumping women. Books about guys just cutting those chicks loose are hotter than hot. There's such a hunger for it!"

Who knew? I thought the fact that in my book my main character dumps his girlfriend would be an unattractive quality that would have to be overcome, but there's actually a hunger for it! A hunger! I was a lucky bastard.

"Who specifically is ready to eat this stuff up?"

Craig pointed at me, winking.

"Nice. Extending the metaphor. Keeping the ball in the air. I'm impressed."

Okay then.

"Thanks."

"To answer your question, the publishers have taken a

look at the marketplace and seen that there are no books servicing the bastard market. There are plenty of books for the women who get dumped, or as we like to call it, chick lit. There are also some books for guys who've been dumped, dickless lit. Sorry, inside joke. It's pretty funny if you're in the know."

"I'll bet."

"But nothing for the heartless shitheads doing the dumping. Who tells their stories? Who gets inside their heads? The publishers see this untapped market and they can't wait to stick a finger up in that mother. And that's where you come in, Davey."

"David."

"David, you bet."

"That's amazing. So there's a real market for my stuff?"

"Yep! Everyone is talking about it. There are already forty books getting ready to hit the stores. But there are still plenty of houses looking to get in on the action. I can sell your book in a week, no sweat."

"Really? A week?"

Craig slammed his hand down on the desk.

"A week! I swear. This time next week, your book will be sold."

"That's great!"

"Isn't that great?"

"Well . . . yes! It's great."

"It sure is great."

"Great."

We lapsed into silence, tangled up in our mutual dependence on the same word. I couldn't believe this was happening. Sensing my joy, Craig went in for the kill.

"So am I your man? I mean you can go home and think about it all you want. Ask around, we have a great reputation."

I arranged my expression into one of calculation. Time to be business savvy.

"What kind of stuff do you do?"

"All kinds. Nonfiction, self-help. Romance, sci-fi, horror. It helps to have a genre. Straight literary fiction is a hard sell, believe me. But dump lit, that moves books."

"Have you done anything I've heard of?"

"I'm sure. The Batemen books. Kenneth Koulter, the Jews for Jesus guy. Though he does young adult fantasy now. Follow the heat, you know? I just sold a proposal for Warwick Davis's autobiography."

"That name sounds familiar."

"The lead from *Willow.* He was the main Ewok in *Return of the Jedi* as well. Real firecracker. What a life, believe me. Sexaholic. Deathly afraid of bees. You should hear his stories."

"I love *Willow*!"

"It's a great flick."

Caught up in the moment, I let my mouth run as I tried to think of more questions.

"Isn't it amazing how many midgets they got for that movie? Where do they come from, that's what I want to know. There must be a midget union or something. My buddy Dustin says there's a midget farm out in Idaho, but he still thinks Jawas are based on real creatures that live in the Gobi Desert, so you know he's an idiot."

I froze, suddenly hearing what I was saying. Fuck! What if he really was a midget? A really tall midget! Why is it I never listen to what I'm saying until it's too late! I blew it! I winced, awaiting the fallout. To my everlasting relief, Craig laughed.

"I think there is a union. Can't stand midgets myself. They freak me out."

He shuddered for effect. Okay, that's weird. After all, he can fit into their clothes. It's amazing how people lay fierce claim to their places in the world. No one hates midgets more than the people who are only two inches taller than them. And that's how the Man keeps us down.

Craig leaned back again.

"I can go on and on with my client list, if you want."

Any business sense I had went flying with the midget comment.

"That's okay. I'll be happy to go with you."

After all, you are the only one who ever got back to me. And I couldn't ignore the kitsch factor. Craig's face lit up.

"Fantastic! I'll get to work straight away with sending out the manuscript. A week! Mark it down! This will be a big one, I can feel it!"

I sat still in my chair, unable to move if I wanted to, but frozen as well by the prospect of my life actually reaching the heights I'd aimed for. It was all worth it. All of it. Because this one will be a big one. This had to be one of the happiest moments of my life. And it felt good. Damn good. I sat in that tiny office with that tiny man and I felt wonderful. My moment had arrived.

* * *

I called everyone I'd ever met. Mrs. Hickenbothem got a call. The doctor who pulled me from my mother's womb got a call. My friends went crazy, as excited as I was. They were all so happy for me. Everyone should have such friends. My mom almost fainted, though I think that had more to do with the stress of her first show that weekend. My dad told me I'd finally earned his love. I think he was kidding. Alex immediately told a girl in the bar he was sitting in when I called him, trying to use my success as a pickup line (it failed). And Janey was great. She stopped by with pizza and champagne and we celebrated by candlelight. Everything was forgotten as we encircled each other, diving into each other, letting our scents take over. Success never smelled sweeter.

Chapter Twenty-two

Colossal Stupidity

It took a while to find the gallery where Mom's masterpiece was being shown. Situated between a tiny pottery store and an Armani Exchange, it sported no sign, no art in the windows, nothing beyond the street number. I warily pushed through the front door, not sure what to expect. Usually, when you push through these unmarked doors in nondescript buildings, you expect to walk into a huge loft filled with people, all the cool hipsters who don't bother walking the streets, traveling instead by special tube that deposits them directly at the bar. This was not that kind of door.

I stepped into a tiny room with eight pieces of art on the wall, none of which bore any resemblance to me. A small bar was set up in the back, serving wine and Diet Coke in plastic cups and cheese on Ritz crackers. A small group of people stood by the bar nervously, not sure what to do. Snuggled among them were my parents. I walked up to my mom, who looked terrified.

"Hey, congratulations, Mom!"

"Congratulations to you, too. My author son!"

I gave her a big hug. Dad took a sip of wine, making a face.

"I think this stuff came out of a box."

"Hi Dad."

"Good job with the book. Your mom's a mess. Be nice."

Mom hit him lightly.

"I'm fine. Just nervous. I've never been shown in a gallery before."

"It's a huge step. Hey, Alex."

My brother walked up, his smile larger than his shoulders.

"Have you seen it?"

"Not yet. Where is it?"

He pointed.

"Right over there."

I followed his finger. Sweet. Lord. Above. There I floated mid-wall, directly next to the entrance, larger than life. Nothing but white for five feet in every direction. Nothing to get in the way of my big moment.

"Wow."

Mom glanced at me nervously.

"Do you think people will notice it? I didn't want it right by the door."

Dad smirked.

"They'll notice it."

I slowly walked up to it. The light above seemingly shone through my painted translucent shirt, for a disconcerting realistic effect. Mom stepped up beside me, face expectant.

"What do you think?"

I swallowed hard.

"It looks magnificent."

At least no one but my family and Janey would be seeing it. So all in all this shouldn't be too painful. An older woman with steel-gray hair and some kind of hot pink leopard-print wrap hanging off her shoulders stepped up beside us.

"It's breathtaking. The celebration of life through dance. I adore it. You are obviously the subject."

"Yes, I am."

Breathtaking? Okay then. My mom took my shoulder.

"David, I want to introduce you to Helen Jukt. This is her show. She graciously invited me to display a piece here when she saw the painting in class."

Helen rubbed her hands together.

"When I laid eyes on this wondrous piece, I felt dwarfed by what your mother has accomplished. My work, it pays the bills, but your mother's work pays the soul!"

"It is something special, Ms. Jukt."

"Helen. Feel free to wander. Good luck, Elaine."

Helen wandered away, back toward the bar. My dad had obviously been introduced, because he made sure to step back out of sight as she approached. Mom's eyes filled with tears.

"She is such a wonderful woman. Can you imagine? Letting a nobody like me display during her show."

I pulled her into another hug. Despite what I might think of her choice of subject, this was still my mom's big night and I was proud of her. Alex walked back from the bar and handed me a drink, which I chugged like a frat boy. I looked over his shoulder at Dad, sipping his wine alone in the corner.

"How's Dad?"

Mom answered me.

"He's all right, so far. Moving is tough on him. It's tough on us both. There's nothing left in the house, really. Most of it's been shipped ahead. I'll need your help with the final few pieces. Do you think you could come and help us with that?"

"Of course."

"Good. We like to see you."

She kissed my cheek while patting Alex's arm. He smiled at me, strained, his eyes swimming with worry. Mom looked toward the door.

"Where's your new girlfriend?"

"She's having dinner with her dad. She should be here in an hour."

"I can't wait to meet her."

The room was fairly empty. Apparently the Helen Jukt experience didn't exactly pull them in. I wandered around to look at her work. Most of it seemed to center on dolls being mutilated, with blood everywhere and slits in the sky that just might be airborne vaginas. The dolls wore either ratty lingerie or nothing at all. Staring at her work made me want to see a Disney movie, just to try to recapture some of my innocence. My mom bravely tried to ignore the rest of the show, exclaiming loudly at how forward-thinking Helen was. My dad stood in the corner and tried not to be seen. I glanced up at the painting of me again. At least no one else I knew would be seeing it.

"David!"

My mouth dropped. Cameron and Mary walked up to me, hand in hand.

"What are you doing here?"

Cameron smiled and handed me a postcard with one of

Helen Jukt's unlucky dolls on the cover. Turning it over, I read the invitation to come see my mother's big debut.

"Who sent you this?"

Cameron patted my back.

"Beats me. But I'm here. This whole teach Barbie a lesson she won't forget stuff isn't your mother's work, right?"

I wish I could claim it as my mom's, but the minute they spotted the real deal, the gig would be up. Mary spied it first, a spasm running through her. She reached out and grabbed Cameron's arm, forcing him to turn. Cameron's eyes bulged as he took in Disco David, his brain imploding under the stress. Before he could release the pressure, my mother walked up.

"Cameron! You came! Lovely to see you."

Still red, Cameron leaned in and kissed my mom on the cheek. He couldn't speak, however, so I had to jump in with the intros.

"Mom, this is Mary, Cameron's lovely lady."

As Mary and my mother exchanged hellos, Cameron desperately tried to swallow his reaction. To add fuel to the fire, Dustin stode through the door, alone. He waved as he walked up, his face puzzled as he took in Cameron's quivering lips.

"What's up with him?"

Cameron wordlessly pointed. Dustin spun around to face my mother's painting and made the kind of face one normally makes when faced with a gargantuan chocolate sundae. He whispered softly to himself.

"It's Christmas."

"Dustin! I'm so happy to see you!"

My mother gave him a hug, but Dustin couldn't look away from my painted self. His lips moved soundlessly as he went through every joke he could think of. As my mom released him, Zach appeared. I turned to Mom.

"You invited Zach, too? How did you even know where to send the invitation?"

Mom looked confused.

"I didn't send him anything. I haven't seen him in years."

Zach stopped short when he saw us.

"What are you guys doing here?"

Huh?

Helen saw him from across the room and immediately rushed over.

"Zach! How are you!"

"I'm wonderful. Your work looks marvelous."

"You are too kind. Zach here has been to all my shows. He even owns one of my pieces. You know Elaine?"

"I am old friends with her son. How do you know each other?"

"I'm showing one of her paintings!"

Zach smiled widely.

"Really! That's amazing, Mrs. Holden. Which one is it?"

Mom pointed.

"Turn around."

She spun him around to face the work of art. Zach's eyes bulged.

"My goodness. Oh my goodness."

"What do you think, Zach?"

"It's . . . wonderful. The lines are so clean. The effect with the translucent shirt . . . it works perfectly. The treasure trail of hair down to the leather pants is a bold choice that completely works here. The bright, almost otherworldly lights behind him . . ."

"They're disco lights."

"They highlight the otherworldly nature of movement. I love it. Brava, Elaine. Brava."

Mom could have floated away. She hugged the life out of that poor boy instead. Zach smiled weakly.

"Brava."

Helen led my mom away to meet some people, leaving Cameron and Dustin to mouth "Oh my God!" in unison. Zach shook his head sadly.

"This is how we deal with art. We mock it. David, your mother's painting is beautiful. She is truly talented."

"Um. Thanks."

"It looks just like you."

Dustin snorted.

"Right down to the leather pants."

They shook in silent laughter again. I took a deep breath, riding it out. Eventually Cameron composed himself.

"She really captured you."

"What do you mean? I'm not like that. That's my mom's strange vision of me."

Dustin clapped my shoulder.

"I don't know, buddy. I've seen you in a club. You do kind of dance like that."

"I don't dance like that. I would never wear a see-through shirt."

A giggle escaped Cameron's lips.

"But I can so see it on you."

Zach placated me.

"It's not like anyone thinks you're gay, David. I know plenty of gay men who are manlier than you."

Dustin almost peed himself. Mary broke in before it went too far.

"Look, this isn't a bad thing. I think those overly macho qualities are unattractive. You, on the other hand, I'd consider a catch."

Dustin put his arm around me.

"We all love you, dude. You don't need to be able to break through a brick wall with your forehead. I mean, I can do it, but that's me."

The door opened to admit Annie and Rat Boy, of course, the last stragglers to my humiliation party. I hadn't seen her since the morning she showed up at my place, and the sight of her now made my stomach jump. She waved and bounced over to us.

"What's wrong with you people? Dustin, are you crying?"

Dustin spun her around to see. For half a moment I entertained the hope that she'd break out into a profane, joke-laden tirade and show Rat Boy her true colors, but instead she simply shrugged.

"Yeah, that's pretty much David."

I just couldn't catch a break.

I snuck a look at Annie as she stood there admiring the painting. A chill ran down my spine as I recalled the dreams I'd been having. But they didn't mean anything, right? I'd had my chance, if I'd wanted it, and I let it go. We were friends, best friends, and that was that. But I had to admit, now that I was truly paying attention, the blond hair suited her, transforming her into a sexier version of the Annie I'd known before. And those eyes, the same eyes I'd known for fifteen years, now seemed deep and mysterious. Could this be something . . . but look at her, she isn't even trying to make fun of me. Maybe she really has changed. Maybe she's not even my friend anymore. Maybe her happy has pulled her away too far.

Leaving Rat Boy to peruse the other paintings, Annie stepped up alongside me and whispered into my ear.

"How's my little Dancing Queen holding up?"

I repressed a snort of laughter. She was still in there, buried but alive. We had so much in common. I thought about Janey, who'd soon be arriving to meet most of my friends for the first time. We were so different. She had problems I had no idea how to solve. She ate comfortably in the nicest restaurants in the world, she slept next to priceless artwork, she floated so far above me I was surprised I could see the bottom of her shoes. But Annie and I . . . was this why I held back with Janey? Was this the barrier I felt? I had to know.

"Can I talk to you for a second?"

Grabbing her by the hand I led her into the back, into a small room filled with soda, cheese and boxes of wine. I knew this was stupid, I could feel it as I did it, but I needed to know. She looked up at me, puzzled.

"What's going on, David? Is this another pep talk about how useless my fiancé is, because I'd rather not hear it."

I didn't answer. I didn't know what to say. I stared at her, at those familiar features I'd known for half my life. I thought about her saving me from those assholes in high school, and the feel of her fist paying me back for my ingratitude. I thought about all the times I sat in her kitchen as she baked me cookies and listened to me complain about some woman who just couldn't understand me. I thought about the first time I met her, back in freshman year, when she sent me that rose in a vain attempt to court me. I wasn't ready then. Was I ready now? Only one way to find out. I leaned in to kiss her. Caught off guard, she just stood there like a deer in headlights, unable to avoid the crash.

I was inches away from her lips when I realized my mistake. Up close, her face seemed so different. She turned into a whole new person from this angle. The scent of her breath was strange, the aroma alien to me. I'd never been close enough to her lips to sample it. I'd never realized what a huge gulf lay between our friendly distance and her lips. And now that I'd crossed that divide, I could see that the picture was completely different up close. I didn't belong here. This wasn't what I wanted. If I traveled those last few inches and brushed against her mouth, everything would be ruined.

I pulled up, brakes squealing as I struggled to avoid the collision. Thankfully, she backed away once she got over her shock and stared at me in disbelief from the farthest corner of the room.

"What the fuck do you think you're doing?"

What could I say? I had no idea. She placed a curled hand over her mouth.

"Were you going to . . . *kiss* me?"

The repulsion in her voice offended me, even as I felt relief that I hadn't gone through with it. A kiss from David isn't exactly like making out with Jabba the Hutt, you know. She continued on, not needing any answers from me.

"What were you trying to prove? Why the hell . . . what is going on, David?"

Finally I opened my mouth to explain myself, but neither

she nor I ever found out what I would have said, because she'd already decided she knew. Her bewildered look transformed into disgust.

"This was your last ditch effort, wasn't it? Anything to break me and Josh up, is that it?"

I found my voice, alarmed that I'd been accused the one time I wasn't guilty.

"No! That's not it at all."

"That's a low blow, David. A low, low blow."

"I promise, that wasn't what I was . . ."

"You are a piece of work, David Holden. A piece of goddamn work."

She brushed by me and headed for the main gallery. As she hit the doorway, she turned one last time.

"And don't think this gets you out of taking Josh out for his bachelor party. You owe me big time, now. Man, you are something else."

And she disappeared through the door, leaving me feeling like the biggest asshole in the world. Still, all in all, it could have gone worse. Of course, it took only about a minute for me to prove that wrong.

I followed Annie back into the gallery and there was Janey, the hurt look in her eyes telling me exactly what she was thinking. Here was worse staring me in the face. Shit. I thought quickly, trying to find a spin that would make this work, but I came up blank. There was only one recourse. I'd have to tell the truth.

I quickly walked up to her and pulled her over to the corner. She whispered fiercely.

"What were you doing back there with her?"

She looked terrible. Her eyes were red, though I don't

know when she had time to cry, and her hands were shaking. Was she really that jealous? She held a dark red plastic cup in her hand, no doubt already filled with soothing wine from a box. I had no idea why she'd fallen apart so quickly, but I rushed to contain the damage.

"When you asked if I had a thing for Annie, it threw me. I'd never thought that that might be a factor. I couldn't get it out of my head. So tonight, when I saw her, I took her in the back to see if that was true, to be fair to all of us. But it wasn't! I couldn't even kiss her. So everything's fine now. She's only a friend and that's all she'll ever be."

I expected this little speech to put all of Janey's fears to rest. Imagine my surprise when she seemed to get even angrier.

"What is going on, David? Something is going on and I don't know what it is."

I was taken aback by the anger in her voice.

"Nothing. Nothing is going on."

"We've been strange around each other ever since I told you I was falling for you. And now you tell me that you needed to see if you had a thing for a girl you've known for fifteen years to be fair to me? Now you have to go searching for reasons to break up?"

Where was this coming from? I was caught flatfooted.

"No! No, of course not."

"Then what's going on?"

Her voice was rising and I could see my friends muttering to themselves. She must be drunk off her ass again. What a great first impression. I spoke softly, trying to lead by example.

"Nothing is going on. I just told you that it was all nothing."

"And that's supposed to make me feel all warm and happy inside? If you want to break up with me, just break up with me!"

"Why do you keep saying that? Why would I want to break up with you?"

"You've been pulling away. And why shouldn't you? I'm no picnic, right? I mean even my own dad thinks so. You know what he did? I just found out today from my landlord. He tried to get me evicted, offered my landlord a hefty chunk of cash to throw me out so I'd have to come back home. It was only after my landlord found that he had no legal recourse to kick me out that he told me. Aren't I lucky! So I confronted my dad at dinner tonight and he didn't even look embarrassed. 'It's for your own good,' he tells me. That control freak motherfucker. And now you're looking for an excuse to ditch me. What did I do? Try to be too real? Try to expect something of you? Tell me. What the hell did I do?"

The entire gallery was listening to us now. I had no idea what to say. I should have felt ashamed, but what did I do wrong? Nothing. And here she was screaming at me for no reason. I felt bad about her dad, that was a really shitty thing to do, but why was this my fault? She lifted her glass to her mouth and I felt something snap.

"Maybe you've had enough."

Her hand froze, her eyes hardening into diamonds.

"What did you say?"

I should have stopped there, but I was feeling put-upon and reckless.

"That's not going to make this better."

"What the hell is wrong with you? You don't know a thing about me! Here I'm afraid of telling you too much, and you don't fucking hear a thing I say anyway. You are a coward, David. Nothing but a fucking coward!"

I heard a cough and I turned to see everyone staring. My mother, my father, my brother, my friends, Helen Jukt, everyone. I'd never been that embarrassed, not even when I got the stiff one at naked hula hooping. Determined to put an end to it, I reached out to grab Janey's hand and take her outside. Unfortunately, she recoiled violently, and in the process one of her feet hooked behind the other. I grabbed for her hand, but all I got was her cup as she stumbled backward toward my mother's infamous painting.

Whack.

A hush fell over the crowd as we all stared at the large hole in my portrait where Janey's flailing arm had punched right through. She turned around in alarm, unhurt, her face now horrified at what she'd done.

"I'm sorry. Oh, Mrs. Holden, I'm so sorry."

No one replied. We were all too busy staring at my painted twin, his huge cheesy smile undimmed even though the treasure trail of hair now led down to a huge hole in the crotch of his leather pants. Whether he'd been manly before is open to debate; he was definitely unmanned now.

Shocked by this accident I glanced down at the cup in my hand. A soft fizzle greeted me as I stared hard into the dark, bubbly sea of Diet Coke.

* * *

Janey sat facing me, her face pale. I'd met her in a small coffee shop near her apartment. I didn't feel angry anymore. I didn't feel anything. I poked at my muffin until she broke the silence.

"Please tell your mom how sorry I am about that painting."

"I will. I did."

My mom was already planning a new portrait of me, this version sitting me at my desk with a huge quill writing out my masterpiece. But I asked for the old, maimed painting anyway. I kinda liked it now. It really did look like me. We lapsed back into silence until this time I felt the need to speak.

"How're things with your dad?"

Her voice trembled despite her wry smile.

"We're not speaking, of course. I shouldn't be surprised. He'll do anything he can to get his way. Maybe I'll be a stripper."

"That would show him."

"I just hate that my mom was right. I'll have to bring the shirt back now."

She took another sip of coffee. I was reminded of our first real date. No pretending this time, though. Nothing hidden in the cup. That thought prompted me to speak.

"I'm sorry about the whole drinking thing."

Might as well get all the sorrys out of the way. She didn't look up.

"Yeah, that was pretty shitty. When was the last time I got drunk? You never even noticed that."

"I noticed."

"Okay."

"I am sorry."

"Me, too. I overreacted, to all of it. I guess that shit with my dad pushed me over the edge."

More silence. I wondered if I could have loved her if she'd been a little easier. I thought about her hand in my back pocket as we walked by the East River in the soft twilight and I knew that part of me already did. But that didn't change anything. If last night had proved anything, it proved that my life was complicated enough without her worries dropped on top. They crushed me. Why couldn't everything be simple? It was up to me to make it so.

"Look, I know what happened with your dad was awful. It really was. It's just . . . I can't handle all of this. It's too much for me right now. It's all too much. So I think it would be better if . . ."

She spoke into her coffee cup.

"You're breaking up with me, huh?"

I felt my heart drop at her frozen voice, but I would not waver.

"I'm sorry."

She didn't move, just stared at me, everything right there in her eyes. My stomach tightened, threatening to squeeze my insides into shapelessness. This is what women did. To look at me at that moment, you would never know I was about to sell my book and become what I've always dreamed of, what I'd worked toward ever since I quit my useless job. Everything was coming to fruition, and instead of perfect joy, I felt like I'd been beaten senseless, betrayed by everything I relied on. Love should be a rock, something you can always trust to stay stable beneath your feet as you reach upward. It shouldn't pitch and roll like a carnival ride. It shouldn't be a roller coaster in the dark. It tore at me to stand up and walk away. I could feel something ripping inside me. But I did it. Because I wanted to be happy. The big happy. And I knew it didn't feel like this.

Chapter Twenty-three

The Preemptive Strike

I didn't want to deal with anything, so I put the entire bachelor party into Dustin's hands, which maybe in retrospect wasn't the best call. He met me at Barnes and Noble to discuss, his face a thunderstorm in full swing.

"She dumped me. That bitch dumped me!"

"Donkey Girl dumped you? When?"

"Last night! Told me on the phone! I mean, fuck!"

I awkwardly patted his shoulder.

"Did she say why?"

"Oh, sure. She wouldn't fucking shut up about it. 'I never tell her what I'm thinking. I'm so fucking secretive.' Women just want to burrow in like those bugs in *Wrath of Khan*. It's all about mind control."

"Why didn't you just say what you were thinking?"

"I did! She wouldn't believe me! I told her I was thinking about work and some stuff I needed to pick up from the drugstore and that funny joke you forwarded me. The one about the dying yaks."

That was pretty funny. But I could see where he went wrong.

"You didn't say you were thinking about her? Even if you're not, you always say it."

"Oh, I said it. But she didn't want to hear that. She wanted me to be thinking about *us*. It wasn't that I never told her what I was thinking. It was that I wasn't thinking what she wanted me to be thinking."

"You weren't thinking about what she was thinking about. Which meant you could be thinking about anything."

Dustin shook his fist at the unfairness of it all.

"I don't want to talk about it anymore. I want to talk about this bachelor party. We're men, David! That's what this night will be all about! We've been getting too soft with all this relationship crap! They dig at you and they chip away until your balls just fall right off, and if you stick your hands down to catch them, that's when they dump you. We need to celebrate our manliness, our refusal to let our balls roll away on the floor."

All this talk of balls rolling away was making me queasy. I turned to the Urban Fiction section in embarrassment.

"Dustin, no strip clubs. The law's already been laid down."

"Man! Pussies! You're all pussies!"

"This is about Rat Boy, and he doesn't want strip clubs."

Dustin picked up a *Shopoholic* book without looking at it.

"This is not at all about Rat Boy and who cares what he wants! The bachelor party is for the friends, not the groom. He's not allowed to do anything, but we are! Rat Boy's lucky we're inviting him along."

"No strip club, Dustin. It's final."

He knocked the book on his forehead.

"Then I'll think of something else. We're going to be men, damn it. We need to rise up!"

I pointed to the paperback in his hand.

"You know that's a chick lit book, right?"

Dustin hastily dropped the book like an estrogen-laden hot potato.

A few nights later Dustin's backup plan was revealed as Rat Boy, Cameron, Zach, Dustin and I met up outside Hogs and Heifers. Hogs and Heifers is one of the many fake biker bars that cling to the outskirts of Manhattan. With hot belligerent women behind the bar and huge Harley goons with long beards and head scarves guarding the door, these facsimiles of real badass hangouts appeal to the thrill-seeking (up to a very safe point) yuppies of which Dustin is a proud example. They're the Disneyland versions of the real thing, about as authentic an experience as dinner in Morocco in Epcot Center. First off, who ever heard of a line at the door of a biker bar? Especially a line that contains baseball-hat-wearing twenty-five-year-old Goldman Sachs associates in khaki pants, talking with their buddies on their cells, mentioning large monetary figures for no reason except to impress the women in capri pants and twin sets behind them. How many true to life biker joints boast at least five bachelorette parties a night? I've been in a real biker bar. My buddy Jim almost died in one while wearing a sundress. So I can tell the wheat from the chaff; and we were definitely in chaff city.

Though he obviously didn't approve, Rat Boy kept his

mouth shut, willing to go where we go, playing nice. Cameron liked the idea of hot bartenders, as did I, so we didn't put up too much of a fight. The problem stemmed from an unlikely place: Zach.

"This looks dangerous, guys. I'm not too sure about this."

We thought he was kidding, but one look at his worried face assured us otherwise. Zach, the man who'd traveled through West Africa alone and once spent the night with a strange experimental German couple he'd called blind from a number posted on a bulletin board in Hamburg, was scared. I couldn't keep the incredulity off my face.

"That girl in line has a Hello Kitty sticker on her purse. I think we'll be okay."

Zach shook his head.

"Look at all the bikes. These types of places have fights all the time. And they never have anything good to drink. You ask for a mojito and they hit you with a bat. I don't like it."

Rat Boy looked at the rest of us with hope in his eyes.

"Maybe we can go somewhere else?"

Dustin shook his head firmly.

"No. We are doing this. Aren't we guys?"

I couldn't believe we were trying to muster the manliness to go into a bar that was featured in *Time Out*. I nudged him.

"Zach, it's just a bar. I bet you they'd make you a Buttery Nipple if you asked politely."

Zach tried to peer in the window, but he couldn't see past the glowing beer neon signs.

"The first sign of trouble, I'm leaving."

I clapped him on the shoulder.

"Just get in line."

We stepped behind two college guys in rugby shirts. Dustin's face glowed.

"This is gonna be awesome. I hear that the girls get on the bar and dance. And they pour water on each other!"

He was almost panting when we reached the door. Cameron checked his pockets.

"It's not too expensive, right? I'm trying to save money for when Mary and I move in together."

Dustin shook his head forcefully.

"Don't be a pussy, Cameron. This is drinkin' time. Money means nothing here. You can always make more."

"I'm not buying everyone in the bar drinks this time, Dustin."

"Of course you are. That's why I always buy you the first two shots. It pays dividends for the rest of the night."

"It's not gonna happen."

Zach looked around, worried.

"Do you think anybody has a knife? Or a gun?"

I peered at the people in line.

"They live on the Upper East Side. They have doormen."

And through it all, Rat Boy stayed silent, watching us. We made it to the door, to be greeted by a huge biker bouncer. Zach took an involuntary step back.

"This doesn't look good."

Dustin stepped up with his ID in hand.

"Don't be a dickless wonder, Zach. It's a bachelor party. Tonight we are men. Even David."

One by one we walked through the door, though I had to pull Zach by the elbow. The place was packed, to the point where you could barely move. It looked like a typical bar, with a pool table, dartboard and a TV above the pool table playing

Sportscenter. If a single badass hid out there in the crowd, he had to be be quite short, because I couldn't see him. All I could see were scores of baseball caps atop every type of frat boy imaginable, mixed in with the blown-out hair of the slumming Connecticut girls and the hipster wannabes. About as intimidating as a college dorm party, with fewer bongs. Zach was shaking.

No girls danced on the bar, though the bartenders were as hot as advertised, one a brunette in a cowboy hat and halter top and the other a tall blond in a tight belly-baring number. Dustin fought his way to the front and came back ten minutes later with five shots. He handed them out, with Rat Boy taking his with obvious distaste. I leaned in.

"It's just one shot. You don't have to if you don't want to."

"That's okay. I should. It's my night."

He said it with the sad air of a guy who really wanted to be doing some yoga. Dustin lifted his shot glass.

"To Josh and Annie!"

We raised our glasses and tossed back the fire water, which made me cough as my eyes watered.

"What the hell was that?"

Dustin smiled.

"Straight tequila. We are men!"

Zach spit his back into the glass.

"I wonder if they make cosmos."

He wandered up to the bar, trying not to be touched by anyone. Dustin took Cameron up to get him loaded, leaving Rat Boy and me standing side by side. I turned to him.

"Beer?"

"Do you think they have water?"

"We can ask. But you're doing the asking."

"Okay."

We found the blond bartender down at the end and Rat Boy shouted his request into her ear. She gave him a look of profound disgust, grabbed the water tap, and sprayed it directly into his face, sending him reeling back into me. The crowd went wild. She grabbed two Buds, popped the caps with her belt, and handed them over without a word. I handed one to Rat Boy.

"I think you wanted a beer."

"That girl should be fired for that."

"She's hot. There's nothing we can do."

"This is a rough place."

"No rougher than Fort Lauderdale."

We stood there awkwardly, sipping our beers almost unwillingly in the hope no one would spray us again. Rat Boy moved his bottle in tiny circles, staring through the lip at the brown liquid within. This was going to be a long night.

Time passed with the two of us standing there. Cameron and Dustin were pushed right up against the bar the whole time, staring hungrily up at the various dancing ladies above them, who never bothered to stare back. Zach stayed at the bar as well, caught by one of the bartenders who refused to let him leave, fascinated as we all were by his strange gentlemanly charm. I think I even saw her slip him a fruity drink, though I couldn't be sure. It didn't seem to help much. He still looked terrified. And through it all, Rat Boy and I stood side by side, a conversation no-fly zone, until out of nowhere Rat Boy seemed to work up the courage to speak.

"Annie told me what happened."

Great. Now Rat Boy was going to try to beat me up.

"Really?"

"I don't really blame you. How could I? She's wonderful. But she loves me."

I'd rather he punched me so we could get it over with. Instead, I shrugged.

"I knew it was a mistake as I was doing it. You have nothing to worry about there."

"I know. She's still your friend, you know. She'll forgive you. She's just making sure you think about what you did."

"That's good to hear."

Not that it mattered. It was all over after the wedding, anyway. But at least she didn't hate me. Rat Boy rubbed his finger along the rim of his beer bottle.

"I admit, I'm still learning things about her. That Dirty Telephone Game . . . that was something."

He shuddered involuntarily. I took a swig before answering.

"That's Annie. She may try to change, but that bite will always be there. You know that, right?"

He nodded, moving forward out of the way of an unruly Dartmouth grad getting tossed out by the bouncer.

"She has her flaws. And I have mine. You know, in Phoenix, it's so much easier to look inside yourself and get a good sense of who you are. It's harder here with all the people and taxis and street construction at six in the morning. But in Phoenix, out in the desert, I could take a good look and see how I might do some things the wrong way and overreact and be judgmental and all that stuff that can hurt other people. And coming here to be with Annie, I wanted to change all that, be better for her. I told myself I wasn't ever going to do anything that hurts her. And she told me the same thing. And it took us, what, two weeks to break that promise?"

"Maybe that's just who you are."

To my surprise he agreed with me.

"That is who I am. That's the problem with the desert. You can see the problems, but you also see no reason why you can't just fix them. Everything's so cut and dried out there. But here, you have to compromise. And with the nudity and the crass talking and all of it, we found out that there are things we can work on, but can never really fix. And now that we've accepted that, we can compromise. Instead of expecting these extreme changes, we can change just enough to be happy."

But what is the difference between a compromise and a capitulation? I guess it depends on what you really want. Which means you have to know what you really want. So what did I want out of this new, compromised world? Rat Boy smiled up at me tentatively and told me what he wanted.

"I want us to be sort of friends. Not best friends, of course. But you're important to Annie. And you may not be the best influence on her, but she smiles when she talks about you and that's important. Promise me you won't disappear because of me, okay? I'd feel awful."

I didn't know what was going to happen, but I had to tell him what he wanted to hear.

"I'm not going anywhere, I promise. Though I'll always be a bad influence. It's my right as her old friend."

"A small part of me likes that unpredictable side of her. I like knowing she's a little bit of a loose cannon. It keeps me guessing."

What was she, Mel Gibson? But almost against my will, his words made me feel better. At least after the wedding, after I'd been left behind like a childhood toy long outgrown, she'd be with someone who wouldn't bury her, who'd let a little of the Annie I loved thrive. At least she'd have a chance for happiness.

Cameron and Dustin came up, a wide and sloppy smile adorning Dustin's face.

"They're gonna do the water dance! This is what bachelor parties are all about, Josh! Watch and fall in love!"

A Melissa Etheridge song came on the jukebox, prompting the two bartenders to leap up onto the bar. They each held a pitcher of water in their hands, their hips swaying to the music. The frat boys went crazy, screaming for the show to start. The two beauties danced around seductively, kicking at rambunctious hands that got too frisky. The song hit the chorus and with a flourish, they upended the pitchers over their heads. Dustin almost fainted with joy.

"They're wet! You see! They're all wet! Sweet Jesus, they have water on them!"

Rat Boy stared upward, uncomfortable with the vulgar display, but not looking away either. I enjoyed the aquatic performance, nodding with appreciation as the two ladies poured another pitcher over their chests. Good clean family fun. But even the spectacle of two women dousing themselves couldn't keep my mind from dwelling on how empty I felt. Janey could compromise, too. I'd seen her try. Why was Rat Boy so willing to do the work and not me? Was he stronger than I was? Well, there's a big difference between an inappropriate comment about cock-gobbling and an art-desecrating spectacle. Anyway, look at Rat Boy, standing there with his beer barely touched, flinching every time someone hit a ball with a pool cue. He was getting so much more than he could ever have expected with Annie. But me . . . I expected so much more.

I thought about Janey sitting across from me at Aureole,

listening to me hem and haw. Listening to me backtrack. I couldn't tell her that I loved her. But I couldn't tell her that I didn't. I still couldn't tell myself that I didn't. Even now, with all my expectations lined up and agreed upon, I couldn't tell myself that I didn't love her. What did that mean? Instead of saying I love you, could I say I don't not love you? Would that have helped matters? She probably wouldn't have understood what I meant. But that meant something. I wasn't sure what, but it meant something.

The song ended and the crowd went wild. Zach walked up, his eyes glazed and unfocused. I grabbed him by the shoulder.

"What are you doing? You're drunk!"

"I felt threatened! I have to fit in or they may sense weakness and pounce."

"How many have you had?"

"I have lost all mathematical ability. You are not allowed to count here in hillbilly country. Wait a sec, Martina's calling. We had a nice conversation about nipple piercings. She's had them done as well."

Sure enough, the brunette bartender stood on the bar, pointing to Zach and demanding that he get over there. Zach timidly stepped up into Martina's reach, and she took him roughly by the shoulder, spinning him around to face the crowd. She dropped down, wrapping her legs around his waist and encircling his neck with one arm. With her free hand, she yanked Zach's head back, opening his mouth wide. Then she reached back and grabbed a bottle of rum, upending it directly into his open mouth until he began to spit it up. She threw the half empty bottle to her co-worker and sealed her handiwork with a kiss on the lips, before throwing Zach back into the crowd. The frat house went wild, rushing the bar for similar treatment, prompting Martina to start kicking meatheads in the face. Zach staggered back toward us, stinking of hard liquor.

"My shirt is a mess. It's Hugo Boss!"

Cameron whistled, eyes red and half closed, completely bombed.

"That was awesome! Hey guys, guys, hey, hey guys, listen, guys. Guys? Guys. I got this round!"

Dustin clapped him on the back.

"Why don't you buy one for the whole bar?"

"Good idea!"

And he ran off to the bar to do just that. Zach swayed on his feet, prompting me to lean in to look at his dilated pupils.

"You all right there, Zach?"

He nodded, smiling.

"Of course. I feel great."

With that, he rushed off to the bathroom. Dustin laughed.

"That's what you get when you order a Buttery Nipple. Isn't this place awesome?"

It really struck me how different my friends are from me. We all have the same sense of humor, I guess, but we looked at the world through such different eyes. How did we manage to stick together for any length of time? If I could lose Annie this easily, how soon before I lost the rest as well? How soon before I lost everyone? Before I could get too morose Zach came barreling out of the bathroom, wiping his mouth with one hand while his other hand was violently shaking by his side. He reached us and whispered furiously.

"We have to leave. Now."

I didn't understand the rush.

"Are you okay?"

"Right now! Come on! Now!"

His voice rose with panic. Alarmed, Dustin ran over to the bar to grab Cameron and we all pushed our way through the crowd. We could hear shouting behind us as we reached the door, sweeping by the biker bouncer out onto the street. Zach didn't stop, booking it down the side street. Unsure what to do, we raced after him. I yelled ahead.

"Why are we running?"

Zach screamed back to me.

"Come on! Faster! I don't want to die!"

We hit the corner and made a turn. Without slowing, we swerved to the right, down another side street. Zach could really run for such an urbanite. Must be all the hula hooping. Eventually we slowed down, coming to rest by the stairs of a tall brownstone. Zach looked furtively down the street.

"I think we lost them."

The rest of us could barely speak, bent over double, trying to keep from dying of heart attacks. Finally, I found the breath to ask the question on all our dried lips.

"What the fuck was that?"

Zach chanted under his breath. I poked him in the shoulder, prompting an irritated stare.

"I'm doing my mantra. Give me a moment."

Dustin stood upright.

"Just tell us what the fuck happened back there before I kick your ass personally."

Zach took a deep breath.

"It was horrible. You know how rough and tumble that place was. I was very tense. And that last half bottle of rum upset my stomach. So I ran into the bathroom, kicked open the stall, and purged myself all over the place."

Cameron leaned up against the stairwell, still trying to regain his breath.

"So? That happens. Was the bathroom attendant mad about the mess or something?"

"That place is a pit. There was no bathroom attendant. There was only one other person in the bathroom. Unfortunately, he happened to be sitting on the toilet in that very stall, directly in front of me, staring in horror at the fruits of my inebriation, which now covered his lap."

Dustin let out an amazed chortle.

"You puked on a guy sitting on the john! That is classic!"

"That's not everything. You have to understand, it's a rough place. I could tell what kind of people frequent it. They are harsh, angry people. They work with their hands, their big calloused hands. So they're not averse to beating the life out of someone who crosses them. I knew this man that I had just befouled would be angry, furious. How could he not? And I didn't want to get hurt. I'm wearing a Hugo Boss. Vomit comes out, blood does not. So I did a preemptive strike."

I started to get the picture. It wasn't pretty.

"What did you do . . . ?"

Zach looked mildly embarrassed.

"I punched him in the face and ran."

We stared at him in shock. Dustin came to his senses first.

"Before he could do anything?"

"Yes."

"Just popped him and ran."

Zach nodded. Dustin looked away, picturing the scene in his head. He stared back at the rest of us, eyes wide with awe.

"That is the coolest thing I have ever heard."

"Stop making fun of me. I could have died."

I tried to get Zach to see the enormity of what he'd done.

"Look at it from his perspective. This guy, who probably works at Deutsche Bank during the day, goes out with some friends to this cool joint where girls dance on the bar. He has to hit the bathroom, some bad sushi or something, and sits down on the can to do his business. He sits there a few minutes in peace and quiet, thinking about some work he left at the office, when suddenly someone kicks open his stall and pukes all over his lap, then, for no reason at all, slugs him in the face and runs back out the door. You probably changed his world perspective in there."

Dustin clapped his hands together.

"Life really is beautiful!"

Rat Boy touched Zach's shoulder lightly, causing Zach to flinch. Rat Boy pulled his hand away quickly, but still looked concerned.

"Are you all right?"

Zach thought about it, doing the internal checkup.

"I could eat something."

Cameron looked back the way we came.

"You feel better than that poor bastard, I bet."

Zach smiled a little at the thought.

"I just transferred a little stress."

And we walked off in search of a late-night snack, oblivious to the destruction in our wake.

* * *

After a round of chicken fingers at a nearby diner, Rat Boy decided to call it a night, heading home to his woman with obvious relief. Cameron staggered off to Grand Central to catch the last train home to his mate, who waited for him at home in the 'burbs. Dustin, unwilling to give it up, headed to the East Village to give Coyote Ugly a try. Zach and I let him go, tired of all the macho pretending. I turned to him.

"Headed home?"

Zach looked down at his watch.

"Actually, Keith is working at his bar tonight. It's right around here, I think."

"So he's a bartender?"

"Just to help with the bills until he gets more work as a Pilates instructor. He's very good, you know. I think he'll do quite well."

"I'm sure he will."

"You know what? I want you to meet him. I mean, really meet him."

I tried not to gasp in shock. Zach has never introduced a single significant other of his to any of his friends. He always maintained that it's better to keep those worlds separate. The only reason I knew what Keith looked like was because of the hula-hoop night, and I still hadn't been allowed to talk to him. But this . . . this was very different.

"You really like him, don't you?"

Zach smiled shyly.

"He's different from anyone I've ever known. So sweet and tough, all at the same time. I think . . . don't make fun of me. But I think I may be falling in love."

"Come on. You barely know the guy."

"I feel something. I don't recognize it. So I could be wrong. But I think I may be. I don't know whether to spin around with arms outstretched or run to Paraguay."

"Which will it be?"

"We'll have to see. Come on. Just make sure you don't tell the others. I don't want to deal with their callous attempts at humor. I'm very raw right now."

We headed down the street, into the West Village, eventually coming to a small lounge on the corner of Jane and Hudson. A pink neon sign blinked THE PLACE. Zach pointed.

"This is the place."

"I can see that."

"Be nice, okay?"

"Of course."

"He's a great guy."

"You told me."

"You'll love him, I know it."

"I'm sure I will."

"But be nice, anyway."

"You don't even have to ask."

I'd never seen Zach this nervous before. He led me into the dark lounge, looking around for his sweetheart. I picked the guy out a split second before Zach laid eyes on him, and I will always wish I'd been able to keep him from seeing what he saw. The love of his life, the best guy in the world, making out with a tall bald black man in the corner of the bar, their two perfect chins grazing each other, threatening to start a stubble fire. Even through the music and the din of the crowd, I could hear Zach's heartbreaking gasp. Keith must have heard it, too, though I know it was impossible, because he broke away from his kiss and turned to see Zach standing in the doorway. His look surprised me. He wasn't mortified or anything like that. At best, he seemed mildly embarrassed. Patting his friend, he began to walk toward Zach. Zach whispered to me out of the side of his mouth.

"Please wait outside."

"I can help . . ."

"Please."

"Okay."

I backtracked through the door, moving over to the window to peer in. Zach and Keith stood surrounded by dark figures, arguing. Zach was about to cry. It was awful to behold, like something unnatural. I'd never seen him cry about anything. Keith kept shrugging, like he had a twitch. After a few minutes, Keith put up a hand and walked away, terminating the discussion. Zach watched him go, devastated, unable to move. After a moment, he gathered himself, wiping his cheeks, and turned to walk out the door. By the time he got to me, his face was stone.

"I don't think it's going to work out."

"He's a dick, I can tell."

"It's not his fault. We were never exclusive. He likes to play the field. I can't fault him for that. I should never have let it go so far."

Zach began to walk quickly down the street. I jogged to keep up.

"So you felt something. You can't fault yourself for that."

"Of course I can. I don't want to be feeling like this all the time. This is awful. How do you stand it?"

"You get through."

"We were dating only a few months. That's nothing. I shouldn't feel this bad."

"It doesn't matter how long. It digs in quickly."

"He was so . . . I thought we had this . . . a connection or something. I'm delusional. I'm overreacting, obviously."

"Come on. This is good for you."

"How is this good? In what possible light is this agony good?"

"Because it might have worked."

"But it didn't."

"But it might have. And then you'd feel what you felt when you walked up to the bar all the time. I've never seen you like that. It's a good thing. You shouldn't run from it."

Zach stopped at the street corner, standing unnaturally straight as he waited for the light to change.

"I've been reading this book, *The Unbearable Lightness of Being*, and I truly identify with it. It's all about people with burdens who are happy and people who go through life without burdens, light as a feather, but disconnected and alone. I've been reading this and thinking, I feel like that. I have a million small wonderful experiences, but I float above them, never really attached. So when I met Keith, I felt this was my chance to take on a burden and see if the magic formula really works. And for a very short time it did. But now, look at me. My burden has driven me into the ground. I'd give anything to be floating right now. Anything."

"Something tells me it's not just about burdens, Zach. It's about the right burden. The burdens that are really gifts you don't mind carrying. You don't take on just any burden, and it's when you realize it's not the right burden, when you get nothing in return for your labor, that you shed it."

Ever since my conversation with Rat Boy, my picture of Janey, which always danced right on the edge of my mind, had been pushing against the walls that kept her where she needed to be. I could miss her, but not dwell on her, that was the arrangement that kept everything stable. But she'd found a way to whisper past my defenses and now I could hear her demanding to know what kind of burden she was. The wrong kind obviously. But then why did I feel heavier now that she was gone? Zach didn't want to hear any of this.

"How? How do you leave this behind? I guess I can head to Spain again. Though it's a bit hot this time of year."

"Or your friends can help you. You can stay here and let us try to put it all into perspective, so maybe next time it won't be so hard."

"That doesn't sound like floating, David."

"You can try to float again. And maybe you'll manage it. But at one point the balloon pops. At one point you will come down. Which would you rather? Learning how to land now? Or letting it go, never sure when it will all come crashing down? Look, you got hurt. It happens to everyone. But it doesn't have to be a bad thing. We can help you make sense of it. So it doesn't blindside you next time."

Zach crossed the street, not answering me. I walked quickly, keeping up. He didn't answer for a time, staring down at his feet as he strode up the sidewalk past the closed stores and dark cars. Eventually, he turned to give me the most naked look I'd ever seen from him.

"Would you really do that?"

"Of course."

"Why?"

"You're my friend."

"Oh. Right."

We walked on. Zach maintained a constant distance between us, but he kept going in my direction. He could hop a cab at any time, but for now, we walked.

Chapter Twenty-four

The Big Happy Arrives

I stood in the tiny elevator heading up to the eighth floor of the generic, nondescript apartment building that housed my new agent. He'd left me a message telling me to come in to discuss a fabulous deal he'd worked out for me with a big publishing company. He said I'd be falling over myself with joy. I could feel my hair standing on end as I watched the numbers rise up above the maze of silver buttons. I had pushed Janey to the back of my mind again, hoping she'd fallen out (though the memory of her scent informed me otherwise). I hadn't slept more than three hours a night all week. Excitement, of course.

I skipped down the faceless hallway, right up to the plain, featureless door that now seemed to me to be the most beautiful door in all the world. I pressed on the buzzer, dancing in my shoes. The door opened to reveal a short woman in jogging clothes.

"You must be David. I'm Robin. Grab a seat, Craig will be with you in a moment. You need anything?"

She led me to the small couch right by her desk. I sank

down, still marveling at how I could read the refrigerator magnets from my seat.

"No thanks, I'm good."

"If you need anything, just holler!"

And then she sat down right in front of me, her back five inches from my nose. A minute or two passed and a woman popped her head out of the back office.

"Robin? Do you have the contracts for the Birchman book?"

"Right here, Karen."

"Thanks."

She slipped back in. I realized Karen couldn't have been taller than five three. I felt like Shaq in this place. I had to be careful not to step on anyone. I felt a hand on my shoulder.

"David! Buddy! Come on in!"

I stood up, quickly pumping Craig's hand, almost tearing it off in my excitement. We stepped back into his minuscule office, and I once again wedged myself into the chair of honor. Craig leaped straight to the point.

"I've got an offer here from Pocket Books that is just so good, there's no way anyone will match it. It's a preempt, which means we can't go to auction, but with what they're willing to do, I think this is the way to go."

He bowled me over with his enthusiasm. I resisted the urge to clap.

"Great! Wow! So, what's the offer?"

"Okay. Here goes. Are you sitting down?"

As if I could have stood up without a shoe horn if I wanted to.

"You bet."

"Then get ready to wet yourself."

He picked up a sheet of paper and glanced down at it, his eyes glowing. He made a drum roll noise with his tongue, both amping up my excitement and grossing me out a little, before stopping the roll with a slap of his hand on the hard desk.

"Pocket Books has offered you . . . a four-book contract! Can you believe it! That is never done, and I mean never, but they liked your style and they think this genre is going to be huge, so they want to lock you up for a while! It's amazing. I can hear myself say it and even I don't believe it!"

My mouth flew open in shock. Four books! I'd be set for the next few years! Maybe I could buy an apartment! A beach house! I could ease my dad's troubles with his job, buy them their new house or something. Four books! That was amazing!

"My God. I think I did just wet myself."

"It's okay! I put paper down!"

"Well, give me the good news. How much is the contract worth?"

"Five thousand for the first book, ratcheting up to fifteen thousand for the fourth book!"

The world froze. The music scratched. The dog whined. The cartoon character did a double take, with spit. Everything ground to a halt.

What the hell?

I swallowed, hard.

"Dollars?"

"You bet."

"That's it?"

"That's pretty good."

"It is?"

Craig's eyes softened, letting out a sliver of sympathy.

"Hey, this isn't Hollywood. Books don't do the same business, especially if you're a first-time author. If one of your books takes off, the royalties will be nice, trust me. But you don't get into this business for the fame and fortune. That's what the movies and television and music are for. You write books because you love to write books. And this deal lets you write four books—dump lit books of course—and assures you they'll get published. That's one of the sweetest deals around."

A shudder ran through me as my big happy crashed and burned. But why? Wasn't this what I wanted? What else did I expect? Who was I kidding? I knew what I expected. I expected to sell this book and look around to see I'd made it to the pinnacle, the very apex of achievement, where I could be happy forever. But now that I was here, I could see that I'd only pulled myself up the first step, and a mountainous staircase loomed ahead of me, the top far out of sight. Off to the sides of this climb lay the littered remains of friends and family, experiences and simple pleasures, all cast aside in the single-minded rise up the stairs. The only thing that could sustain me would be the love of what I was doing. The love of writing. But did I love to write? Or did I just love to be read?

"This is a great deal. Really. Can I think about it?"

Craig nodded vigorously.

"Of course. Of course you can! But don't wait too long. They may get spooked and take the offer off the table and we don't want that!"

Of course we didn't. Right?

On the way out, Craig pulled me toward the main office.

"I want you to meet Julian. You'll love him. Julian, you in here?"

"Come on in, Craig!"

Stepping into Julian's office, the first thing I noticed was the huge shaggy rug. Like the floor had an extremely hairy back. The furniture, white and ultramodern in the way that seemed long out of date, lay spread around the room haphazardly. This must be where all the space in the old apartment ended up. Julian, a graying gentleman in huge round sunglasses, took his unlit cigar out of his mouth to say hi.

"David! I've heard so much about you. Four-book deal! Huge!"

"It's nice to meet you, Julian."

Julian stood up to shake my hand and, to my considerable lack of surprise, he barely came up to my shoulder. I glanced over at Craig, who stood even shorter. Thinking back on Robin and Karen, I solved the mystery. All of Julian's employees were shorter than he was. That's one way to be tall that doesn't involve shoes with eight inch soles. Here in munchkin land, Julian was a giant among men. Not a bad way to live, all things considered. Be just a little taller than your expectations. Then you'll never feel small.

* * *

In the elevator back down to the lobby, I leaned up against the wall, shell-shocked. Five thousand dollars? Fifteen by book four? Writing that first book took me a year, at least. I couldn't live off that money. I'd be DJ-ing weddings and bar mitzvahs forever! This wasn't a big happy! This wasn't even a miniature happy. This was a pig fuck. A big, giant, pig fuck. What do I do now? I tossed aside everything for this moment. Everything that would distract me from my goal. And now, I've reached it, and I have never been more disappointed in my life. This is why people drink wine out of boxes. Everything was leading up to this moment. And now . . .

Now what?

* * *

I helped wrap up my parents' living room, taking the pictures off the walls and cushioning the lamps with a year's worth of the *New York Times*. The moving people would be coming over the weekend to take care of the big stuff, and they'd reassemble them in some strange room in some strange town out in mythical, foreign Connecticut. My childhood memories would be rearranged between different walls, with new vistas outside the unfamiliar windows. Enough will be similar to make the new all the more striking and disquieting. Alex worked in the garage, trying to take apart some strange machine that was all the rage twenty years ago for melting snow. My dad loves fads. Without them, we'd probably still be snowed in from the blizzard of '84, or so he maintains. He'd be the only one alive, having eaten the rest of us long ago.

I hated to see my entire life boxed up for transport, especially since the more important pieces, like the walls and the floors and the trees and the graffiti behind the toilet, would be staying behind. Nothing remains frozen, and it hurt to see it thaw. Mom had to wipe her eyes every ten minutes, her hand lingering on a thousand memories of her family. I wished we lived in one of those Victorian novels, where houses stayed in the family for generations, having as much if not more personality than the people who inhabited them. Our house had lasted most of my life. Beyond that, nothing. It had no name, no dark secrets, no countless generations of my forefathers floating around in the attic. It was the place my parents raised a family, and now that the family was raised, they had to move on. We always seem to be moving on.

I didn't mention my book troubles. No sense adding to the stress, especially with my mom crying over dirty tennis balls found behind the grandfather clock, or a ten-year-old plastic Easter egg filled with fossilized jelly beans discovered inside the arm of one decrepit old easy chair. I did let them know that I'd broken up with Janey, thinking that it would make my mom feel better to know I wasn't with the girl who destroyed her work. Her answer surprised me.

"I'm sorry, David. I felt so bad for her. It was an accident, after all. She sent me a lovely note, you know. I got it yesterday. Apologizing and hoping I forgave her. I appreciated it. I hope you didn't break up with her because of that."

And she went back to weeping over the cups we got for free from the gas station when I was four. I felt like weeping over my life. What did I have now? I had no real job. Maybe a deal writing books about dumping people. That sounded like fun. My home would soon be gone, my family broken up, with my brother up north and my parents out in the wilds of Danbury. My entire plan crumbled at my feet. And all I could think about was Janey's face as I said, "I'm sorry," not realizing how true those words were. Ah well, right? Fodder for book two, what with the dumping and all.

I slipped into my room to make sure I didn't leave anything behind. Not finding anything of me anywhere, I slid into the corner, staring out at the backyard scene I'd grown up looking at. I was practically thirty and it was all almost gone.

"I'll miss it, too."

My dad stepped into my room, staring at the ceiling, which was covered in small yellow shapes.

"Though why you ever put up those stupid glow-in-the-dark stars I'll never know."

I shrugged.

"I wanted to look at the constellations."

"Which constellation? I can't recognize any of them."

"I made up my own. That's the Harvey star cluster, in the shape of my invisible friend Harvey. The Big Anteater and the Small Anteater. The Great Gummy Worm, or the Roll of Quarters, I can't remember which. And the star of David, my own little joke."

"Well, they won't come off, so you might want to leave a cheat sheet for the next folks."

"Maybe I will."

We lapsed into silence, staring at the fake stars on the ceiling. Dad shifted uncomfortably.

"Your mom doesn't want me to tell you, but I think I should. I got laid off last month."

I tried to act surprised, but failed horribly. Dad nodded to himself.

"Of course you know already. I knew I should have told you sooner."

"What happened?"

"I worked there for thirty-five years and they decided to phase me out. Gave me a new job that they created just for me, and then, two months later, they downsized it. Impressively sneaky, I thought."

"So what now?"

"I try to consult. I still get a pension, which will kick in soon. But it won't be anywhere near what your mom and I are used to. We'll have to change our lifestyle. The glory days have passed by."

"But you'll still have money, right?"

"It won't be the same. It won't ever be the same. Your mom wants to stay home and paint. I want to travel. We'll have to compromise somehow. We can't afford to travel the way I thought we would when I retired. Nothing's working out the way I thought it would."

He sounded so down. I tried to cheer him up.

"It could be worse. You still have two sons, right?"

"Yeah. Yeah, I do. You always talk about happiness, right? It never lasts. Even the best things that you think will last forever slide by eventually. I loved my job. I got to travel the world and deal with important financial people, even though I couldn't explain any of it to my own family."

That was true. I still have no idea what my dad did. It had something to do with Wall Street, travel, money and making Sandy Weil beg. My dad continued.

"But now it's gone. You guys are gone, too. It's back to your mother and me, just like before. Like the last thirty years never happened. Except for the back pain and the strange new wrinkles. So what now? That's what I keep asking. What now?"

My back began to ache as I could feel my muscles tense. My dad had never talked to me like this before. He'd never really shown any weakness. He got angry, and sad, but he never talked about it. What was I supposed to do? Say something helpful? I could try.

"You can retire. Spend more time with Mom."

Dad gave me an incredulous look.

"It'll just be the two of us in the house all the time. We'll rip each other to shreds."

"Does the new house have a panic room to hide in if someone goes all *Shining*?"

He smiled wanly.

"We'll figure something out. We have to. I just don't know what it is. I wish I knew."

Another roller coaster in the dark. Didn't anyone get to ride by the light of day?

"I'm sure you'll be fine."

"It's a lot of work, David. It's more work living with your mom than I could ever get across to you. So much work."

"But Mom always says you guys were in love from the start. From the time you picked up her friend and her at the airport to go to that cruise."

"We were in lust. We couldn't keep our hands off each other. But that doesn't guarantee love. The love part was work."

"What kind of work?"

"The way I look at it, people fall in lust all the time. I fell in lust once or twice before your mom, and I might have married one of them if I'd really wanted to work at it. But I didn't, I broke up with them. Just like people break up every day. Your mom, though, that was different. I lusted after her, but there was something else."

"Love at first sight."

"Nah. Not that. That stuff is bullcrap. I don't believe in it. Most of those love at first sight couples break up in the first six months. Those people believe that because they have these strong feelings, everything else is predestined to work out. And it isn't. People are fragile. I think what really happens is you meet someone you have a connection with. Someone you want to be around and talk to and laugh with. You know what I mean. And that connection is a great gift, believe me. But that isn't a promise. That's just a starting point. And then the work begins."

"How hard did you have to work with Mom?"

Dad whistled.

"It wasn't easy, let's say that. We got married after eight months of dating and we almost didn't make it through the first year. The things she did to a roast beef. Criminal. And she'd get angry when I said something. It's an expensive cut of meat. You don't massacre it like that. I might as well buy a skirt steak if you're gonna do that. And maybe I was a little arrogant. Just a bit. We came this close to divorce."

I was rocked. I'd never heard any of this before.

"Over roast beef?"

"Over what was behind it. You know what I think the most important ingredient of any successful relationship is? The one nobody talks about? The fact that both people want it to work. If both people are willing to keep at it, that more than anything can tip the scales. And it was worth it. The second year was fantastic. I'm not saying you should keep plugging away when it's awful. But if the good times make you happy enough, and the bad times aren't horrendous, then it just might be worth the work."

"Then this new phase isn't so bad. It's just a little more work."

Dad made a face.

"The problem is, we got into a groove for the past few years and I've gotten lazy. I'm out of shape for this new round. I am not looking forward to it. But we'll be fine. Don't worry. After all, we both want it to work, right?"

He gave the room one last look and walked out.

I sat still in the corner, thinking. Janey wasn't easy. I looked into the future with her and saw years of work ahead of me. I wanted someone nondemanding, like Julie the Relapse Girl. She'd been so simple to date. Almost like a dating doll I had to play with only when I wanted to. But look how that worked out. So no matter who I dated, it would be hard? No matter what I did with my life, it would be hard? There'd be no big payoff? My parents worked at their marriage for thirty-four years, and now they still had to work? The rough edges never completely smoothed out and the bad habits never really washed away? It never stopped? I thought I'd make it to my big happy and from then on I'd coast. But it never stopped. Big or small, I still had to deal with the next day and the next and the next. I still had to do it again. I slumped back into my corner, tired just thinking about it.

* * *

That evening I sat at my computer and thought about writing novel after novel. Doing it again and again, finishing one and then starting up the next. Working a day job to pay the rent and then coming home to type away late into the night. On my way home I'd stopped in the bookstore to stare at the shelves. There were so many books. Why did anybody buy one in particular? What would make my book stand out from the rest? I'd probably have to hope for a few people giving my first one a try, and maybe by the fourth I'd have a small following. Or maybe not. Maybe I'd still be plugging away, working at it, forever. I stared at that blank computer screen, getting tired just thinking about it.

Chapter Twenty-five

The Perfect Wedding

Friday dawned, or so I'm told. I slept through it. Don't worry, I always sleep through it. Unless sometime in the future the day happens to dawn around eleven, I'll have to take this whole sunrise rumor on faith. Of course, it didn't help that this particular day brought with it a sense of foreboding and dread. After all, it was the best day of my best friend's life. If that wasn't cause for depression, I didn't know what was.

Annie gettin' married. The thought of it twisted my stomach. I could see her sinking into the depths away from me like Leo in *Titanic*. This was the last day of my friendship with Annie. After she said I do, I would see her only for a few more forced meetings when she remembered to schedule them, followed by infrequent phone calls and finally the inevitable phasing out of all communication. If you didn't get along with the spouse, you were history. And though I didn't hate Rat Boy, and he said he didn't hate me, the fact that I brought out the cynical, non-granola-eating side of his wife would never sit well with him, despite his assurances to me at Hogs and Heifers. He'll never say anything, but Annie will pick it up nonetheless. And you have to side with your spouse. No matter what. I would never fault her for it. Even though I'm the sacrifice.

I lay in bed in my tiny apartment, not wanting to face the end of an era. The apartment didn't bother to try to kill me anymore. It could sense that my life was hardly worth it. I never would have thought that I'd miss my apartment's murderous side. In retrospect, the attacks made me feel like I was worth assaulting; something in my life was worth snuffing out. Now that the attacks had stopped, I felt defeated. I dreaded putting on the suit and the tie and the smile, pretending that this was all so fantastic. Annie was being sucked into the life of a shiny, happy, boring person and there was no way I could save her. When the priest gave his benediction, he'd really be giving the last rites to the best part of my old friend. From then on out, all ordinary, all the time.

An hour later, I drove up into Westchester with my tie on the seat next to me, laughing at how uncomfortable it would soon make me, as ties often do. I had a gig after the reception, a simple bar night that I couldn't get Bill to take on, so I'd thrown my equipment into the back of my Jeep. I couldn't wrap my head around the fact I was going to Annie's wedding. It felt more like another job, another performance where I would dance around with a big fake smile and try to make everyone happy. But no tip this time. Not even the leftovers from the dancing Greek. In fact, I'd be poorer by the end.

I pulled up to the church, a modern (read: tacky) version of the Catholic cathedral, and parked around back. A small addition wrapped around the back of the church like a fanny pack, an ugly two-story collection of walls where the kids learned their Jesus after school three times a week. After the ceremony, Annie would be leading us all into that depressing building for the hastily assembled reception. As I hopped out of my car and slipped on my suffocating tie, I wondered how I would be able to get through this. The most depressing, ill-advised wedding I'd ever worked would be a fairy tale compared to this tossed together nightmare. Maybe it was fitting. Maybe the surroundings should reflect the mood. I tightened my tie as a self-flagellating gesture while I made my way around to the front of the church, gathering myself before stepping into the big day.

I felt like an interloper, like I would be asked to go around back with the help. You really do become your job, no matter what that job is. I felt so much more like a DJ than an author. On either side of the aisle, people filled about a quarter of the pews. This would be no Kennedy wedding. Rat Boy's people milled about on the groom's side. I half expected to see an entire hippy commune stagger out of a smoke-filled VW bus, singing John Denver songs to the sounds of a hastily assembled drum circle, every one of them buck naked. Instead, you couldn't tell whose people were whose. Rat Boy's family and friends looked like everyone else, with no long-haired, mustache-wearing burnouts with exposed genitalia in sight. Everyone seemed shaven and clean-cut, actually. If anyone looked strange, it was the people on Annie's side. Her wicked aunts sat in one row, sharing the one eyeball between them. Annie's cousins sat on either side, including, to my shock, my ex-girlfriend Beth. The only girl I'd ever loved sat next to her mother, and now she saw me.

Fuck. I wasn't prepared for this. I hadn't even thought about the possibility that she'd show up. What was I thinking?

She's Annie's first cousin. How could she stay away? Beth smiled uncertainly and stood up, walking toward me. She looked different, somehow. Well, two years had passed. That's a long time, an eternity. Her body had changed, filled out the way all women's bodies do unless they never eat anything again, and it suited her. She walked with a bit more confidence, a bit more ease. But her face . . . her face had changed the most. Somehow, somewhere down the road, she'd become ordinary.

Not that she was ugly. She just didn't glow the way I remembered. She didn't have the vitality, that energy that I'd loved. She used to force my eyes to her without saying a word. This woman in front of me now would have merited maybe a second glance in the grocery store, but nothing more. Where had that glow gone?

"Hello, David."

The voice. Her voice remained the same. Her voice brought me back to dinners and late nights and later mornings, to trips and dancing and happy after happy. But it seemed incongruous coming from this different, lesser person.

"Hi, Beth. It's been a while, huh?"

"It sure has. How've you been?"

"Good. Very good. I'm an author now."

What, did you think I wouldn't mention that first thing? Come on.

"Good for you. I'm working in education, myself."

"Sounds great."

We sputtered out. We both knew the next question, the only mystery remaining was who would ask first. I made the sacrifice.

"Seeing anyone special?"

Her eyes lit up and she was off. She'd been living with this guy for a year now and they were very happy and he was so great and she couldn't believe how lucky she was and on and on and on. Her face regained a little of that glow I remembered as she spoke and I realized that I had in a way supplied it. We'd lit each other up like we shared the same battery. And now someone else made her light up, bringing out her beauty. I probably should have felt a pang hearing about how happy some other guy made the only girl I'd ever loved, but instead all I experienced was a twinge of nostalgia for the sound of her voice. I'd been so happy to listen to her blabber on about whatever thought happened to pop into her head. I loved to hear the way her mouth formed the words. In fact, I'd often closed my eyes to listen to her, not even paying attention to the words, just focusing on the sounds. I thought of Janey's big eyes peering up at me, her ridiculous lip gloss shining below. Beth went on and on about her new man and I drifted away to kissing Janey's teeth while she smiled. I had to stop her before I became buried by regret.

"He sounds fantastic. I need to check on Annie. I'll talk to you later, all right?"

"Sure. It was good to see you."

"You too."

She wandered back to her family, her final mission to show how well she'd moved on successfully discharged. She probably heard the regretful edge in my voice and attributed it to her tale. But my regrets, like my life, had moved on. I spun and made my way back to the little room where Annie waited to change her life.

I knocked on the door.

"You decent?"

"Come in, David."

I slipped inside. And stopped up short.

"Wow."

Where Annie found that dress on such short notice I'll never know. But no matter how rushed and slipshod the rest of this day may turn out, no one could ever say she looked anything short of magnificent. I don't know much about dresses. I'm more of a how-much-skin-does-it-show type of fashion aficionado. But even a classless idiot like myself could appreciate how beautiful Annie looked surrounded by white as she sat nervously biting her nails. I smiled sincerely.

"You look amazing."

Annie blushed at my earnest tone.

"Not from you, David. You're supposed to come in and make fun of all the frills."

"Sorry. I'm struck dumb. In all senses of the word. Hello, Florence."

Annie's mother sat in the corner, on the phone talking to some client out in L.A. She waved and went back to her conversation. I walked over to sit down beside the blushing bride. We sat in silence for a moment until I broke it.

"Are we okay?"

Annie smiled, flicking my arm with her fingernail.

"Of course we are. Idiot. Is everyone here?"

"Yep. Including your cousin."

"Ouch. That's right. Are you okay?"

"I'm fine. She seems happy now."

"From what I hear. I don't think she'll stay long at the reception. I'm hoping most of my family cuts out right after the cake cutting. I want to have a good time."

"You will. I promise."

I looked around the small room, uncertain of what to say. A thought occurred to me.

"Who's giving you away? With your father gone, who does that?"

"No one, actually. I thought about using Eddie since he's my cousin, but he's a little too creepy. He's wearing a shoestring tie, you know. I don't really have any other male family to do that."

What the hell.

"I'll do it, if you want."

Annie shook her head softly.

"Thank you, but no. I'll walk down myself. Why does someone need to give me away, anyway? I'm not going anywhere. Why do I have to lose to gain?"

I knew the answer to that question, and she could read it on my face. She grabbed my cheeks in the kung fu grip of her iron fingers.

"Ow!"

"Don't you do it. You better not abandon me after this wedding is over. I don't care what anyone says. You're my best friend, David. I don't have a brother. I have you. You're family. You don't give up on family, all right?"

Her hand threatened to pop my jaw. My answer came out strained and muffled by her clutching fingers.

"Aw wight. Aw wight. I pwomith."

She let go.

"What?"

"I said, I promise."

We lapsed into silence. I was family? I never really thought of it that way. Then again, who else but family would go to such lengths to sabotage a relationship they didn't approve of? Of course we were family. Families never really break up, do they? The bonds never really dissolve. Hell, Annie's awful aunts sat whispering hatefully in their pew to prove it. Mary's mom would be at the wedding of her daughter and Cameron, the sum of all the ethnic groups she despised, if it came to that. It would take a lot of work to keep in touch, let alone remain close. But something about that thought of permanence, that promise still to be there after the dust kicked up by our various quests for happy settled, that comforted me. I may not like the life she was embarking on, but I'd always have a place onboard. She smacked my knee.

"The way things are going, you'll probably end up living above my garage anyway."

"Great. I can sleep between the bags of organic wheat."

"Wiseass."

Her hand made its way onto my hand and we sat there, still, staring at the door to the future, feeling change rushing toward us like a tidal wave that gave us just enough time to take a breath before crashing over us and sending us down deep into the unknown.

* * *

Okay, the service ended up being nice. They both couldn't stop smiling, though the sight of Rat Boy's incisors peeking out between his lips didn't thrill me. Per Annie's request, Dustin, Cameron and I stood by Rat Boy as ushers, while his four sisters stood by Annie as bridesmaids. Four sisters. It explained a lot about him. There were no maids of honor or best men. The genders didn't match up. After the priest pronounced them man and wife, Cameron and Dustin and I turned to one another at the same time, sharing in our grief at the world's refusal to stay where we put it. Zach stood in the audience, clapping enthusiastically with the rest. After all, it didn't affect him much either way.

I ducked out of the cocktail hour to check on Bill, who was setting up in the main hall. The ceiling rose up maybe a foot above my head. My agent would have felt right at home. Bill's feet poked out from under his table, muffled curses drifting out in a steady stream.

"Bill? You all right?"

Bill smacked his head, in time-honored fashion, before sliding out. He'd foolishly donned his tux before setting up, resulting in a dust covered black jacket and a partially torn bow tie.

"I'm fine, David. Great."

"You know the drill, right? You spoke with Annie earlier."

"Yep. It's all down."

"Then what were you doing under there?"

"Nothing. Just trying the figure out where this thingy went."

He pointed to the wire in his hand.

"You mean the speaker cable?"

"I guess."

"It goes in the speaker. There's a clue in the name if you look hard enough."

"Which speaker?"

"Where's the other speaker cable plugged in?"

Bill's eyes went wide.

"There are two of these?"

I spent the next fifteen minutes setting up Bill's table for him. He'd already managed to break one of his CD players when he tried to plug the electric cord into the back of the amp, causing a short. I had to run out and grab some of my equipment to replace it. By the time I had him up and running, a sneaking suspicion had wormed its way into my brain.

"Bill, weren't you supposed to do that wedding at the Inn in Rye last weekend?"

Bill looked down.

"Yeah."

"Did you?"

"Sort of."

"What happened?"

"They sent me out with an assistant, to help me out, you know? He had to take over."

"Your assistant took over the wedding?"

"Yeah."

"Had he ever done a wedding before?"

"Not really. He was pretty good, though."

"So you've never done this before?"

"I've seen it done."

"Oh. Okay. That's okay, then."

Bill looked ready to cry. I awkwardly patted him on the back.

"Don't worry. It'll be fine. You'll be great."

Tears began to fall, making streaks in the dust on his face.

"I don't want to let you down."

"You won't. Don't worry. It'll be fine. Just focus on the game plan. Okay? All right."

He brought himself under control and put on a brave face.

"I'll be a superstar."

"Sure you will."

He went back behind the table to prepare. I stood staring at him for quite some time. I couldn't. I was in the wedding party. But if I didn't, if I left that idiot in charge . . . who knows what could happen? What should I do? A shudder ran down my back. I turned and locked eyes with Janey, who stood by the table, dressed in her waitress uniform. She held a stack of bread dishes in her hand, about to place them around the table. She looked more beautiful than I'd ever seen her. I couldn't have walked away if I tried.

"What are you doing here?"

She put the pile down on the table before she answered.

"Malena is sick, so . . ."

Silence as our eyes stayed locked.

"This is a little awkward."

"I'm sorry."

I didn't know what to say. I felt lightheaded. Words came out of my mouth without consulting my brain.

"There's a problem with the DJ. He's an idiot."

She blinked, her mouth twitching. She struggled for a moment before looking away.

"You better go deal with it, then."

She turned and hurried back into the kitchen, leaving the plates stacked on the table. I considered following her, but instead I walked across the room, back out to the cocktail party like a coward.

I approached the boys standing in the corner. Mary, who was fast becoming Annie's only female friend, kept by her side, making sure her wineglass was full, glowing as brightly as the bride. I smirked at Cameron.

"Looks like your lady is getting ideas."

Cameron looked pained, but not too pained.

"I hope she's not in it to piss off her mom, that's all. That's my job."

Dustin nudged him in the ribs, hard.

"Go on, tell him. Fine, I'll do it. They're moving in! The sucker is letting the girl shack up with him!"

I turned to Cameron in shock.

"You guys have been going out for, like, three months. That's nothing."

Cameron gave an embarrassed but defiant shrug.

"Her lease is up and she can't really afford a nice place, so why not?"

We all knew why not, but I decided to play it diplomatically.

"Congrats, man. You're on the first step to having all of this!"

I waved my arms around the cramped room, just as a girl with a tray of potato skins walked by. Only her limbo skills kept us out of an embarrassing accident. Cameron took me at my word.

"You'll all have to come over sometime."

Dustin shook his head in disgust.

"For a dinner party?"

Zach sighed wistfully.

"I love dinner parties. Good conversation for hours, plus food. What's not to love?"

Cameron agreed.

"So you'll have to come."

"Well, actually, I'm heading out to Tuscany the day after tomorrow."

I looked at him sharply, but he avoided my eyes. Dustin was impressed.

"I want your life, dude. For how long?"

"A few months. We'll see."

"We'll miss you, buddy."

"Likewise."

He still wouldn't look at me. We both knew it might be longer than that. We'd seen the other night how long he could run. Cameron changed the subject for us.

"How's it looking in there, David?"

"Good thing his family didn't demand a Jewish wedding. Otherwise, we'd put them on the chair and end up running their heads through the ceiling."

Dustin looked around at the people milling about.

"One of Rat Boy's sisters is kinda hot. Man, I love weddings. I look so good in a suit, it's almost not fair. I think I'll give her a whirl."

He stepped past us to go talk to the young lady in question, who didn't look as impressed by his suit-wearing skills as he was. Mary swooped in and grabbed Cameron to meet some friends of Rat Boy's family, who coincidentally went to the same summer camp as she had. Zach and I stood there awkwardly for a moment, neither wanting to bring anything to the surface. After a few minutes, Zach stepped away to grab another drink and tell Annie's friend from work what the Sistine Chapel looked like up close. I stared around at the party, feeling apart and alone, and made my decision. You don't let down your family.

* * *

Everyone found their seats in the main room. Bill stood behind me, relief gushing from his face, as I picked up the wireless mic and brought it up to my mouth.

"Ladies and gentlemen, can I have your attention please? My name is David from the All-Stars DJ Company. You may recognize me as groomsman number one from earlier today. I'd like to ask you to direct your attention to those double doors, because there are some people I'd like you to meet!"

I threw on "In the Mood," and stepped out from behind the table as Cameron entered, a sister on his arm.

"First off I'd like to introduce to you the beautiful Marissa, on the arm of Cameron, a strapping young man if ever I saw one!"

They applauded as Cameron led his charge onto the floor.

"Say hello to Deborah and Kylie, on the arms of an extremely lucky Dustin!"

Dustin came out, a sister on each side, grinning like an idiot. He'd strike out with both of them, but for now why don't we give him his moment.

"Now put your hands together for Kathleen, escorted by a dashing gentleman with a body to die for, David!"

I ran back through the doors and reemerged with Kathleen on my arm. The crowd laughed and gave me an alcohol-soaked cheer as I led her onto the floor and then ran back behind my table to turn down the music.

"And now, ladies and gentlemen, please rise and join me in welcoming, for the first time in public, the new Mr. and Mrs. Mendlesohn!"

Everyone stood and cheered, clapping wildly, as Annie and Rat Boy stepped into the room. They glided onto the floor as I played the theme from *Rocky*, just to make Annie smile. I turned it down and spoke softly into the microphone.

"And now the happy couple will dance their first dance."

I put on their song, an old R&B classic called "Always and Forever." I have no idea why they love it so much. It doesn't reflect either of their tastes. They won't tell me. They moved out onto the floor and began to dance, slowly, while the guests stood around and watched with smiles on their faces. You couldn't help but smile. Watching them move, I pulled away from the scene, seeing it not as a friend, but as the DJ doing his job. I've seen hundreds of weddings. Some beautiful, some modest, some smooth, some disasters. But for some reason, this wedding took me back to a gig I had in my first month. I ended up in the basement of the Knights of Columbus in Jersey City, working the reception for two of the happiest people I'd ever seen. Everything about the party was poor: the food was potluck, the decorations were handmade from paper cutouts, no one even dressed up except the couple. But the bride and groom were so happy they couldn't stop smiling. It truly was the greatest day of their lives. After I spoke with them, I realized why no one was overdressed. Both the bride and the groom were mentally disabled. They'd never thought they'd be allowed to get married at all. So every moment of that reception was magic.

I'm not saying that Annie and Rat Boy are mentally disabled, though about Rat Boy I wouldn't be surprised. But that look of unfettered joy, that look that doesn't care about the party or the flowers or the cake or any of that, that only cares about the friends and the rings and the one slow song, that look lit their faces like it lit the couple in that Knights of Columbus basement. It was beautiful, and it made me ashamed.

Once the song ended and everyone clapped their hearts out, I threw on a long first-course song and rushed back into the kitchen. Rialto stood behind the counter, filling the room all by himself.

"David! This place is a dollhouse! I feel like a giant!"

"Sorry about that, Rialto. I need to steal one of your waitresses."

"She's back there getting ketchup. Try not to get any on the napkins."

I followed his pointing finger down a side hallway, where a small storage closet stood with the door open. I couldn't pick up her scent from so far away, but somehow the air seemed to carry her to me. Maybe what I call pheromones someone else might call love. Or, as my dad might say, the chance for love. Maybe what I call pheromones is just my body kicking me in the ass, trying to force me to look past my expectations. Can anything kill happiness quicker than expectations? Thank God for pheromones or I might have walked on by. I knocked and Janey stuck her head out. She froze when she caught sight of me.

"Oh. Hi."

"Expectations, that's the problem, really."

Her face went blank.

"Is it."

"You know what it is? It's like weddings. Your wedding is supposed to be the best moment of your life. But we've seen a million weddings, right? How many looked like the best moments of anyone's life to you? You're surrounded by people your parents made you invite, never actually having time to touch the food you were so keen on making sure they cooked, never having time to dance to the music you spent days picking out. You have maybe five minutes in a limo with your new wife or husband, and the rest of your time is spent either making sure the perfect wedding in your head goes off without a hitch, or just running along trying to keep up with somebody else trying to make the perfect wedding in his or her head go off without a hitch. And there are hitches. So many hitches. Cakes collapse and grandparents do strange dances with knives and uncles pass out in the laps of bridesmaids. Songs skip and names are mispronounced and sometimes people won't get up and dance no matter how many times you play 'Get Down Tonight.' And even if none of those things go wrong and it's the party of a lifetime, you still don't get to enjoy it. You whiz around like you're in a roller rink, thanking everyone for their punch bowls and Cuisinarts and matching dining room placemats, telling everyone how much you love them, even if you have no idea who they are or how they got in. Before you know it, you've taken off the garter with your teeth and thrown your bouquet to the pack of ravenous wolves who can't wait to be the next one to float through their own perfect weddings without actually enjoying them. And then you're running through rice and diving into a car that looks like a grafittied subway train from the eighties, and you lie back and look at each other and sigh and say, 'Thank God we made it through.' You need those photos and you need that video, because without them you'd never remember a thing. The best day of your life, completely forgotten.

"But years pass, and you watch the video and you look through the photos and you remark at how happy everyone looks and gradually, in your mind, it turns into the wedding you always wanted it to be. It was the perfect wedding. You don't actually remember it, so it might be true. It probably is true. Look how big our smiles are in this photo! And then you look down at your little girl and tell her that one day she'll get married and it will be the happiest, best day of her whole life. And you'll believe it.

"But we've seen so many. We can compare. We know the

truth. It's a party, like any other party. Some are good parties, some are bad parties. But if this can be the happiest day of your life, why not the anniversary, or the sweet sixteen, or the bar mitzvah? They're all parties, right? We play the same music and invite the same guests and eat the same food. Actually you go to dozens of parties in your life just like your wedding, maybe hundreds, maybe thousands if you have a house in the Hamptons. So why are they different?"

Unsure whether it was her turn to talk, Janey waited a moment before hazarding a guess.

"Expectations?"

"Exactly! So what's the difference between having dinner with a friend and having dinner with the mayor? Winning twenty-five dollars at a talent show and hitting a home run at Yankee Stadium? Going on a perfect date or getting your book published?"

"Wait a minute. Is this about your book? What happened with your book?"

"They offered me a four-book deal."

"That's amazing."

"I turned it down. I'd do only a one-book deal."

"Why? Was it not enough money?"

"It was no money, but that wasn't the problem. It just showed me the way to the problem. The problem is that I hate writing. My book was a fluke. I don't enjoy the process and I never have. I had one idea and I wrote about it. The prospect of writing three more books makes me sick to my stomach. I thought my book would be my big deal, but it wasn't anything but another thing that happened. A small success that I can be proud of, but nothing more than that. If you don't enjoy the process, the outcome means nothing. Being a writer would be miserable, no matter how happy being published may make me. So I turned it down."

Janey sighed, disappointment shining in her eyes.

"I see. So you're not a writer. Thanks for coming back and telling me. I like to be kept up to date."

She turned to disappear back into the closet. I put my hand on her shoulder to stop her.

"Wait. That got me thinking."

"No. Really? How much thinking can one guy do?"

"About us. About why I ran from you. About why I couldn't handle the thought of falling in love with you. You're not easy, Janey. You're challenging and there are times when you have to deal with stuff that has nothing to do with me, stuff I can't do anything about. We went out only a few months and I could see that. I look down the road and I don't know what we'll end up being. And that's what scared me. I couldn't see it, it could go so many ways, you know? But I was really loving the process. Even though I ran, I really was loving the process. That's what my problem has always been. I want to be happy, but I don't understand what makes me happy. I've either avoided it or chased after the wrong thing because of some Ditto in first grade. If I wanted to, I could float above it, going for the surface happys, never touching down. But I don't want that. I'm too greedy. Maybe there is no big happy. Maybe it's an illusion, a dream like the thought of the perfect wedding that exists only in anticipation and in retrospect. But there is some kind of happy. I may have to change what I expect, but it's there, and I want it."

Janey acted unconcerned, but her eyes glistened.

"What the hell are you trying to say? Is this good news for me or bad news or did you take up dictating because you're too lazy to write?"

I hesitated, not sure how to put it. Her eyes rolled.

"Motherfucker. You're still slow revealing, aren't you? I was so scared of frightening you away, I never had the guts to say what I felt. Well, fuck that. Here's the truth. Up until you dumped me, I was on the road to falling in love with you. I didn't know where it was going either. But that's where I was."

"What about now?"

"I don't know now. I just . . . I want to trust you, I really do."

Then I'd better be honest, with both of us.

"I think I'm falling in love with you. That's what I'm trying to say."

Janey didn't move. She was listening.

"Hear that? The song stopped. You talked longer than 'Scenes from an Italian Restaurant.' You could have just said that and you wouldn't have a dead silent reception hall right now."

But she couldn't stop the smile from creeping across her face. Shouts started drifting in from the next room, begging me to throw on another song, but I ignored them. My life had been restarted clean, without expectations or even big, overarching dreams, and all I knew was that there were things I loved, like my friends, like my family, like Annie, like maybe this woman standing before me with a gradually widening smile that threatened to take over her face entirely. I was pretty sure they loved me back. You need to work with what you have if you want to get anywhere. So while I may not have known what kind of happys lay waiting out there for me, or whether I'd be able to grab on to them when they popped up, I had to like my chances.

Acknowledgments

The first time I did one of these, I admittedly went a tad overboard, thanking practically everyone I'd ever met. Blame it on the arm cream. This time around, I'm going to be less specific in my gratitude, in an effort to be nice to trees and people who couldn't care less. So first off, I'd like to thank everyone who ever hired me to DJ their wedding, bar mitzvah, middle school dance, etc. You could have tipped better (much better), but I'm not bitter. Your stories are worth more than gold. Thanks to the wonderful folks at Miramax for being so steady, even when events would have dictated otherwise. Thanks to Johnny Saunders for pushing me outside my comfort zone; it hurt, but it hurt good. Thanks to David Dunton for being such a good friend as well as agent. Thanks to my sassy circle of friends, who've inspired me and challenged me and never let me fall. Thanks to my wonderful family who've been so actively supportive they could qualify as a political party in the next election. And a special thanks to Kristina Grish for surrounding me with more love than I could ever hope to deserve. Yes, I know. I'm such a dork.